Praise for Vince Flynn's bestselling thrillers

'Sizzles with inside information, military muscle, and CIA secrets. Vince Flynn remains the king of high-concept political intrigue' Dan Brown, bestselling author of *The Da Vinci Code*

'Vince Flynn is Tom Clancy on speed. He grabs you by the scruff of the neck on Page 1 and doesn't let you go until the end' Stephen Leather

'Mitch Rapp is a great character who always leaves the bad guys either very sorry for themselves or very dead' *Guardian*

'A fast-paced political rollercoaster with a razor-sharp edge, featuring a CIA superhero that George Bush would no doubt give his right arm to have at his disposal' *Lads Mag*

'A thriller with deadly aim . . . moves at the speed of a stinger missile' *People*

'A Rambo perfectly suited for the war on terror' *Washington Times*

'First-class political intrigue from a master storyteller' *Booklist*

'A sharply plotted thriller . . . Flynn knows his politicians and pits his characters against impossible odds with non-stop action and suspense' *Publishers Weekly*

VINCE FLYNN

SEPARATION OF POWER

POCKET
BOOKS

LONDON • SYDNEY • NEW YORK • TORONTO

First published in Great Britain by Simon & Schuster UK Ltd, 2003
This edition published by Pocket Books, 2008
An imprint of Simon & Schuster UK Ltd
A CBS COMPANY

3 5 7 9 10 8 6 4 2

Simon & Schuster UK Ltd
1st Floor
222 Gray's Inn Road
London WC1X 8HB

Simon & Schuster Australia
Sydney

www.simonandschuster.co.uk

A CIP catalogue record for this book is available
from the British Library

ISBN: 978-1-84983-257-1

Printed and bound in Great Britain by
Cox & Wyman Ltd, Reading, Berkshire

To

Emily Bestler

ACKNOWLEDGEMENTS

First and foremost, I have to thank my lovely wife, Lysa, for her patience and understanding while I labored over this novel—especially the last three months. Darling, you make it all worthwhile. To my agent, Sloan Harris, for all of his wise counsel and good humor. It has been great watching all of your successes over the last year. To my editor, Emily Bestler, for giving me the time and cover to finish this book. Once again, you've taken it to another level, and did so without giving me any anxiety attacks.

To Larry Johnson, an incredibly knowledgeable counter-terrorism specialist, whose advice is always welcome. To Pat O'Brien, an old high school friend and a man who knows his way around the Hill. To Bill Harlow, an excellent author and the director of the CIA's office of public relations, thank you for patiently answering my questions. To Fred Manget of the CIA's office of general counsel, for educating me on national security non-disclosure documents and Congressional Notification. To all of my sources who wish to remain anonymous, I once again thank you for your help. To Sessalee, Karen, Tommy, Edward, and Paula for our annual lunch in New York, where we always talk about much more than books. And as always, to all of the booksellers and readers, your enthusiasm and support make this a very fulfilling job.

SEPARATION OF POWER

PRELUDE

D r. Irene Kennedy stood over the fresh mound of dirt and wept. It had been a small funeral; relatives and a few close friends. The others had already left the windswept cemetery, and were on their way back into town for a light lunch at an aunt's house. The forty-year-old director of the CIA's Counterterrorism Center wanted to spend a few moments alone at the grave of her mentor. Kennedy lifted her head and wiped the tears from her eyes as she took in the landscape. She ignored the biting chill of western South Dakota and let it all out. This would be her last chance to grieve so openly for the loss of the man who had taught her so much. After this it was back to Washington, and perhaps the greatest test of her life. During Stansfield's final days the director of the CIA had told her not to worry. He had made all the proper arrangements. She would take his place as the next director of the Central Intelligence Agency. Kennedy did not relish the confirmation process that awaited her, but what really had her worried was measuring up to her old boss. He was the greatest man she had ever known.

Thomas Stansfield died on a cool fall morning surrounded by his children, grandchildren and Irene Kennedy. It was exactly as he'd wanted it to be. Just two weeks before his eightieth year, he wanted to go no further. Those last few days he had sat in his leather chair, a calm haze of morphine dulling both his mind and the stabbing pain of the cancer that was ravaging his insides. He stared out the window as the last of fall's leaves fell. This was the final autumn of his life.

Thomas Stansfield's rise to the top of the Central Intelligence Agency was the stuff that legends were made of. Born near the town of Stoneville, South Dakota, in 1920, he came of age during two of his country's most difficult decades. The carefree days of his youth had been squelched by dry hot summers and apocalyptic dust storms that rose up from the southern plains and turned day into night. The Great Depression had taken its toll on the Stansfield family. One of his brothers, an uncle and several cousins had been lost along with two of the four grandparents.

Stansfield's parents had met in their teens, both fresh off the cattle cars that had sprinkled countless European immigrants across America in the years that followed World War I. His father was from Germany; his mother from Norway. Thomas Stansfield grew up mesmerized by the stories his parents and grandparents told of their homelands. He learned English in school, but at night by the fire it was the native languages of his parents and grandparents that was spoken. He excelled in school, and from an early age showed far less interest in farming than his brothers. He knew that someday he would return to Europe and explore his family's history. When he was given the chance at the age of seventeen to attend South Dakota State University on a full academic scholarship, he didn't hesitate.

College was not difficult for Stansfield. He majored in engineering and history and graduated at the top of his class. As the hot and hungry days of the thirties wound to a close Stansfield recognized something far more ominous on the horizon. While most of his classmates and professors were turned inward, obsessed with America's problems, Stansfield kept an eye on the rise of fascism in Europe. His intellect told him that something foreboding was on the horizon.

Franklin Delano Roosevelt also knew that something innately evil was occurring in Europe and the Far East. But there was nothing Roosevelt could do in the late thirties. The political will to intervene was not there. America had lost too many of her sons in the first World War, and its citizens weren't about to jump into another so quickly. It was Europe's problem. So Roosevelt, always the keen politician, bided his time and prepared for war as best he could. One of the things he did was to call on his close friend Colonel Wild Bill Donovan. Donovan, a New York lawyer, had been awarded the Medal of Honor for leading the Fighting 69th infantry regiment in France during World War I and was one of Roosevelt's most keen and intense advisors. At the urging of Donovan, Roosevelt authorized the formation of the Office of Strategic Services. One of the first things Donovan did was to scour the armed forces and American universities for young men with the language skills that would aid the OSS in analyzing intercepted Axis power messages. Donovan also had something else in mind. He knew it wasn't a question of if America would enter the war but a question of when. And when it did he wanted to be ready to insert Americans behind German lines to organize resistance forces, gather intelligence and if called on, assassinate the enemy.

Thomas Stansfield was one of Wild Bill Donovan's greatest recruits. The thin farm boy from the western steppes of South Dakota was fluent in German, Norwegian and spoke decent French. During the war Stansfield was parachuted into both Norway and later, France. Still in his early twenties, he was the leader of what was to become one of the OSS's most effective Jedburgh Teams. After the war General Eisenhower would say that the invasion of France would not have been possible if it were not for the efforts of the courageous Jedburgh Teams to organize French resistance, provide detailed intelligence reports and ultimately disrupt and confuse German troop movement during the first days of the invasion. Thomas Stansfield had been one of those brave men who had operated behind enemy lines for months preparing the way for the invasion force. In the predawn hours of D–Day Stansfield and his Jedburgh Team demolished a major rail line and a phone junction box.

After the war Stansfield continued to serve his country. When the CIA was formed in 1947 he became one of its first employees. He stayed in Europe for much of the next four decades, almost all of it behind the Iron Curtain. He was one of the Agency's most effective recruiters of foreign agents. In the eighties President Reagan was so impressed with the man's steely demeanor he made him the Moscow Station Chief because he knew Stansfield would drive the Russians nuts. After Moscow he was brought home to become the deputy director of operations and then finally director of Central Intelligence. He had served his country well and had sought no recognition. On his deathbed President Hayes had come to visit him. The president told Stansfield that preparations were under way for a full military burial at Arlington National Cemetery. The president also expressed his interest in eulogizing Stansfield himself. It was the least the country could do for a man who had given so much. Stansfield in his typical humble way declined, and told the president that he wanted to be buried where he'd been born. No pomp and circumstance, just a simple private ceremony for a very private man.

Kennedy brushed a moist strand of brown hair from her face. She missed him. Standing in the cold wind, the gray bleak sky overhead, she felt alone and isolated, more so than at any other time in her life. When she lost her father to a car bombing in Beirut it had been extremely painful, but there was one major difference. Back then nothing was expected of her. It was all right to check out for six months and travel the world in search of answers. This time she had no such luxury. First there was Tommy, her extremely inquisitive six-year-old son. There was no running from that responsibility. Tommy's father had already done that and Kennedy wasn't about to disappoint the most important person in her life for a second time. If it were only Tommy, she could handle it. But it wasn't. There was Washington.

Kennedy looked to the west, at the rise of the Black Hills and their strange ominous beauty. For a moment the thought of running flashed across her mind. Take Tommy, quit the CIA and run. Never look back, and avoid the whole mess. Let the self-serving vultures go after some-one else. She lowered her eyes to the grave of Thomas Stansfield and knew she could never do it. She owed him too much. She knew he had counted on her to keep the CIA politically neutral. Kennedy could think of no one she admired more than Thomas Stansfield. The man had given close to sixty years of his life to his agency, his belief in democracy and his country. And she had given him her word. She would return to Washington.

Kennedy sighed heavily and took one last look at the grave. She let the rose in her hand fall to the mound of black dirt, and she wiped the last of her tears from her face. A final silent good-bye was uttered and a simple request; that he would guide her through the difficult months to come. Kennedy turned and started for the car.

1

Williams Island was one of hundreds of tiny land masses that made up the Bahamas. But unlike other similar islands in the Bahamas, it had a new landing strip capable of handling executive jets. This was due to a prominent inhabitant who owned a private compound on the island's western end. With the sun less than an hour away from setting, the distinctive whine of turbine engines could be heard in the distance. A gleaming Gulfstream personal jet suddenly appeared with the bright orange orb of the Caribbean sun as its backdrop. The plane steadily descended, its approach looking like a mirage as the heat shimmered off the runway. With barely a noise, the wheels gently touched down and rolled along the runway. There was no control tower at the small airport, just a hangar and maintenance shed. The plane came to a stop in front of the hangar and the engines were silenced.

A shiny new Range Rover was parked by the hangar, the driver standing next to the vehicle, hands clasped in front of him in kind of a nonmilitary version of parade rest. The native Bahamian had been sent by Senator Hank Clark, the man who owned the compound at the other end of the island. He was also the man who had helped to secure financing and donations for the new runway.

The door of the glistening jet opened and out stepped a man and woman in business attire, both of them in their early thirties, both of them with black leather Tumi laptop bags over their shoulders. The two were barely on the tarmac and out came the phones. They punched the numbers in as fast as they could and waited impatiently for the phones to connect with the nearest satellite. After a moment a third individual appeared in the plane's doorway. This man was not dressed in standard business attire.

Mark Ellis stood perched in the doorway for a moment and surveyed the scene through a pair of black Revo sunglasses. He had a well-trimmed brown beard that helped hide the acne scars of his youth. Ellis was dressed from head to toe in expensive Tommy Bahama casual wear. Silk tan pants, a short-sleeved silk shirt with a tropical design and a blue blazer. With the shoes the outfit cost close to a thousand dollars. His personal shopper from Semi Valley purchased the entire ensemble. The woman brought Ellis racks of clothes to look at each month. He never perused the bill and never asked if the items were on sale. Ellis usually listened to the woman's suggestions and the entire affair was almost always over in fifteen minutes or less. The woman would clip the tags and hang the clothes in his 1,200 square foot master bedroom closet. On the surface the closet might seem a little large, but in relation to the rest of the 36,000 square foot home, it was fitting.

Mark Ellis was a billionaire. At the height of the dot com craze *Fortune* magazine had put Ellis's net worth at twenty-one billion dollars. With the recent dot com bust the number was now half that and it was driving him nuts. The recent downturn in his portfolio was why he was visiting the tiny island. Ellis was one of the biggest hitters in Silicon Valley, but unlike many of his neighbors Ellis made nothing. He didn't develop hardware, software or cutting edge technology; Mark Ellis was a professional gambler. Venture capital was his game. He bet on companies, preferably startups that no one else knew anything about. Fast approaching the age of fifty, Ellis had been in the VC game since the age of twenty-eight. Supremely confident, and sometimes competitive to a fault, he worked long hours and expected those around him to work even longer ones. Mark Ellis had a temper, and nothing could bring it out quicker than failure. Failure meant losing, and he hated to lose with a passion that surpassed even his zest for wealth.

There had been a lot of failures of late and Ellis was literally losing his mind, allowing it to be taken over by anger instead of rational calculation, which was what he needed. The only good news for him was that he recognized the problem. The bigger issue, however, was the solution, and there was only one, to reverse the trend of losses.

Ellis stroked the edges of his brown beard as he started for the Range Rover. Despite his reputation as a gambler, he hadn't been to the track or a casino in well over a decade. As far as legal gambling was concerned, he had two big problems; he didn't like the odds, and he didn't like playing by their rules. Mark Ellis didn't like playing by other people's rules—period. Whether it was the Catholic Church, the Securities and Exchange Commission, the Internal Revenue Service, or the government in general. Mark Ellis, born in Buffalo, New York to the son of a steel worker, believed that rules were designed to keep you down. They were designed to keep the masses in check. From an early age he had understood this, and he had made it his personal goal in life to never live by their rules.

SENATOR HANK CLARK was a large man who inside the Beltway was affectionately referred to by some as John Wayne. Clark had the size, the swagger, and most notable, the gift of making people feel important when they were around him. Not to say that Hank Clark was altruistic. He wasn't. Clark had no aversion to making enemies in life; he just found it suited his needs much better when the other person thought he was a friend. He was, after all, a politician. Like a well-schooled assassin, he knew that it was much easier to slit someone's throat when they allowed you to get close. That was why, in an increasingly divided Washington, the Republican senator from Arizona was one of the few politicians left who could truly reach across the aisle. Clark made no public enemies, and he made very few in private. He was a likable man, and he used his amiable style to find peoples' weaknesses. Senator Henry Thomas Clark was a truly dangerous man.

Clark looked out over the beautiful blue water of the Caribbean and smiled. He had done very well for himself. His private compound on the tip of the island had its own lagoon and over fifty acres of lush privacy. Inside the compound were a gatekeeper's house, a guesthouse that overlooked the quaint lagoon and the grand main house with commanding views of the ocean. All three were done in a tasteful Mediterranean style. Clark was standing on the terrace of the main house. Thirty feet below the surf pounded into the sheer rock cliff. Standing as he was, leaning out over the water, was like being on the bow of ship. The bright orange sun was slipping over the horizon. It was another day in paradise.

He'd gone from trailer trash to the U.S. Senate. Clark smiled, took a drink and thought, *Only in America could a kid grow up in poverty with a father and mother who were drunks and go on to become a multimillionaire and a U.S. senator.* Clark knew there were those who would find the line pat, but he doubted they had started out so low in life and risen so high. Not Clark though. Not a day passed when he didn't think of how far he had come, and how far he still intended to go.

His father was an abject failure in every sense of the word. So much so that he blew his head off when Hank Clark was a boy. The memories of his youth were a constant reminder of how bad things could be. No father, a mother who was drunk every day of the week and the stigma of living in a trailer park. Fortunately for Hank Clark his parents had unwittingly given him one true gift: a 90-mph fastball and a wicked curve. That was his ticket out: a full ride to Arizona State University. After school Clark had gone into commercial real estate and development in a fledgling suburb of Phoenix called Scottsdale. Clark's life from that point forward had been one success after another. By thirty he had made his first million. By thirty-five he was set for life and decided to go into politics. He served one term in the U.S. House of Representatives and then it was on to the Senate, where he was now in the middle of his fourth term. One would think that this would be enough for most people, but not Hank Clark. He wasn't done achieving yet. There was one more job he wanted.

Unfortunately, several people in Washington weren't cooperating at the moment. That, Clark knew, was why Mark Ellis had decided to make his unscheduled trip to the tiny island. Clark was a wealthy man, but he had no intention of throwing away all of that hard-won money. That was why he needed Ellis and his friends. They had serious money, they weren't simple millionaires, they were billionaires, and they weren't shy about doling some of their billions out for access and information.

Clark sighed and shook his head at the tedious road ahead. Information, that's what this whole mess was about. Knowledge truly was power, and men like Ellis

understood that Clark could help give them the knowledge they needed to grow their billions and protect their
kingdoms. Even over the roar of the surf Clark heard Ellis
enter the house. Clark and Ellis shared a thirst for power
and that was about it. Where Clark was calm and discerning, Ellis was volatile and brash. The man had a way of
wearing people out through frontal assault after frontal
assault. Nothing tricky, no feints, he just hammered you
into submission. Clark found it all very interesting. He
was a true tactician, and often relished outmaneuvering
people like Ellis, but tonight, in the warm Caribbean air
he would prefer drinks, some light fare and the smooth
skin of a young woman flown in from Miami.

Ellis strode out onto the terrace at full speed like an
impetuous prince delivering bad news from some far-off
front. His demeanor was very out of place in the laid back
atmosphere of Clark's private retreat, and the senator
made an effort not to let his irritation show.

There was no hello, no comment on the weather or
the beauty of the setting sun. Ellis forcefully slapped down
a copy of the *San Francisco Chronicle* on the small wrought
iron table near Clark and kept his eyes focused on the
man. "What in the hell is this all about?"

"Good evening, Mark. How was your flight?"

"Never mind my flight," barked Ellis as he looked up at
the much taller and more substantial Clark. "Explain this
to me." Ellis pointed at the paper, but kept his eyes on the
senator.

Clark glanced down at the paper and said, "Mark,
you'll have to read it to me. I don't have my glasses with
me." Clark smiled as Ellis snatched the paper off the table.
This might be enjoyable after all: the bull and the mata-
dor.

"The headline reads, New CIA Director. Sources close

to the president say that next week he will nominate Dr. Irene Kennedy to become the next director of the CIA. If Kennedy is confirmed she will become the first woman to head the spy agency." Ellis threw the paper back down on the table in disgust. "You told me you would take care of this mess."

"Yes, I did tell you that, and, yes, I am taking care of it."

"How, just how in God's name are you taking care of this, Hank? You are not my only source in Washington," spat Ellis. "I'm hearing things."

Clark took a drink and gauged the sincerity of the thinly veiled threat. "What are you hearing?"

"I'm hearing Kennedy won't play ball. I'm hearing if she finds out about our little arrangement she will blow us out of the water."

Shaking his head, Clark replied, "As for your first point, I'm not entirely convinced she won't play ball, and as for your second point, she would never go public with our business dealings."

"How can you be so sure?"

With absolute sincerity, Clark replied, "She'd probably have you killed instead."

Taking half a step back Ellis gave the senator a questioning look. "You can't be serious?"

"Oh, I'm very serious. I don't know who your other sources are, but I will guarantee you they don't know Dr. Kennedy as well as I do. She was taught by the best. That agency has never seen anyone as competent, efficient and lethal as Thomas Stansfield, and I doubt they ever will . . . but Kennedy will be the next best thing. I have no doubt that Stansfield has left her with his files." Clark turned and looked out over the water. "All the secrets he compiled during his fifty-plus years of service in the intelligence business. I know some very powerful men in

Washington who are very nervous about her nomination."

Ellis clenched his fists in a show of frustration. "Then why in the hell don't you guys tell the president to withdraw his nomination and get someone in there who we can manage?"

"It's not that easy, Mark. These men are afraid of her. They are afraid of what she knows, and they would prefer not to draw any attention to themselves."

"Bullshit! I don't care how many of them are afraid of her. I don't care how many of them lose their jobs or their wives or whatever it is they are afraid of losing—"

"How about their freedom?" Clark asked with an arched brow.

"What do you mean, freedom?"

"Some of them would like to stay out of jail."

"Oh, come on."

"You'd better get some new sources in Washington, Mark." Clark started back toward the house. "I'm going to get another drink. Would you like one?"

Ellis hesitated for a moment and then followed. "My sources are fine." He stared skeptically at Clark's broad back and concluded, "I see what you're trying to do. You're trying to scare me into backing down. And I'm telling you right now I'm not going to."

Clark stepped behind the simple granite bar with two large bay windows behind it. The bottles were kept on a speed rail beneath the bar. Reaching for the Scotch, he said, "Your little investigative firm that you use in Washington"—Clark allowed himself a slight chuckle—"I suppose they're fine if you're looking for a little dirty laundry on one of my colleagues or a reporter you don't like . . . or if you want to look through the garbage of one of your competitors." Clark stopped. "Oh, I'm sorry, I forgot, they got caught doing that." Grabbing a glass for Ellis, he poured him some tequila. "That was rather embarrassing for you, wasn't it?" Clark flashed his guest a smile, and then raised his glass in a salute before touching it to his lips.

Ellis muttered several swear words under his breath and took a drink. The situation the senator was referring to was a disaster for the billionaire. He had hired a private investigative firm in Washington to spy on the lobbying office of one of his chief competitors. The sleuths attempted to bribe the night cleaning crew by giving them cash for garbage. The cleaning crew reported this to their employer and the cops stepped in and busted the employees of Leiser Security. It was later learned that Ellis had hired the firm. Ellis hid behind a shield of lawyers and no charges were ever filed, but on a personal level the incident was the talk of Silicon Valley. Ellis avoided the social scene for months and was on the wrong end of some very scathing jokes.

Knowing no other style, Ellis refused to be deterred by the senator's embarrassing reference. "That has nothing to do with what we're talking about. I don't buy this crap that a bunch of senators are scared of Kennedy, and if they are, that's all the more reason to block her. You're not making any sense." Ellis shook his head and frowned.

"Mark, it's basic risk reward," intoned Clark as if he were speaking to a teenager. "Not everyone in Washington wants to raid the CIA like you do. Most of them think that Kennedy will do just fine, in fact probably better than anyone else we could find. To them there is no reward in blocking her nomination." He took a drink of Scotch and added, "Only risk."

"I'll offer them some reward. I'll fill their reelection coffers with cash."

The senator thought about this for a second. "That might work on a few of them, but not enough to make it happen. The only way to stop her nomination at this point is to find something damaging in her past. The senators on my committee will not vote against her over differences of opinion. She has too good of a reputation for the work she's done as the head of Counterterrorism."

"Then we'd better find something in her past and end this thing before it gets started."

"I've looked, and there isn't anything."

"Bullshit. You don't get to where she is without breaking some of your stupid oversight rules."

Clark knew in fact that Kennedy had trampled all over those rules, but she had done so because Clark and several other very important senators had asked Thomas Stansfield to do something about the increase in terrorist attacks against the U.S. The result was the formation of the Orion Team. An organization supported by the Agency but outside the Agency. Their job in a nutshell was to take the war to the terrorists. The hunters became the hunted. To use the Orion Team against Kennedy would be a very risky proposition. If she decided to take others down with her, it could get very ugly indeed. That particular information was far too valuable to trust Ellis with, though, so Clark just shook his head and said, "There is nothing. Believe me, I've looked."

"Maybe your sources aren't as good as you thought," replied Ellis, who was very proud of himself for using Clark's own retort against him.

Unflappable as ever, Clark flashed a big grin and said, "I am my own source."

"Well, I'm going to have some people check her out."

"Be my guest, but be very careful."

"Why? What in the hell do I have to fear from her?"

"Oh, Mark, you don't know where you tread. Do you know anything about this woman's mentor?"

"Stansfield?"

"Yes." Clark grinned in admiration for the old spymaster. "Thomas Stansfield was not afraid to have people eliminated."

"You mean killed."

"Of course, but only those who were stupid enough to plot against him and let their identities be known."

"So you think Kennedy has the same ruthless side that her boss did."

"Oh, I never said it was ruthless. Thomas Stansfield was not a ruthless man. He was very calculating. If you tried to do this country harm, or his agency, or him personally," Clark shook his head, "you were apt to end up dead."

"You didn't answer my question," Ellis stated with irritation in his voice. "Is Kennedy capable of having someone killed?"

"I'm not sure, but I sure as hell don't want to find out."

The billionaire stomped his foot on the ground like a petulant child. "Dammit, I am getting killed! My portfolio is down forty percent! My investors are down over fifty percent! It's bad enough that the market is in the tank, but it's unacceptable that I'm flying blind! I spent way too much fucking money on Echelon!" Ellis pointed to himself and shouted, "I want a return on my fucking investment!"

Clark was about to tell Ellis to calm down, but thought better of it. The man was beyond recovery at the moment. His thoughts turned to Echelon, the supersecret program started by the National Security Agency back in the seventies. Through a series of ground stations located around the globe and satellites in space the agency began intercepting telexes, faxes and phone calls. Using supercomputers and highly advanced voice recognition software the NSA was able to sift through millions of calls daily, and sort out the ones that were interesting. Somewhere along the way some people got the bright idea of targeting certain foreign companies that were direct competitors of U.S. firms. The information was then passed along to, for example, a certain U.S. telecommunications company that was up against a French company for a lucrative bid. Echelon continued to morph into the nineties. Worried about the spread of U.S. technology, the super-snoops at the NSA began to monitor communications in and out of Silicon Valley. Senator Clark, as Chairman of the Senate Select Committee on Intelligence, got to see what was being discovered firsthand. The information he got was valuable to men like Mark Ellis. Who was working on what? How close were they to bringing their product to market? Who wanted to buy whom? Ellis had made a killing on the information. Clark had helped to create a monster, and now he was forced to deal with it.

After the long moment of thought Clark said, "It is not my fault that Echelon was shut down."

"Well, you guys should have killed that bitch when she went to the press and blew the whistle."

The "bitch" Ellis was referring to was an employee of the NSA who had heard one too many intercepted phone calls and decided it was a bad thing for the U.S. government to be spying on its own people. "Mark, we like to avoid killing people after they've gone to the press. It looks rather bad."

"Don't patronize me. There are ways."

"And we tried all of them." Ellis was actually getting under Clark's skin. "We made her look like an absolute nut and scared everybody with the exception of *60 Minutes* away. You aren't in jail; I'm not in jail . . . no one is in jail. No one has even been brought up on charges, Mark. I'd say we did a pretty good job of handling what was very close to being a disaster."

"This is a disaster!" snapped Ellis. "Didn't you hear me? My portfolio is down forty percent. My clients are getting killed and some of them are threatening to walk."

Clark breathed a heavy sigh and placed a hand on Ellis's shoulder. Leading him back toward the terrace he said, "Two years from now, your portfolio will be back up. Ten years from now it will be double what it was before this whole mess started. Everybody is getting killed right now."

"I'm not everybody," moaned a frustrated but slightly calmer Ellis. "I want Echelon back. I want a CIA director who will play ball. I need that information."

Clark kept his hand on the billionaire's shoulder as they stopped near the edge of the terrace. "Mark, I will get you the information you need. I promise."

"What about Kennedy? You've told me before we have no chance of controlling her."

"I said it would be difficult, not impossible." While squeezing Ellis's shoulder Clark looked out across the water and thought of a possible solution. The trick was to get someone else to do his dirty work. He had to stay above it all. He had to stay close to the president and maintain his confidence. Then when everything was right he would strike.

2

Mitch Rapp woke up on his stomach. He reached over to find Anna but she wasn't there. He had no desire to move so he simply lay there, thinking about how tired he was. His left shoulder was painfully stiff. He would have liked to think it was from the time he dislocated it playing lacrosse for his alma mater Syracuse University, but he knew it was something a little more serious. The real damage had been done by a bullet. At thirty-two Rapp was a beat-up old man. He had barely taken a break since graduating from college. For years he had been obsessed with the fight against Islamic terrorists, obsessed with killing as many of them as he could before they had the chance to do the same to innocent people whose only crime was that they disagreed with the zealots' bastardization of Islam.

There were days when Rapp wondered if he had really made a difference. After all, the crazies were still out there threatening to bring Armageddon to America. In his rare moments of self-pity, he thought it was all for naught. He knew deep down inside, though, that he'd made a huge difference. He had never bothered to count each and every person he'd killed. The obvious reason was that he preferred not to know, and the more practical one was that there was no way he could ascertain the actual number. Machine guns and explosives, the indiscriminate weapons of war, made the tally impossible, but the number was large. Rapp knew it was well over fifty and possibly one hundred, and those were only by his hand alone. If he counted the times he'd helped lead Special Forces units on takedowns, or the times he painted a target so U.S. jets could drop laser-guided bombs, the number was easily double if not triple.

Those days were behind him, or at least he hoped they were. It was not going to be easy to walk away from the action after all these years. He was extremely good at what he did. And what he did when you stripped everything away was kill. Yes, he had great intelligence. He spoke Arabic, French and Italian fluently. He had keen analytical abilities and organizational skills, but when you stripped it all away he was an assassin. He was America's assassin, though. He was the very tip of the U.S. spear, the man on the ground getting things done, taking the battle to the very enemy who had sworn to bring a reign of terror and death to the people of the United States. Mitch Rapp was *the* front line soldier in the most singular sense of the word. In this era of laser-guided bombs, cruise missiles and surgical strikes, he was a neurosurgeon, operating in countries like Iran and Iraq for months at a time with virtually no aid from his handlers in Washington. He stalked his prey carefully, got in close and then when the time was right, he eliminated them. Despite all of his success, only a handful of people knew of his existence. The Orion Team and its members were one of the closest held secrets in Washington, and fewer than ten people even knew the name of the organization.

Rapp knew there were those in Washington who would absolutely lose their minds if they found out what he had been up to for the last decade. Part of him was sensitive to the problem. God knows he had seen some abuses of power during his tenure, but not by himself or

Kennedy. There was a definite need for congressional oversight, but there was also a need for black operations. Politicians were politicians after all, and throughout the history of governments they had proven themselves incapable of keeping secrets. By virtue of their need to talk, raise money and peddle influence, all but a few were simply unable to keep their mouths shut. This was the standard feeling among the intelligence and military types in Washington, while on the other side of the issue the politicians looked at the people at the CIA and the Pentagon as a bunch of crazy cowboys who needed to be kept on a short leash lest they shoot themselves in the foot.

In a way Rapp agreed with both of them. There was enough blame to go around on both sides. The Agency had certainly launched some harebrained schemes with almost no chance of success, schemes that flew in the face of congressional oversight and more importantly to Rapp, common sense. There were also those on the Hill who had intentionally leaked classified information to the media to embarrass political enemies. This was how Washington worked, and had worked for years.

Americans had grown soft with all of their rights and personal freedom. They had no idea how harsh the rest of the world was. On the surface most Americans would be shocked by the things he had done. But they would be shocked from the comfort of their homes, having no idea what things were like in the Middle East. Women would judge him the harshest, and they would do so without thinking how they would be treated by the men he killed. Women in these fundamentalist Islamic communities weren't even treated as second-class citizens. They were property owned by their fathers, and then by their husbands once a marriage was arranged. No, America didn't have the stomach to be confronted with what he had done. That was why secrecy was essential.

Rapp stood and looked out the window of his small Cape Cod-style home. Down below, the water of the Chesapeake Bay looked cold. All of the leaves were off the trees and the cold gray skies of November had settled in. Standing in only his boxers, Rapp shivered briefly and then headed downstairs. There wasn't much enthusiasm in his step as he descended. He had a ten o'clock meeting at Langley that he had some serious reservations about. When he reached the first floor his new best friend Shirley the mutt was waiting for him. The dog was incredibly smart and obedient. Rapp patted her on the head and said hello. He had picked her up at the Humane Society one night several weeks earlier. Rapp had needed the canine to give him a little cover for some lurking that he had to do. Due to his normal unreliable schedule owning a pet was out of the question, but things were about to change. His days of globe-trotting were over. Or at least he hoped.

Rapp entered the kitchen to find the love of his life sitting at the table eating a bowl of cereal and reading the *Post*. He walked over and kissed Anna on the forehead. Without saying anything he went straight for the coffeepot and poured himself a cup. No sugar, no cream, just straight black coffee.

Anna Rielly swallowed a mouthful of cereal and looked up at Rapp with sparkling green eyes. "How are you feeling this morning?"

"Like shit." He moved his shoulder around in an effort to loosen it.

"What's wrong?"

"I'm getting old. That's what's wrong." Rapp took his first sip of the hot black liquid.

Rielly grinned. "What are you talking about? You're only thirty-two."

"I might as well be sixty-three with the life I've lived."

Rielly studied her man for a second. They had met under the strangest of circumstances, and at the time she didn't realize how ruggedly handsome he was. But she'd had ample time to notice since. She looked at Mitch's olive-skinned body. There wasn't an inch of fat on the man. He was one lean muscle from his broad shoulders to his sleek calves. There were some flaws, although Rielly never thought of them that way. Mitch liked to refer to these flaws as the chinks in his armor. Rapp had three visible bullet holes: one on his leg and two more on his stomach. There was a fourth, she knew, but that one was covered up by a thick scar on his shoulder where the doctors had torn him open to get at the bullet, pull out the bone fragments and reconstruct his shoulder socket. Besides that there was a scar left by a knife that had skewered his right side. And there was one more scar that he was particularly proud of. It was a constant reminder of the man he had sworn he would kill when he started on his crazy journey ten years ago. It ran along the left side of his face, from his ear down to his jawline. The plastic surgeons had done a great job minimizing the mark to a thin line, but more important to Rapp, the man who had given him the scar was now dead.

Rielly smiled at Rapp and stuck out her arms. "I think you look great."

"I still feel like shit." Rapp stayed where he was, leaning against the kitchen counter.

"My, you're in a sour mood this morning." Rielly let her arms drop. She studied Mitch briefly and then it dawned on her what was bothering him. "You don't want to go see Irene today, do you?" Rapp mumbled into his coffee cup and Rielly said, "I knew it."

"It's not Irene. I don't mind Irene . . . I look forward to seeing Irene."

"Then it's going to Langley?"

"Yeah . . . I don't know . . . I suppose."

Rielly had worried about this, but had kept it to herself. Rielly was a reporter and her job was to observe things . . . people, really. From what she observed as NBC's White House correspondent, she had serious doubts as to whether Mitch could make the transition from undercover operative to bureaucratic employee. He was too used to calling the shots and working on his own. At Langley he would have to be part of a team, and he would have to take orders. But worst of all, Rielly knew, was that he would have to watch what he said. Washington was a town where people often wanted to hear anything but the truth.

Rielly stood and went over to him, kissing him on the cheek. "Whatever you decide to do, honey, I will support you. If you want to stay at home and raise the kids I would think that's just great."

Rapp set his mug down and held up his hands, forming a "T" like a basketball referee. "Technical foul. No overt discussion of marriage, weddings or children until you have a ring on your finger."

Rielly scoffed at him. "That's your stupid rule, not mine. You know we're going to get married, and I know we're going to get married." She pinched his waist and with a playful smile said, "So let's get the show on the road."

Rapp grabbed her by the shoulders. "I've been just a little busy lately." He glanced over at a spot on the other side of the kitchen where just two weeks earlier he'd shot and killed a man. "I'd like to get some things straightened out before we take the big step."

Rielly waved off his caution saying, "Yeah . . . yeah, there's always something." She turned to leave. "I have to get to the White House. I'll call you later."

Rapp followed her to the front door. "You're not mad, are you?"

"No," Rielly said in a light voice. "I really do have to get to work, and you," she grabbed him by the chin, "have to get ready for your meeting." He rolled his eyes, and she kissed him on the lips. "It won't be that bad. Try to go into it with an open mind. Now I really have to get going. Call me and let me know how it goes."

"Unless you have access to the president's secure phone I think we'll have to wait until tonight to discuss my job offer."

"Oh, that's right. I always forget how paranoid you people are." Rielly opened the door.

"Hey, what do I always tell you? Just because you're paranoid—"

Rielly was halfway across the porch. Without turning around she yelled, "I know . . . I know . . . just because you're paranoid doesn't mean someone isn't following you."

Rapp smiled as he watched Anna open her car door. Shirley followed her and did a quick lap around the car. "I love you," he yelled.

Rielly stopped, and with a genuine smile, she looked at Mitch in his white boxer briefs and said, "I love you, too. Now get back in the house and put some clothes on before the neighbors see you."

3

The sun shone brightly through the colonnade windows of the West Wing's Cabinet Room. The gray morning skies had cleared a bit. It was a classic Washington photo op. The president's handlers had set it up, and the commander in chief had gone along without endorsement or complaint. It was a part of the job and he had learned to tolerate it. The cameras were like a bad back; they were always around and there wasn't much you could do about them. President Robert Xavier Hayes was seated in his leather chair at the middle of the long table, his back to the windows. His chair was taller than all the others, just in case anyone forgot who the most important person in the room was.

On the president's right was Senator Moeller, a Democrat and the ranking minority member of the Senate Select Committee on Intelligence. To his right was chairman of the Joint Chiefs General Flood. On the president's left were Senator Clark, the chairman of the Senate Select Committee on Intelligence and the president's national security advisor, Michael Haik. Aides and staffers filled the remaining seats. Photos were snapped almost continually by two photographers from the White House press pool while a cameraman from one of the networks shot video of the meeting. Two reporters waited dutifully for the signal from the White House press secretary to give them the nod to start asking questions. They had been briefed on the purpose of the meeting and were told what would be permitted and what was out of bounds.

President Hayes, a moderate Democrat from Columbus, Ohio, knew both men on either side of him well, from his years in the Senate. He conversed freely with them and even cracked a few jokes while the cameras snapped away. It was what was called in Washington a staged love-fest: the two parties coming together, putting aside their differences and doing the right thing. President Hayes was handsome in a clean-cut way. A shade over six feet, he had thin brown hair that was turning grayer by the month. Hayes stayed thin by putting in thirty minutes on his treadmill or bike four or five days a week. He almost always worked out first thing in the morning, knowing it was usually the only time when someone wasn't trying to get a piece of him.

Hayes checked his watch and then nodded to the press secretary, signaling that it was time to start the questions.

Because space was often limited, it was not possible for the entire White House press corps to attend every event. Instead, there was a pool out of which reporters and photographers would take turns covering events, and then share the material they collected. It was Anna Rielly's lucky morning to unearth the obvious. The White House correspondent for NBC hit the record button on her Dictaphone and smiled at Hayes.

"Good Morning, Mr. President. Will there be a memorial service here in Washington to honor Director Stansfield?"

"No. Director Stansfield was adamant before he died that he wanted a simple private burial in South Dakota. The CIA is planning on erecting some type of monument to his service out at Langley, and I'm looking into placing a permanent marker at Arlington honoring his service during World War Two."

"Have you come to any decisions on who will succeed him at the CIA?"

"As a matter of fact we have." Hayes looked to both of his former colleagues. "We have stumbled across one of those increasingly rare moments of mutual agreement." Hayes laughed and the others joined in. "With very little difficulty we have decided on the one person who is best suited to take over as the new director of Central Intelligence." The president looked to his left and said, "Hank, why don't you do the honors."

Rielly was slightly surprised. This truly was a unified front to have a Republican senator announce the nominee of a Democratic president. Rielly turned her green eyes on the well-liked senator from Arizona and asked, "Senator Clark?"

"The truth is, we didn't have to look very hard, or very far, to find the best man for the job." Clark winked at Rielly over his intentional disregard for the politics of political correctness. "The best man for the job is a woman who is currently running the CIA's Counterterrorism Center. Dr. Irene Kennedy is our hands-down choice to be the next DCI."

The five men smiled and nodded at each other while flashes from the cameras lit up the room. Not to be left out of the spotlight, Senator Moeller cleared his throat and said, "This is truly a historical moment. Dr. Kennedy will be the first woman to head the CIA, and for that matter the first woman to head up any of the agencies that make up our intelligence community."

Rielly was busy writing something on her notepad and without looking up she said, "That is of course, if she's confirmed by the Senate."

"That goes without saying," Clark said. "But Senator Moeller and I can tell you that she will have no problem making it through our committee."

"Assuming there are no surprises."

Clark stared at Rielly. She really was a beautiful woman, with a brain and a little spunk to boot. He wondered briefly if she knew the type of person her boyfriend was. The number of people he had killed. "There are no guarantees in this town, Ms. Rielly, but assuming there are no surprises, I am very confident that Dr. Kennedy will sail through the confirmation process."

Rielly directed her gaze at the president. "Was Dr. Kennedy your first choice, Mr. President?"

Without hesitation Hayes replied, "Yes."

"Was Dr. Kennedy Director Stansfield's choice to succeed him?"

"Director Stansfield felt that Dr. Kennedy was more than up to the task."

Smiling, Rielly said, "I assume that means Kennedy was Stansfield's choice."

"Director Stansfield thought that Dr. Kennedy was more than qualified to head the Agency." The president answered Rielly's question in such a way as to leave little doubt that he would not answer the same question if it was asked a third time.

Rielly took the hint and checked her notes. "Will Deputy DCI Brown stay on as the number two person at the Agency or will he be leaving?"

Michael Haik, the president's national security advisor, fielded the question. "I spoke to the DDCI this morning, and he said he will stay on for as long as he is needed."

"Does that mean that he plans on leaving as soon as Dr. Kennedy is confirmed?"

"No. Brown has the utmost respect for Dr. Kennedy

and is looking forward to working closely with her."

"Is he disappointed that he didn't receive the nomination from the president?" Rielly didn't look to Hayes for an answer. She kept her eyes on Haik.

Haik knew he had to throw Rielly a little bone here or she would keep digging. "Of course he's a little disappointed. Brown is extremely qualified. We were fortunate enough to have two great candidates to choose from. Brown respects the choice of Dr. Kennedy and is looking forward to helping her transition into the top spot."

"I would like to add something here," interjected Senator Clark. "Brown has been invaluable to the CIA, the Senate Intelligence Committee and this country." Clark leaned forward to elicit a nod from Senator Moeller. "There is no reason why just because one of them got the job the other should have to leave. If Brown were to decide to vacate his position I would be extremely upset. I would expect Dr. Kennedy to rely heavily on Brown to get the job done." Clark's words were intended for one person and one person only: Irene Kennedy. He could ill afford to lose Brown right now. Kennedy needed to understand that if there was any house cleaning to be done, Brown was to remain untouched.

Rielly flipped to the second page of her spiral notepad. "There have already been some rumblings from the Hill about Dr. Kennedy taking over the top spot at the CIA. Are you sure this confirmation is going to be as easy as you think?"

"I'm not familiar with these rumblings," the president said. "Would you care to identify the rumblers or rumbler you're referring to?"

Rielly smiled briefly at the president and said, "Chairman Rudin has gone on the record stating that he thinks nominating Dr. Kennedy as the next DCI is a huge mistake."

"The last time I checked Chairman Rudin was in the House, not the Senate," said the president flatly. He had a recent history of run-ins with the fellow Democrat, and he was none too fond of him.

Rielly looked a little confused. "Yes, but he is the chairman of the House Permanent Select Committee on Intelligence."

"He sure is, but that also means he will have nothing whatsoever to do with the confirmation of Dr. Kennedy."

"But, he runs the committee that approves the Agency's budget. Aren't you the least bit concerned that Chairman Rudin considers Dr. Kennedy a disastrous choice?"

The president forced a smile. "I wouldn't be alarmed, Anna. Chairman Rudin isn't truly happy unless he has something to complain about." Hayes winked at Rielly and then turned to his press secretary. On cue, the press secretary sprang into action and ushered the press pool from the room, leaving the president and his guests to discuss business in private.

4

Rapp showered and took his time getting dressed. He put on a dark gray, three-button suit, a white shirt and a burgundy tie. He left his house a little later than he should have, but he didn't care. As he worked his way around the Beltway from the east side of town to the west, he kept the radio off and tried to go over the details of his last mission one more time. During Rapp's affiliation with the Agency he had always felt secure that his identity was kept a very close secret. He moved freely around Washington without fear of being recognized by someone who might know that he did more than run a small international computer consulting business. The only people he really associated with were the handful of other world-class triathletes who lived in the Baltimore-Washington area. They trained with each other from time to time, but even that had stopped several years earlier when Rapp retired from the sport.

As Rapp picked his way through traffic he sifted through the details of what had happened on that last mission in Germany. That was where it had all started to unravel. Just a month earlier Kennedy had called on him to handle a very delicate mission. A German industrialist named Count Heinrich Hagenmiller had been caught selling highly sensitive equipment to the Iraqis, the kind of equipment that was crucial in the manufacturing of nuclear weapons. Rapp's job was fairly straightforward, not unlike others that he had done before. He flew to Germany where he met up with a husband and wife team, Tom and Jane Hoffman. They had been in place for a week running surveillance on the count. Posing as agents from Germany's federal police, the BKA, they gained access to Count Hagenmiller's estate during a party that the count was throwing. Rapp entered the mansion with Jane Hoffman, while her husband waited outside in the car.

Everything had gone as planned. The count had left his guests and joined them in his study. He was accompanied by his lawyer and a bodyguard. None of this had been a surprise. Rapp killed the count with one well-placed shot from his silenced .22-caliber Ruger pistol and then disabled both the lawyer and the bodyguard without having to kill them. When Rapp turned to ask Jane Hoffman to help him cuff the lawyer, he found himself looking down the barrel of her gun. This was where everything fell apart. She shot him twice in the chest, the bullets sending him back and over. He hit the ground hard, and with a whiplash effect, his head slammed against the bottom rung of the bookcase ladder and everything went black.

What the Hoffmans didn't know was that Rapp had bulletproof Kevlar sewn into the liner of his leather jacket. When he awoke almost five minutes later the Hoffmans were gone, the bodyguard was dead and a pool of Rapp's blood covered the floor from the gash on the back of his head. Rapp's next course of action came instinctively. Create a diversion and run like hell. He set fire to the study, destroying his own blood, and then stole a car that one of the guests had arrived in. Rapp never went into a mission without planning in detail his escape routes if something went wrong. The experience paid off and by afternoon the next day, without any help from the Agency, he was safely out of Germany.

For the first time in Rapp's career in counterterrorism he was confronted with a very ugly side of his business, the possibility that he had become a liability. And in his world, liabilities had a tendency to be erased from the balance sheet. Rapp could think of nothing worse than being betrayed by either Stansfield or Kennedy. He trusted them more than anyone in the world. Fortunately, upon his return to America he discovered that his handlers had not betrayed him. There was another problem. A leak. Somewhere, somehow, someone had found out about him, and they had set him up. Stansfield and Kennedy discovered that a man named Peter Cameron had hired the Hoffmans to kill him. Rapp was just about to confront Cameron's neck when he discovered him dead in his office.

In the weeks since Cameron's death they had learned some interesting things about the former employee of the CIA, but they had run into a dead end when it came to finding out who he had been working for. Kennedy had a special team within the Agency who were still poring over every detail of Cameron's life in hopes of finding out who had hired him and why, but Rapp knew not to expect much from them. Cameron had been killed by the man who had hired him. Rapp was sure of it.

Rapp wanted out. There would be no more targets, no more assassinations. He wanted to be done with death, and move on to creating some life of his own. He loved Anna more than anyone he had ever known. It was destiny that he'd saved her life and they'd fallen in love. The thought of losing her, of not spending the rest of his life with her, gave him a sickening feeling, and worse, it was affecting his instincts. He was losing his edge. Ironically, now that he was finally ready to walk away from the Orion Team, he couldn't. Right now, there were just too many unanswered questions.

He had to find out who in the hell had hired Peter Cameron and why. It was one thing to have to look over his shoulder when he traveled in the Middle East, but it was an entirely different matter to do it here in the U.S. It would be no way to raise a family, worrying every time he left the house that someone would harm his loved ones. No, Rapp knew he would have to see this thing through to the end. Most probably a bloody one.

By the time he arrived at the main gate of the CIA he was already five minutes late for his 10:00 A.M. meeting. As he approached the intimidating checkpoint he stayed to the left and got into one of the employee lanes. At the barrier he stopped his car and showed his fake credentials to a black-clad man from the CIA's Office of Security. The man had an MP-5 submachine gun slung across his chest and a bulky automatic in a nylon holster at his hip. A dozen more of his compatriots were out on post monitoring the gate, and there were even more standing behind the tinted bulletproof glass and brick of the blockhouse that was dressed up to look like a fancy highway weigh station. The unseen men and women inside carried even bigger guns plus a stash of LAW 80 shoulder-launched rockets just in case some heavy vehicle tried to crash its way onto the grounds. The CIA took its security very seriously.

The man studied Rapp's credentials for a moment and then handed them back to him. "Have a nice day, sir."

Rapp nodded and drove ahead, passing through the bright yellow spring-loaded crash barricades. The heavy steel devices were designed to pop up at a moment's notice to bar any unauthorized entry and potential car bombers. He proceeded to the underground parking garage of the Old Headquarters Building where he had to again show his credentials. He parked in a spot reserved for visitors to the director's suite, and passed through an unmarked door into a small lobby. Another guard was waiting and gestured for him to enter the elevator. Rapp stepped in by himself and the doors closed. The elevator went straight from the underground garage to the director's suite on the seventh floor. When the door opened two stocky men in suits were waiting for him. The shorter of the two looked Rapp over from head to toe and gestured for him to enter the office of the director's administrative assistant.

Rapp did so without comment and stepped into the spacious office. The woman behind the desk stood and surprised him by saying, "Good morning, Mr. Rapp. Could I get you anything to drink before your meeting?"

"Coffee would be fine." He wondered how the woman knew his real name.

"Any cream or sugar?"

"No thanks. Just black."

She pressed a button on one of three phones and said, "Dr. Kennedy, Mr. Rapp is here for your ten o'clock."

"Thank you, Dottie. Send him in."

Dottie got up from behind her desk and poured Rapp a mug of coffee in a blue Central Intelligence Agency mug. After handing the mug over to Rapp she showed him into Dr. Kennedy's office and closed the door.

Kennedy was at the far end of the long office amid a bevy of file boxes that were stacked on the conference table. Rapp had been in the office on only two previous occasions and glanced around to see what had changed since Stansfield's death. It appeared not much. The old spook's photos and awards were still hanging on the walls. He wondered if this was an oversight, or a sign that Kennedy was having trouble letting go of her old boss and mentor.

Kennedy grabbed her jacket from the back of one of the conference table chairs and put it on. She was wearing a stylish gray European suit with flared notched lapels. The color was very similar to Rapp's suit. The uniform color scheme would have made a student of George Orwell smile knowingly.

"Sorry about the mess. They moved everything from my old office while I was at the funeral." Kennedy smiled sadly. "Orders from Thomas. Even from the grave he's still running the show." Kennedy held her arms out and offered her cheek to Rapp.

He held the coffee mug clear and wrapped his free

hand around her waist. After kissing her cheek he said, "I'm sorry I couldn't make it to the funeral, but things are a little—"

"No need to explain." Kennedy squeezed him tightly. "You're still not used to showing your face in public. Thomas more than anyone would have understood."

"Well, you know I always had a lot of respect for the old codger."

Kennedy released him, stepping back and motioning for Rapp to take a seat on the couch. "He had an immense amount of respect for you, Mitch." She sat in an overstuffed leather chair. "You know that, don't you?"

Rapp shrugged off the words, uncomfortable, as always, with praise.

"Well, he did. He told me once that in all the years he had been in this business he thought you might be the best." Kennedy sat back in the chair and watched Rapp struggle with the compliment for a moment. She desperately wanted him to come inside and work in the Counterterrorism Center. Rapp's understanding of the Middle East, its different terrorist cells and how they operated would be invaluable to the Center. She could not begrudge him his wish to cease field operations. No one stayed in his line of work forever. It was just too taxing, both physically and mentally. In fact, she had actually begun training Rapp's replacement four years earlier and the young man was coming along just fine. Now, however, with her new duties as director there was no way she could continue to run the Orion Team. She wasn't sure she could trust the team's delicate missions with anyone other than Rapp.

Beyond all of that, she needed someone inside the Agency to watch her back. The blown operation in Germany still loomed large. Someone out there knew things they were not supposed to. They either worked at the Agency or they had someone who did. Kennedy thought it was the latter, and so did Stansfield. Before his death, he had warned that Rapp was not the ultimate target in Germany. Yes, someone wanted him dead, but not for the common motive of revenge. Rapp was meant to be found dead next to Count Heinrich Hagenmiller. The scandal was meant to embarrass the Agency, and in Stansfield's keen analysis, ultimately finish Irene Kennedy's career and maybe the president's. The prize, as Stansfield had put it, was the directorship of the CIA. Someone, for reasons unknown, didn't want Kennedy to take over as the head of the world's premier intelligence agency.

"How's Tommy?" asked Rapp of Kennedy's six-year-old son.

"He's fine. Still growing like a weed. He asked about you the other day. You should come by and see him."

"I know." Rapp grimaced. "Things have just been a little difficult lately. The last thing I'd want would be for some of my problems to become his."

Kennedy appreciated his thoughtfulness and told him so. They would get around to discussing their mutual problem later. "How is Anna?"

"She's great."

"Have you talked to her about the job offer?"

"Yes."

"And . . . what does she think?"

"Well, anything is better than what I'm doing right now, but I'm not so sure she thinks it's such a good idea for the long run."

"Working for the CIA?" Kennedy asked.

"Yeah, I suppose. You know she's a reporter. She'd never admit it to me, but they think we're a bunch of fascists."

Kennedy nodded knowingly, tucked a stray lock of her shoulder length brown hair behind her ear and with a smile said, "And they're all a bunch of communists."

"Pretty much, except now they prefer to think of themselves as socialists since the whole communism thing didn't turn out too well." Rapp laughed at his little cheap shot and Kennedy joined in.

Privately, Kennedy wondered how Mitch and Anna would deal with the difficulties of two careers that were so diametrically opposed. Kennedy could see Anna's friends poking fun at her boyfriend who worked for the CIA. She had repeatedly envisioned a horrible scene where some smart-ass reporter, who'd had one too many glasses of Chardonnay, decided to prove his intellectual superiority by making light of Mitch's career. The dream always turned out the same way. The smarmy man ended up on the floor in a pool of blood with his nose no longer in the center of his face.

Kennedy pushed the picture from her mind and got back to the subject at hand. "Look, I'm not going to hold you to what you told Thomas before he passed away. I don't think it was fair of him to pressure you at that time. I know you have some reservations about coming to work here at Langley, but I want you to know that you would be invaluable to the Counterterrorism Center." Looking down for a second she added, "And, Mitch, I could really use your help."

It was the last part that got to him. Rapp had an overwhelming sense of loyalty when it came to Kennedy. He knew he couldn't say no to her when she made it personal, but he had to at least try. "I've been doing some thinking. Hear me out for a second." He shifted and crossed his legs. "I've worked outside the Agency for years and have been very effective. I'm not so sure it wouldn't be better for me to remain out of sight and continue to help in a more subtle way."

Kennedy had thought of this and so had Stansfield. Neither of them liked the idea because of the logistical issues it created. Kennedy and Rapp needed an official cover so they could converse in the privacy of her office on a moment's notice. "We haven't filled you in on all of your new job requirements. You'd be far more than just an analyst in the CTC." Kennedy paused. "I want you to run the Orion Team for me."

Rapp looked surprised. "Really." What he hadn't come out and said, what he was slightly embarrassed to admit, was that his reluctance to come in from the cold was grounded in a fear of being trapped in an office environment five days a week. He'd never done it before and he wasn't so sure he wanted to start now. Rapp knew himself better than anyone with the exception of maybe Kennedy. He was a lone wolf, used to operating with minimal interference from the outside. He was not a team player, but the chance to run the Orion Team was extremely appealing.

"I would need you very close to me," Kennedy said. "As you know from your own experience, most of our decisions must be made on very short notice."

"I would love to run the Orion Team, but I'm not so sure I like the idea of working in the CTC."

"Why?"

Rapp shrugged. "I'm just not all that excited about punching the clock. I know enough about this place to know that I'd end up . . ." He struggled to find the right phrase. "I'd be stuck in meetings all day. It would drive me crazy. I'd end up telling some desk jockey to shove it up his ass."

Kennedy smiled at the delicious thought. They could

probably use a little of that around here, but she knew it wouldn't go over real well. "I'm not worried about that. Yes, you might have to keep your temper in check and watch what you say, but Mitchell, you're used to doing that. When you were undercover you couldn't just speak your mind. You had to practice restraint."

"Oh, so I should act like I'm being inserted behind enemy lines." Rapp cracked a smile. "Do you have any idea how stressful it is when I do that? I can't let my guard down for a second."

"My point is that you are surely capable of practicing a little restraint."

"I'm fully capable, but *my* point," Rapp stabbed himself in the chest with his forefinger, "is that I'm not so sure I want to." Turning away, he looked out the window at the gray morning sky. "I'm not sure what I want to do, period."

Kennedy studied him for a long moment and then asked in a knowing tone, "Mitch, what else are you going to do with your life?"

"I don't know." Almost as an afterthought he hearkened back to his conversation with Anna. "Maybe I'll stay at home and raise the kids."

"What kids?" asked an amused Kennedy.

"The kids I plan on having someday."

"Isn't there something else you have to take care of first?"

"Like what?"

Grinning, Kennedy answered, "Like getting married."

"Oh, yeah. I'm working on that." Rapp smiled at the thought of his plan to get engaged.

Kennedy couldn't hide her joy. Mitch deserved some happiness. "Any details you'd like to share with me?"

With a smirk, he replied, "I have to share them with someone else first."

"Of course." Kennedy held the thought for a while and then, changing back to the original subject said, "Don't worry about the mundane stuff that goes on around here. I can protect you from most of it. And what I can't . . . well you know how to handle yourself. I'm sure I'll have to smooth some things over from time to time, but that's to be expected." Kennedy changed gears and went ahead with the assumption that Rapp had nowhere else to go. At least nowhere else that would provide the same challenges. "I'll start you out with an annual salary of sixty thousand, and you'll get another hundred and fifty for running the Orion Team. Tax free, of course, and deposited into your offshore account."

Rapp nodded. Money wasn't the overriding issue, but it was at least nice to know he'd be taken care of. "What would my official position be?"

"I'm working on that. We could easily put you in the CTC as an analyst, but I'd like to give you something with a little more clout. Possibly special assistant to the DCI on Middle Eastern affairs."

"I still need to think about it. When would you want me to start?"

"Today," Kennedy said with a straight face.

"That's not going to work. I need some time to take care of a few things, and Anna and I are going to Italy for seven days."

This was not good news to Kennedy. She stood and walked over to her desk. Grabbing a videotape, she returned to the sitting area and put it into the VCR. With the remote control in hand she stepped away from the TV and pressed play.

On the screen a woman stepped from an elevator and started down the hallway. Rapp had already watched the tape a dozen times. The woman looked innocent enough, shoulder length blond hair, a little taller than average, her figure concealed by a roomy sundress. Bangs and large tinted glasses obscured her face, and she was careful to keep it directed away from the security camera. She was a pro. Halfway down the hall the woman stopped and knocked on an office door. The building was Funger Hall, located on the campus of George Washington University. The door was opened. You couldn't see who she was visiting, but both Rapp and Kennedy knew it was Peter Cameron, the man who had tried to have Rapp killed in Germany.

Kennedy pushed the fast forward button and sped through a section of the tape where the corridor was empty. Suddenly the blond-haired woman reappeared in the hallway and went in the opposite direction toward the staircase. Just as she reached the fire door, almost on cue, the elevator doors opened and two men stepped into the hallway. The woman briefly glanced over her shoulder. Kennedy froze the tape and zoomed in on the face.

"Any idea who she is?"

Rapp stared at the grainy image. He remembered the whole thing very well. It had been less than two weeks since he'd stepped off that elevator with Scott Coleman. They had only moments earlier discovered the identity of the man who had failed to kill Rapp in Germany and then attempted to lure him into a trap at his own home. The man was Peter Cameron, and by the time Rapp and Coleman made it to his office he was dead. A sharp object had been shoved through his ear and into his brain. Cameron's death had been extremely painful, but quick.

In response to Kennedy's question about the girl, he shook his head and said, "No." It was a lie. He knew the second they found Cameron's dead body who she was.

The way she moved, the way Cameron was killed, it all pointed to one person. Her name was Donatella Rahn and Rapp owed her much.

"I'm having Marcus run a search on her against known assassins."

Feigning indifference, Rapp simply nodded.

Kennedy sat and pointed at the TV. "She is our only link right now. Somebody hired Peter Cameron to make sure you didn't make it back from Germany. They wanted the CIA to be embarrassed. They wanted the Orion Team exposed, and if our thinking is right, your dead body would have been all the proof they needed. Whoever is behind this knows things they aren't supposed to."

Rapp rolled his eyes at the obvious. "And what exactly do you want me to do about it?"

With a genuine smile Kennedy said, "I want you to go to Italy and ask Anna to marry you." She paused and took joy in the surprise she saw on his face. It would be nothing compared to his next reaction. "And then I want you to stop by Milan and ask your old friend Donatella who hired her to kill Peter Cameron."

The grin that had spread across Rapp's face melted away at the mention of Donatella. Rather than say anything stupid he stayed silent and let Kennedy make the next move. She got up and walked over to the safe behind her desk. Returning with a file, she dropped it on Rapp's lap.

"It's all in there. Most of it you already know. Some of it will be new to you, and some of it you might like to correct. You know her better than anyone in this building."

He looked down at Donatella's file. It was rather thick, at least two inches. He tossed it back onto the coffee table without opening it. "How did you know?"

"An educated guess, and then I had Marcus do some digging. Customs shows her arriving in New York the day before Cameron was killed." She tilted her head and asked, "Why didn't you tell me?"

"I wasn't sure," shrugged Rapp.

"It didn't have anything to do with the fact that you were involved with her?"

He thought about it for a second and said, "I'm not sure. On some level it may have . . . but . . ." Rapp gave up on trying to explain.

Kennedy pressed on, asking, "But what?"

Rapp respected Kennedy a lot, so he chose his words carefully. "You have enough to worry about right now. I wanted to run this down on my own and make sure, before I brought it to you."

"You didn't trust me." Kennedy stared unflinchingly at him.

He looked away and said, "I trust you."

"Then what's the problem?"

"The problem is that you have a leak." Rapp sat forward on the edge of the couch. "No one was supposed to know I was going to Germany, but someone did. I know Donatella. She'll talk to me. If it really was her who killed Cameron, I'll know. If you send someone else to pick her up, either they'll end up dead or she will, and that's the last thing we need right now."

She wasn't pleased to have to admit it, but he was right. Still, though, she didn't like being kept in the dark. "Do you want me to send along any help? Have some of our people over there keep an eye on her until you get there?"

"No. The fewer people who know about this the better."

Kennedy nodded and thought about the importance of

Rapp's trip. After a moment of reflection she said, "Mitch, she's our only link."

Rapp looked away from his boss and out the window. He thought of how desperately he wanted to close this chapter in his life and said quietly, "I know."

5

WASHINGTON, D.C., MONDAY EVENING

Approximately two miles north and a little west of the White House is one of the most formidable embassies in Washington. Located atop a hill off Connecticut Avenue, the large encampment is fitting for a nation that has felt threatened throughout its entire existence. Most native Washingtonians didn't even know that the embassy belonged to Israel. To them the series of buildings seemed to possess nothing more than an interesting architectural style and a commanding view. The more informed observer saw a fortress. The buildings were designed with small windows that were used sparingly. The architectural device was one that was used in the Middle East to combat the hot sun, but here in Washington it was employed as a security measure. The windows were all bulletproof and designed to neutralize audio listening devices. The buildings were set back a very comfortable distance from the street and a blanket of steel mesh was hidden beneath the varying façades. The perimeter fence looked normal enough, but was in fact reinforced to stop anything short of a tank.

The Israelis had ample experience with car bombs, and

that experience contributed greatly to the design of the embassy compound. Humans are creatures of survival, and there is perhaps no greater modern day example of a tribe fighting for its survival than Israel. The western world is very familiar with the horrific atrocities perpetuated against the Jewish people by the Nazis in World War II. Unfortunately, in Israel's opinion, the west considers the Holocaust a historical event: the Nazis are gone and Israel now has a country of its own. What most of the west has failed to realize is that Israel is a piece of land surrounded on three sides by Arab countries that have at one time or another over the last fifty years, attacked the tiny Jewish state and threatened to wipe it off the face of the earth. In addition to their neighbors, the Jews must also deal with a threat from within. The Palestinians, the people who occupied the ancient lands before Israel settled there after World War II, have also sworn to destroy Israel. Israel is a country, a people, a tribe that must fight every day for its very survival. When dealing with the Israelis this is something that must always be remembered.

Senator Hank Clark never lost sight of this important fact. People who had to fight for their survival tended to be quite a bit more motivated. The senator's limousine pulled up to the main gate of the Israeli embassy. As the limo's headlights bathed the sturdy gate and the security personnel who were dressed in tuxedos, he thought of how much he admired the Jews and their tenacity. After the car was thoroughly checked it was allowed to pass.

Parties at the Israeli embassy were never known to be lush affairs. Now the French, for all of their complaining and lack of devotion to their allies, were an entirely different matter. The French knew how to throw a party. The Israelis tended to be quite a bit more serious about life, and their parties had a rather austere atmosphere.

Even so, Senator Clark made it a priority to attend as many functions at the embassy as he could. Everyone simply assumed Clark was pandering to the Jewish vote in Phoenix, but that wasn't the case. Clark enjoyed immense popularity in his home state, and his getting reelected did not depend on whether or not he attended a party. But it was fine, if his staffers, his colleagues and the press thought he was currying favor with the Jews. Like most things with Clark, one had to dig a little deeper to find his real motive.

The tall senator stepped into the main foyer of the embassy by himself. He had left wife number three at home. She didn't care for the serious, cut-to-the-chase approach of the Israeli diplomats, so she had decided to sit in a warm bath and indulge herself in an aromatherapy session and an expensive bottle of wine. This suited the senator fine. He had enough on his mind tonight, and the last thing he needed was to baby-sit number three. In fact, Senator Clark would love nothing more than to replace number three with a number four, but he was afraid it didn't fit into his current plans. The American people would give him a pass on two divorces, but a third would really be pushing it.

Clark had barely made it through the entrance when the Israeli ambassador's underlings besieged him. Hands were firmly squeezed. Clark doled out a few backslaps and greeted everyone with his best smile. One of the more senior diplomats, who knew Clark better than the others, helped whisk him away so he could take care of the first order of business. Thirty seconds later Clark was standing in the large ballroom with a tumbler of ice-cold Scotch in his hand. A full head taller than almost everyone at the party, Clark scanned the crowd for the face he doubted he would see. The man he was to meet with tonight did not like to be seen in public.

After about an hour of schmoozing, Senator Clark was led away from the other guests by an unremarkable man in his forties. The senator had no idea who the man was and had no interest in finding out. After a brief stop at the men's room, Clark was handed off to another individual who led him past the Shin Bet security personnel and into the working part of the embassy. None of the security officers asked for identification, much less looked at him. Everything had been arranged, Clark knew, by the man he was going to meet. By the time they reached the elevator the sounds of the party were a distant roar.

The entire embassy was considered a secure facility by Shin Bet, the Israeli agency charged with handling security for all of the country's embassies and consulates. But nowhere in the embassy was security taken more seriously than in sub level three. The entire floor was without windows and partitioned from the rest of the facility. It housed the offices of the military's various intelligence organizations, AMAN, AFI and NI, as well as those of Mossad, Israel's vaunted foreign intelligence service. The area could be accessed in only two ways; by a single elevator or staircase. The staircase, however, could only be used in the event of a fire, which to date had never happened. All traffic to and from the floor was by way of the elevator.

Clark stepped into the elevator by himself and descended four stories beneath the earth to an area where electronic eavesdropping was more difficult. When he stepped from the elevator, he was greeted by a sterile combination of bright lights, white floor and white walls. The only noticeable feature in the room was a heavy secure door with a camera mounted above it and an automatic fingerprint recognition pad to the right. Clark heard the metallic click of the lock on the door being released and he opened it. Standing on the other side was a woman who Clark guessed to be in her mid thirties. Without speaking, she gestured for the senator to follow, and they were off. Midway down the corridor the woman took a right and then stopped several doors later. With a polite smile and an open palm she motioned for Clark to enter the dim room.

Clark found his friend sitting at the other end of a rectangular ten-person conference table. He stepped into the room. The thick spring-loaded door closed automatically with an airtight *click*. The walls and ceiling were covered with a gray foam that looked similar in pattern to the inside of an egg carton. The senator knew the foam was designed to keep whatever was said inside the room, which was exactly what both men wanted.

The man at the far end of the room closed the file he was reading and switched his cigarette from his right hand to his left. Standing, he extended his hand to the senator and greeted him warmly. "Good evening, Hank. It is a pleasure to see you, as always."

"Thank you for making the trip, Ben. I really appreciate it."

Ben Freidman shrugged as if to intimate that traveling halfway around the world from Tel Aviv was no big deal. Freidman gestured for Clark to sit, and he turned to a small portable bar that was behind him. Like Clark, Freidman also enjoyed his alcohol.

"I had to come anyway. I need to see the president in the morning." He poured two drinks and then eased himself into the chair at the head of the table.

"Anything important?"

"I'd say so," Freidman replied with a troubled look.

"Can you tell me about it?"

"It involves Iraq. You will hear about it soon enough, but let's not talk about my problems right now. Let me hear yours." Freidman was a pit bull of a man in both personality and physique. He was aggressive, tenacious, and loyal. If he did not love you, he was a man to be feared, but if he did love you, he was as dependable as a eunuch guarding a vestal virgin. Freidman loved his country first and foremost, and after that he loved those who helped protect Israel. Senator Clark fell into the latter category.

Freidman kept his head shaved, and rarely wore a tie. Most of the time, like tonight, he wore a pair of dress pants with a plain short-sleeved dress shirt. A good fifty pounds overweight, the five foot ten inch spy liked to keep his shirts untucked. Not only did he find it more comfortable in the often oppressive heat of Tel Aviv, it also helped to conceal the gun he always carried in a holster at the small of his back. Born in Jerusalem in 1949, Freidman came of age just in time to distinguish himself in the famous Six Day War of 1967. He was in a front line unit that was overrun during the initial hours of the war. Instead of lying low and waiting for the Israeli Defense Forces to push the Egyptians back across the border, Freidman grabbed two men from his squad, and against the orders of his squad leader, set off into the night to harass the enemy. They succeeded brilliantly in their mission, infiltrating the perimeter of a mobile Egyptian command post and wreaking utter havoc. His bold actions did not go unnoticed, and after the famous Six Day War, AMAN, Israel's military intelligence organization, got their hands on him. By the age of thirty Freidman had risen to the rank of colonel and had fast gained a reputation as a man who got results. It was then that he had been recruited, or as some in the military felt, stolen by the Mossad.

Over the next two decades Freidman became a legend within the Mossad. What was even more miraculous to some was his uncanny ability to avoid highly embarrassing situations. Whether it was luck or cunning, no one could be quite sure, but Ben Freidman had risen to the very top of what many considered the most effective intelligence agency in the world. He was a man to be respected and feared. He was the director general of the Mossad, and rarely did a month pass where he didn't send someone to their death.

Freidman took a sip of his Polish vodka, and looking at his guest, surmised that he would most likely keep the trend going. Tilting his head slightly, Freidman asked the chairman of the Senate Select Committee on Intelligence, "What troubles you, my friend?"

"Oh, many things, but one thing in particular."

"Dr. Kennedy?"

"Ummm . . . yes and no. She is an issue, but at present there's someone who is a bigger priority."

A thin mischievous smile creased Freidman's lips. "Mr. Rapp?" Shaking his head he added, "I told you, you should have never got him involved in all of this. He is far too dangerous a man."

"Yes, you were right about that, but we can't turn back the clock." Clark hesitated for a moment, as if he were struggling to suppress a bad memory. Freidman had indeed advised him to avoid Mitch Rapp. He had been very specific on that point, warning him that four continents were littered with the corpses of people who had gone toe to toe with America's top assassin. At the time Clark had thought that Freidman had refused out of some respect for Rapp, some common bond they had forged while fighting the same enemy. That was the rationale the senator had used when he had been stupid enough to trust Peter Cameron.

Just the thought of Cameron caused Clark to grimace.

He had recruited him personally. As the trusted chairman of the Senate Intelligence Committee, there wasn't much that Clark couldn't get his hands on. He had chosen Peter Cameron after several years of studying the man's every move. Cameron was a twenty-four-year veteran of the CIA's Office of Security; the CIA's own little private Gestapo. One of the Office of Security's chief jobs was to watch the watchers, to spy on the spies.

Cameron knew things and had contacts that the senator was more than willing to compensate him for. After more than two decades of mediocre pay, Cameron leapt at the chance to become a well-paid mercenary for the senator. It had been Cameron's idea to kill Rapp and leave him in Germany for all the world to discover.

Despite all of his suppressed anger Clark had to be honest with himself. The plan had been a bold one. Clark had shadowed Rapp and Kennedy and intercepted the orders. Cameron had used his contacts inside the Agency and paid them well. Clark was sure of that, for he had been the one handing over the suitcases of cash. If the plan had succeeded, Chairman Hank Clark would have presided over the most sensational hearings this country had seen in decades. The facts Clark was prepared to slowly unearth would have destroyed President Hayes, and wounded the Democratic Party for at least the next two general elections. It would have allowed the senator to virtually handpick the next director of the CIA. A director who would be more than willing to open up the treasure trove of secrets formerly known as Echelon. And more important than all of it, the entire affair would have allowed Hank Clark to launch his bid for the White House. He would have had the money from Ellis and his associates in Silicon Valley, the nationally televised committee hearings would have given him the all important face time and name recognition, and his party would have been beholden to him for bringing the Democrats to their knees. It was a lock. They had come so close. If only Peter Cameron had succeeded.

Clark had failed to listen to Freidman and he was now paying for it. When the Germany operation blew up in their faces Cameron assured Clark that he could handle the CIA's top killer. Clark had given him one more chance, and Cameron had screwed that up too. Disguised as FBI special agents, Cameron and his cronies had picked up Anna Rielly and brought her to Rapp's house. Once again, Cameron underestimated his target, and before the night was over more men had died at Rapp's hands.

That was when the senator had decided to cut his losses. In a brief coded e-mail to Freidman, Clark had arranged for Peter Cameron to meet his maker. Twenty-four hours later Cameron was dead and Mitch Rapp had run into a brick wall in his pursuit to find out who had ordered the hit on him in Germany.

If Clark had learned anything from his experiences of the last month it was to be extra careful. The lure of ultimate power had caused him to make some poor decisions, and he was not going to let it happen again. He would heed the advice of Ben Freidman, and from this point forward he would be more careful.

Leaning back in his chair, Freidman gestured with his hands, telling his friend to unload his burden. "How can I help?"

Clark hesitated briefly and then said, "The woman you sent to take care of Cameron?"

Freidman raised an eyebrow. "I never told you it was a woman."

"The CIA has tapes of her."

"When you say the CIA, who do you mean specifically?"

"Kennedy."

"What do the tapes show?"

"They show her coming and going."

Freidman noticed that Clark seemed very disturbed by this bit of news. Always with one eye on the end game, he decided to play the whole thing off as unimportant. "She's a pro. I doubt they will find anything on those tapes."

"But what if they do?"

Freidman acted as if he were giving the senator's words serious concern. He scratched one of his muscular forearms and said, "I'm not worried. Even if they got lucky and found her, they would never get anything from her."

The thought of the CIA finding the woman caused Clark's chest to tighten. He reminded himself to keep breathing and stay calm. "I'm worried," he said flatly. "I would like this potential problem to go away. No loose ends. Rapp got close enough last time."

Freidman grimaced at Clark's words as if he were wrestling with an idea he didn't like. "This woman is very good. One of my best. I have put years and years of training into her."

"Five hundred thousand."

Freidman liked the number. It was easily double what he had expected. That was another thing he really liked about Clark and his cowboy attitude. There was no dicking around when it came to money. After considering the issue for a bit longer, Freidman nodded and said, "I'll take care of it, but it will have to wait until I return. This is too delicate to handle from America."

Clark felt as if a heavy weight had just been lifted from his shoulders. Relieved, he asked, "When are you heading back?"

"Tomorrow afternoon."

Smiling, Clark said, "Ben, I can't thank you enough for

coming all this way. I really appreciate it. I should have listened to you when you warned me to steer clear of Rapp."

"Don't worry." Freidman shrugged off the comment as if it were trivial. "You have been a good ally, and when you are president," the director of the Mossad raised his glass in a toast, "you will be an even better ally."

6

MARYLAND, MONDAY EVENING

The stars were bright even with the fire. Anna had given him a portable wrought iron fire kettle for his birthday, and Mitch had put it to good use. The temperature was around fifty and dropping. Rapp sat on the deck of his small cottage overlooking the Chesapeake. A slight breeze was coming in off the water, just enough to keep the smoke from billowing into his face. He was dressed warmly in jeans, a beat up sweatshirt and an old brown Carhartt jacket. He was sitting all the way back in a white Adirondack chair with his feet up on a footstool that was barely a foot from the flames. Shirley was lying at his side quietly. All he needed to make the night perfect was for Anna to get home.

Ten minutes later he got his wish, or at least he hoped. Shirley heard the car first. Her head snapped up, which alerted Rapp. He listened carefully to the sounds with his eyes closed for a moment. The dog leapt to her feet and scampered off the deck and around the side of the house to investigate. Rapp continued to listen while his left hand slid between the folds of his jacket in search of the cold hard comfort of his 9-mm Beretta. The harsh reality of Rapp's life was that people wanted to kill him. During the first ten years of his career in counterterrorism he could always count on coming home and letting his guard down. His job required it. The weeks and sometimes months that he spent abroad on missions was absolutely draining. The sheer amount of information he had to memorize for a mission was sometimes overwhelming: maps, codes, specifics on his target, the local authorities, political groups and competing terrorist groups. It all had to be memorized, and that was before being inserted.

Once he was in the country it got even worse. Without letting others see, he had to be hyperaware of everything that occurred around him. Imagine walking through a sea of people in the vibrant city of Damascus. Not only did he have to track those he had been sent to kill, but he also had to constantly look over his shoulder to make sure no one was following him. This was no easy task in a part of the world where ninety plus percent of the men had black hair and mustaches and most of the women were covered from head to toe in the traditional Muslim wrap. If his true identity were discovered he would be painfully stoned to death without a tribunal, and that would be the easy way out. If he were caught by the police, or a foreign intelligence service, he would be brutally tortured. And not just slapped around and screamed at. This was the Middle East. No part of his body would remain unviolated. He would be forced to endure the most inhumane conditions imaginable. Rapp regained control of his wandering imagination and pushed the horrible thoughts from his mind.

This was why he needed a safe place. A place where he could let his guard down and recuperate. That had been taken away from him, though. Someone in America knew about Rapp's secret life. They had tried to kill him twice now: once in Europe and once back in the States. Europe was bad enough, but setting a trap for him in his own home and using his girlfriend as the bait was way too close. Someone knew too much about Rapp and as each day passed it strengthened his resolve to find out who that person was. Before he could get on with his life he had to close this chapter. And Rapp desperately wanted to get on with his life. He wanted Anna, and he wanted children. He wanted a normal life, but he knew as he looked into the kitchen and saw Anna standing in front of the refrigerator that it would have to wait. He would have to do what he was trained to do. He would have to hunt down the person who had hired Peter Cameron, and he would have to kill him.

Rielly stepped out onto the deck with Shirley following close behind. She had a beer in each hand and a sly grin on her face. She bent over and kissed Rapp on the lips. "How was your day, honey?"

"Just great," he replied with a noticeable lack of enthusiasm. "How was yours?"

Rielly straightened up and handed him a beer. "Fine." Turning, she said, "I'm going to put some jeans on. I'll be back in a minute."

Rapp smiled at her as she went back into the house. *That was easy,* he thought. He'd been dreading the interrogation she would give him about his meeting with Kennedy. Rapp took a swig of beer knowing that as soon as she came back down she would dig in. He wondered how he should edit his story so it would come out in the best light. There were certain things he couldn't tell her for reasons of national security and others that he just couldn't tell her because he feared she would think less of him.

When Rielly came back outside she had on jeans, one of Rapp's flannels and an old wool blanket draped over her shoulders. She plopped down in her chair, tilted her chin up, pursed her lips and closed her eyes.

Rapp leaned over and kissed her on the lips. "Thanks for the beer."

"You're welcome." Rielly took a sip of her own and said, "Now tell me all about the meeting."

"You know . . . we talked a little bit about this and a little bit about that. It lasted about an hour. No big deal, really. Anything happen at the White House today?"

"Nice try." Rielly grinned. "You could care less about what happened at the White House today, and I have no idea what a little bit of this and a little bit of that means. So cut the crap and tell me what happened."

"I'm not sure where to start." Oh, he loved her. She was so beautiful and strong, both physically and mentally. Rapp was equally drawn to both. He knew himself well enough to know that if he were to ever survive in a long-term relationship he would need a woman who would keep him in line from time to time. Rapp had been a loner for far too long and had picked up some habits that weren't very helpful in running a successful partnership.

In an intentionally condescending tone Rielly said, "Why don't you start from the beginning?"

"Well, I wore my gray three-button suit and that tie you bought me for Father's Day." Rapp stopped and looked at her with a shitty grin. "Why did you buy me a tie for Father's Day, by the way? We never settled that. Was it wishful thinking on your part, or were you trying to imply that I may have some children that I don't know about?"

"I've got all night, Mitchell, my darling. We can do this the easy way or the hard way. You can just tell me, or I can wear you down hour by hour."

Rapp smiled as he took another drink. "I can hold out."

"Oh . . . I'm sure you can. But two can play at that game." Rielly gave him a devilish smile and turned her attention to the fire.

"What's that supposed to mean?" asked Rapp with a little more eagerness than he would have liked to show.

"No sex."

Rapp groaned, "Oh God. Don't you pay any attention to all of those stupid relationship books that you and your friends read? They all say the same thing. *Never!* And I repeat, *never* use sex as a weapon."

"I'm not using it as a weapon." Rielly shook her head. "If I decide to abstain I will do it on religious grounds."

"And what would those be?" Rapp laughed.

"That I shouldn't be giving myself so freely to a man who I am not married to, much less engaged." Rielly quickly took a drink of beer to hide the smile that was spreading across her face.

Rapp watched her for a second and said, "So you want to become some sort of born-again virgin?"

"Yeah, something like that."

Rapp laughed. "That's the dumbest thing I've ever heard. Only a sexually repressed Irish Catholic girl from Chicago could come up with something so ludicrous."

"We'll see how ludicrous you think it is after a couple of weeks of cuddling and nothing else."

Still laughing, Rapp held up his hands in mock surrender. "Okay, okay. You win. What would you like to know?"

Rielly smiled triumphantly. "What was the new job offer?"

"Come to work in the Counterterrorism Center. She hasn't decided on a title yet. I'd be attached to the Middle East desk in some form or another. Either as a senior analyst or a special assistant to the DCI on Islamic terrorism."

Rielly raised her eyebrows in exaggerated excitement. "I like the second one. It sounds very important."

With a grimace Rapp said, "I'm not sure I like either of them."

"Why?"

"I don't know, honey. I don't know if I can go to work in that damn puzzle palace."

"What do you mean?"

"I'm not used to punching the clock, and as you know, taking orders is not my strong suit."

"Yeah, but what else are you going to do?"

Staring into the fire Rapp said, "I don't know. I'll stay home and raise the brood."

"Oh no, you won't." Rielly shook her head. "The last thing I want is a brooding husband raising the brood. You'll go nuts, Mitchell. You need challenge in your life. Don't get me wrong. I think you'll be a great father, but a Mr. Mom you're not."

"Yeah, I know, but—" Rapp stopped and took a drink.

"But what?"

"I don't think I'm cut out to play all of the Mickey Mouse games they make you play at Langley."

Rielly reached over and touched his hand. "I think you should do it. At least give it a try."

"Really?" Rapp said, a little surprised.

"Yeah. And don't forget, you've got the director in your corner if anything goes wrong."

Rapp studied her. "Hmm."

"What?"

"I just didn't expect you to tell me to take the job."

"We all have to do something, honey. You were very good at what you did for the last ten years." Rielly reached out and touched his cheek. "I got to see it firsthand." Softly she added, "You saved my life." A warm smile washed over her face and she leaned over and kissed him. "And now that I've fallen in love with you, you are going to have to retire from the front lines and take a desk job." She pinched his cheek. "The transition might be a little difficult at first, but you know too much about the Middle East to just walk away."

"It doesn't bother you at all that you'll have to tell your family and friends that I work for the CIA?"

"Are you kidding me?" Rielly grinned. "My girlfriends all drool over you as it is; when they find out you're a spy they're gonna lose it." She laughed.

"No, I'm serious. Won't it affect how you're treated at work? You know . . . sleeping with the enemy."

"No." She shook her head and then after thinking of a couple of potential problems added, "And if it does, I'll deal with it."

Thinking about what she had just said, Rapp slowly nodded his understanding. "Well, that makes me feel better about it."

"Good. What else did you talk about?"

Rapp thought about Kennedy asking him to take over the Orion Team, but that was strictly off limits. He had never uttered the words to her, nor would he. "Not much else. Just salary and some administrative stuff."

Rielly gave him a skeptical look. "Come on. What else?"

"Nothing that I can talk about."

"Mitchell?"

"Anna," Rapp replied in a mocking tone. "You're going to have to get used to this. If I take this job, almost everything that I touch will be classified. I won't be able to come home and chat about it."

Rielly rolled her eyes. "Your whole life is classified."

"Honey, we might as well come to terms with this right now. If you won't respect the fact that I can't talk about ninety percent of what I do or see at work then I might as well tell Irene right now that I don't want the job." Rapp stared at her intensely to make sure she knew he was extremely serious about the issue.

"I'll respect it, I'll respect it. Don't worry."

"Good." Rapp leaned over and gave her a long kiss. Her lips felt so good. He was head over heels in love. He knew it was affecting his judgment, but there was nothing he could do about it. There was no turning back, no slamming on the brakes; he didn't even have the willpower to tap them. After a while he worked his way to her ear and asked, "Can we go upstairs and have sex now?"

Rielly purred her response, and they rose together and went into the house, leaving behind the warmth of the fire.

7

OVAL OFFICE, TUESDAY MORNING

"What in the hell is this meeting about?" President Hayes tilted his head down so he could look over the top of his specs at the three people standing in front of his desk. He was still drinking his morning coffee and reading the day's schedule when the three of them had come waltzing in with apprehension on their faces. They then proceeded to dump something in his lap that was unusual, to say the least.

Valerie Jones, the president's chief of staff, spoke first. "I just heard about it for the first time five minutes ago." Jones turned to look past Michael Haik, the president's national security advisor, to Irene Kennedy.

Kennedy spoke. "I received the call early this morning. He was very serious, but then again, he usually is."

Hayes leaned over on the left armrest and stroked his chin. This whole thing was strange, a first for him in his relatively short career as president. Nothing good could come of it, he was sure of that. Looking up at Kennedy, he asked, "Have they ever done something like this before?"

Kennedy thought about her dealings with the Israelis over the last two decades. "They request backdoor meetings with us from time to time. Usually for the obvious reasons: they don't want the press or any opposition to find out," Kennedy shook her head slightly, "but I don't seem to ever remember them going straight to the top."

"This can't be good. The director of Mossad flies to the United States and pretty much demands to see me. I don't see anything positive that can come out of this." Hayes looked up at his NSA. "Michael, what's going on over there? Any flare-ups in the peace process that I haven't been told about?"

"No, it's the same old thing. Arafat demands XY and Z and then walks away from the table. The bombs start to go off and then a month later they sit back down at the peace table and start over again."

"It's not that," Kennedy said in a thoughtful tone. "If it had something to do with the peace process they wouldn't fly Ben Freidman all the way in from Tel Aviv. Their ambassador would take care of it, or the prime minister would call." She paused and thought about another possibility. "No," she said making up her mind. "Ben Freidman means real trouble. Something is going on over there that we don't know about. Something serious."

"Great," the president grumbled. With more than a little frustration he said, "And none of you have any idea what it is."

"Sorry, sir," was all Haik could say.

The president thought about the situation for a moment. He was tempted to pick up the phone and call the Israeli prime minister, but caution got the better of him. The PM was due to visit the U.S. in two weeks. There was obviously a reason for sending Freidman. The president looked to Haik and said, "Get General Flood over here. I want him to sit in on this."

Haik grabbed the white handset of the bulky secure telephone unit sitting on the president's desk and hit the speed dial button for the chairman of the Joint Chiefs. Seconds later, General Flood was on the line and the national security advisor was explaining the situation. The general said he would be there just as quickly as his limousine could take him across the Potomac.

President Hayes checked his watch. It was a quarter past eight. "Freidman will be here at nine?"

"Yes," Kennedy answered.

"All right, between now and then I would like the three of you to try and come up with some idea of what this is all about." President Hayes snatched his glasses from his face and glared at three of his most trusted advisors. All he got in return were blank stares.

COLONEL FREIDMAN AND his bodyguard caught a taxicab on Connecticut Avenue. Freidman could have easily requisitioned one of the embassy's limousines for the trip but he preferred to keep a low profile. Anyone arriving at the White House in a limousine was sure to get his or her photograph taken. There were other cities where Freidman wouldn't dare to move about unless he was entombed in an armor-plated limousine, but Washington was not one of them. All of the various groups of the Middle East knew the rules. To attempt an assassination on American soil would be suicide, both financially and politically.

As the taxi headed toward the White House, Freidman stared out the window at the embassies they passed. The concentration of power in this town was unlike any other in the world, and Freidman was here to make a huge power play. He respected America; it was, after all, his country's greatest ally. Every year the Americans pumped billions of dollars into the Israeli economy, and the military aid they supplied was invaluable, but then again America had riches beyond her needs. There were many in Freidman's country though, who felt the Americans could give more, that they could do more to secure the borders of the only true democracy in the Middle East. Freidman was one of those people.

Trusted with the security of his tiny homeland, Freidman would stop at almost nothing to get what was good for Israel. He respected America, but in the end that respect was greatly overshadowed by his ultimate loyalty to the Israeli cause. America wasn't always willing to do everything they asked, and that was where Freidman often came in. The ugly secret was that the Mossad spied on the U.S. Not only did they spy, but from time to time they also ran covert operations against their greatest ally. That's not what this meeting was about, at least not yet. Played in the best possible light, it was about two allies taking on a common enemy. In the perpetually cynical eyes of Ben Freidman, it was getting the U.S. to do Israel's dirty work.

The taxi dropped them off two blocks from the White House, and the two men nonchalantly approached the northwest gate. They cleared security and were escorted to the White House Situation Room by one of the president's aides. Without having to be asked, Freidman's bodyguard headed down the hall to the White House Mess. His boss was secure inside the White House. The man would use the opportunity to get a cup of coffee and see if he could overhear any useful conversations. When Freidman entered the small conference room in the basement of the West Wing, he wasn't surprised in the least that there were only five people in attendance.

He was a little surprised, however, that no one rose to greet him. He took note of the mood and the lopsided seating arrangement. The president was where he expected him to be, at the head of the table; Kennedy was opposite the commander in chief at the other end and the chairman of the Joint Chiefs; the national security advisor and the chief of staff were all on one side of the table. Freidman draped his overcoat over one of the four empty chairs on his side of the table and looked to Kennedy to break the frigid air.

Smiling, the head of Mossad said, "Thank you for arranging this on such short notice, Irene."

Kennedy nodded, but offered no words.

Freidman took the hint and sat. Their moods would change when he showed them what he had in his briefcase. Turning to the president he said, "Thank you, Mr. President, for meeting with me. I hope you know we wouldn't have asked if it wasn't extremely important."

Like Kennedy, Hayes nodded, but gave no answer. Yes, the Israelis were their friends, but Hayes was not as blind to the often selfish goals of the Jewish state as some of his predecessors. He had given specific instructions to the others. No warm greetings were to be extended to the head of Israeli Intelligence. Freidman had called this meeting, and it would be his responsibility to do the talking.

"Have you noticed anything alarming out of Baghdad recently?" Freidman looked to Kennedy.

Before Kennedy could answer the president said, "Mr. Freidman, I'm rather short on time this morning. I think it would serve us best if you told us what this is all about."

Freidman placed his elbows on the table and said, "We have unearthed some very alarming news, Mr. President, and I'm afraid you aren't going to like it one bit."

Freidman reached for his briefcase. After entering the combination, he popped the clasps and retrieved a large red legal file. The file was sealed with a string and wax. Freidman broke the seal and extracted a sheaf of papers with a four-by-seven, black-and-white photograph clipped to the front. Sliding the photo over so the president could view the image, he said, "This is Park Chow Lee. He's North Korean. As you might imagine, he sticks out like a sore thumb in Baghdad. Park is a doctor." Freidman extracted several more photos and slid them in front of President Hayes. Where the first photo was posed and clear, these were taken from some distance and were slightly grainy.

"That first photo, Mr. President, of Park in the white lab coat, is him walking into the Al Hussein Hospital in Baghdad." He paused briefly to see if anyone was going to ask any questions. They didn't, so he continued. "There's only one problem with the photo. Mr. Lee is not a medical doctor, he has a Ph.D. in nuclear physics." Confident that he finally had their attention, Freidman decided to sit back and pause for a second.

Kennedy sat at the far end of the table and observed. She could see where this was going. Her daily intelligence briefings had contained some flash reports about Saddam doing business with the economically bankrupt state of North Korea. Saddam was sending them oil, and in return North Korea was sending him arms and technology. It also appeared from where Ben Freidman was heading that they were also trading talent. Kennedy watched as President Hayes briefly looked at her. She gave him a slight nod, confirming that the information was most likely legitimate. She noticed a hint of irritation in the president's face, and wondered briefly if it was directed at her. It probably was. When Freidman was gone she would have to explain why Mossad had beat the CIA to the punch. That was fine. Kennedy had no problem admitting that where the Middle East was concerned they could not compete with Mossad when it came to putting people on the ground.

"We have photographed Mr. Lee coming and going from the hospital for almost three months. He arrives early, leaves late and sometimes even stays for several days."

The photos of Lee were being passed around the table. National Security Advisor Haik picked up on something Freidman had said. "How do you know he's spending the night? Isn't it possible you missed him leaving?"

"It is, but," Freidman pulled out several more photos, "we also know where he and the other North Korean scientists are staying." Freidman passed the photos across the table to Haik.

The president was not in a patient mood, so he asked rather abruptly, "Where is this going, Mr. Freidman?"

"It's going to a very bad place, sir." Freidman exhaled a deep breath. "With the help of Mr. Lee and the other North Korean scientists, Saddam is about to get his greatest wish. In less than one month Saddam will have added three nuclear weapons to his arsenal."

President Hayes blinked and said, "What?"

"By the end of the year Saddam will have three fully operational nuclear weapons."

"How is that possible?" Hayes looked to his advisors. "Everything I have been told says we're two years away from having to deal with this. Not a month!"

"Those estimates, sir," stated Kennedy, "were based on Saddam rebuilding his own nuclear program. They did not include him bypassing the developmental stage and purchasing technology, components and scientists from North Korea."

The president was seething. His administration had been making great strides with the North Koreans. At this very moment they were trying to push through a billion-dollar aid package to try to help the anemic North Korean economy get back on its feet. Kim Jong Il himself had told Hayes that he would personally bring an end to North Korea's state-sponsored terrorism. The president told himself to put North Korea out of his mind for the moment. That would have to be dealt with later.

Stabbing his index finger at the photos in front of him, Hayes asked, "How accurate is this information?"

"I consider it to be very reliable, sir." Freidman kept his eyes focused on the president and did not waver.

"How reliable?" Hayes wanted more.

"This is, of course, not to leave this room." Freidman took a moment to look each of the president's advisors in the eye. The mole he had cultivated in the Iraqi regime was the highest Mossad had ever turned. To lose him would be devastating. "We have someone on the inside, and I can tell you nothing more. He is well-placed and highly reliable."

"Under a goddamn hospital," was all General Flood could say. His military mind was already trying to come up with ways to level the building.

"What type of weapons are we talking about?" asked Haik.

"Two of them are ten-megaton nukes designed to be delivered by the new Scud Three missile, and the third is a five-megaton nuke designed to be delivered by bomber or specialized artillery."

The room fell deathly silent. All of them had sat through enough intelligence briefings to know the level of carnage just one of the bombs could cause. Each of the three individually was more than sufficient to level Tel Aviv.

"Mr. President, none of us are happy about this. Least of all the leaders of my country." Freidman paused for a second before continuing. "I have been sent here by my prime minister to inform you that we will not allow these weapons to be deployed." Freidman's tone was calm but determined. Though he had been sent to Washington to get the Americans to do Israel's dirty work, there was no mistaking the resolve of his people. If the Americans failed to act, Israel would.

President Hayes nodded slowly. He had already deduced as much. There was no way Israel would let a megalomaniac like Saddam join the nuclear club. President Hayes wasn't about to allow it, and he was more than five thousand miles away. The Israelis were separated by only five hundred miles.

Finally, President Hayes asked, "When are you heading back to Israel?"

"I leave this evening."

Hayes drummed his fingers on the table while he thought of the next step. "Mr. Freidman, I appreciate you making the trip. Could you wait outside for a minute while I have a word with my advisors?"

Freidman collected the photos and placed them back in his briefcase. When he had left the room Hayes took off his suit coat and began pacing. He thought about taking his new director designate of the CIA to task for allowing him to be blindsided, and then decided it wasn't fair, and in the end probably counterproductive. Instead he said, "Around the horn. I want to hear opinions on what we just heard. Starting with you, Valerie." The president stopped and looked at his chief of staff.

"I think before we do anything we need to confirm that this is really the case."

"Oh, it's for real," moaned General Flood. The bear-size warrior had his elbows on the table and his face buried in his hands. "They would never send Ben Freidman all the way to Washington if it wasn't. Besides, we know how eager Saddam is to get his hands on one of these things. He's just found a way with the help of the North Koreans to cut a few years out of the process."

"Michael?" asked Hayes.

The national security advisor replied, "We need to make sure this time line is correct, and then we need to get a guarantee from the Israelis that they will not act before we have time to come up with a solution."

"General?"

Flood lifted his face from his hands. "I hate to say it, Mr. President, but we need to level this facility, and my guess is Tomahawks aren't going to do the job. We are going to have to put planes over Baghdad. We might lose some people, but they are definitely going to lose people. I mean they put the damn thing under a hospital for a reason. They don't think we have the stomach for it." Flood was extremely concerned. He had been warning everyone who would listen about the problem of nuclear proliferation for years. He leaned forward and looked at the president's chief of staff. "I'm telling you right now, Valerie, I know how your mind works. You're ten steps ahead of the rest of us. You're thinking of the political fallout this will create. You're imagining the reporters standing in front of the hospital while they pull the twisted bodies of children from the rubble. Well, let me replace it with some different pictures. Imagine an entire U.S. Navy carrier battle group patrolling the Persian Gulf. Now blink your eyes and they're gone. Over seven thousand men and women vaporized. Imagine a nuclear warhead exploding over the oil fields of Saudi Arabia. Now imagine the entire world economy plunged into a depression because those oil fields are rendered useless for the next hundred years due to radioactivity."

Flood paused just long enough to catch his breath. "That's just for starters. Now imagine Saddam throwing two of these things at Israel, figuring he can wipe them off the map before they have the chance to retaliate. There's only one problem with that plan. The Israelis aren't stupid. They keep their nukes spread out in secure underground hardened bunkers. Some of those weapons will survive, and whoever is left won't hesitate to return the favor to Saddam. We'll have a full-scale nuclear war in the Middle East. The initial blasts will kill millions. God only knows how many more will die from the fallout, but it won't be pretty. The region will shut down, oil production will screech to a halt, and the economic tidal wave will make the Great Depression look like a hiccup."

The president had stopped pacing halfway through the general's rant. Looking at the military's top officer, Hayes was slightly unsettled by the fact that he agreed with everything the man had just said. So much so that a brief shiver ran down his spine. Finally looking to Kennedy he asked, "Irene?"

Kennedy also agreed with everything that had been said so far. "They want us to take care of the problem for them."

"You mean Israel?"

"Yes." Kennedy folded her arms across her chest. "But make no mistake about it—if we don't act, they will."

"Shit." The president walked back to his chair and sat. He tried to decide on a course of action. Leveling a hospital with God only knows how many innocent civilians inside was not a pleasant thought, but taking no action at all, and being confronted with one of the scenarios that General Flood had described, was horrific.

For the first time in his presidency he was honestly scared. He would have to call the Israeli prime minister at some point, but that could wait for a day. The list of people he would have to tell domestically was long, but due to secrecy concerns, most of them would have to wait until the last possible moment. The best move right now was to delegate and manage.

As if he were pulled out of a trance, the president lifted his head and said, "Irene, I want you to take Freidman back to Langley and debrief him personally. Get as much information as you can from him, and then as quietly as possible try to confirm it. But, before you bring any of your people in on this, I want you to call me and tell me what you've learned."

Pointing at the chairman of the Joint Chiefs, the president said, "General, put your best people on this, and give me some options. I want to be prepared to move at a moment's notice if needed."

"Whoa," cautioned Valerie Jones. "Let's slow down a bit. Don't you think we should explore some diplomatic options? We've made a lot of progress with the North Koreans lately. Maybe we could put some pressure on them to pull their people out. I mean, hell, we have an awfully big aid package we can hold over their heads." Jones stopped when the president started shaking his head.

"We're not going to call North Korea, we're not going to call Saddam, the Jordanians or the Saudis, and we most definitely are not going to call the U.N. If Saddam gets the slightest whiff that we're on to him, it's over. He'll move those bombs, and we're back to square one." The president shook his head. "No. We've given him enough chances. He's been told to stop pursuing weapons of mass destruction, and he has ignored the international community at every turn. This time he gets no warning. Those bombs have to be taken out."

8
___

MARYLAND, TUESDAY MORNING

Congressman Albert Rudin walked through the men's locker room of the Congressional Country Club with a white towel thrown over his shoulder and a pair of shower sandals on his feet. Rudin grew up in the days where swimming at the YMCA required literally nothing. Swimsuits were not just optional, they were forbidden. A towel was for drying oneself, not wearing. Consequently the sixty-eight-year-old politician from Stamford, Connecticut was not shy about parading through the locker room buck naked. Gravity had taken its toll over the years, and his skin hung loose from his bony runner's body. It was not a pretty sight.

Rudin normally worked out at the congressional gym on the Hill, but today he wanted to talk to one of his colleagues from the Senate, and he wanted to do so in private. That was why he had requested that his friend meet him in the steam room of the golf club. The locker room was a virtual ghost town from November to March every year, and that was what Rudin wanted. A recent string of events in his life had caused him to reassess who his allies were. Rudin opened the door to the steam room and stood there for approximately five seconds. His purpose was to let enough steam out and make sure no one was lurking in the room.

Finally satisfied that he was alone, he entered the room and laid his towel down on the tile bench. With great deliberation he began kneading his loose skin as if he were working some lethal poison from his pores. Representative Albert Rudin was a cranky, crass old politician who was having a very bad year. The worst he could remember in a long time, and it was all the fault of a centrist president who had turned his back on the base of his party. Albert Rudin had been a loyal soldier to the Democratic Party for over thirty years, and this just wasn't fair. All he was trying to do was his job.

Rudin was the chairman of the House Permanent Select Committee on Intelligence. It had been his one request for all of his hard work. It was not much to ask for. The House Intelligence Committee wasn't one of Washington's glory jobs. Most of their meetings were conducted behind closed doors, and rarely were cameras ever allowed in the hearing room. If Rudin had been greedy like the others he would have asked to sit on the Appropriations or Judicial committees. But he hadn't. He had simply asked to run the Intelligence Committee. All he wanted to do was serve his party. It was Albert Rudin's goal in life to see the CIA shut down and dismantled. In his mind there was no bigger waste in the federal budget than the black hole that was known as Langley.

They spent billions a year on gathering intelligence,

and what did the government get in return? Nothing. The vaunted CIA had failed to predict the two most signifi-cant events of the last twenty years: the fall of the Soviet Union and Iraq's invasion of Kuwait. Rudin sometimes felt like he was losing his mind. It seemed that the more vociferously he pointed out Langley's failures, the more people shunned him. It drove him nuts. It was right there for all to see. The CIA had been feeding them grossly overestimated reports on the Soviet economy and military preparedness for years, and in Rudin's keen mind there was only one reason for them to do so. The CIA and the Pentagon were conspiring against their own government. They didn't want their budgets cut so they went out and grossly exaggerated the strength of the Evil Empire.

Rudin wiped a thick layer of sweat from his face and cleared his throat with a rumbling hack. Turning to the far corner, he deposited his spit with a well-aimed shot. *It was probably that damn Reagan's fault,* Rudin thought. Reagan was to blame for most things in Rudin's mind. If there was ever a face that could be put on evil it would be that of Ronald Reagan. Rudin had little doubt that the former president had directed the CIA and the Joint Chiefs to inflate the Soviet Union's numbers so they could get the budget increases they were after. After Reagan it had been his successor Bush, a former director of the CIA, who had decided to cozy up to Saddam Hussein. The maniacal leader went from being a trusted ally to enemy number one overnight. It was just another example of how dupli-citous and incompetent the CIA was.

Rudin was right. He knew it in his deepest being. The others were wrong. Even members of his party had turned their back on him and it was all because of that damn Thomas Stansfield and President Hayes. At least Stansfield was dead, but that didn't solve his problems.

Now he had Kennedy to deal with. He had to figure out some way to stop her. She couldn't be allowed to take over at the CIA. They needed someone who would go in there and tear the roof off, exposing all of the vermin to the light of day. Rudin would take great pleasure in watching them scurry for cover. He needed someone he could trust as director. He needed someone who would cooperate with his committee when he held hearings. He needed someone who would clean house.

Kennedy was not the answer, but his hands were tied. Just weeks earlier, he had received the most vicious ass-chewing of his life at the hands of President Hayes. The rest of the party leadership had been present for the event. In Rudin's mind it had all been unwarranted. All he had been trying to do was stop Thomas Stansfield from turn-ing the reins of power at the CIA over to Irene Kennedy. The only thing that would accomplish would be to replace one liar with another, and Rudin had been lied to enough. Thomas Stansfield was probably the most adept liar Washington had ever seen. He had been lying to Rudin's committee for the better part of two decades, and Rudin now thanked God every morning that Stansfield was finally dead.

That, however, didn't help the fact that the president had announced Dr. Kennedy as his successor. Rudin had tried to prevent that. During Stansfield's final days, Rudin had met with Senator Hank Clark, the chairman of the Senate Intelligence Committee and Secretary of State Charles Midleton. Midleton was a good fellow Democrat who shared Rudin's concerns about the CIA. It was an agency run amok, an agency that was continually getting in the way of diplomatic relations and negotiations. It was in Midleton's best interest to replace Stansfield with someone who was not so loyal to the CIA. This common bond against the CIA was why they had asked to meet with Senator Clark. Clark was a Republican after all, and in charge of the very committee that would have to confirm or block Kennedy's nomination. He was their trump card in torpedoing her career. Clark was really the only Republican that Rudin could count as a friend, the only one who he could actually tolerate.

Rudin felt that they could reason with Clark. Show him why it was in his best interest, in the Republicans' best interest to kill Kennedy's nomination before it ever got to his committee. Clark had been sympathetic, but ultimately uncooperative, and that left Rudin and Midleton to stop the changing of the guard. Rudin's first move was to call Kennedy before his committee in an attempt to catch her in a lie. At the same time Secretary of State Midleton began to use his significant resources and clout to undermine the support for Kennedy.

Disaster struck when somewhere along the way, the president found out what they were up to. Unknown to Rudin, Secretary Midleton and President Hayes didn't have the best of relationships. Apparently a deal had been struck during the campaign. Midleton, a senator at the time, had finished third in three consecutive primaries. Midleton came to Hayes, the party's front-runner, and offered to bow out of the race and throw his support behind Hayes. Like all things in politics, Midleton's offer came with some strings. No, he didn't want to be vice president. Midleton didn't like his odds of eventually becoming president if he took that post. Secretary of state was a much more glamorous post, and one where if the need ever arose, he could distance himself from President Hayes.

Midleton never quite got it through his head that Hayes was now his boss. The arrogant secretary of state had been caught and warned several times for sticking his nose in other departments' business. President Hayes had very clearly warned him that he was to stay out of the CIA's business. It appeared Hayes had found out that Midleton had ignored his orders and was attempting to undermine Irene Kennedy's career. President Hayes hit the roof. He called Midleton to the White House and forced him to resign on the spot.

Midleton was not the only person the president had been angry with that day. Literally minutes later Rudin had been escorted into the Situation Room by the speaker of the House. When the president entered the room Rudin knew something was horribly wrong. He didn't know President Hayes was capable of such anger. In a screaming match, Hayes told Rudin that who he chose to become the next director of the CIA was none of his goddamn business and if he heard another peep out of him, he would do everything in his considerable power to strip him of his chairmanship and make sure he suffered a humiliating defeat in his next reelection. Rudin had left the meeting in utter shock.

That night he received a phone call. The person on the other end informed him that Secretary of State Midleton had committed suicide. Before Rudin could respond, before he could take a breath, in the time it took him to blink his eyes he became terrified. Albert Rudin had been around Washington too long to think that Charles Midleton would kill himself out of embarrassment. The man was vain, but come on. To end your life over being forced to resign, especially so early in an administration? If Hayes floundered as president, it would have made Midleton look like the smart guy for getting out. There had to be something more to it, and in Albert Rudin's mind that something more was Thomas

Stansfield. Rudin felt it way down in his creaky old bones. Midleton had been murdered. He had been killed by Stansfield for something that he had done, or tried to do. It had been his final warning to all his enemies before he died. *Don't mess with Irene Kennedy.*

In the weeks since Midleton's alleged suicide, Rudin had spoken to no one of his suspicions. But now that Stansfield was dead, he was going to begin making some inquiries. He had to. There was no way after all these years that he could quit the fight against the CIA. His own party had turned his back on him. They had moved to the center with that smug bastard Hayes leading the charge. Sure their polling numbers were up, but those could change overnight. He needed to stay true to the core beliefs of the party. The CIA needed to be reined in, and if it cost him his job, so be it. He needed to do what was right. The soothing combination of hot steam and an overwhelming sense of righteousness gave Rudin the belief that he could do it, that he could do anything. If he just stayed the course, he would find a way, and President Hayes would be made to pay.

THE DOOR TO the steam room opened, revealing the silhouette of a big man in a white towel. Senator Hank Clark, being a bit more modest than his congressional colleague, had his towel wrapped around his waist. Clark swaggered into the hot misty room. Despite the haze of the steam, he easily picked out the cragged profile of Rudin.

"Good morning, Albert." Instead of sitting, Clark began his search for the eucalyptus bottle. He found it on the top bench, and after shaking it, he went about spraying it in the areas around the steam jets.

"Not too much of that stuff," grumbled Rudin.

Rudin went on to mumble something else, but Clark couldn't decipher what was said, nor did he care. Albert Rudin was a chronic grumbler, and Clark had learned to ignore it. He had in fact learned to ignore many of Rudin's irritating habits. The senator set the bottle down and then reclined his large body on the bottom bench across from Rudin. Clark leaned back, stretched his arms out and rested his back against the upper bench. After letting out a satisfying moan and taking in a deep breath of the eucalyptus-laced steam he asked, "What's on your mind today, Albert, and why are we meeting in the steam room? You haven't decided to come out of the closet, have you?" Clark had a difficult time suppressing his desire to laugh. He had thought of the line on the way to the club, knowing it would irritate Rudin immensely. The man had absolutely no sense of humor.

"I don't find your humor very funny."

Clark choked on his laughter. "I'm sorry, Albert, but I couldn't resist. You've never asked me to meet you in the steam room before." The steam jets kicked on, and over the hissing there was more mumbling from the other side of the room.

Rudin finally decided to enunciate his words and said, "You'll have to excuse me, but I'm a little paranoid these days."

"And why is that?" Clark began rubbing the warm water into his face.

"You know why." Rudin's words had more than a hint of accusation in them. He struggled over whether or not he should raise his suspicions over Charles Midleton's suicide. After a brief pause he decided he needed to test the water a little. "I saw the footage of you at the White House the other day. How in the hell could you sit there next to that phony?"

"Which phony are you referring to? There's an awful lot of them in this town."

"The biggest phony of them all. Hayes!" The president's name came out like a hiss.

Clark let his head fall back and looked up through the steam at the ceiling. "Come off it, Albert. There are far bigger phonies in this town than Robert Hayes."

"Not in my book."

All Clark could do was shake his head.

"How in the hell could you sit next to him and agree to Irene Kennedy as the next director of the CIA? How?" Rudin asked in exasperation.

"Albert, I don't know how many more times I'm going to have to explain this to you, but I don't see Dr. Kennedy as a bad choice."

"Oh my God! I can't believe you're serious. What did Hayes offer you?"

"I resent your implication, Albert. He offered me nothing. I think you need a refresher course in civics."

"What in the hell is that supposed to mean?"

"It means that you've been in this town long enough," Clark's voice took on a slight edge, just enough to let Rudin know he shouldn't push it too far today. "The president has the power to appoint. It says so clearly in the Constitution."

"I know," snapped Rudin. "I've read it more times than you have. It falls under the Separation of Powers. The Chief Executive has the power to appoint and nominate and the Senate has the power to confirm. The fundamental principal is separate but equal," hissed Rudin. "You have every right, no, you have a duty to block Irene Kennedy's nomination."

"In the Senate we have something that you and your friends in the House are unfamiliar with. It's called decorum. When the president appoints someone to a position we almost always give him his choice unless there is some skeleton in their closet."

"Well, I think you'd better take a look in Kennedy's closet, because it's full of them."

"And what proof do you have of that?"

Rudin leaned forward. "Oh, come off it. You know exactly what I mean. She's so dirty she's got shit coming out of her ears."

This was not easy for Clark. The logical side of him wanted to slice Rudin's weak arguments to shreds, but he had to suppress that desire. The goal here was to make him even more resolute. Not to give him reason to rethink. But at the same time, Rudin couldn't know he was being played. Clark had done a masterful job thus far. He had been the one who had told President Hayes that Rudin and Midleton were plotting against him and his choice to be the next DCI. Fortunately for Clark, Rudin hadn't the slightest idea that his friend in the Senate had betrayed him. His overwhelming paranoia of Thomas Stansfield had caused him to attribute almost every bad event in his political life to the now dead spymaster.

Clark now leaned forward. The two men were eye to eye, three short feet separating them. "You are very quick to point out, Albert, that it is in my power as a senator to confirm or block the president's nominee, but you very conveniently leave out the fact that your committee has the power to investigate. If you think Irene Kennedy is corrupt, then investigate her." Clark stared through the steam at Rudin's deep-set eyes, waiting for the inevitable. The senator knew Rudin had no choice but to back down. There was nowhere else for him to go, and then Clark would have him exactly where he wanted him.

Rudin blinked as a bead of sweat dropped from his

brow down onto his prominent nose. It hung there on the tip for a second and then slowly broke free. Rudin sat back and wildly waved a hand in front of him, signaling to Clark what he thought of his idea. "I can't do that," was his terse reply.

"Why not?" egged Clark.

"I told you what happened. I told you what the president and the party leadership said. I'd be done. My career would be over. They'd strip me of my chairmanship, and I'd never be heard from again."

Clark could feel it coming together. He smiled openly. "I find it impossible to believe that they could silence you."

"You weren't there when they let me have it. Hayes threatened me." Rudin pointed to himself. "He said he'd make it his personal goal in life to see that I was defeated during the next election."

"Calm down, Albert. I think you've gotten yourself so far into this you're not seeing clearly."

"What could I possibly be missing? The speaker of the House picks me up in his limo, drags me over to the White House, I'm ambushed by my own party's leadership, and I'm threatened by the president himself." With a grimace Rudin added, "Please tell me what I'm missing."

Clark was tempted to remind Rudin that he'd brought it all down on himself, but decided it would be counterproductive to the task at hand. "Albert, I think you're selling yourself short. When was the last time you were challenged in a primary? Ten years ago?"

"Eight."

"When was the last time my party gave you a serious challenge?"

"It's been a while," he conceded with some real pride.

"So, how is the president going to stop you from going on to an eighteenth term?"

"I haven't been challenged from within my own party because there has never been an alternative, but if the president were to lean hard enough on the people who run the party back in Connecticut . . . if he were to promise to infuse a bunch of cash into their coffers, they'd dump me in a heartbeat."

"Maybe so, but that's a risky proposition for the president. Voters don't always like bigwigs from Washington interfering in their local politics. You could spin it in the media that the president had a vendetta against you. If you played it right you could make yourself into a victim of petty Washington politics. The local voters and media would love it."

Rudin thought about it for a moment and saw that it might work. Maybe he wasn't in as dire of a spot as he'd thought. "But what about the present? If I launch an investigation they'll cut my balls off."

"It might be too late for them to do anything if the media gets behind the story." Clark folded his arms across his chest and gave this some time to sink in.

Rudin gave the idea some serious consideration. "That would be a risky play."

Clark could see his words were having the right effect. It was time to lead him to action. "Albert, I know you as a man of great integrity. I don't always agree with your politics, but you've stayed true to your party through the worst of times, and frankly I don't think you deserve to be treated like this." He studied the malleable congressman while he spoke. All he was doing was telling Rudin exactly what he wanted to hear. "Great men are often hated and envied by their peers. It is usually not until they are gone that their greatness is recognized." Clark shook his head as if saddened by the whole affair. "I don't think you should be treated like this. Being threatened by the president is wrong."

"Why don't you say that to him?" asked Rudin in earnest.

Clark shook his head emphatically. "In this town we have to fight our own battles. You know that, Albert. As a Republican my opinions on a dispute within your party would not be welcome. No . . . that wouldn't work at all. You have always been a man of principle and conscience, and I don't think you should change now." The senator searched Rudin's face for a sign that he was with him, and that his ego was inflated to the proper degree. Satisfied, Clark went for the kill. "Albert, you should follow your conscience. If you truly think Irene Kennedy is corrupt," he hesitated as if it were painful for him to give such advice. Leaning closer, he finished by saying, "If she is as bad as you think she is then you really have no other choice."

Rudin let his head drop into his hands. The struggle he was having was apparent. In a pleading tone he said, "But it will be political suicide. They will kill me."

Oh, he was so close. He had to tread very carefully. "I have already told you how you can neutralize them. Let the media get the ball rolling and then call hearings. The president wouldn't dare do anything to you at that point."

"How in the hell am I going to get the media to cover this? I've been bitching about the abuses at Langley for so long none of them listen to me anymore. I need some help. I need your help. All you have to do is get her in front of your committee during the confirmation hearing and hammer her."

"No way." Clark shook his head vigorously. "I'm going to tell you this for the last time, Albert. I like Dr. Kennedy. I think she will do a good job. If you think she's as bad as you say she is, then it's up to you to prove to the rest of us that she's rotten."

"But I can't," Rudin practically shouted. Regaining some control he said, "I know what I know, but I don't have the kind of proof that I could take to the press. All you'd have to do is ask her some questions that I'd prepare, and I will guarantee that she'll cave in."

In your wet dreams, Clark thought to himself. Irene Kennedy was not the type of person to wilt under the bright lights of a confirmation hearing. Not unless she was confronted with real evidence. Clark decided that a little anger was needed. Raising his voice, he said, "Albert, I'm not getting involved in this. If you want to derail her then it's up to you. I'm here as your friend, but if you ask me again to ambush her in my committee room, in front of the cameras, after I've given my word to the president, I will get up and leave!"

Rudin backed down. "All right. I understand your position, but what the fuck am I going to do? When I heard that bastard Stansfield had cancer I jumped for joy. I thought, finally we can clean out that rats' nest. And now this . . . it's just too much for me. I've given too much of my life to public service. I just can't sit back and watch the blatant corruption continue."

There was a long silence. Finally, Clark decided Rudin was ready. "I feel bad for you, I really do. . . ." he said. "It's just that I've given my word." The senator looked away thoughtfully, as if he were struggling with a tough decision. "There is one thing I can do that might help." Clark paused to see just how eager Rudin was. It was painfully obvious on the congressman's face that he would gladly accept what his friend had to offer.

"I know of someone who is quite remarkable at digging things up." Clark stared his fellow politician in the eye. "Things that people don't want dug up. I will articulate that you'd like to have a talk with him."

"Is he expensive?"

Clark moaned inside. Rudin was the cheapest bastard he'd ever met. In truth the man *was* expensive, but Clark was willing to subsidize the job. "He's actually quite reasonable." With a grin Clark added, "Or so I've been told."

"When can I meet with him?"

"I'll see if he can stop by your office this afternoon, but I can't make any promises. He's a very busy man."

"The sooner the better. I don't have a lot of time to derail this train."

Clark nodded. "And one more thing, Albert. Keep me out of this. All I'm doing is giving you someone's name. What you do from this point forward is up to you."

"Don't worry, Hank. I'll never forget that you were there for me during my darkest hours."

With a soft smile, Clark said, "Don't mention it. That's what friends are for." Clark kept the smile on his face, but inside he was elated. Rudin was about to be spoon-fed just enough information to bring about the end of Irene Kennedy's bid for the directorship of the CIA. The Democratic Party was about to be blindsided.

9

TEL AVIV, WEDNESDAY MORNING

The sleek, black Mercedes sedan moved quickly through the streets of Tel Aviv. The sedan had tinted bulletproof windows, anti-mine flooring and armor-plated sides and roof. Ben Freidman sat in the backseat by himself. Two Mossad bodyguards were in

front, one driving, the other riding shotgun. A small arsenal of weapons was stashed throughout the vehicle in case
of an attack, which was a very real threat. So real that
Freidman had two armor-plated cars, the Mercedes and a
Peugeot. Freidman was switched from one car to the
other throughout the day, always in an underground
garage or a secluded area away from prying eyes.

Colonel Ben Freidman, the director general of
Mossad, was perhaps the most hated man in the Middle
East. Yes, characters like Saddam Hussein and Yasser
Arafat had their enemies, but they were Arabs, and make
no mistake about it, the Middle East was overwhelm-
ingly Arab. The multitude of factions and tribes that
made up the Arab people had fought each other for mil-
lennia. The feuds ran deep, rich in historical lore. Despite
the tiniest of differences from one group to the next
they rarely got along. There was, however, one exception, and that exception was an almost universal hatred
of Israel.

Amongst Arabs, the most hated and feared organization
in all of Israel was Mossad. They were a den of assassins
and thieves given official sanction by the government of
Israel to conduct an illegal war against the Muslim peoples of the world.

This reputation did not bother Ben Freidman. In fact,
he did everything in his power to perpetuate the fear. If
one of the fallouts was that he had to lead a life in which
he was constantly surrounded by bulletproof composites
and heavily armed men, then so be it. The Arabs had
sworn to crush the Israeli state and he had promised to
defend it. They were in a war and had been for over fifty
years. This sham of Middle East peace perpetuated by
American do-gooders and soft Israeli politicians had
made his job more difficult, but Freidman was not one to

complain. He was always adapting, always preparing for the next battle.

For the first forty years of Mossad's existence the agency had been cloaked in secrecy, so much so that the various directors general were unknown to all but the prime minister and his or her cabinet. Times had changed though, and in the nineties Mossad became a victim of Israel's increasingly partisan and volatile politics. The agency's anonymity was stripped away and the office of the director general became one of the hottest seats in the government. Ben Freidman's name was regularly printed in the papers and his picture was shown frequently on television. Any terrorist with half a brain could pick him out of a crowd and blow his head off.

The purges that Mossad underwent in the nineties had taught Freidman to be leery of all politicians. His allegiance was to his country and Mossad. The prime minister, and the rest of the squabbling politicians, could take a backseat. They had nearly destroyed the most effective spy agency in the world with their incessant desire to meddle. From 1951 to 1990, only six different directors general ran Mossad, but during the political bloodletting of the nineties four men had held the post. The lack of any sustained leadership had disastrous effects on recruiting and the morale of Mossad's employees. Despite all of this, when Ben Freidman was named to the post by the current prime minister he had gladly taken the job.

Freidman understood something his four predecessors didn't. To run the world's most effective spy agency you had to act like a dictator, not a politician. And to be a dictator you had to have power. Freidman had spent a fair amount of time in America over the years and had worked closely with the CIA in a mutual effort to battle terrorism. He learned that the CIA had been forced to adapt far earlier than Mossad had to the political game. Washington was a much more political town, and the media in the U.S. was absolutely unwieldy compared to the rags in Israel. Thomas Stansfield had shown Freidman how to get results in a supercharged political environment.

Stansfield made it very clear that his agency was not interested in politics. The first thing he did was develop assets outside the normal channels so he could act without the politicians on the Hill knowing what he was up to, and then he began to use the Agency's mounds of information against any politician who tried to make political hay out of the CIA. Most of the politicians in Washington understood that the CIA had a dirty job to do and they steered clear, but there was always a handful of opportunists who were looking to advance their own careers, or their party or both. Stansfield focused on building dossiers on the ones who were really aggressive, and over a period of years he performed admirably at keeping the wolves at bay.

Freidman had learned that the politicians in Israel were no different. The ones who were looking to ascend to upper levels of government all had something that they were currently involved in, or something from their past, that they wanted kept quiet. Freidman collected that information into a tidy insurance policy that helped to keep the prime minister and the opposition parties quiet. With his flanks protected, he could go about the real business of his job, which was waging war against the terrorists who had sworn to push Israel into the sea.

It was midmorning in downtown Tel Aviv, and as was almost always the case, the sun was out and the temperature was a comfortable eighty-one degrees. Both pedestrian and motor traffic were moderate. Moving fast, the limousine approached the prime minister's office building. The driver radioed ahead to say they were on their way in. The security guards out front expertly scanned the street for any signs of an ambush, and then radioed the car to say it was clear. When the armored car came around the block the heavy barrier to the underground parking garage was down and four intense-looking individuals armed with Uzi submachine guns were fanned out to secure the area.

The Mercedes zipped into the garage and the heavy spring-loaded barricade popped up almost instantly. This was life in Israel and none of the men who had just participated in the brief exercise gave it a second thought. They had all been raised on the front line. They had been taught from the earliest of ages to never pick something up in public that was just left lying around, to be very suspicious of strangers and call the police at the slightest sign of something out of the ordinary. Their enemy walked among them, and a day never passed where they didn't think of it. To let one's guard down was to invite death and become one of the thousands of casualties that had been racked up since the birth of the tiny country.

Freidman stepped from the back of the car leaving his specially made metal briefcase with his men. He was wearing light-colored slacks and a loose fitting, short-sleeved, tan dress shirt. The shirt was, of course, untucked, and his pistol was firmly secured in his belt holster at the small of his back. Two security officers escorted him into the elevator and took him up to the prime minister's suite. Freidman spoke to no one as he walked through the outer office and into the secure windowless conference room. He sat in one of the chairs and drummed his thick fingers on the shiny wood surface.

A moment later David Goldberg entered the room and sat. The former army general was a no-nonsense hard-ass. Heavyset and set in his ways, he was the head of the conservative Likud Party. Despite holding just nineteen seats in the 120-member Knesset, Goldberg had been elected by the overwhelming majority of the Israeli people. They had grown tired of the ever-increasing concessions made by the Labor Party in their dealings with Yasser Arafat. Goldberg had been swept into office on a wave of national unity and given a charter to put the bloodthirsty Palestinians in their place. This was a campaign promise he intended to keep, and Goldberg was smart enough to know he couldn't fulfill it without the aid of Ben Freidman.

Goldberg had a mane of thin white hair, which framed a tan face and heavy jowls. Physically he shared many of Winston Churchill's characteristics. He was a large man, but not muscular. If anyone bothered to look under his clothes they were apt to discover a body like a pudgy baby's. Some might perceive this as a weakness, but those who understood Goldberg knew better. The man had a biting temper, and the balls of a bull. He had distinguished himself on the battlefield during the Yom Kippur War and had never forgotten the despicable sneak attack by Israel's Arab neighbors on one of the holiest days of the Jewish year.

Israeli governments had changed frequently over the last two decades, racking up one failed peace accord after another. And when each gambit for Palestinian and Israeli harmony failed, and the blood began to flow, the country turned to Goldberg's party for guidance. Like Churchill, his country had no use for him unless things were dire.

Goldberg smoothed his tie and let his hand rest on his belly. Leaning back he asked, "So tell me how things went with the Americans?"

Freidman had refused to call Goldberg after his meeting with the president. Knowing all too well the capabilities of the NSA, he had opted to deliver his news in person. "It got off to a slow start, but I think our goal will be achieved."

Goldberg liked President Hayes's tough record on terrorism, but was suspicious of the man. In the year that he'd been in office he'd made it quite clear that he would not be pushed around by the American Jewish lobby. Goldberg understood better than most that Israel's ace in the hole had always been their fellow Jews in America. "Why the slow start?"

"I don't think President Hayes liked the fact that it was me and not you making the call."

"Surely he understands why I didn't call him."

"Like I said, after I told them what we've discovered, his attitude changed."

"And what was his response?"

Freidman grinned, remembering the tension on Hayes's face. "He was not happy."

Goldberg found these conversations with Freidman very tedious. The man never simply told a story. You had to extract information from him bit by bit. "What did he say?"

"Nothing. He didn't need to, though. The anger on his face said it all."

"Who else was at the meeting?"

"Dr. Kennedy, General Flood, Michael Haik and Valerie Jones."

"Did anyone speak?"

"No."

Goldberg's heavy face twisted into a concerned frown. "I find that very unusual. Don't you?"

"No. President Hayes has made it very clear that

America's best interests are not always the same as ours."

Anxious to disagree, Goldberg said, "That may be, but it doesn't explain why they wouldn't speak. For God's sake, we're their only true ally in this whole bloody region."

Inwardly, Freidman smiled. Goldberg would not have gotten far in the intelligence business. He was far too emotional. "The president clearly didn't like the way I requested a backdoor meeting. My guess is he instructed everyone to keep their mouths shut while I was in the room." With a shrug, he added, "This is not unusual, David. Being the head of Mossad often guarantees a frigid welcome. Even in one's own country."

Goldberg nodded his acceptance. Freidman was right. There were members of his own cabinet who turned mute when the intimidating director general of Mossad entered the room. "So what was the outcome?"

"I spoke with Dr. Kennedy afterward. They are taking this very seriously, and will be in contact with us. She asked that we be patient and do nothing until they have a chance to find a solution."

Goldberg sprang forward in his chair, concern on his face. "Didn't you tell them exactly what I told you to? There is only one solution to this problem, and it isn't diplomacy or economic sanctions! Military action is the only solution!"

Freidman held out his hand and gestured for his prime minister to calm down. "Don't worry, David. I intimated your every word to Dr. Kennedy. As I told you before I left, with Saddam's recent show of defiance, President Hayes is looking for an excuse to bomb Saddam . . . and this is a very good one."

"But those bombs can be moved!" Goldberg had not calmed. "If Saddam gets the slightest whiff that we, or the Americans, know about the bombs, they will be scattered across Iraq in a second!" Goldberg slammed his fist down on the table. "This is our only chance!"

"And you don't think the Americans know that?"

"I don't pretend to understand the American mind," spat Goldberg. "They often do things that make no sense to me."

"Well, not this president. He hates Saddam for reasons that we know all too well, and he is going to do exactly as I told you."

Goldberg shook his head and thought about Freidman's plan. "I don't know. I can see them going to the U.N. or pulling some stunt like going on television." He wagged his finger at Freidman. "Never underestimate the ego of an American politician. They love to grab the spotlight, and I don't think I am being irrational by worrying that President Hayes might decide to go on TV and announce to the world that Saddam is in the final stages of completing a bomb. It would be the safe route for him to take, to build another coalition. Hell, the damn Arabs would line up against Saddam in a heartbeat. The Saudis and the Iranians fear him as much or more than we do."

Freidman calmly shook his head. "He can gain their support after he turns that hospital into a mound of sand. None of us want him to join the nuclear club. President Hayes is a very decisive man. He doesn't relish what he has to do, but he knows it's the right thing."

"What about the hospital?" pleaded Goldberg. "The Americans are loath to be sullied by the pictures that will follow."

Freidman hesitated to respond for a moment, knowing that Goldberg had a good point. "There is no doubt this aspect is troubling, but they know to do nothing is worse."

"I am not saying they will do nothing. I'm saying that their course of action will be to take to the airwaves, not to the skies."

"I know what you're saying, David, but I disagree with you. I know this president. The bombs will be falling within two weeks and the Americans will have solved our problem for us."

The prime minister lowered his chin and studied Freidman. His jowls spilled over the collar of his white dress shirt. "I wish I could share your confidence, but I don't. I have already asked our air force to make preparations for a strike. I will not sit around and wait for the Americans to act, and if they try to take this to the U.N. or go to the media with it, I will send in the planes immediately! I will not give Saddam a chance to move those bombs!"

Goldberg's words brought a smile to Freidman's face. He admired the man's fighting spirit. If there were more like him they would have never gotten themselves into this mess with the Palestinians.

"What do you think is so funny?" asked an angry Goldberg.

"You misunderstand my smile, David. It is one of admiration. The Americans will attack exactly because of what you just said. They know if they don't take care of the problem, you will. And that, my friend, is a problem they don't want to deal with. President Hayes will order the strike and take care of our problem for us. Just be patient, and give them the time they need to put it together."

"I will give them some time, but I will not be patient. Under no circumstances will I allow Saddam to bring those weapons into service. If it means we have to go to war with Jordan, Syria and Iraq, I would welcome it. Our air force would make mincemeat out of their fliers and our army would crush anything they throw at us."

"And what about Egypt?" asked Freidman.

"They have no stomach for fighting. They know what will happen if they try to cross the Negev. They will be slaughtered just like the last time they tried. Besides, they are not as easily influenced by Saddam as Syria and Jordan are." Goldberg confidently shook his head. "No, they will do nothing. You are a fighter like me, Benjamin. You know deep down inside the Arabs want nothing to do with us. We have pummeled them one too many times. They would rather talk tough and do nothing."

The prime minister's words brought a smile to Freidman's face. He agreed with everything Goldberg had just said. It was very nice for a change. "You are a tough old warrior, David. The people of this country probably have no idea how lucky they are that you are in charge during these difficult times." Standing, Freidman looked at his prime minister and said, "The Americans will come through for us. I promise."

10

It was unseasonably cold in the nation's capital, even for November. The president had asked Irene Kennedy to arrive early, earlier than the others. He wanted to have a few words alone with her. At 7:00 A.M., the White House was a relatively calm place. It was still thirty minutes to an hour away from the start of another busy day. The Secret Service agents and officers were dutifully standing their posts, but that was about it. The deluge of media, employees and visitors were still sleeping or getting ready for another day at the nation's most famous residence.

Kennedy entered the West Wing on the ground floor. She was dressed in a conservative but stylish dark blue suit. Under her arm she carried a locked pouch containing the president's daily brief, or PDB, as it was known by all in the national security community. The brief was essentially a daily newspaper put together by the CIA's top analysts. It was a highly classified document and was distributed to only the most senior people in an administration. Each copy was collected at the end of the day and destroyed. Normally someone junior to the director of the CIA delivered the brief, but Kennedy had decided to handle it herself this morning.

She made her way up to the first floor and into the president's private dining room off the Oval Office. President Hayes was waiting for her, an array of newspapers spread out on each side of his place setting, a bowl of Grape-nuts in the middle and a piping hot cup of coffee on his right. Hayes was a very organized and determined man. He had told Kennedy recently that he wasn't going to let the job destroy his health like it had his predecessors'. He spent thirty minutes on the treadmill and bike four to five days a week. In fact, this was when he normally reviewed the PDB. This morning, however, he had scheduled several early meetings. The situation in Iraq had him on edge. When they were done with their coffee they were to head down to the Situation Room to receive a briefing from General Flood and his staff.

Thus far, Kennedy had talked Hayes into keeping the

amount of people involved in the crisis to a bare minimum. The secretary of defense was in Colombia until
Saturday. He would be briefed when he returned. The
Joint Chiefs and the secretaries of the various services
were to be kept in the dark until the last minute and the
remaining members of the Cabinet, with the exception of
Michael Haik, were also to be left out of the loop.
Kennedy had convinced the president that the last thing
they wanted to do was give Saddam a heads-up that
something might be coming his way.

The president didn't bother to look up from whatever
paper he was reading when Kennedy entered the room.
"Good morning, Irene. Have a seat. Would you like anything to eat?"

"No thank you, sir. Coffee's fine." Kennedy poured
herself of cup from the sterling silver pot sitting in the
middle of the table. These early morning meetings with
the president in the small dining room were becoming a
weekly event. Kennedy was starting to feel very comfortable in her dealings with the man.

"What's new today?" Hayes shoved a spoonful of the
tiny brown rocklike cereal into his mouth.

"Well," Kennedy extracted a key from her jacket and
started to open the pouch. "Pakistan is making threats
again to launch another offensive to take back the dis-
puted land with India . . ."

The president waved his hands in the air and then
wiped a drop of milk from his lip. With his napkin still in
hand, he said, "Put the brief away. I'll look at it later.
Unless there's something that needs my immediate attention, I'd like to talk about this mess your Israeli friend has
dumped in our laps."

Kennedy briefly wondered if the use of the word *friend*
was more than a random selection. It was apparent that

the looming crisis with Iraq had the president upset. "What would you like to know, sir?"

Hayes set his napkin down and pushed his cereal out of the way. He took a second to rearrange the things in front of him while he organized his thoughts. "I want to throw something at you, and I want you to keep an open mind." Hayes made direct eye contact and added, "I want you to give me your honest answer."

Kennedy kept her expression neutral, her brown eyes locked on the president's. She nodded for him to continue.

"Can we trust the Israelis on this thing?"

Kennedy instantly disliked the question. It was fraught with problems, too broad to give a well-crafted answer. "Could you be a little more specific, sir?"

"This information they've given us, can we trust it? Is it possible they have it wrong . . . or that they've been fed this information by the Iraqis?"

She thought about the question for a moment and answered, "As you know, sir, anything is possible, but I think this information is pretty accurate."

Hayes grimaced. He wanted a more concrete answer than what she'd just given him. "What makes you say that? Is it because you trust Colonel Freidman?"

Kennedy got her first hint of what might be bothering the president. "I trust Ben Freidman, sir, but only so far. I know better than anyone where his loyalties lie. He does nothing unless it helps Israel."

"That's what worries me. I don't like being manipulated by any country, but I especially don't like it by a country that owes us its very existence. Quite a few of my predecessors allowed Israel to lead them around by the nose, and several of them weren't even aware of it. Not me." Hayes angrily shook his head. "I won't allow it. I want to make damn sure this information is correct before we start dropping bombs. Do we have anyone in Baghdad who can confirm what Freidman told us?"

"This is awkward, sir." Kennedy hesitated for a second. "Our resources in Iraq are limited. As you know, we have a few people in the regime who are on our payroll, but to ask them to look into this would be extremely risky."

"Isn't that their job?" asked the president with a hint of irritation in his voice. "Isn't that what we pay them to do?"

"Yes," Kennedy conceded, "but for them to go outside their area of concern and start asking questions . . ." her voice trailed off and she uncharacteristically grimaced. "It would almost certainly get them tortured by Saddam's secret police."

The president was undeterred. "Well, listen, before we start dropping bombs on a hospital I'd like to be absolutely sure that those nukes are in fact there."

"Sir, I can ask one of them to look into it, but I think they will ignore me. It's too risky. Besides, we have no reason to doubt the Israelis on this."

"I can think of several reasons why I should doubt them." Hayes rolled his eyes.

Kennedy ignored the comment and extracted a file from the pouch. "I thought you might be interested in these." She slid a sheaf of black-and-white satellite photographs across the table. They were of downtown Baghdad. The Al Hussein Hospital was circled in white. "I had my people go back through the files to see what they could dig up on the hospital. This is what they found." Kennedy removed the first photo, revealing a second one that showed just the hospital and the surrounding one-block radius. On the east side of the hospital, where the alley was located, several vehicles were bracketed in white and next to them were two simple words: Dump Truck.

"This all started a little over three years ago. Dump trucks all day long for a month straight. My experts estimate that over a thousand tons of earth was removed from beneath the hospital." Kennedy flipped to the next photo. It was the same setup, except this time the vehicles in the alley were labeled as cement trucks.

"My people counted the number of trucks that came to the site and feel pretty confident that they weren't just laying a new foundation. They say the only time the Iraqis use this much cement is when they are trying to build a bunker."

"How in the hell did we miss this?" Hayes asked angrily. "Isn't this why we spend billions on the spy satellites?"

"The problem, sir, is that we leveled a good portion of the country. Since the end of the Gulf War it's been a nonstop succession of dump trucks and cement trucks."

The president flipped through the remainder of the photographs without comment. When he was finished he took his time putting them back in a neat stack and then handed them to Kennedy. "You think this corroborates what Freidman told us?"

"Yes, I do."

The president stood and walked over to the window. He gazed across the way at the Executive Office Building. Kennedy watched him in silence, speculating if he wasn't telling her something. She was in the midst of wondering if the Israelis had done something she didn't know about, when the president turned around and spoke.

"How many people are in this hospital?"

"I'm not sure, sir." Her answer was less than truthful. One of her analysts had given her a range, but she didn't

think now was the time to tell the president the number.

"Hundreds?"

"Possibly."

The president turned around again and looked out the
window. Kennedy felt for him. It would probably be aviators who would drop the bombs, but they were trained
from day one of flight school to deal with it. Not the president. He was ultimately the one who would be ordering
those people to their deaths. Kennedy feared that he was
going through the hospital wondering how many children would be killed, how many mothers, fathers and
grandparents. It was an ugly business they were in.

Without looking away from the window, the president
shook his head and said, "You know, right now I really
hate the Israelis for putting me in this position."

Kennedy frowned at the president's words. Emboldened
by a career of making difficult decisions she said, "You
don't mean that, Mr. President." When Hayes turned
around she said, "The Israelis didn't put this facility under
a hospital. Saddam did. He is the one who has put those
people in harm's way. He's the one who's put us in this
position."

11

SITUATION ROOM, WEDNESDAY MORNING

General Flood was traveling light, so as not to
attract too much attention. He'd brought along
only four aides, one each from the air force, the

navy, the marines and the army. When the president and Kennedy entered the Situation Room, the five military men were arrayed around the far side of the table. Simultaneously, the warriors snapped to their feet.

"Good morning, gentlemen. Please be seated." The president pulled out his leather chair at the head of the table and sat.

Michael Haik, the president's national security advisor, arrived on their heels. He and Kennedy sat next to the president. The president's chief of staff had not been invited to the meeting, and General Flood was very appreciative. He didn't want the president to be distracted by Valerie Jones inserting political issues into the meeting. The task at hand was to apprise Hayes of his military options and give him a realistic estimate of the time it would take to move the right assets into position.

General Flood was seated opposite the president at the far end of the table. He was an imposing man at six feet four and almost 300 pounds. Flood leaned forward, placed his forearms on the table and started. "Mr. President, as you have requested, my staff and I have prepared several contingencies for you. The first plan is one you are familiar with. Within minutes of you giving us authorization, we could launch a salvo of Tomahawk cruise missiles that would level the target. This plan has only one redeeming quality in my opinion. It guarantees us that we won't lose any air crews." Flood paused briefly. "We are also of the opinion that a strike with Tomahawks would not guarantee the destruction of the primary target."

The president wasn't sure what the general meant, so he asked, "Please elaborate?"

"Dr. Kennedy has provided us with satellite imagery that suggests a command- and control-type structure was created underneath the hospital. Tomahawks don't work against these types of hardened targets. We would merely level the hospital and incur some collateral damage."

"General," growled the president with a look of disapproval on his face.

"I'm sorry, sir," apologized the general, who had momentarily forgotten the president's severe dislike of sterile military terms. "We would merely level the hospital and kill most, if not all, of the people inside. We would, of course, also run the risk of an errant Tomahawk hitting something other than the target, but depending on how many missiles we use in the attack the chances of that happening is somewhere in the neighborhood of five to ten percent."

"What's the next option?"

"The next one involves using F–117A stealth fighters from the 48th Fighter Wing out of Holloman Air Force Base in New Mexico. These platforms would give us maximum stealth and the ability to deliver precision-guided munitions to the target. Our odds for success in taking out the nukes are much better, but still somewhat limited."

"How so?" asked the president.

"To go after a hardened target like this we need to use penetration bombs. The weapons bays of the F–117's are limited as to the size of the bombs they can carry. The largest penetration bomb they can deliver is the GBU–27/B. It's a good weapon, and in most cases I think it would suffice, but with this strike, sir," Flood adopted an uneasy tone, "I'm afraid we're only going to get one chance to take these things out."

The president nodded. "I share your concerns, and agree that we are only going to get one chance at this. If we send in the stealth fighters, what are our odds for success?"

General Flood looked first to his left and then to his right. "We have some disagreement on what the number might be." The general nodded to a man in a dark blue air force uniform.

"Mr. President, I'm Colonel Anderson. It is my opinion that a flight of four F-117's, each one armed with two of the twenty-one hundred pound GBU-27/B laser-guided paveway bombs, would be more than enough to destroy this target."

"So you're talking eight bombs."

"That's correct, sir."

"And you're confident that the nuclear devices will be destroyed."

"I am, sir. This is the weapon we used on many of the hard targets during the Gulf War, such as aircraft shelters and command and control centers."

"How confident?"

The colonel thought about it for a moment and replied, "Ninety percent, sir."

The president wasn't sure he liked the answer. He noticed that one of the general's other aides was frowning in such a way that it was obvious he disagreed with his fellow warrior. The man was a marine, and Hayes noted the birds adorning his epaulets. He looked the officer in the eye and said, "Colonel, you seem to be in disagreement."

Without hesitation the marine replied, "Yes, I am, sir."

"What's the problem with Colonel Anderson's plan?"

The marine looked across the table at his friend and said, "I have a lot of respect for Colonel Anderson, but we are in disagreement as to what would be the more effective plan of action here. I don't feel that a ninety percent success rate on this mission will cut it. If the stealth fighters don't succeed in penetrating the bunker beneath the hospital all they will do is add a layer of rubble to the top of it, making the target even harder to penetrate if we need to conduct follow-up strikes."

"Then what do you suggest?"

"Are you familiar with Deep Throat, sir?"

The president was a little miffed by the question. The first thought that entered his mind was Watergate, quickly followed by the porno movie of the same title. He decided it was best to say nothing, and simply shook his head.

"Deep Throat, sir, is the name for our super penetrator bomb, the GBU-28/B. Colonel Anderson is correct that the GBU-27/B was very successful against hardened airplane shelters and other low-level command and control centers, but it should be noted that the weapon was absolutely ineffective against Saddam's big command and control centers." The marine looked briefly at General Flood and then continued. "During the war the CIA located what they thought was Saddam's main command bunker. It was at the al-Taji Airbase about twenty miles outside of Baghdad. Early in the air war we launched three separate sorties with F-117's carrying GBU-27/B laser-guided penetration bombs. We dropped over twenty bombs on the target, sir, and we barely put a dent in it."

The F-117 strike was sounding less appealing by the minute to the president.

"We realized that if we ever wanted to get at Saddam and his generals we would need a bomb that could penetrate these superbunkers. The air force's Air Armament Division was asked to find a solution, and do it quickly. In record time they came up with Deep Throat, a forty-seven-hundred-pound behemoth that was twice as long and twice as heavy as any other penetration bomb in our arsenal. It was so big, in fact, that the stealth fighter couldn't carry it. The bomb was designated the GBU-28/B. On the last night of the war, sir, two F-111's took off from the Royal Saudi Air Force Base at Taif. They each carried one GBU-28/B. The bombs were dropped from high altitude. One missed, and the other scored a direct hit."

"What were the results?"

"All five of the bunker's blast doors were blown off their hinges, sir. From the inside out." The marine paused to let the president think about the destructive force. "The target was obliterated."

"Who was in the bunker?"

"Dr. Kennedy can answer that question better than I can, sir."

"Irene?"

"At least a dozen of his top generals, some of Saddam's family members and a number of high-ranking politicians."

The president momentarily reflected on how much easier his life would be if Saddam had been in the bunker on that night. Unfortunately, he wasn't. "What would a bomb of this magnitude do to the hospital?"

"It would completely level it, sir," answered the marine.

"What about the surrounding buildings?"

"The collateral damage—" the marine caught himself and said, "If we hit the target, the number of people killed in the surrounding buildings would be minimal."

"And if we miss?"

"Whatever this bomb hits, sir, it will destroy."

Hayes thought of the finality of such a statement and then said, "Taking into account the very real potential of missing the target, what are the odds for success if we use Deep Throat?"

"One hundred percent, sir. We can stack the sorties and bring them in two planes at a time at whatever staggered intervals are deemed appropriate. The targeting pods on the F-111's can give us real time imagery. We'll know within seconds if the first sortie was successful or not. If it fails, we green light the second one and so on until we get it right."

The president brought his left hand up and scratched his chin while he thought about these superbombs raining down on innocent civilians. He pushed the image from his mind and asked the obvious question. "Why would I go with the stealth fighters if at best you can only give me a ninety percent success rate?"

General Flood fielded the question. "If we use the stealth fighters, sir, and the smaller penetrating bombs, it is a relatively simple, low-risk operation. The number of assets involved is very manageable. The stealth fighters can get in, drop their bombs and be on their way out before the shooting starts. If we decide to use Deep Throat it changes the scope of the operation significantly. The F-111 is the most stable platform we have that is capable of carrying Deep Throat. As you know, the F-111 is not a stealth aircraft. That means we would have to launch a major attack against Iraqi radar and SAM installations to make sure we don't lose one of the planes. An attack of this nature would involve navy and marine F-18's operating off the USS *Independence* in the Gulf, cruise missiles launched from the battle group, air force units operating out of Saudi Arabia and Turkey, and it would also likely involve some units from the Joint Special Operations Command."

"So we'd have to let a lot of people in on our secret?"

"No, not necessarily. We are constantly working these

units up to conduct just this type of operation. We could wait until almost the last minute to hand down the target for the sortie of F-111's."

"How much time do you need?"

The general hesitated for only a second. "If we're up against the wall, we could get an attack under way in less than twenty-four hours, but I'd prefer to give my people a week to make sure all of our intelligence is up to date, and brief the air crews on a full list of targets."

The president looked to Kennedy. "What do you think?"

Kennedy thought about the two options and said, "I think we should use Deep Throat."

"What if Saddam gets wind that we're getting ready to hit him?"

Kennedy shrugged her shoulders. "He expects us to hit him. Once a year we go in and clean out his SAM sites and a few industrial targets. Knowing Saddam, if he gets wind that we're preparing to attack, he'll slap himself on the back over how smart he was to hide his bombs under a hospital." Kennedy shook her head. "He won't move those bombs. He thinks they're safe right where they are."

"All right." The president looked at his watch and then stood. The general's four aides leapt out of their chairs, but before anyone else could get up Hayes told them to sit. "I have to run to another meeting." Hayes looked at General Flood. "I want both of these options on the table, and anything else you can think of. I want to be able to react quickly if we need to, so do whatever it takes to get these assets into position." Looking to Kennedy, he said, "I want your people to get together with General Flood's. Show them all of those photos, and try to give me a more definite answer as to whether or not we need to use Deep

Throat." Hayes turned to leave and then stopped at the door. "One more thing. No one is to mention this hospital as the target until I say so. If there are any leaks, heads will roll."

12

TEL AVIV, WEDNESDAY AFTERNOON

What to do with Donatella? The director general of Mossad sat amid a cloud of smoke in his office and wrestled with the question. She had been a great recruit, one of his best. Ben Freidman was not a disloyal man, but he, like almost everyone else, had his price, and $500,000 was a lot of money. It would be a welcome addition to his personal pension plan. Freidman saw nothing wrong with taking money, as long as what he was asked to do didn't go against the interests of Israel. He wasn't so pure as to not take financial advantage of the significant power that he wielded.

On the flight back from America, he had struggled with the dilemma of killing Donatella. Senator Clark wanted her dead, and he was willing to pay a lot of money. Besides, Freidman had to admit that the specter of Mitch Rapp finding out that he was involved with the good senator from Arizona made his skin crawl. Having Rapp mad at you was not a good thing. Freidman did not relish what he must do, but there was no doubt that the right thing to do was wipe out the trail.

Donatella had been very loyal to him over the years, and more important, she had been one of his best kidons, an assassin of the first order. A dark-haired beauty, Donatella had lured almost a dozen men to their death, all of them enemies of Israel. After a number of very productive years Freidman had released her from her official commitment to the Mossad. The files in the basement stated that she wanted out, but the truth was that Freidman had urged her to enter into a partnership with him. It was all part of the colonel's plan to set up a network for which there was no political oversight. The dark side of global economics was that there was always a billionaire or two who needed some dirty work done: A former employee who had gone to a competitor with valuable information, or worse, gone to the authorities or the press. A wealthy father who didn't like the way his son-in-law treated his little princess. Accidents were arranged and these people ceased to be problems. The real global captains of enterprise acted no differently than their predecessors had for centuries. There wasn't a problem that the right amount of money couldn't solve. Freidman had made a tidy fortune brokering Donatella's talents to this elite group. But now that would all come to an end.

Freidman stabbed his cigarette out in an ashtray that two hours ago was clean, but was now brimming with stubby butts. He lit another and inhaled. Looking down at the photo of Donatella, he sadly shook his head. She really was a gorgeous woman. One of the most beautiful he had ever laid eyes on. And that was just on the surface. To watch the woman in action was almost indescribable. She exuded a sexuality that was truly intoxicating. She had even managed to seduce the great Mitch Rapp, although Freidman had wondered on more than one occasion who had actually seduced whom. Yes, she and Rapp had been lovers. Freidman had never even admitted it to himself, but he had been jealous. Rapp had acted where he had not. Freidman had been forced to restrain himself on many occasions. He desperately wanted to experience Donatella's full range of passion, but he knew it would be a monumental mistake. He always knew that someday he might have to kill her, and he could not allow that decision to be clouded by love.

Freidman reached down and touched the photograph. He admired her stunning mane of black curly hair, her sultry dark eyes and her high cheekbones. The woman was a goddess. Even knowing better, Freidman regretted more than ever that he had not acted on his feelings and taken her to bed. It was a shame to have missed such an opportunity.

The intercom on the desk buzzed and a woman's voice announced, "Mr. Rosenthal is here to see you."

Without taking his eyes off the photograph, Freidman reached out and pressed the intercom button. "Send him in."

The head of Mossad looked down at the image and sadly shook his head. What a waste, but it had to be done. Mitch Rapp could not be allowed to find out that he'd been involved in any of this.

MARC ROSENTHAL WAS one of Freidman's most trusted kidons. At thirty-two he had been with the Mossad for almost fifteen years. He had always been small and even now could pass for someone in his early twenties. When he had joined the Mossad at nineteen he could have passed for a twelve-year-old, and that was exactly what he did. Freidman used the teenager to run sensitive information in and out of the occupied territories and to scout out areas before raids were launched. By the time he reached his twenty-first birthday Rosenthal was garroting terrorists in the back alleys of Hebron and Gaza.

Freidman had only a handful of people he could trust with this operation and Rosenthal was one of them. There were two others who Freidman could think of, but both of them had worked with Donatella, and he did not want her powers of persuasion to get in the way. Thus he was left with little Marc Rosenthal. He was a Mossad man through and through, and more important, he had been recruited and trained by Freidman himself. He would do as he was told and would ask few questions. And if things went wrong, he would keep his mouth shut.

"Marc, I have something very delicate and important that I need you to take care of." Freidman stabbed out his cigarette and closed the file. Picking it up, he handed it to Rosenthal and said, "Her name is Donatella Rahn. She used to work for us." Freidman lit another cigarette and exhaled a billowing cloud of smoke. "She's good . . . very good. Unfortunately, she's been doing some things that could be very embarrassing to us."

Rosenthal nodded. Nothing more needed to be said. The boyish-looking man began looking through the file. "When do you want it taken care of?"

"As soon as possible."

"Do you want me to do it solo or bring my team?"

Freidman let loose an ominous laugh as he thought of Marcus trying to take Donatella down all by himself. It was possible, but not wise. "Bring your team, Marcus. This woman is very dangerous. She's killed more men than both you and I combined."

The comment elicited an arched eyebrow but nothing else. "What about the body?"

"Use your judgment. If you can, I'd like you to dispose of it yourselves. If things get hairy, leave the body and get out." Having worked in the field for years, and detesting interference from HQ, Freidman tried whenever possible to give his people the freedom to make decisions them-selves.

While still looking at the file, Rosenthal said, "I can be in place by tomorrow morning."

"Good." Freidman pointed the tip of his glowing ciga-rette at Rosenthal. "Use only your best people, and take care of it as quickly as possible." The colonel leaned back in his chair, took a drag off his cigarette and then added, "And of course . . . don't get caught."

CAPITOL HILL, WEDNESDAY MORNING

SENATOR CLARK SAT behind his massive desk in the Hart Senate Office Building. It was cold and windy in the nation's capital. He stared out the window, studying the weather, putting off for at least another moment a more pressing problem. The last vestiges of fall hung stubbornly from the burly oak trees on the grounds across the way. Only a few dark sodden leaves were left. Winter was on the nation's doorstep, and the thought of it brought a sense of dread. Clark did not do well in cold climates. A native of the southwest, he thought that D.C.'s winters were anything but mild. To Clark, if it snowed for even a day the city was too cold.

Looking out the window at the gray sky, he decided he would get out of town for the upcoming weekend: either Phoenix for golf or down to the island for a little fishing. Wife number three had something planned in New York, so he didn't have to worry about trying to convince her. He would be on his own, which at present was what he preferred. Number three was becoming increasingly con-frontational and demanding.

This was something he couldn't understand. He had come into the marriage knowing exactly what he wanted, and he had made his intentions very clear. For Christ's sake, he was sleeping with number three while he was still married to number two. What did the woman expect, that after all these years he was going to change just for her? Well, he wasn't going to change. Things would have to be managed. Another divorce at this juncture was out of the question. It would torpedo his chances at running for president. He would have to strike a deal with her at some point. He had, of course, made her sign an ironclad prenuptial. Under that agreement she would get a million-dollar lump sum payment and another $250,000 a year until she remarried. If things got ugly he could put some more money on the table and get her to play nice for a few more years. That would be a last resort, though. The real jewel to entice her with would be the White House. Being First Lady, after all, wasn't a bad deal.

A voice from the recesses of Clark's constantly plotting mind came up with another option. Have her killed. *No, he told himself, she's not that bad, at least not yet.* The morbid idea gained a little more weight with him as he thought of the potential advantages. The grieving spouse role might really help him connect with the soccer moms. The more he thought about the idea the more potential he saw. Wife number three was an extremely attractive and polished woman. They looked very good together. At least they did when she was happy, but she had a bitchy streak in her that was impossible to hide. When she was mad at him, she liked to make it a point to tell others. That could become a real liability during a long campaign. The press sooner or later would pick up on it and pile on. Clark doubted number three had the mental toughness to withstand such a barrage. No, he would have to decide on a course of action long before it came to that.

Clark returned his focus to a file on his desk and

decided the problems of wife number three would have to wait for now. At present, he had a more pressing issue that needed his attention. Mark Ellis and the other moneymen from California could not be put off indefinitely. They expected a return on their investment, and they had their sights set on the CIA and its treasure chest of valuable industrial secrets. The problem for Clark was not a new one. He needed to effect the outcome of an event without anyone knowing that he'd had a hand in it. He'd built his entire political career on this simple concept. He had gained the president's confidence by professing his support for Kennedy, and now it was time to get someone to do the dirty work. Someone was going to have to take Kennedy down, and Congressman Albert Rudin was just the man. Clark had planted the seed in Rudin's head during their last meeting. His own party was wronging him. His years of loyalty had been casually tossed aside by the party's leaders, and for what? For the nominee to a post that any one of a thousand people could fill.

Clark sensed that Rudin was ready to take the gamble of his political life. He was ready to go against the party in order to save the party. At least that was the self-righteous reasoning that Rudin would use. All the congressman from Connecticut needed was one good push. *No,* Clark thought. *He didn't need a push; he needed a trail of crumbs.* Clark looked down at the file on his desk and grinned. The information in the file would become that trail.

Clark closed the file and pressed the intercom button on his phone. "Mary, would you please send in my next appointment." The senator stood and buttoned his suit coat. When the door opened, Clark walked around his desk to meet his visitor. Extending his hand he said, "Good to see you, Jonathan."

The deputy director of the CIA shook the hand of his

patron. "Good to see you also, Hank. You look nice and tanned."

"I was down at the island last weekend." Clark was distracted for a split second as he thought of his meeting with Ellis. "I'll have to have you down sometime. You'd love it. Do you like to fish or sail?"

"Both."

"Good, then. If all goes well in the next few weeks we'll have to fly down and celebrate our victory." Clark gestured to a wing chair. "Have a seat. May I get you anything to drink?"

"No, thank you." Brown sat in the chair and watched as Clark walked around the coffee table and sat down on the large brown leather sofa.

Clark unbuttoned his jacket and laid his arms out casually across the back of the couch. "This is the part where it gets tricky, Jonathan."

With a laugh that was more nervous than humorous Brown said, "I thought we were already in the tricky part."

Clark chose to ignore what he took as a sign of weakness and pushed on. "Rudin is ready to jump, or almost ready. All he needs is a little push from us, and he'll bring Kennedy's confirmation to a screeching halt."

Brown knew Clark didn't call him to his office to simply fill him in. "Where do I come in?"

"I'm meeting with someone tomorrow. Former FBI. His name is Norb Steveken." Clark winked. "Very trustworthy."

The former federal judge wasn't impressed that the man had worked for the FBI. There were times on the bench when he thought the FBI was every bit as ruthless and corrupt as the people they were after. "What does he do now?"

"He's an investigator."

"For whom?"

"For whoever happens to be paying him."

Brown accepted the senator's answer. He'd learned long ago that Clark had acquaintances from virtually every walk of life. "Who's paying right now?"

Clark batted away Brown's concerns with a wave of his hand. "You don't need to concern yourself with that. The important thing is that when you talk to him you need to seem very reluctant to give him what he needs, at least at first."

"And what does he need?"

"He needs information that Congressman Rudin can use to launch hearings."

Brown knew it would come to this eventually but it didn't lessen his discomfort. Used to keeping his cool on the bench, he pressed forward. "What information?"

Clark casually crossed his legs and said, "Give him the goods on the Orion Team."

Not quite sure he'd heard right, Brown asked, "You want me to tell a former FBI agent about the Orion Team?"

"Don't worry," Clark cautioned. "I've convinced Congressman Rudin to meet with Mr. Steveken. I've told Albert that I don't want to get involved in this, and I don't intend to get you dragged into it, either."

"Then why are you asking me to meet with this Steveken fellow?"

"Steveken will do what I tell him, and I'm going to tell him if you give him anything it will be off the record, and it's to stay that way."

"What about sending the info to Rudin anonymously?" Brown was desperate to come up with an alternative.

Clark shook his head. "It won't work. Albert is already in deep shit with his party. If we're going to get him to put his nuts on the line, he needs to hear this from a real person who can tell him they heard it straight from the mouth of someone at Langley."

Brown expressed his apprehension through pursed lips. "I don't know. It's one thing to pass information on to you, Hank, but talking to a former Fed about the Orion Team doesn't sound like such a good idea." The potbellied Brown squirmed in his seat. "People who get caught locking horns with this group tend to disappear."

"Peter Cameron was too cocky. You don't have that problem."

"I don't know," said Brown with obvious reservation.

Clark kept his voice reasonable. "Jonathan, you know the plan. I promise you this is the last big step. Once Albert starts his investigation there will be no turning back. The press will be all over this thing, and you and I both know Kennedy doesn't stand a chance at surviving that type of scrutiny." Clark pointed to his friend. "And then I will make sure you become the next director of the CIA, and a very wealthy one, I might add."

Brown was looking to cash in after years of public service. Besides, America was a nation of laws, and Kennedy needed to be held accountable. "All right. How do you want me to do it?"

With a smile Clark asked, "Do you still walk that dog of yours every night?"

"Yes."

"Good. You can expect Steveken to approach you in the park by your house. Probably tomorrow night."

"And what do you want me to tell him?"

Clark thought about it for a moment. "I want you to act real nervous at first. Tell him you don't want to talk to him. Try to walk away. Don't worry, he'll follow. He's a very persistent fellow."

Brown repeated his question, "And what do you want me to tell him?"

"Nothing," smiled Clark. "At least not tomorrow night. Tell him you need to think about it. Tell him to come back the next night, and you'll have a decision for him."

13

MARYLAND, WEDNESDAY EVENING

Rapp was ready to go. The cab was waiting in the driveway. He'd already gone out and said hello to the man, telling him he was waiting for his girl-friend to arrive and then they could leave. Anna was late, which was to be expected. As Rapp went over his mental checklist one more time, he decided he might have to implement the thirty-minute rule with her. Yes, he decided it was time. If they needed to be somewhere at 8:00 he'd have to start telling her 7:30. She was thirty minutes late for everything unless it was a live broadcast.

She'd actually held up Air Force One last month for close to fifteen minutes. Jack Warch, the special agent in charge of the presidential detail, had been kind enough to call Anna on her cell phone and ask her if she was going to make the flight. Anna was stuck in traffic and pleaded forgiveness. The Secret Service agent, used to these flights being delayed, had no problem buying her some time. Besides, they were going to California and would be able to make up any lost time in the air. It helped that Anna Rielly was a favorite of the president. It also helped that Jack Warch and President Hayes owed their lives to Anna Rielly's boyfriend.

Rapp checked his watch more out of a nervous habit than a need to know what the exact time was. They were flying out of Baltimore International in less than two and a half hours. They still had plenty of time, but Rapp didn't like to be rushed when he was sneaking weapons onto a flight. From his vast arsenal, he had decided to bring his Heckler & Koch HK4 pistol. His version was designed to carry the 9-mm short round. Rapp had disassembled the weapon and concealed individual parts within various items in his suitcase.

The people at Langley's Science and Technology division purchased everyday common items like blow-dryers, shaving cream cans, alarm clocks, radios and luggage. They then modified the items by creating false or hidden compartments while always maintaining each item's ability to perform its task. If a customs officer or border guard plugged in a blow-dryer and it didn't work it was a huge red flag. The people from S&T were experts in this field. They even went so far as to test everything they designed on state-of-the-art airport X-ray machines. They could tell you the make and model of almost every X-ray machine and metal detector used in every major airport around the world, and more important, they could tell you the best way to pack your suitcase to minimize the risk of an operator discovering an illegal item in your luggage.

Anna would flip if she knew, but such was his life. Traveling the streets of almost any Italian city without a weapon was a risk he did not want to take. The plan was to tell her when they were settled into their hotel in Milan. Telling her before they left might put some undue stress on her when they had to clear customs in Italy. Like most reporters, Anna was a good actor when she was after something, but helping your boyfriend sneak a weapon, a weapon you didn't want him to bring in the first place, into a foreign country . . . that was pushing it. No, Rapp told himself again, not telling her was the right thing to do. Besides, she would be more concerned about the other thing he was sneaking onto the flight.

It had cost him double what he thought it would, but the second he saw it, he knew it was for her. It was classic and simple. A flawless, ideal cut, one carat diamond perched atop a platinum band in a Tiffany setting. She was going to melt when she saw it, and he was going to enjoy every minute of it. The ring was safely tucked away inside a compartment of his leather jacket. On impulse he reached down and ran his finger along the inside of the liner, feeling for the telltale bump. It was still there.

Rapp checked his watch again. Oh, how he wished she would get home. The urgency he felt to get to Italy surprised him a little. He'd been thinking about it all morning. It was the beginning of a new life. This would be the watershed moment for which he'd been secretly yearning.

He heard tires squeal. Rapp looked down the long driveway. The unsettling noise brought a smile to his face. It would be Anna making the turn onto their street. He'd been through all of this before, standing, waiting for her on the front porch, and hoping that she was okay. Hoping that some demon from his past hadn't tracked him down and taken her. Praying that some sicko, who had seen her on TV, hadn't decided that Anna was to be his possession.

Anna laughed it off when he told her she should call if she was going to be late. She was always slightly apologetic, but showed no signs of changing. Her defense was that she was a very busy person whose job made it almost impossible to be punctual. At the time Rapp had been tempted to tell her that was the dumbest excuse he'd ever heard, but over the past year he'd learned to choose his words carefully, or better yet, just keep his mouth shut. Being right wasn't always worth it.

Someday soon he would make her see the need to be on time or at the very least, to call. There were real security reasons involved, and there was his mental health to consider. Some people had overactive imaginations and when mixed with a little paranoia, could lead to real problems. But with Rapp it wasn't imagination; it was reality. He had been on the front lines. He had seen what the enemy was capable of. He had seen them kill innocent women and children without hesitation. As far as Rapp was concerned, this was the major difference between them. In all of his years, in all of the operations he'd conducted, his record was clean. He had yet to kill a noncombatant. He did his killing up close, usually with a knife or a gun and on rare occasions he'd used explosives. He was immensely proud of this, and had come to realize that it was probably the only thing that allowed him to sleep at night.

The tires squealed again, and then Rapp's black Volvo S80 careened onto the driveway. All Rapp could do was smile and shake his head as his future wife sped down the driveway and then skidded to a halt next to the cab. *Thank God she's a good driver,* he thought. He couldn't be mad at her for being late. He was too excited to start his new life.

Rielly jumped out of the car with a sheepish look on her face. "Sorry I'm late, honey. I got hung up . . ."

Rapp wasn't interested in excuses. He'd heard them all. He just shook his head and smiled. "Your bags are in the cab. Do you need anything from the house?"

With her purse over her shoulder she moved quickly

toward the front door. "I'd like to brush my teeth, and take some of this makeup off." Because Rielly often had to give reports from the White House throughout the day, she was stuck wearing a thick layer of makeup for long periods of time. Whenever she came home it was her first order of business to scrub it from her face.

Rapp looked at his watch. "We're late."

"I know." Rielly paused just long enough to give him a quick kiss and then blew past him and into the house. "It'll only take a minute."

As Rapp watched her set her purse down and start up the stairs he mumbled, "More like ten."

Rielly yelled over her shoulder, "I heard that," and continued up the stairs.

A little frustrated, Rapp said, "Well, it's true. Maybe you could reapply it on the way to the airport." Rapp had been here before. *It'll take a minute* was code for ten to twenty minutes.

She yelled down from the upstairs bathroom, "Don't worry, we've got plenty of time. Flights never leave on schedule anymore."

"Is that what you told the president when you held up Air Force One last month?" Rielly didn't know that Rapp knew about her little incident.

She appeared at the top of the stairs with a toothbrush in one hand and a tube of toothpaste in the other. "Where'd you hear about that?"

"It was in the *Washington Times* this morning." Rapp said this with a straight face despite the fact that he was making it up. He knew Anna never read the *Times* due to the fact that she thought it was a biased newspaper. Every time this was brought up, he liked to remind her that the *Post* wasn't exactly known for its well-balanced staff.

Rielly's little knob chin dropped and she said, "Please tell me you're kidding."

Rapp smiled. "Okay. I'm kidding."

"Then how in the hell did you know about that?"

"Never mind." Rapp gestured with his hand to get her moving. "Let's go, we're late."

"I want to know how you know." She was serious.

"Never mind. I have my sources." Rapp turned. "I'm going to put the car into the garage. Hurry up!"

Rielly watched him disappear for a second and then returned to the bathroom. While she loaded up her tooth-brush she looked into the mirror and said, "You've got a seven hour flight to get it out of him." With complete confidence that she would succeed, she stuck the tooth-brush into her mouth and went to work.

THE BIG AMERICAN Airlines 747 was parked on the tar-mac at BIA. They waited at the gate until all of the pas-sengers had presented their boarding cards, and then they got in line. It was one of Rapp's rules, and of course Anna had wanted to know why. Getting used to the idea that he was going to spend the rest of his life with her, he decided to explain. They were flying in first class. If they had boarded the plane right away, when the first class ticket holders were given the opportunity to settle in, they would have been the center of attention for the other 250 fliers as they waltzed up to the gate. Mitch's way, they waited until the end and slipped onto the flight without anyone paying any attention to them. It was all about keeping a low profile.

Rielly had accepted the reasoning without comment. They sat at the bar and had a beer while the rest of the passengers lined up like cattle and started the boarding process. She thought about Mitch's attention to detail. It permeated everything they did as a couple. There was, of course, the restaurant thing. It was a little irritating at times. He could never sit in the middle of a room. He always had to have his back to a wall, and always upon arriving, excused himself to go to the men's room. At first Rielly didn't notice and then the O'Rourkes, some friends of hers, had pointed it out. Anna had asked Mitch about it, and after some weak attempts at deflecting her queries, he copped to it. It was standard operating procedure, or as Mitch liked to say, SOP. Check the bathrooms, the emergency exits and the basic lay of the land. That way if anything went down you knew what your options were.

There was also the gun thing. At first it didn't bother her too much. Her father and two of her brothers were cops. She grew up with guns around the house, and in fact owned a snub-nosed .38-caliber revolver herself. She kept it locked up, but had the permit to carry it if she wanted to. She usually only did so if she'd received some weird letters or calls from a viewer. But Mitch wouldn't leave the house without a gun. Literally, if he didn't have a gun on him it was within arm's reach. He even mowed the lawn with a gun stuck into the waistband of his shorts. When they went out on the boat he kept a gun in the glove box. There were at least three guns stashed in various places around the house.

She had pressed him on the issue once, hinting that he might be just a little too cautious. He had told her that the only reason he was still alive was because he was so cautious. He had gone on to tell her that if any of those people from his not so distant past ever showed up, she'd be very happy that he was armed. At that point she had thrown a hypothetical at him. What if we get married and have kids? He thought about it for a moment and told her that some things would have to change. The answer had satisfied her at the time.

Rielly took a sip of her beer and looked at Mitch. Leaning in, she asked in a whisper, "You're not carrying a gun, are you?"

Rapp pulled his beer away from his lips and said, "No. Just my love gun."

Rielly laughed and then purred like a cat.

Rapp felt a slight twinge of guilt over his answer. But then again she hadn't asked, are you bringing a gun, she had asked are you carrying one. His gun was nowhere near his person. It was carefully packed away in a half dozen pieces, stored in the bowels of the jumbo jet.

They sipped on their beers for a couple more minutes, and when the line was down to just a few people they picked up their carry-on bags and walked hand in hand across the waiting area to the gate. Rapp handed over the first class tickets and they proceeded down the jetway with their boarding cards. When they made the left hand turn for the plane they stopped at the end of the line of backed-up passengers. Rapp held Rielly close and looked into her beautiful green eyes. He could tell by the sparkle in her eye and the grin on her face that she was a little popped up from her one beer. After thirty seconds a man came down the jetway and replaced them as the last in line.

Rielly looked up with a telltale smirk on her face and said a little too loudly, "Maybe he's a spy."

Rapp pulled her head into his chest as she giggled louder and louder. All he could do was shake his head and smile. After she calmed down he said, "Get a hold of yourself or they won't let you on board."

"What are you talking about?" Rielly exaggerated her state of drunkenness by intentionally slurring her words.

"They won't let you get on a plane drunk. Its against FAA rules."

"What if I'm drunk on love?" She closed her eyes pursed her lips for a kiss.

Mitch laughed and gave her what she wanted. After that the line moved quickly, and before long they were settled into their first-class seats. Anna was next to the window and Mitch was on the aisle. While the plane pushed away from the gate, they got their reading material together. As they taxied over to one of the main runways, Rapp looked out the window and checked the weather. It was at least another hour before sunset, the temperature was in the fifties, and there was no sign of rain. The take-off should go smoothly.

Anna started paging through one of her magazines and then stopped. She closed it and looked at Mitch. "You never told me what exactly it is that you have to take care of while we're in Milan."

"Just a little bit of business. Nothing that will take up too much time." Rapp opened his book and hoped that Anna would go back to her magazine. Unfortunately, he knew it was wishful thinking.

"What kind of business?"

"Official business."

In a mocking tone Anna lowered her voice and said, "Top secret business."

"That's right, baby." Rapp winked. "Now why don't you just sit back, look pretty and peruse your fashion magazine? I'll take care of everything else."

Rielly expertly jabbed him in the ribs. "Don't give me that crap. I think you can tell me a little more than, 'official business.' "

"No, I can't." Mitch said emphatically. They'd been down this road before, and he was tiring of it. He leaned in close to her ear and said, "There are certain things about my job that I will never be able to tell you. I've been up front about it from the start and you said you could deal with it. Now are you going to abide by that or are you going to change the rules on me?"

He was right, and she knew it, but it still pissed her off. "No, I'm not going to change the rules, but I think there are times where you don't need to be so vague. I mean you get all freaked out when I'm fifteen minutes late, and you expect me to just sit in our hotel room in a foreign city while you run off and take care of official business." Rielly leaned in so close her nose touched his cheek. "I mean for Christ's sake, for all I know the damn CIA is sending you over here to kill someone." Rielly moved away and stubbornly folded her arms across her chest.

Eyeing her with caution, Rapp thought about what she'd just said and then had to admit she had a pretty good point. He owed her a better explanation. "I'm sorry. You're right. I have to meet with someone . . . someone I used to work with."

"Will it be dangerous?"

"No." He shook his head and meant it. He would be very cautious, but in truth he wasn't expecting any trouble.

"Does this person know you're coming?"

"No."

Rielly frowned, not sure that she liked the answer. "Is this person someone you can trust?"

"Yes. Very much so." Rapp's words were sincere. "Don't worry, honey. Everything will go fine. I'll take care of it the first day we're there, and then we'll have the rest of the trip all to ourselves."

The plane stopped for a moment, and then the engines came to life. A few seconds later the big jet began to roll down the tarmac. Rapp reached over and grabbed Anna's hand. He kissed the back of it and said, "I love you." Rielly kissed him on the lips and told him the same. As the plane began to lift off the ground Rapp's thoughts turned to the person he would be meeting in Milan. Donatella Rahn was much more than someone he used to work with. She was someone he used to share his bed with. For reasons that had nothing to do with national security he had decided to keep that a secret from Anna. That was all ancient history. It had nothing to do with the situation at hand. Rapp helped rationalize the omission by telling himself that he had never asked her about her ex-boyfriends. This almost worked until he realized that she, as of yet, hadn't flown three thousand miles to have a secret meeting with one of her former lovers.

Rapp didn't like the way the argument was working out so he pushed it from his mind. *In and out,* he told himself. *No big deal. I'll go to dinner with her, ask her who hired her to kill Peter Cameron, and I'll be done with it.* Rapp grimaced as he looked out the window and down at his favorite body of water in the whole world. The Chesapeake Bay slid by, while a large container ship worked its way north toward the port of Baltimore. Rapp knew it wasn't going to be that easy. In his heart of hearts, he hoped he was just being his paranoid self. For once he wanted something to be easy. All he wanted was a name. The name of the man who had tried to have him killed in Germany, and then he could make things right and get on with his life.

Anna nestled in and rested her head on his shoulder. Rapp kissed the top of her head and took in the soft fragrance of her light chestnut hair. She was worth seeing this thing through to the end. He would get the name from Donatella, and he would eliminate the problem. Then they could start their family, and he would feel safer knowing that whoever had tried to kill him in Germany was dead. They could do no harm to his family.

14

MILAN, THURSDAY MORNING

The transatlantic flight went well with one exception; neither Anna nor Mitch had slept. Rapp hadn't really planned on it, but he was hoping the two glasses of champagne that Anna had consumed would knock her out. They didn't. In fact, the spirits only heightened her excitement for the week ahead. Two days in Milan filled with shopping at the major fashion houses and a night at the famous Teatro alla Scala, Milan's grand opera house, and then they would board a train and head south for warmer weather and the romance of Sicily. They had talked excitedly about the trip. The anticipation of what lay ahead was absolutely intoxicating. But for fear of ruining the moment, neither of them spoke directly about engagement, wedding rings, marriage, or children. There would be plenty of time to discuss all of that later.

For Rapp, there was also a second reason why the elation was somewhat tempered. Before he could get on with his new life he had to confront his past, and not just anyone from his past, but someone with whom he had been romantically involved. Just being in Milan brought back a deluge of emotions. Most of them were good, but there were some bad ones too. Italy was his favorite place in the entire world. The history, the architecture, the smells, the people, even the dirt, it was all so real.

Getting through customs at Malpensa Airport proved to be relatively easy, as the testosterone-charged Italian customs officials were more concerned with Anna's lingerie than the various weapons that Mitch had stashed throughout his luggage. With the time difference, and the seven-hour flight, they arrived in Milan just in time for the morning rush hour. On the way into the city Anna was all eyes, taking in the sights of the capital city of Italy's Lombardy region. While at the University of Michigan she had spent a semester abroad in Paris. During that time she had taken a week to visit Rome, and that was the extent of her exposure to Italy. They had debated the merits of the two countries, Anna siding with France and Mitch siding with Italy. Rapp planned on changing her opinion by the end of the week. He would be the first to admit that France had many redeeming qualities, but unfortunately that beauty was often overshadowed by the arrogance of its people.

Not in Italy, though. If anything the people added to the passion and history of the ancient country. There was genuine willingness to connect with and help foreigners, especially Americans. Their cabdriver was a perfect example. As they plodded their way through rush hour he pointed out, in English, the various sights of interest. During the early part of the commute Anna was slightly disappointed at how modern and industrial Milan was. Mitch assured her that once they reached the heart of the city she would not be disappointed.

He was right. As they turned onto the Via G. Mengoni, Mitch practically had to restrain Anna from leaping from the moving cab. The Duomo loomed so large she had to stick her head out of the window so she could take in the full height of the intricate spires.

"Oh my God! I think that is the most beautiful church I've ever seen."

The cabdriver nodded proudly and answered, "And one of the biggest."

Anna continued gawking at the architectural marvel as the cab rolled slowly along the cobblestone street. "What's it called?"

"Duomo!"

"I have to see it. Can we see it?" She turned to Mitch. "Can we see it right now?"

Rapp laughed at her obvious excitement. "It's a short walk from the hotel. Only four blocks. After we take a nap this will be our first stop."

"Nap?" she asked incredulously. "I'm not taking any naps, I'm too excited."

Rapp smiled and shook his head. It was nice to see her this way. Maybe this would work out for the best. If they stayed out all day she would collapse around dinnertime, and then he could sneak out and meet with Donatella. Then if all went well, he could get the information he needed and be done with the whole mess. As they passed the Galleria Vittorio Emanuele II, Rapp knew that was a lie. The harsh reality was that in all likelihood, whatever Donatella told him would only drag him in deeper. Donatella was one link in a chain that might be very long. Rapp would have to decide for the first time in his adult life if he was willing to turn something over to others and walk away. Anna kissed him on the cheek as they rolled down the old cobblestone street. Mitch pushed the depressing thought from his mind and forced a smile onto his lips. Maybe it would be simple. Maybe Donatella could answer all of his questions, and explain why he had been set up in Germany. Maybe? Mitch turned away, the smile melting from his face. This type of stuff was never easy, and it was one of many reasons why he needed to get out.

THE ALITALIA FLIGHT pulled up to the gate at Linate Airport. It was one of more than a dozen Alitalia flights that would arrive from Rome throughout the day. Of the two major airports that service Milan, Linate handled mostly domestic flights. It was located just two miles from the center of the city, whereas Malpensa 2000 was more than thirty. The flight had left Rome shortly after nine in the morning and had taken less than an hour and a half to make the journey north. When the door opened a steady stream of businesspeople marched off the plane. An unremarkable man near the middle of the group scanned the faces of the people waiting for the flight, but was careful not to look too interested. He was dressed in a pair of olive slacks, a light blue button-down and a blue sport coat. A pair of dark sunglasses concealed his piercing eyes.

On his first visual pass of the crowd he saw the man he was to meet, but instead of making his way over to him, he continued with the others toward the main terminal. This was Marc Rosenthal's second flight of the day. The first had left Tel Aviv well before sunup. After his meeting with the director general of Mossad he had wasted no time in moving his assets into position. Within hours he had two of his people on their way to Milan, each on different flights, and each stopping in another country before entering Italy. One was to obtain weapons and transportation and the other was to establish surveillance with the target. Freidman had given him the go-ahead to use one of the safe flats in Milan despite the fact that officially Mossad had nothing to do with the operation. Rosenthal had told Freidman that the alternative was to use a hotel; a less than ideal situation, since it was highly likely the Italian authorities would be investigating Donatella's disappearance and possible homicide. In a perfect operation they would take her out without a single witness, but that could not be counted on. There was always the chance that some neighbor, co-worker or passerby might notice several men who seemed out of place. At some point the description of those men would be checked against the security tapes at the local hotels. If they found any matches the next step would be to check the security tapes at the airports, and so on and so on.

When Rosenthal reached the main terminal he continued through the baggage claim area without stopping and walked out onto the curb. Along with the other travelers he got in line at the taxi stand. He noted the number of people in line ahead of him, tried to gauge who might be traveling together and who was traveling alone, and then he counted out the waiting cabs. Rosenthal marked the one that he would most likely be riding in and kept an eye on it. When his turn came, he took one last look around and climbed into the official white taxi. In fluent Italian he told the driver to take him to the Grand Hotel. It was not where he was staying, but that was none of the driver's business.

It was a sunny day, and unfortunately for Rosenthal, the tourists of summer were gone. It was nearing 11:00 A.M., and the streets were not very crowded. He frowned with concern as he looked out the window of the moving taxi. Rosenthal's early experiences as a kidon had left an indelible mark on him. He had been assigned to penetrate the deepest circles of the enemy. There was no more dangerous assignment that could be thrust upon an agent of Mossad than to enter the Palestinian camps. He had been asked to go behind enemy lines and identify the leaders of the various terrorist cells. He'd had to assimilate with the very people he hated.

Those early years had left scars. The shrinks at Mossad knew none of this, nor did anyone else. These were Rosenthal's own private demons. The solitary bravado of his early years had cracked. He hated operating alone. As a predator he had gone from a lone wolf to developing a pack mentality. Never again would he hunt alone. He would never go back to the camps, never go back to the sleepless nights, worrying that he might let something slip in his dreams. No, that was all behind him. Now he did everything possible to stack the deck in his favor.

And his discerning eye didn't like the lack of cover on the streets. Over the last twenty-four hours Rosenthal had scoured the file Freidman had given him. It was obvious it had been heavily censored. Much of it was blacked out, and there were large gaps where entire operations had been omitted. Rosenthal had no doubt the old man had personally removed the information. Part of it was for reasons of compartmentalization and secrecy, but Rosenthal knew the old man too well to think that was the only reason. Freidman had removed information that might cause Rosenthal to hesitate rather than assassinate. Rosenthal was no novice. Although he had not yet reached the age of thirty he had been doing this work for close to a decade. Despite the heavily censored file, Rosenthal knew that this Donatella Rahn had done a lot for Israel, but this was the ugly side of his business. One day you're a prized asset; the next day you're a liability.

As the taxi neared The Galleria Vittorio, Rosenthal told the driver they were close enough to the hotel and asked him to stop. He paid the man and got out. He gave a quick glance over both shoulders and then entered the magnificent nineteenth-century architectural structure. The Galleria

Vittorio Emanuele II was laid out in the formation of a cross, the north–south section connecting the Piazza del Duomo and the Piazza della Scala. Instead of open air between the buildings the large bisecting avenues were covered with an ornate iron framework and glass. It was closed to all but foot traffic. The floor was made of an intricate mosaic of colorful tiles and elegant shops lined the walk.

Rosenthal stopped into a bookshop and purchased a copy of the London *Times.* He loitered near the front of the shop for a moment to see if he was being followed and then continued on his way out the north end of the structure and across the Piazza della Scala. On the other end of the plaza he leaned against a light post and acted as if he were reading the paper. After several minutes a maroon Fiat sedan pulled up to the curb and Rosenthal got in.

It was the man from the airport. He pulled back into traffic and said, "You're clean."

"Good. And the woman?"

"She's at her office. Yanta followed her to work this morning. She got there at nine and hasn't left."

"What about her apartment?"

"We decided to wait for you before we made that move."

Rosenthal nodded. The man driving the car was Jordan Sunberg. Although he looked a good ten years older than Rosenthal he was actually two years younger. Sunberg had a thick black beard and an unruly head of curly hair. The two had worked with each other on many occasions in recent years. They were two of Freidman's favorite katsas. "Did you get the things I requested?"

"Yes. It's all back at the flat."

Rosenthal checked his watch. "Good. We'll make our move this evening."

15

Rapp watched Anna twirl around the middle of the beautiful room, her arms spread and her little chin tipped up toward the vaulted hand-painted ceiling of the fifteenth-century monastic cell. She could not believe this was their hotel room and not a museum. Rapp couldn't have been happier over her reaction. Watching her spin around in circles made him think of what Anna must have been like as a little girl. He felt a brief pang of sadness that he'd missed so much of her life. It was irrational, he knew. There was no way they could have known each other. She had grown up in Chicago and he in Virginia. Besides, if they had met it would have virtually guaranteed that they would not be together right now.

Anna moved across the room and out onto the small balcony overlooking the inner courtyard. Mitch followed her and wrapped his arms around her waist. They stood together, front to back, looking down on the immaculately manicured courtyard. Every tree, every bush, every table, every umbrella was perfect.

Anna reached up with her left hand and touched Mitch's face. Turning her head back she found his lips and gave him a long kiss. As their lips parted she said, "I love you so much."

"I love you, too." He squeezed her tightly and began kissing her neck. After a minute he led her back toward the king-size bed.

"What are you doing?" asked Anna in a playful tone.

"I'm trying to seduce you." He held her tight, continued the kissing and made the last step toward the bed.

Anna grabbed his hands, twisted free and pushed him onto the bed. Mitch willingly let her win and landed comfortably in the middle of the bed. With his hand held out he gestured for Anna to join him. To his great disappointment all he got was a defiant pose; hands on hips with a shaking head. "Come on, honey," he pleaded.

"Nope. We're only in Milan for a day and a half, and I'm not going to spend it in bed."

"Why not?"

"Don't ask stupid questions."

"Come on," he said baiting her. "It won't take long."

"Maybe for you."

Rapp laughed. "Now . . . now. Be nice."

"It has nothing to do with being nice. I'm being a realist. If I get into bed with you, we'll have sex, and then you'll fall asleep. I don't want to sleep right now. I want to get out and see the city." She started for the bathroom. "Besides, you're always better when I make you wait."

Rapp stared up at the mural on the ceiling. "I'll have to work on that." He let out a loud groan that was mostly for show and then got off the bed. After peeling off his clothes, he strutted into the bathroom.

Anna turned from the mirror where she was touching up her makeup. She looked at her boyfriend's naked body and asked in an incredulous tone, "You can't want it that bad?"

"You wish," grinned Rapp as slapped her on the butt and continued past her and into the shower.

After the shower Rapp went out into the bedroom and put on a fresh set of clothes. He stood over his suitcase and wondered what was the best way to handle his next move. He was tempted to assemble the gun and slip it into the specially designed interior pocket of his leather jacket, but he knew that was an invitation for disaster. Anna would wrap her arms around him the second they got outside and she would check for the weapon. She always did. She had gotten used to it, at least in America. She had been raised in a house full of guns. Her father was a cop as well as two of her brothers. Rapp had met the family, and like all good Chicago cops they carried their sidearm with them when they were off duty.

The best way to handle it with Anna was to be up front, but then again if the room was bugged he didn't want to get into it with her here. He made the decision to tell her when they got outside. Rapp picked up his suitcase and carried it into the drawing room. After setting it on the ottoman he quickly grabbed the hair dryer, the can of shaving cream and the radio and pulled them apart. In less than two minutes he had the weapon assembled and the items put back together. Rapp's leather jacket was on the arm of the chair. He opened it and put the automatic into an inside pocket designed to conceal the weapon.

When Anna was ready they went downstairs to La Veranda for a quick bite to eat. They had the restaurant to themselves. It was post breakfast and just prior to the lunch rush. Anna ordered a bowl of soup and Mitch ordered a roast beef sandwich for which he received a concerned look from his girlfriend.

"Doesn't the mad cow thing scare you a little?"

Rapp looked quickly over both shoulders. "Where? Is one on the loose?"

Anna laughed and shook her head. "You know what I mean."

"Yeah, I know what you mean, and I appreciate your concern, but I stand a better chance of getting hit by lightning than contracting mad cow disease."

Anna decided not to make a big deal out of it. She took a drink of water and then asked, "When are you going to take care of your business?"

With a serious look he said, "I'd tried to upstairs but you shut me down."

"Oh," she smiled. "I can see you're in a real juvenile mood today."

"Just in love, darling. That's all."

"Can we be serious for a minute?"

"Absolutely." Rapp grabbed a bread stick and bit off the end.

"When are you going to meet with this person?"

Rapp took another bite of the breadstick and said, "I'm going to try to make contact this afternoon."

"Is this going to interfere at all with our plans for this evening?"

He thought about it for a second and then said, "It shouldn't."

Anna shot him a disappointed look.

"Darling, you're not being fair. I told you I had to take care of this. We're going to have a great trip, but I have to take care of this first." He took another bite from the breadstick and waited for her to give him a sign that she wasn't upset. When she smiled he reached across the table for her hand and said, "Besides, I have a sneaky feeling that you're going to be wiped out by the time tonight rolls around."

Their food arrived in short order and they ate quickly. Before leaving Rapp ordered a double cappuccino for a little extra burst of energy and suggested that Anna do the same. He didn't care how beautiful the Duomo was, tours made him more tired than a two-mile swim. Anna ordered a single cappuccino. The hot drinks came in to-go cups. Rapp signed the check and they left the hotel.

It was a bright sunny day. The temperature was in the mid fifties. It was perfect walking weather. Anna was dressed quite a bit more stylishly than Mitch. The fact that Milan was the fashion capital of the world was not wasted on NBC's White House correspondent. Instead of heading directly for the grand church, Rapp led Anna half a block to the north and took a right onto Via della Spiga. A short block later they took a right onto Via Sant'Andrea. It was at about this point that the tour of the Duomo was put on hold. The first fashion designer that came into view was Hermès, quickly followed by Fendi. Rapp knew the street well, and it was having its intended effect on Anna. He was guessing that it would take them several hours to travel the next full block. They would have to run the gauntlet of Prada, Moschino, Chanel, Gianfranco Ferre and Giorgio Armani. Prada alone could take two hours.

Anna stood gawking at the window of Hermès. Rapp could see her struggling over what to do. Finally, she looked at him and said, "I want to go in for just a minute."

Rapp laughed loudly. "Commercialism over Catholicism. Your mother would be very disappointed."

Anna scowled at him. "It'll only take a minute."

"Don't worry, honey. We've got all day. We can always see the Duomo tomorrow." Rapp opened the door and gestured for Anna to enter. Before following her he looked down the street in the direction of the House of Armani. Donatella was in the building somewhere. Or at least she was supposed to be. Rapp had had Marcus Dumond do a little checking before he left for Italy. Dumond was the Counterterrorism Center's resident computer genius. He'd hacked his way into Armani's network, and with the help of Rapp's linguistic skills they'd figured out that Donatella was scheduled to be in Milan for the entire week. Rapp had memorized her entire schedule for the two days he was to be in Milan. He glanced at his watch for a moment and thought the timing might be perfect. Another thirty minutes of shopping and he'd slip away.

Rosenthal had Sunberg park the car several blocks away and they walked to the café. When they rounded the corner onto Sant'Andrea, Rosenthal was pleased to see David Yanta sitting at a small wooden table talking in his always animated fashion to two drop-dead gorgeous women. Models no doubt. The city was crawling with them. Rosenthal was pleased that Yanta was talking to the women because he was hoping they would score a little sex while on the mission; he was also pleased because in their line of work, nothing stood out more than a lone man sitting at a café. The picture had surveillance written all over it.

As they approached the table Yanta stood up and enthusiastically introduced his two co-workers to the beautiful women. The cover story and names were a variation on ones they'd used before. They worked for an international telecommunications company, and were based out of Paris. They were in Milan to try and get the Pirelli-Armstrong Tire Corporation to carry one of their new products.

Yanta ordered more coffee for the table and produced a fresh pack of cigarettes. Everyone lit up and no one bothered to take their sunglasses off. This was Milan. Looking hip was of paramount importance. Yanta continued to entertain the models with wild stories of their travels. Rosenthal watched him with some slight amusement. Yanta was the biggest natural bullshitter he'd ever met. The man could strike up a conversation with anyone.

He was a bit of dork, which he used to his advantage by piling on the self-deprecating humor and putting those around him at ease. The women more often than not fell for this ploy. Yanta always said he was playing to their instincts as natural healers. Rosenthal thought it had more to do with getting them to lower their guard and making them laugh. Whichever it was though, it worked.

As the conversation bounced around the table, Rosenthal feigned interest. From time to time his eyes strayed across the street to the House of Armani. The showroom was on the first floor and the offices were on the floors above. Somewhere on the third floor was the office of Donatella Rahn. The file Freidman had given him outlined all the pertinent aspects of her life. Her flat was just eight blocks away in a nice upscale part of Milan on the east side of the Giardini Pubblici. She walked to work every day. In the summers she took her holidays at a small villa on Lake Como and in the winter she took ski trips to the Swiss Alps and warm weather trips to Greece. Her job required a fair amount of travel and brought her to Paris and New York on a monthly basis.

She was the perfect honey trap. A gorgeous woman that the Institute could use in a variety of ways to tempt the enemy into letting their guard down. Rosenthal also guessed that they'd used her to seduce and blackmail quite a few powerful men over the years. The file that Rosenthal had received from Freidman had been so sanitized that it mentioned nothing of the woman's operational missions, but Rosenthal could take a pretty good guess at it. He'd seen it done before. She was bait used to lure their enemies into an ambush.

One thing was bothering Rosenthal, though. Back in Freidman's office, the old man had told him that this woman had killed more men than the two of them combined. By Rosenthal's conservative count that put the toll at over twenty people, a huge number for anyone in their business and unheard of for a woman. Rosenthal had decided on the flight up from Rome that the old man must have left out the word *helped*. *Helped kill more men than you and I combined* must have been what he meant.

After all, the woman was a model strung out on heroin when Freidman had recruited her. From what he could gather in the file she had been brought up in a relatively normal environment in Italy. Nothing stood out that would lead him to think she was a highly skilled assassin. *No*, Rosenthal thought, *she's nothing more than a high priced call girl who's been doing a little too much talking. Either that or she's hit Freidman up for some extra cash one too many times.* Rosenthal cringed at the thought.

He decided to let his curiosity rest. Freidman had ordered the woman dead and that was enough. What she had done to deserve it didn't matter. Rosenthal had gone into battle for Freidman many times and would continue to do so without question. The man was a true patriot and Rosenthal would not let him down. By midnight tonight his bidding would be done. Israel's problem would be dealt with, and the world would be none the wiser that agents of Mossad had had a hand in the death of a beautiful Italian model.

16

Donatella Rahn stood in front of her mammoth glass desk and studied a series of ten-by-eight Polaroids that had just been couriered to her office from a shoot that was going on across town. After more than twenty years in the business, the first ten in front of the camera and the next eleven working for the House of Armani, she had a pretty good eye for what worked and what didn't. It was glaringly obvious from the Polaroids that the shoot was not going well. She swore to herself as she counted the thousands of dollars that were being wasted. It looked like she might have to get into a cab and go throw a fit. That was the way it worked.

It was the way it had always worked. Theirs was a business driven by passion. No passion and everything was mediocre. From the designers, to the photographers, to the stylists, to the models, if any one of them wasn't excited about the clothes and the shoot, the outcome was lukewarm at best. And when it came to the House of Armani, lukewarm just didn't cut it.

Many words could be used to describe Donatella Rahn, but lukewarm was not one of them. She had the practicality and decisiveness of her Austrian father and the creativity and passion of her Italian mother. It had taken her a good portion of her life to sort out these traits and learn to control them, or at a bare minimum channel them into the right areas of her life. It was easy for people to never make it past Donatella's stunning beauty, but in reality she was an extremely complex person. Many men over the years had failed to see that she was more than a pretty face, and they had either been left with a broken heart or no heart at all.

At thirty-eight, Donatella looked and felt better than at any other time in her life. Yes, there were a few more wrinkles around her eyes and her skin didn't have the glow that it did when she was eighteen, but she had grown into herself. There was an air of confidence in everything she did. This had not been there when she was modeling, at least not in the early years. She was five feet ten inches of statuesque woman, with a mane of silky black hair. The hair had a slight kinky curl to it that hinted at her wild side. She had a pair of full firm breasts that had been surgically enhanced back in her modeling days, and from time to time she'd gone to see her favorite plastic surgeon to have some problem areas dealt with, but the face was untouched. Her body was the perfect mix of elegance and athleticism. Gone was the rail-thin anemic look of her modeling days. Her heroin polluted body had been cleansed, replaced by a layer of well-toned muscle. In short, she was the type of woman that men lusted after.

DONATELLA'S GOOD LOOKS were all the more amazing when one considered the type of life she'd led in her early twenties. At the time she had been impressionable, too concerned about her weight and about pleasing the photographers and creative directors. But more than anything she had been stupid and weak. Donatella had been seduced by the dark side of modeling. Every night of the week was a Friday night. And not just in Milan. The whole world was her playground. There were wild parties in exotic places with wealthy men. It had turned into one long party. Her life had been spinning out of control for almost a year when everything came crashing down around her.

She'd flown to Tel Aviv for a shoot and run into a bit of a snag trying to get through customs. Two ounces of heroin had been found in her luggage, and she'd been thrown into the clink. She had not been treated well. She couldn't remember all of the details, the whole thing was a bit hazy, but there'd been a lot of screaming. They'd even slapped her a few times, but more than anything she remembered the cold. It had been so cold and then after what seemed like an eternity, a man had shown up.

It was rather ironic that the first image she had in her mind of Ben Freidman was that he was a caring and compassionate soul. He had brought her a blanket; he had brought her warmth. And then after a brief visit he had brought her a doctor who gave her a shot to help with her heroin withdrawal. It was then that the stocky man had offered her a deal. It was a deal she couldn't refuse. She could either spend the best years of her life in an Israeli jail or she could come to work for him. At the time it hadn't been a difficult decision, since she had no idea what coming to work for him entailed. All she knew was that she didn't want to stay in jail.

Freidman had made all the arrangements. Donatella was checked into a treatment clinic in Israel. She called her booking agent in Milan and informed her that she had finally hit bottom and was seeking help. The agent wasn't surprised. She'd seen it happen before and would see it again. She wished Donatella the best and told her to get well. There would be plenty of work for her when she was better. Next there was the tearful phone call to her mother. Her mother was relieved, as was Donatella that the charade was over. Now she could go about healing herself. As per Freidman's instructions, Donatella explained to her mother that they could talk only once a week on Sundays. She gave her mother a phone number to use in case of an emergency and said good-bye. The phone number was not to the rehab clinic; it was routed to Mossad headquarters where a person would answer in the name of the clinic and relay any messages.

There never was a clinic. Donatella was taken to a military facility near the town of Abda in southern Israel. A doctor and staff of nurses monitored her health closely. A constant stream of instructors pushed her hard. There was small-arms training, self-defense courses, grueling physical exercise, memory exercises and much more. She was pushed from dawn until dusk every day of the week. There were many times where she didn't think she was going to make it. There were moments of despair where she thought that prison might have been the better alternative, but every time she was about to hit rock bottom Ben Freidman would show up. He'd made a habit of it over the years.

It wasn't until much later that she caught on to his little game. He wanted to be seen as the savior. The one person she could always count on. During those cold nights at the desolate camp, Freidman would show up with a bottle of wine and some bread. He would sit with her for hours, listening to her stories, trying to find out as much about her as possible. At least that's what she'd thought at the time. In reality Ben Freidman already knew a great deal about Donatella Rahn. He was testing her to find out how honest she was.

As time progressed, and the days became increasingly difficult, Donatella found herself looking forward to her evenings with Freidman. It was the first real intellectual relationship she'd ever had with a man. Thanks to her looks, most of the men in her life had been more interested in her body than her mind. But not Freidman; all he ever wanted to do was talk. At first Donatella thought he might be married, and then she thought maybe he was gay, but in the end it turned out to be neither. He was simply an incredibly dedicated and professional man.

Eventually Freidman did more talking. He explained in detail the tenuous position that Israel was in. He helped Donatella explore her own Jewish roots, and he talked passionately of the horrible injustices thrust upon the House of David. Slowly but surely over the two-month period Donatella grew stronger, and with each step forward came an increasing sense of devotion to Ben Freidman. Her sense of loyalty grew so strong that she would eventually kill for him, and not just once, but many times.

RAPP KISSED ANNA on the cheek and left the Prada store. She had gladly cut him loose after more than an hour of shopping. He was slowing her down. She'd never seen such good prices on designer clothes and accessories. There was serious shopping to be done and she wasn't going to be distracted. He'd explained to her the lay of the land and said that he would catch up with her at Chanel in an hour or so. His mission, as he told Anna, was to find a bookstore and a café that served good coffee.

As Rapp walked down the street he was awash in a steady stream of conflicting emotions. He was not a big fan of lying to Anna, but when it came to his profession he found the need to omit certain details. That's at least what he'd been telling himself since they'd left Baltimore. He was definitely about to take care of a very important piece of business with someone who worked for another foreign intelligence agency, but that someone also happened to be someone he'd been romantically involved with. He'd debated how best to tell Anna about Donatella, but every time he envisioned the discussion it ended in disaster. Maybe he wasn't giving Anna enough credit? After all, he never asked her about her ex-boyfriends and on the rare occasions when she'd talked about them, it hadn't bothered him. She'd had a life before they'd ever met. He could hardly be jealous about men he'd never met.

As he walked down the sidewalk he decided the same should hold true for Anna. Donatella was pre-Anna. She was not the woman he wanted to marry, and that was that. Rapp nodded smugly at his own logical deduction. Satisfied that he was doing nothing wrong, he continued down the sidewalk toward the House of Armani. The smugness vanished a few steps later as he realized that meeting in secret with a former lover while on vacation with the woman you were about to ask to marry you was fraught with trouble. There was nothing about the picture that Anna would like. Rapp grimaced as he thought of her reaction to the whole thing. After wrestling with the idea for a while longer he decided to stop trying to find a solution, for it was painfully obvious that there was none. He could not maintain both secrecy and complete honesty with Anna. It was impossible. He would just have to make sure his past didn't run into his future.

Instinctively, Rapp forced the issue from his mind and began to focus on his surroundings. He was about to conduct a clandestine meeting and it was time to get down to business. As he worked his way down the sidewalk, he studied the vehicles parked on the street. There was only one van parked on the block. Rapp noted the make, model and plate number. It was all memorized in an instant. The van was on the other side of the street so he crossed over to get a closer look at it. As he did so he scanned the cars to be sure they were unoccupied. As he walked past the van, he studied the roof for any antennas or directional microphones. It looked to be clean.

Up ahead there was a florist and then a sidewalk café. Rapp walked past the florist and entered the café. On his way in, he took note of the patrons sitting outside. At the counter he ordered a cup of coffee in Italian and paid for it. Rapp's Italian was decent but nowhere as good as his French and Arabic. With the piping hot cup of coffee in hand he went back to the flower shop. The middle-aged woman behind the counter greeted him warmly and asked if there was anything she could help him with. Rapp walked over to the rose case and expressed an interest. The woman informed him that the long stem red roses were on sale. Rapp thought about it for a second, and then decided that red might send the wrong signal. He decided that yellow would be a safer color. He ordered a dozen of them and waited while the woman put them into an arrangement and wrapped them in tissue paper. Again he paid in cash, and with the flowers in one hand and the coffee in the other he walked across the street.

Next to the glass display windows on the first floor was a door with a security camera mounted above it. To the left of the door was a call box and then under the box a sign in Italian that read, Business by Appointment Only. Rapp instinctively kept his face turned away from the camera and pressed the call button. A second later a woman's voice came over the intercom and asked him his business. Rapp told her he had a flower delivery for Donatella Rahn. The door buzzed, and he entered the small foyer.

A flight of stairs later he was standing in front of the woman who had buzzed him in. She was all legs, and almost every inch of them were on display underneath the glass desk where she was seated. She was very pretty, but unfortunately had the emaciated look that was popular among the fashion crowd. In most other cities she would have probably been a model, but in Milan she was relegated to receptionist. Rapp disarmed the woman with a soft smile and said, "I'm an old friend of Donatella's, and I was hoping I could surprise her with these." Rapp held up the flowers.

The woman gave him a nice smile and eyed him from head to toe as if she were trying to place a value on him.

"You look like Donny's type." The woman gave him a flirtatious smile and then reached for the phone.

Rapp stepped forward. "I really wanted to surprise her."

The woman hesitated for a moment holding the phone at her shoulder. Finally she set it back in the cradle and asked, "Do you know where her office is?"

"Is it still down the hall at the end on the left?"

"Yes."

"Thank you. You're a sweetheart." Rapp gave the woman a wink and headed down the hall. As he neared Donatella's office door he slowed his steps and took note of the fact that his heart had started to beat faster. He knew it had nothing to do with a sense of ambush or violence. It was the anticipation of seeing Donatella. They had been through a lot together, both in the trenches and between the sheets.

The door was open. Rapp neither knocked nor did he enter. He just stood frozen, looking at the curvaceous silhouette of Donatella's figure. She had her back to him, standing over her desk looking at something. Rapp watched as she placed one hand on her hip and with the other pulled her thick hair to one side and began kneading the muscles at the back of her neck. The woman exuded a sexuality unlike anything he'd ever seen. She was wearing a pair of black leather pants that complemented her figure to perfection, a white blouse and a pair of black spiked boots. Just the sight of her long tanned fingers resting on her leather-clad hip brought back a flood of erotic memories. Rapp felt a tinge of betrayal for such thoughts and forced himself to get his mind back on the business at hand.

There was a genuine reason why he wanted to surprise Donatella. He would know almost instantly by the expression on her face if she had been involved in the plot to kill him in Germany. He didn't think she had been or at least he didn't want to believe she had been. As he had already discussed with Kennedy, it didn't make any sense for the Israelis to ambush him. Mossad had been known to do some pretty ruthless things, but there was no recognizable benefit to killing Rapp and humiliating the CIA and America. Rapp was doing the dirty work for them and had been doing so for years. No, Rapp believed Donatella was doing some free-lancing on the side and he had a plan to get her to come clean.

He cleared his throat and waited for Donatella to turn around. When she did her dark almond eyes opened wide, and her full lips parted to form an inviting smile. Donatella threw her arms out and walked quickly across her office. Rapp smiled back. He couldn't help it. He stepped forward and met Donatella's embrace. With the familiarity of an old lover Donatella brought her arms inside Rapp's leather jacket. Her hands shot up, grabbing his taut shoulders and she pressed her breasts firmly against his body. With her eyes closed she found his lips and gave him a passionate kiss. After a moment she buried her head in his chest and squeezed him with all her considerable might.

"Oh, I've missed you," she said in Italian.

Rapp awkwardly held the flowers in one hand and his coffee in the other. He kissed the top of her head and said in Italian, "I've missed you, too."

Donatella gave him one more squeeze and then released him. Closing the office door she said, "Why didn't you call me?"

Rapp innocently shrugged his shoulders. "I was in the neighborhood so I decided to stop by. I'd expect you to do the same if you were in America." It was in that instant that Rapp knew Donatella had been the woman he'd seen at George Washington University. She averted her eyes from his for the briefest of moments. She had killed Peter Cameron.

"Are these for me?" Donatella thrust her arms out and took the flowers from Rapp. She walked over to a long credenza in front of a window that overlooked a court-yard. "This was very nice of you. You didn't have to bring me flowers." After unwrapping them, she turned to Rapp, the bouquet in her outstretched hands. "What is this?"

Rapp looked at the flowers, and then the look on Donatella's face. He wasn't quite sure what she meant.

"Yellow," said Donatella in a disappointed voice. "Yellow is for your secretary, not a woman whose bed you've shared." She dropped the flowers on the credenza and folded her arms across her chest.

Rapp felt bad for just a second and then remembered Anna. He couldn't very well be planning to ask her to marry him and go around giving red roses to former lovers. "They are very pretty flowers."

"Yes they are, but they are not red." Donatella eyed him suspiciously. "There is someone else, isn't there? Someone very important?"

"Yes," he replied with a mix of pride and dread. Donatella meant a lot to him, and he did not want to hurt her feelings.

She studied her old lover for a moment and could sense that this was very hard for him. Determined to hide her true feelings she wrapped her arms around his shoul-ders and gave him a big hug. Inside, however, she could feel herself plunging toward darkness. Part of her, however foolishly, had always hoped that someday, she and Mitch would walk away from their respective intelligence agen-cies, get married and have a baby. Deep down she had always known it had been an irrational indulgence, but she had allowed it nonetheless.

Now she kissed him on the cheek and said, "Congratulations. Do I get to meet her?"

Caught off guard, Rapp stammered and then said, "I don't know . . . maybe."

"Is she here in Milan?" Donatella locked onto him with her piercing brown eyes.

Rapp thought of lying and then quickly decided against it. "Yes, she is."

"You don't want me to meet her."

"No . . . I didn't say that. It's just that it might be a little tricky."

"Please tell me she knows what you do for a living. Or I should say what you really do for a living."

"Yes." Rapp nodded. "Unfortunately, she knows more than she should."

"Then what's the problem? I'd love to meet her."

The meeting wasn't going exactly as he'd planned. "We were lovers, Donatella. I have no burning desire to meet any of her ex-boyfriends."

Donatella chose to focus on the first part of his comment. "Yes, we were lovers." She cocked her head to the side in a confident manner and asked, "How is the sex?"

Rapp frowned. "Donatella."

She persisted. "Is it as good as the sex we had?" Her Italian passion was showing through.

"Donatella, I don't think we should be talking about this."

She looked at him with utter confidence and said, "It must not be."

"We have a wonderful relationship."

"Is she an American?"

"Yes, she's an American."

Donatella let out a laugh that was more of a scoff. "Then it's impossible. There is no way the sex is better."

For some reason Rapp felt the need to defend Anna. "Hey, we have great sex."

In a disbelieving tone she asked, "Better than the sex we had?"

Rapp knew there was no way he could answer this question without either angering Donatella or being disloyal to Anna. "It's different, Donatella, okay?"

"Ha," she laughed with an obvious tone of satisfaction. "It is not better. I can see it in your eyes." She walked over to her desk and yanked open a drawer in search of a pack of cigarettes. "I would like to meet her. Maybe we can have dinner tonight?" She found her cigarettes and lit one.

Rapp declined to take one even though he was tempted. He took the opportunity to get down to the real reason he'd traveled all the way from America. "There is something I need to talk to you about."

"What does she do for a living?"

"We are going to change the subject." Rapp stood firmly in front of her desk.

Donatella took a drag from her cigarette and through the smoke she eyed Rapp suspiciously and said, "I don't believe you. There is no way she knows what you've done for your government."

"She does. In fact, she's seen me in action."

"How . . . When?"

"Remember the incident at the White House last spring?"

"Of course. Ben told me you were involved in it."

"She was one of the hostages."

"Ah . . . Stockholm syndrome."

Rapp frowned. Stockholm syndrome was a psychological term for hostages who began to sympathize with their captors. "Donatella, I wasn't one of the terrorists. I was the one killing the terrorists."

"Oh well, then Florence Nightingale syndrome."

"No." He shook his head and smiled. "I wasn't a nurse, either."

"Oh . . ." She waved her hand in frustration. "You know what I mean."

"No, I don't actually, but we don't need to get hung up on this." Rapp stopped abruptly and studied Donatella as she nervously puffed on her cigarette. With a playful grin he said, "I didn't expect you to be so jealous."

"Of course I am, and you would be too if I was the one in love."

Rapp had to be honest. He thoughtfully said, "Yes, I'm sure I would be." He went around the desk and wrapped his arms around her.

Donatella stabbed her cigarette out in the ashtray on her cluttered desk. "This is a lonely fucking life we live. And now I'm all alone and you're not." She buried her head in his chest. "You're the only man I've ever really loved. The only person who really knows me."

Rapp stroked her hair. "I felt the same way about you too, but you know in the long run it would never have worked out between us. We're too much alike."

Donatella looked up at him. There were no tears in her eyes. She was too tough for that. "Yeah, you're probably right." She released him and took a step back. "Have you asked her to marry you yet?"

"Not yet."

"So you are going to ask her?"

Rapp nodded.

"I really would like to meet her." She read Rapp's expression and added, "I'm serious. Don't worry, I won't do anything crazy. If you've fallen in love with her I'm sure she's a lovely woman."

"She's a reporter." Rapp wasn't sure why he'd offered that piece of information.

"You can't be serious."

"I am."

"Does she know about me?"

"No," answered Rapp.

Donatella thought about this twist for a moment. "You obviously trust her."

"Yes."

"Then I'd like to meet her."

"All right. I'll see what I can do." Rapp set his coffee cup on the desk and grabbed both of Donatella's hands. "I need something from you, and it's very important." Rapp looked into her beautiful eyes and waited for an answer.

Donatella could sense that something serious was on its way. She cautiously studied Rapp for a moment and then said, "I have always been there for you, and I always will be."

"Thank you. You know the same goes for me."

"Of course."

"Were you in Washington two weeks ago?" Rapp saw the flicker of surprise in her eyes.

Donatella's mind was reeling as she tried to figure out how Mitch could have known she was in Washington. Her disguise had been perfect, and the hit had gone down without a problem. He had to know something. Whatever the case was she could not talk about it in her office. It wasn't secure. She held her index finger to her lips to signal that it wasn't safe to talk about such matters, and then said, "I was in New York, but not Washington. I'm sorry I didn't call, but I was only in town for a few days."

"That's too bad." Rapp nodded and stepped back. He

pointed to a tablet of paper on the desk and motioned for Donatella to answer him with a pen.

She shook her head vigorously and said, "Oh my God, I forgot all about the shoot." She pointed to the photos on her desk. "I have to tend to this right away. It's a complete disaster. Why don't we meet for a drink after work."

"I'd love to. Name a time and a place."

"Let's say six o'clock, the Jamaica Café."

"Sounds good to me." Rapp pointed at the paper one more time, but she shook her head even more vigorously than before. Reluctantly, he kissed her on the cheek and then mouthed the words, *I need to know.*

17

CAPITOL HILL, THURSDAY MORNING

Norbert Steveken arrived at the U.S. Capitol early. He checked his gun with the Capitol Hill police officer at the security gate and went off in search of his patron. Steveken was the type of guy you had to meet five or six times before you remembered him, which suited him just fine. In his line of work it was an asset not to be noticed. Just short of five feet nine inches tall, he had brown hair and hazel eyes. He had just turned forty, and despite the paunch around his waist, he was still amazingly quick. It was the handball that he played four times a week that kept him nimble. Norbert Steveken was a tenacious little man. He'd graduated from Penn with honors and went to work for Pricewaterhouse for two years. The job as a CPA was a stepping-stone for the vocation he really wanted. Since he was a little boy Steveken had dreamed of becoming a G-man.

His hard work paid off when in 1986 he became Special Agent Norbert Steveken. It had been the greatest day of his life. With his parents and siblings in the front row, the director of the Bureau himself had sworn him in. At first he found the job exhilarating and challenging. Just the thrill of being a part of the most prestigious law enforcement fraternity in the world was enough to keep it exciting for a few years. But after that certain things started to irk him. First and foremost was the fact that after three years with the Bureau he had yet to pursue a real criminal. The bureaucracy was overwhelming; the sheer level of paperwork was staggering. It got so bad at one point that he started to wonder why he even bothered carrying a gun to work. In his fourth year things livened up a bit when he was moved to the Miami field office to help with bank robberies. That unfortunately only lasted two brief years and then it was back to Washington to push more paper. It was in his tenth year at the Bureau that he'd met Senator Hank Clark.

It was standard procedure for the FBI to help the Senate and House conduct background checks on nominees and people being considered for sensitive positions. Steveken was tasked to work with Clark's committee for a one-year period. It was during that time that he got to know Senator Clark very well. It was a watershed year for Steveken. Clark opened his eyes to how things really worked in Washington. It was the beginning of the end of his career as a Special Agent for the FBI.

With the financial backing of Clark, Steveken left the Bureau and started his own security consulting business. Just four years into it he was making three times more money than the director of the FBI himself; he was his own boss, his services were in demand and the mounds of paperwork were behind him.

Senator Clark knew a lot of influential people—people who were willing to pay good money to have future employees vetted. Fathers who wanted their daughters' boyfriends shadowed for a few days. Owners of companies who were willing to pay him $5,000 a day to come in and lecture their employees on industrial espionage and how to take steps to prevent it. It was a move that had worked out very well indeed.

Steveken worked his way through a labyrinth of back hallways and staircases in search of Senator Clark's hide. There were only seventy of them in the Capitol, each of them reserved for the seniormost senators. A few were no better than a broom closet, most of them were good-size offices and several were as plush as a reading room from a nineteenth-century men's club. Whenever a senior senator failed to come back to Washington either through defeat, retirement or death, there was a mad scramble to get his hide. These rooms were the private sanctuaries of the elite. They were used to get away from the staffers and the lobbyists, and from time to time, to cut backroom deals.

Steveken found Clark's hide on the fourth floor and knocked on the old wood door. The senator yelled for him to enter and he did.

Hank Clark bounced out of his chair and came around the desk. "How the hell are you, Norb?"

"Good, Hank. Thanks for asking." Steveken grabbed the towering senator's hand and squeezed hard. They'd been on a first name basis for some time. "I apologize I couldn't get here quicker, but I was out in California working on some stuff."

"That's all right." Clark slapped his back. "I know I'm not your only client." The senator genuinely liked

Steveken. He had a biting sense of humor, a cynical mind, and he was loyal. In short, he trusted him. "I appreciate you getting back here so quickly."

"No problem. What's on your mind?"

"Sit." Clark gestured to a grouping of a couch and several chairs. "Can I get you anything to drink?"

"Coffee if you have it." Steveken looked out the window. This was where he usually discussed business with the senator. It was best to avoid being seen together. The former FBI agent never tired of the view. The large double-hung window was wide open to let in enough cool air to negate the old radiator that never seemed to rest. From high atop the fourth floor, the view looked to the west, taking in the full length of the National Mall.

Clark poured two cups of coffee from a thermos and asked, "How's business been?" The two men sat down, Clark on a dark brown leather couch and Steveken on a matching chair.

Steveken took a sip of coffee and said, "Great. Thanks to you." He held his mug up in brief salute to Clark.

"Well, you do good work, Norb. My friends have very high standards. If you didn't perform they'd be on the phone bitching to me in a second."

"It's all about managing expectations."

"My friends have high expectations."

"Yes, but I never promise them anything I know I can't deliver, and most important, I always put it in writing." Steveken took a sip from his mug. "People tend to have very convenient memories when it comes to verbal contracts."

Clark laughed. "Yes, they do."

"So what's on your mind?"

Clark crossed his legs and tried to get comfortable. "I need you to do some work for me."

Steveken nodded eagerly. Clark always paid well. "You name it."

"It could get a little hairy."

"How hairy?" asked Steveken in a mischievous tone.

"It involves the CIA."

Steveken set his mug on the table. "I'm listening." He sat back and crossed his legs. A deliberately cool expression draped his face.

Clark knew a lot about Steveken. He was a man who loved a challenge. It was the chief reason why he didn't like the FBI. He felt bored and underutilized. Clark also knew that Steveken had a bit of a chip on his shoulder when it came to his former employer and the CIA. He would love the chance to embarrass them.

"What do you think of the president's nominee to be the next director?"

"I don't know her personally, but the word on the street is that she's pretty sharp."

"She is," Clark replied and then added, "Very sharp, but unfortunately there are certain people in this town who don't want to see her take over at the CIA."

"Isn't that pretty much always the case when one of these jobs opens up?"

"Yes . . . yes it is, but this time there might be some legitimate concern."

"Such as?"

Clark shifted his large body again and said, "This is going to be very delicate, Norb."

"Hank," said Steveken with a slightly offended look on his face. "As far as I'm concerned, everything that is ever said in these meetings is between you and me and the wall."

"I know that, Norb, but this could get rather tricky."

Clark's attempts at caution were only serving to pique

Steveken's curiosity further. "You know I'm not afraid to take risks."

"I know." Clark paused to let the tension build. He looked thoughtfully out the window as if he were struggling over the idea of getting Steveken involved. Finally he looked at his visitor and said, "It could turn into a media circus."

Steveken blinked. He distrusted the media. He was acutely aware that it was an insatiable beast that was often indiscriminate in its destruction. Working in a field where it was best to keep a low profile, the press was something he'd gone to great lengths to avoid. Trying to think a few steps ahead he asked, "Depending on what I find, is there a chance that I'd be called before your committee to testify?"

"No." Clark shook his head. "But there is a chance you'd be called before the House Intelligence Committee."

Now Steveken was confused. "Why?"

"It's a complicated story, and one that I'm trying desperately to stay out of." Clark sighed and then continued. "I've given the president my word that I'm going to support the confirmation of Dr. Kennedy as the next director of the CIA, and I'm not going to go back on that word. Having said that, however, I have some reservations about Dr. Kennedy." With a stern expression he added, "That is not to leave this room."

Steveken acted offended. "It goes without saying."

"Well, most of those reservations have been planted by the chairman of the House Intelligence Committee, Congressman Rudin." Clark noted the frown the name brought to Steveken's face and quickly added, "I know . . . I know the man is a major pain in the ass, but he means well." Clark leaned forward. "Rudin swears that Kennedy is as corrupt as they come. He's extremely passionate about it."

"Then why doesn't he investigate her? He has the power to do it."

"He does indeed. Several weeks ago he called Kennedy before his committee and attempted to ask her some tough questions." Clark took a sip of coffee.

"And?"

"And . . . he got dragged up to the White House by the Speaker of the House and read the riot act by the president himself."

"Oh. The president doesn't want any trouble with his nomination."

"Exactly. And as I've said, I gave Hayes my word. I'm not going to go back on it and besmirch Kennedy's reputation during the confirmation hearing all because Al Rudin has a bur up his ass. But at the same time, I would like to avoid backing this nomination if Kennedy has something in her past that could embarrass me."

"So you'd like me to quietly dig around, and see what I can turn up."

"Exactly." Clark sat back and slapped his thighs.

"That shouldn't be a problem. I'll get started this morning."

"Great." Clark smiled uncomfortably and then added, "There is one more favor I need to ask of you."

"Shoot."

"You won't technically be working for me."

"Who will I be working for?"

"Congressman Rudin."

Steveken frowned. "Excuse me for being so blunt, Hank, but the man has a reputation as being a real ass."

"I know he is, but he means well. I promise I'll tell him to be on his best behavior or you'll walk."

The frown had not left Steveken's face. "Does he know

what my rate is? I mean the guy has a reputation of being the cheapest politician on the Hill."

"Don't worry about your fee. I'm going to take care of that."

"No." Steveken was embarrassed. "I can't charge you. You've done enough for me."

"No, I insist, Norb, and I'm not going to argue about it with you. You're worth every penny and then some."

"Hank . . . I don't feel right taking—"

Clark held up his hand and cut him off. "Don't say another word. I don't want to hear it. I'm paying you and that's the end of it. All right?" Clark believed that the best way to keep someone loyal was to pay them well.

Steveken nodded. "All right. But I'm not going to take any crap from Rudin."

"That's fine," smiled Clark. "Now there are a couple more things. I have a contact for you at Langley. He's very high up, and I think he'll be willing to help."

"Who is it?"

"Jonathan Brown. Do you know who he is?"

Steveken mumbled something and said, "The former federal judge?"

"Yes."

"He had a reputation as a real prick when he sat on the bench."

"That doesn't surprise me. He's a by-the-book kind of guy."

"Then he's not going to tell me anything."

"Don't be so sure," cautioned Clark. "He's seen some things at Langley that have troubled him greatly."

"Has he told you?"

"No. He knows if he tells me there's no turning back."

Steveken seemed to struggle with the whole thing. "I don't see why he'd open up to me."

"Because he has a conscience. All he needs right now is for someone to give him the chance to do the right thing." Clark backed off a bit and added, "Now that's assuming Kennedy has done something egregious. Maybe it's someone else, maybe it was Stansfield, but the point is I want to make sure before I vote for Kennedy that I'm not going to get egg on my face."

Steveken accepted the answer. "I think I understand."

"Good." The senator stood and so did Steveken. "Do you know where Wolf Trap Park is?"

"No."

"It's out by the Leesburg Pike."

"I'll find it."

"Good. Brown walks his dog in the park every night when he gets home from work, usually around six. I suggest you bump into him tonight."

Steveken wondered how Clark knew this, but decided not to ask. "How should I approach him?"

After thinking about it for a moment, Clark said, "Tell him you're working for Congressman Rudin. Tell him the congressman is very worried that the wrong person is about to be made director of the CIA. Tell him that anything he provides will be kept off the record. His name will not get dragged into this." Clark placed a hand on Steveken's shoulder. "The congressman is just looking for something to get an investigation going and throw a wrench into the confirmation hearings."

"Don't worry, Hank. I'll handle it."

"I know you will, Norb. And if nothing turns up, that's great. I like Dr. Kennedy, and I think she'll make one hell of a director. I just want to make sure she's not going to embarrass me before I cast that vote next week."

"I understand."

"Good. I told Congressman Rudin you'd stop by his office this morning. Can you swing over there?"

"Yeah. I'll do it right now."

Clark slapped him on the back. "Thanks, Norb." He was about to say good-bye and then he added, "And one more thing. My name stays out of this at all costs. All I did was refer you to Rudin. I never paid you a penny for this job. Right?" Clark winked and the two men shook hands.

18

MILAN, ITALY, THURSDAY AFTERNOON

Marc Rosenthal had killed the enemies of Israel in a variety of ways, by knife, by bullet, even by poison once, but his instrument of choice over the years had been explosives. There were several reasons for this. To start with he found it practical. Explosives enabled him to maximize damage while maintaining his cover. A machine gun could be just as lethal in the right hands, but to stand in the open and hose down a group of people was to open oneself up to return fire. And that was just the start. Such an act made escape very difficult. No, Rosenthal liked bombs. He could study the habits of his targets and get the device into place before they arrived.

He'd pulled off some bold operations during his years with Mossad. Rosenthal knew that during a time when Mossad had had a streak of bad luck, he was one of the few bright stars. That was in great part due to the keen instincts of Ben Freidman. Freidman had sent Rosenthal into the occupied territories to gather information. The baby-faced Jew had proven to be so effective at penetrating the Palestinian terrorist organization Hamas that Freidman couldn't resist using Rosenthal to strike back. The first bomb Rosenthal planted took out several mid-level lieutenants of the organization, but it was his second bombing that proved to Freidman that Rosenthal was an astonishingly brave warrior. The second bombing took place at a streetside café in Hebron. Rosenthal had planted the device in the bottom of a trash can early the same morning and then that afternoon he met several of his Hamas compatriots at the café for lunch. During the meal Rosenthal got up and went to the bathroom. In his pocket he carried a pen that doubled as a trigger for the bomb. Before leaving the bathroom he depressed the pen cap and threw it into the garbage. The bomb was now on a twenty second delay. Rosenthal then walked back and sat down at the table. He had picked his spot carefully. Between him and the bomb was a palm tree in a concrete planter. Rosenthal calmly counted the time and at eighteen seconds he bent over as if to pick up something he'd dropped.

The blast instantly killed three of the four men he was dining with and two other patrons. Rosenthal escaped with a severe concussion, some lacerations from the flying debris and some hearing loss. The fact that he himself had almost died in the bombing served to cement his standing as a soldier of Hamas.

It was this bold move that allowed him to get close to Hamas leader Yehya Ayyash. Rosenthal was brought into the inner circle, and five months later on a bright sunny day he took a call for Ayyash on a cell phone that had been modified by the technicians back at Mossad. When Rosenthal handed Ayyash the phone, he walked away and left the group. Once again he had a pen in his pocket, but this time there was no delayed fuse. Rosenthal never looked back. He pressed the top of the pen with his thumb and the explosion was instantaneous. The shaped plastic charge in the phone tore into Ayyash's head and killed him. That was the end of Rosenthal's undercover work in the occupied territories. He was hated by all of Palestine.

Freidman had taken significant interest in honing Rosenthal's skills as an assassin. The director general of Mossad had significant experience in the arena. In 1972 eleven Israeli athletes were taken hostage during the Munich Olympics by the Palestinian group Black September. Two of the athletes were killed right away when the terrorists burst into their dormitory at the Olympic Village. The terrorists demanded the release of 234 Palestinians held in Israeli jails. Golda Meir, Israel's prime minister at the time, refused to release the prisoners because she believed it would only invite future disasters. After a tense five-day standoff, the German authorities made their move at the airport while the terrorists were transferring their hostages to a plane. The rescue operation was a disaster. The nine remaining hostages were all killed, as were six of the eight terrorists. To add insult to injury, the two surviving terrorists were later released.

Ben Freidman had been at the airport that dreaded day in 1972. He had been standing next to one of his idols, Zvi Zamir. Zamir had been the director general of Mossad at the time, and after the massacre in Munich, it was Zamir who had convinced the prime minister that it was time to take the gloves off. Golda Meir directed Zamir to hunt down the masterminds behind Black September and kill them. Over the next nine months the blood flowed and Ben Freidman proved himself to be one of Mossad's most efficient assassins. His first hit was barely a month after the massacre of the Olympic athletes. Mossad wanted to send a signal to everyone, and their first target was Wael Zwaiter, a PLO representative in Rome. On October 16 Freidman came up behind Zwaiter, put two bullets into the back of his head and left him for dead on the street. Not even two months later Freidman was part of a team that killed Mahmoud Hamshari by placing a bomb in the phone of his Paris apartment. The bomb was detonated by remote control and the PLO representative was decapitated.

Blood continued to flow and Freidman's crowning achievement came on April 13, 1973. He was part of a select force of Mossad agents and Army commandos that launched a raid into the heart of Beirut. The targets that night were three of the PLO's most senior officials. Muhammad Najjar, Kamal Adwan and Kamal Nasser were all gunned down in their homes. The success of the raid had implications far beyond the deaths of the three leaders. Information seized during the raids led to the assassination of three more terrorists with ties to Black September. The success of the raid was short-lived, however.

Just two months after Mossad had experienced one of its greatest successes it experienced its worst nightmare. The disaster occurred in the sleepy Norwegian ski village of Lillehammer. A team of Mossad agents was sent to investigate a possible sighting of the terrorist Ali Hassan Salameh. The inexperienced group incorrectly identified the target and then proceeded to kill Ahmed Bouchiki, a Moroccan waiter. If that wasn't bad enough, six of the team members were subsequently captured while trying to escape. The men and women were put on trial and five of the six were jailed. The international outcry was deafening, and Mossad was officially ordered to get out of the assassination business.

But unofficially, they stayed very much involved in the dirty business and Ben Freidman continued to be one of Mossad's best. He had used those years of experience to train Rosenthal. They studied why certain operations succeeded and why others failed. The Lillehammer fiasco was easy to dissect. After all, they'd killed the wrong man. Everything started with the misidentification of the target. The entire mess could have easily been avoided with some thorough checking. After that there was one other glaring flaw; there were too many agents involved in the operation. This was the result of too much oversight from Tel Aviv. Freidman knew that for a mission to be successful, the man or woman pulling the trigger had to have as much autonomy as possible, but they must always remember to not embarrass Israel.

It was for that reason that there would be no explosives this time. It was one thing to set off a bomb in Gaza or Jerusalem. As strange as it might seem, the people of the Middle East were used to such things. But a bomb in Milan would draw too much attention. The authorities and the press would start to dig and eventually fingers would be pointed at Israel. There were better, quieter ways to handle the situation. Donatella Rahn would have to be killed up close. Preferably a silenced bullet delivered to the back of her head.

Before leaving Tel Aviv, Rosenthal had thoroughly read Donatella's file. He had seized on her heroin addiction and thought that there might be a way to fake her death with an overdose. As convenient as the plan sounded at first, Rosenthal had to be realistic. She was not some waif of a model. She herself was a skilled assassin. There would be no realistic way to subdue her without a struggle. And a struggle would mean noise and possibly witnesses. In addition, a struggle would leave marks on her body that wouldn't be consistent with an overdose. No, the heroin overdose was too complicated; there were too many spots where it could blow up in their faces. They needed something uncomplicated.

Rosenthal had been trying to pick a spot all afternoon. He could always do it on the crowded street while she walked home from work. Rosenthal was an expert at blending into a crowd. His diminutive size made it very easy for him to move almost unnoticed. It would be relatively simple for him to stalk her, put a bullet into her heart and keep walking. The only real risk was another pedestrian getting in the way or trying to chase him after he pulled the trigger. It was a risk that he was willing to take if he had to.

As Rosenthal looked out the window of the rented car, he had something else on his mind. In front of him was the building where Donatella's flat was located. He'd been sitting there for half an hour and had just witnessed a UPS driver deliver a package. It got Rosenthal thinking. The best place to do it would be her apartment. She would have her guard down, and they would have time to clean up and sanitize the apartment when they were done. The apartment it would be. He started to prepare a mental checklist of the things he would need. After another five minutes of watching he told Sunberg to take him back to the safe flat.

THE WHITE HOUSE, THURSDAY MORNING

PRESIDENT HAYES WAS in the Cabinet Room watching his secretary of commerce slug it out with a group of lobbyists that represented the AFL–CIO, the Teamsters, and Amnesty International. The argument was over whether or not the U.S. should continue to grant most favored nation status to China when it came up for review in a few months. In Hayes's mind it was a worthless debate. There was only one way the U.S. would revoke China's most favored nation status and it had nothing to do with the high-priced lobbyists sitting around the large, highly polished conference table. China would have to cause an international incident. Even something so brazen as being caught stealing secrets from American businesses might not be enough. They would have to take military action against Taiwan, and that wasn't going to happen. The Chinese were ecstatic with their new highbred economy. Where the former Soviet Union was in shambles, trying to make the transition from a closed socialist economy to an open one, the Chinese were flourishing. They offered something the Russians couldn't. Stability.

Hayes looked on with mixed feelings of sympathy and disrespect as the union representatives and lobbyists tried to state their cases. He had sympathy for them because they were truly passionate, but he also loathed them precisely because they were so passionate about a dead issue. Unemployment was at a thirty-year low. The alarmists from the unions had said that NAFTA would cost millions of jobs and it hadn't. Wages were up. Continued open trade with China was good for the American economy and hence the American people. The human rights people had a slightly better point, but in the end isolationism was no way to get China to treat its people better. The key was continued trade. Get them to open their economy first and then their minds and hearts.

Hayes felt the meeting was a waste of his time, but in Washington you always had to have your eye on the next election. These people represented a big portion of his base. He needed to lend them a sympathetic ear lest they go looking to back a different Democratic candidate. The president sat in his chair with hands folded neatly in front of him and nodded as the woman from Amnesty International recited a slew of statistics about the number of people unjustly incarcerated in the world's largest country.

When the door opened Hayes was relieved to see Michael Haik enter. The wiry national security advisor came around the table and apologized to the president's guests. He then bent over and whispered something into the president's ear. Hayes nodded several times and then looked to the people sitting across the table.

"I'm sorry, but something has come up." Hayes stood. "Thank you for coming to see me." He walked around the table and shook each person's hand. "You've made some very good points, and I'll take them under advisement."

As the president started to leave, the man representing the AFL-CIO stepped forward and said, "We're sick of losing on this issue, sir. We're prepared to pull out all the stops this time."

Hayes paused and looked at the man. He should have kept walking but didn't. "What's that supposed to mean, Harry?"

"It means come next election, we're going to remember who stood with us on this one."

Hayes took a step closer to the man. "What are you going to do, Harry? Tell your people to vote for a Republican?"

Finding courage in the fact that the president had a less than fifty percent approval rating, the man replied, "With all due respect, sir, you might not be the only person seeking the party's nomination."

Instead of losing his temper, Hayes smiled at the man. He patted the union representative on the shoulder and said, "Good luck trying to get someone to commit political suicide." With that Hayes left the Cabinet Room and made a mental note to keep an eye on the MFN China vote. There were maybe three or four people within the party that might try to challenge him. If any of them voted against MFN status for China it would be a clear signal that they'd decided to challenge him.

As they started down the stairs to the basement of the West Wing, the president asked Haik what the unscheduled visit was about. Haik informed him that General Flood had not wanted to talk about it over the phone. The two men continued to the Situation Room, where they found Irene Kennedy, General Flood and two other army officers waiting. The president recognized one of them, but not the other. The man he recognized was General Campbell, the head of the Joint Special Operations Command.

"Mr. President, this is Colonel Gray. He's the CO of Delta Force. I think you've met on one other occasion."

"Yes, of course we have." The president now remembered the warrior. He reached out across the table and took the man's hand. "Good to see you again, Colonel." As would be expected Gray had a hardened edge to him that commanded respect.

"I'm sorry to interrupt your meeting," continued Flood.

"Don't worry." Hayes rolled his eyes. "You actually saved me from another thirty minutes of sheer boredom." The president sat in his chair at the head of the table and everyone followed suit.

General Flood settled his large frame into the chair at the opposite end of the long conference table. "During our last meeting you asked me to explore all options to achieve our goal. I consulted General Campbell on the mission and he brought in Colonel Gray. Before I turn this over to the Colonel, I'd like to note that Delta Force was conceived to handle extremely delicate and difficult situations. I have confidence in Colonel Gray and his men and I encourage their creative solutions to very difficult problems. It is our job," Flood looked at the president, "to decide how and when to use them." The general glanced over at Colonel Gray and nodded for him to start.

"Mr. President, you may remember during the Gulf War that Delta Force was asked to look into the possibility of going after Saddam and either grabbing him or killing him. There were two schools of thought here. The first was that we were at war and hence we wouldn't be in violation of the executive order banning the assassination of foreign leaders. Many of us in the military argued that Saddam was a soldier. More often than not he wears a uniform, and he is a military dictator. The other camp argued that we would be in violation of the executive order signed by President Reagan. The debate proved to be moot due to the fact that we could never locate the exact whereabouts of Saddam. Along the way, however, we learned a couple of interesting things. Saddam takes his own security very seriously. So seriously that he often leaves his own people in utter confusion. He has an entire fleet of white armor-plated limousines and cars that he uses like a big shell game. These caravans move about the country in a completely nonsensical pattern. During the war we'd get a report that Saddam was in one part of Baghdad only to find out two minutes later that there was a second caravan seen on the other side of town, and then five minutes after that we'd get a report that he was seen in the south meeting with leaders of his Republican guard. The man has over twenty palaces, and we'd get reports all night of motorcades coming and going. He was impossible to track.

"It wasn't until after the war that something occurred

to me. As warriors we're taught to probe for the enemy's weakness, and if we can't find one, we have to find a way to use his own strengths against him." Colonel Gray grinned. "I've found a way to use Saddam's strength against him."

The president was hooked. Sitting up a little straighter he said, "I'm listening."

"Sir, Saddam's own people don't know where he is. They are used to seeing motorcades of white cars racing about the country at all hours of the day. No one ever stops them, because the only person in the whole country who travels in such a fashion is Saddam himself and a few of his select family members."

The president still hadn't figured out where the colonel was heading. "I don't see how you'd use this against him."

"If one of these motorcades contained not Saddam, but a select team of Delta Force operators, they would be able to move about the country unchallenged."

Very slowly a smile crept onto the president's face, and then he began to nod. "I'm intrigued, Colonel. I'd like to hear more."

19

MILAN, THURSDAY EVENING

Rapp was growing impatient. He'd arrived at the Jamaica Café before six so he could check the place out. Anna was back at the hotel sleeping. After a tiring night of travel and a full afternoon of shopping, she'd hit the wall. Rapp had tucked her into bed and said that he'd return and wake her for a late dinner. He noted with a yawn that he could use a little sleep himself.

Rapp had grabbed a corner booth in the bar, which was beginning to fill with customers and smoke. In his left hand he held his Heckler & Koch HK4 pistol with a snubbed silencer. It was under the table covered by a cloth napkin. Rapp wasn't taking any chances and with each passing minute his unease was growing. It was now a quarter past six, and there was no sign of Donatella. Mentally, he began going down the list of possibilities. Rapp agreed with Kennedy that Donatella's activities in America some two weeks earlier were not sanctioned by the Israeli government. Mossad had done a lot of crazy things over the years, but this didn't fit. There was no reason he could think of why the notorious Israeli intelligence service would want to double-cross him and leave him for dead in Germany. Mitch Rapp and the Orion Team had been Mossad's greatest ally for nearly a decade.

They were capable of penetrating the operation. There was no doubt about that. If anyone could do it, it would be Mossad, but they still didn't have the motive. And if director Stansfield had been right, the motive was to stop Kennedy from becoming the next director of Central Intelligence. Once again Rapp didn't see it. As the director of the CIA's Counterterrorism Center she had been a staunch ally of the oldest democracy in the Middle East. *No,* Rapp thought, *Donatella had to be freelancing.* The big question now, was for whom.

As the minutes slid by he began to wonder if he'd ever get the answer to his question. There was the chance that Donatella was hung up at work and running late, but you did not survive long in this business by accepting the most common reason. You survived by thinking of all the possibilities and planning for contingencies. Throwing logic aside for the moment, he wondered what she would do if she had in fact been working for Mossad when she'd assassinated Peter Cameron. She'd have to run. There was no other solution. She couldn't very well turn to the Israelis and tell them he'd contacted her. They'd just as soon kill her rather than protect her. For once and for all, Rapp did away with that possibility. There was no way the Israeli government was involved in this.

There was the list of usual suspects. The Russians, the Chinese, Iraq, Iran, Syria, the Palestinians and the French. Of the group, the Russians were probably the only ones who had the assets to penetrate the operation, and once again, he didn't see the motive. All roads pointed back to America. Somebody wanted him dead, and if Thomas Stansfield had been right, that person or persons ultimately wanted to end Irene Kennedy's career.

Rapp hadn't the faintest idea who they were. He needed Donatella to point him in the right direction, and for that to happen she had to show up. As he looked around the bar for the hundredth time he quietly hoped that she'd been smart enough to keep their meeting earlier in the day to herself. She had to trust him one last time and he would make sure she'd make it through without getting harmed.

Finally, at 6:27 Donatella entered the noisy, crowded bar in a black pant suit with a coat draped over one arm. Like two true professionals they barely glanced at each other. They'd been taught the same thing. Trouble almost always comes from where you'd least expect it. Get the target to focus on one thing and then blindside them. They both warily checked their flanks to make sure no one was coming after them. Rapp watched heads turn as the gorgeous Donatella walked through the bar. His eyes expertly scanned the crowded bar, searching for faces he'd seen before, and looking for a pair of eyes that were watching him rather than the stunning brunette.

Donatella smiled her devilish smile and came around to his side of the booth. She kissed him on the cheek and then with her curvaceous hip she bumped him to the side and sat practically on his lap. Her intent was twofold. First of all, she did not want to sit with her back to the door and second, she did not want to have to talk across the table. It would be much better if they could whisper in each other's ear.

"Sorry I'm late," said Donatella in Italian. She shook her head to the side in an effort to move some of her thick mane out of the way.

"What was the holdup?" asked Rapp in her native tongue.

"It was a disastrous day. We had a shoot that cost a lot of money and produced nothing but crap, and then the only man I've ever truly loved stopped by my office and told me he was getting married." Donatella flagged down a passing waiter and ordered a double Stoly martini with a lemon peel. When the waiter was gone she turned back to Rapp and said, "All in all it's been a really shitty day." With a fake smile she asked, "And how was your day, honey?"

Rapp felt a little guilty. "I'm sorry, Donny. I never meant to hurt you." Taking her hand he said, "You've always been very special to me, and you always will be."

"But not that special." She stared at Rapp with her dark brown, almond-shaped eyes, her full lips pursed as if she might begin to cry.

Rapp put his right arm around her and pulled her tight. He kissed her forehead and said, "You have to have faith that everything will turn out."

Donatella pushed away; her eyes were moist. "That's

easy for you to say. You have someone. You've found the person you want to marry, and what do I have? Nothing."

"You have to have faith that it will happen for you, too."

"My faith was you. However foolish it might have been, I thought one day we'd walk away from all of this crap and live happily ever after."

After brushing a tear from her cheek, Rapp said, "We haven't exactly seen a lot of each other over the past year."

"I know, it was foolish of me, but dammit, I loved you. I still love you."

Rapp swallowed uncomfortably. He knew Donatella to be a very passionate woman, but he didn't expect her to show this much emotion. "Donny, I loved you very much. You know that. We were there for each other during some of the worst times."

She nodded, but kept her head tilted down, buried in his chest. Pulling herself together a bit, she looked up and said, "I'm happy for you ... I really am ... it's just that ..." She couldn't finish the sentence.

"What?"

"This is a lonely fucking business."

Rap knew all too well what she meant. He pulled her close and squeezed tight. "Don't worry, Donny. If you're ready to put it all behind you, I'll make it happen." Rapp decided at that exact moment that he would do whatever it took to bring her in. He would use whatever leverage he had to make sure she was safe.

Donatella sat up and grabbed a handkerchief from her bag. She blotted the tears from her eyes and said, "I'm not done yet. I have a few more years left before I can retire."

Rapp thought of the fate of Peter Cameron and decided she might not have a few more years. At that moment the waiter approached the table and set Donatella's drink down.

"He'll have a glass of your house red wine, please." Donatella dismissed the waiter and turned to Rapp. "If I'm going to cry and drink vodka I'm not going to let you get away with drinking coffee."

Rapp didn't argue. He instead used the opening to get to the point. "Donny." Rapp looked her in the eye to make sure she knew how serious he was. "I'm going to tell you some things, and as always they're in complete confidence. In return I need you to be honest with me."

Donatella set her drink down and moved back a bit. She'd been thinking about how she was going to handle this all day and she as yet hadn't come up with a solution. "I'll do my best."

"What is that supposed to mean?"

"It means I'll do my best."

"Will you be honest with me?"

"I'll be honest with you, but you know there are certain things I can't answer no matter what our history is."

Reluctantly, Rapp conceded the point and asked, "Are you going to answer the question that I asked you in your office this afternoon?"

She'd thought about little else since he'd left, that and the fact that the man of her dreams was going to marry someone else. Her first instinct was to lie. It had nothing to do with Mitch, it was standard operating procedure. Everybody was on a need to know basis, and if someone wasn't in the loop they shouldn't be asking the question. Hence they shouldn't be offended when they found out they were lied to. Mitch fell into a different category, though. They had been through so much, and not just in the bedroom, but in the field. There was an unspoken rule between them. If you can't answer the question, don't. Mitch knew something. She had no idea how, but one thing was clear, somehow he knew she was in Washington several weeks ago.

Rapp leaned in and repeated the question. "Were you in Washington several weeks ago?"

Donatella took a sip of the cold vodka. "Yes."

"Did you spend any time at George Washington University?"

"Who wants to know?"

"I do."

"No one else?" asked a skeptical Donatella.

"Oh, there are others, but no one wants to know as bad as I do."

"And why is that?"

Rapp studied her for a second. They could go on like this for hours, like two tennis players volleying the ball across the net at each other. He was in no mood for such a game; he didn't have the time. Taking a calculated risk he said, "There was a professor at George Washington University that I really wanted to talk to. Unfortunately, someone stuck a pick in his ear and scrambled his brain before I could get to him. Any idea who would do such a thing?"

Donatella fidgeted and looked away at the crowd. She knew he had her. He'd seen her kill that way before. Choosing to deflect his question by asking one of her own she said, "Why did you want to talk to him?"

Rapp's eyes lit up with anger. He leaned in until his nose was just inches away from Donatella's. His response was spoken through gritted teeth. "Because he tried to kill me."

SITUATION ROOM, THURSDAY MORNING

COLONEL GRAY HAD the room's rapt attention. Even the unflappable Irene Kennedy was shaking her head in disbelief at the Delta Force commander's bold plan. Its audacity was absolutely beautiful.

President Hayes looked at the colonel with a slightly

miffed expression and asked, "You've already practiced this?"

"Yes, sir."

"How?"

"We took three MH-47E heavy lift helicopters from the 160th Special Operations Aviation Regiment (SOAR) and loaded them each with one Mercedes sedan and four Delta operators. We flew the planes from Pope Air Force Base in North Carolina to Hulbert Field in Florida. Once we arrived we conducted eight separate infiltration and exfiltration operations over an eight-day period. We tried to make the exercise as realistic as possible. Each night we sent out two MH-53 J Pave Lows with Delta operators in each bird. Their job was to secure the landing area for the arrival of the MH-47E's. The first two nights we made it easy on them. We selected paved roads on remote parts of the base. The Pave Lows arrived at the preselected area and secured and marked the landing strip. The MH-47E's arrived and landed without incident. The cars were unloaded and the Delta operators took off on their simulated mission. The cars were then reloaded and the choppers took off.

"The next two nights the Pave Lows arrived and found the designated area occupied by potentially hostile forces. They had to move onto the secondary landing sites and so forth. With each passing night we made the mission increasingly difficult. We simulated one of the choppers breaking down, we simulated the force coming under attack in the middle of unloading the cars, we threw everything at them."

"And?" the president asked.

"They fared very well. We finished the exercise with an understanding of what should be done to increase the odds for success. We also came away believing that if called on we could put this plan into action in very short order."

The president blinked several times and said, "So you're telling me you think you could fly a couple of these choppers into Iraq, land, unload the cars, drive into Baghdad, hit the target, and get everybody out safely." The president shook his head. "Excuse me if I sound skeptical, but this seems a little over the top."

"I'm in the business of *over the top*, sir. That's what you pay me for."

President Hayes laughed and then leaned forward. "Colonel, do you really think you could pull something like this off?"

"That depends on what type of cover you're willing to give us, sir."

"What do you mean?"

"If what I've just described to you represents the entire scope of the operation," Gray paused for a second while he calculated the odds of success. "I'd give my men a fifty to sixty percent chance of achieving the primary goal and making it out without any casualties."

The president grimaced. "I don't like those odds."

"I can get them closer to ninety percent if you're willing to expand the scope of the operation."

"How?"

Gray glanced at the two generals before continuing. Both Flood and Campbell signaled for him to proceed. "It would be very difficult to get the choppers that deep into Iraqi airspace without them being picked up. To pull this off, we'd need to create some chaos. General Flood has informed me that one of your contingencies is for massive air strikes."

"It's something I'm considering."

"Well, if the fly-boys were to go in and wreak havoc with the Iraqis' air defenses and lines of communications just prior to my boys going in, it would create the perfect environment. And if they could continue bombing until we were back out it would be a huge help."

With a look of disbelief, the president asked, "You want to send your men into Baghdad with bombs dropping all around them?"

"Yes." Gray sat forward and gestured with his hands. "We'd create a safe corridor for the team to get in and out of the city. No bombs would be dropped in that zone, and no bombs would be dropped within, let's say, a six-block radius of the hospital."

"Colonel, I haven't been at this job very long, but I do know that our aviators don't always hit their target. Don't you think it's a little dangerous to send your men into a city that we're bombing?"

Colonel Gray looked his president in the eye and said, "Sir, being a Delta Force commando is dangerous. No one fights for me who doesn't want to be there. If my men wanted a safe job they'd go sell cars for a living."

"Point well taken, but . . ." The president remained skeptical. "This seems awfully complicated and," Hayes looked down the length of the table at General Flood, "you always tell me the more complicated these things get the better chance there is that something will go wrong."

"That is usually true, sir," answered the chairman of the Joint Chiefs.

Colonel Gray wasn't to be deterred. "Mr. President, I'll grant that this is complicated, but I can give you two things that the air force can't." Forcefully, Gray continued. "Let's not forget the primary objective. We need to be sure that we destroy the nukes. I can guarantee that we'll know whether those nukes are actually underneath that hospital. The air force can't give you that guarantee, sir. My men can. They will get into that facility, and they will provide you with a bona fide answer as to whether or not those nukes are actually there. We can destroy the weapons on site, and since they are in a fortified bunker, I'm confident that we could pull the mission off without having to kill all of the innocent people in the hospital." Gray paused briefly to let the president think about what he'd said and then added, "If you do it the air force's way, you will be ostracized by the international community for bombing a hospital. You will have no real proof that those nuclear weapons actually existed. Saddam will bus in the journalists so they can shoot footage of the twisted bodies in the rubble. There will be pictures of mothers holding dead babies covered in dust, and the entire Arab world will hate us even more than they already do. Saddam's control will be further consolidated around a wave of anti-American sentiment and the U.N. will likely vote to end the economic sanctions—"

General Campbell interrupted his subordinate and said, "Colonel, let's stick to our area of expertise, and leave the other stuff to the president and his staff."

President Hayes held up his hand and said, "That's all right . . . that's all right. I think Colonel Gray has very succinctly stated what we've all been afraid to say." President Hayes sat quietly for a moment while he thought about the fallout from the air strikes. The colonel was right. The current coalition against Iraq was in such a weakened state that it wouldn't take much to put an end to it. The bombing would more than likely end all economic sanctions. The Israelis had dumped one hell of a problem into his lap. In frustration, Hayes turned to Irene Kennedy and said, "I'd like to hear your thoughts."

20

Donatella was speechless. In two large gulps she finished her vodka martini and began in earnest her search for the waiter. She caught the man's eye as he was maneuvering his way through the crowd with a tray of drinks. Holding up her empty glass by the stem she asked for another. Her head was swimming and it wasn't from the vodka, at least not yet. She was scrambling to try to figure out how she had been pulled into this. Who had contacted Ben Freidman and hired him to kill Peter Cameron? It wasn't an official Mossad hit. This was purely a freelance venture. She knew because her fee for killing Cameron was already sitting in a Swiss bank account, and Mossad would have never paid her so well.

"Donny, I want some answers." Rapp's anger had not diminished.

Donatella was flustered. The hit on Peter Cameron had been advertised as an easy one, but she should have known better. The fee was too high, even for a rush job. She took a deep breath. "Why did he try to kill you?"

Rapp leaned back in. "You didn't answer my question. Who hired you to kill him?"

She shook her head vigorously. "Believe me, I know far less about this mess than you do."

"You know who hired you."

"Mitchell, please tell me why this man tried to kill you."

"All right, Donny, I'll tell you, but when I'm done you're going to tell me who hired you and why." Donatella turned again in search of the waiter and Rapp reached up and grabbed her sculpted chin. Pulling it back toward him, he looked her in the eye and said, "Give me your word."

Donatella reached up and tried to push his hand away. "Don't start ordering me around."

Rapp kept his hand firmly on her chin. "Donny, I'm here as your friend. There are people in Washington who are really upset about this. Half of them want to put a price on your head and the other half want to talk to your old employers in Israel."

With her eyes closed Donatella began muttering to herself. When she opened her eyes she calmly said, "Tell me why he tried to kill you."

Rapp released her chin as the waiter set Donatella's second drink down. When the man was gone Rapp said, "This goes no further than this table." Donatella nodded. "I was on an operation recently. Two operators were there to assist me. I was the triggerman, they were backup. I took down the target and then they shot me and left me for dead."

A look of concern on her face, Donatella reached out to touch him and asked, "Where?"

"Two shots, right here." Rapp pointed to his chest. He read the expression on her face and said, "I know, very unprofessional." He pointed to his forehead. "They should have double-tapped me, but they had reason to believe that I wasn't wearing body armor. At any rate, Cameron was the man who paid them. I don't know who Cameron worked for, and I don't know what the motivation was to kill me, but I'll tell you this. . . . Those two people who double-crossed me are dead."

"You killed them?"

"No. Cameron did."

Donatella took a drink. "How do you know he killed them?"

"Someone who I trust very much saw it go down. Cameron pulled the trigger. He then turned on the people who helped him kill the two who he hired to kill me, and then he tried to kill me one more time in Washington." Rapp sat back. "And I was just about to get my hands on him when you showed up." Rapp took a drink of wine. "I saw you that day, Donny. You had a blond wig on. I stepped off the elevator as you entered the staircase at the end of the hall. Something struck me as familiar about you, but I had other things on my mind, like torturing that bastard Cameron so I could find out who hired him. When we picked the lock and got into his office, and I saw the way he'd been killed . . . I knew it was you."

Donatella found the need for more of the cold vodka. This was not good business. There was a pattern emerging. It appeared that anyone who'd been hired to fulfill a contract was the next person on the list to be killed. She saw her dreams of getting out of the business vanishing before her eyes. With her eyes closed she nodded and said, "It was me."

"Thank you for being honest. Now will you please tell me who hired you?"

Donatella looked into Rapp's piercing eyes. She needed time to think, even if it was just a few minutes. It was obvious she had gotten herself into a mess. Whoever had hired her had shown a propensity for killing the very people he employed. That meant she could easily be next on the list.

"Donny, for your own good, tell me who hired you."

Donatella held firm. She loved Mitch and she felt a

loyalty toward him, but her ultimate loyalty was to Ben Freidman, the head of Mossad. She couldn't give Ben up, at least not until she thought it through. She needed time. Donatella opened her purse and grabbed some money. She threw enough to cover the tab on the table and said to Rapp, "Come on. We need to take a walk."

SITUATION ROOM, THURSDAY MORNING

THE MOOD IN the Situation Room was tense. Colonel Gray had done a thorough job of pointing out the problems of going after the nukes with air strikes. The president had asked Kennedy for her opinion on the matter, and his nominee to become the next director of the CIA was taking her time crafting an answer.

With all eyes on her, Kennedy announced, "I think Colonel Gray's plan is ingenious. I think it has a better chance of succeeding than even he knows."

The president was a little surprised by Kennedy's overwhelming endorsement. "What makes you say that?"

"The psychology of the Iraqi people. They fear Saddam so thoroughly that they wouldn't consider challenging him."

"But it's not him," countered Michael Haik. "It's a bunch of white cars." It was obvious by his tone that he wasn't as enamored of Colonel Gray's plan as Kennedy was.

Kennedy stuck to her guns. "To them, those white cars *are* Saddam, and no one ever challenges Saddam. He's killed members of his own family; he's killed dozens of his top generals. No one challenges him for fear of losing their life." Kennedy looked at Colonel Gray. "I really have to commend you. I'm embarrassed that the CIA didn't come up with this idea first."

"Isn't there a real risk of this blowing up in our faces?" asked the president.

"Yes, there is, but I don't think it could be any worse than the fallout from bombing a hospital."

"But Saddam put those damn nukes under that hospital. He's the one putting those people at risk."

"I agree with you, sir," said Kennedy, "but I doubt the international press will."

The president lowered his head in frustration and rubbed his temples. Without looking up he asked, "General Flood, what's your take on all of this?"

"Sir, I think the important thing right now is to keep our options open. We should have Colonel Gray move his assets into the theater of operations. That way if you decide to play this card, we can do so on short notice."

"And if we go ahead, what is your opinion on providing air cover?"

The chairman of the Joint Chiefs hesitated for a moment and then said, "I am not a believer in half measures, sir. As we've discussed before, I do not think we should have ended the Gulf War when we did. We were enamored with our own technology and forgot that the way you win a war is to put troops on the ground. We should have gone all the way to Baghdad and made sure Saddam was ousted." Flood paused long enough to let out a sigh of frustration and then said, "We chose not to do that and for the last decade the man has continued to be a big pain in our ass. If he has in fact got his hands on some nukes, and is about to make them operational, I think we need to hit him hard, and I mean really hard. I would recommend, whether we implement Colonel Gray's plan or not, that we launch a comprehensive bombing campaign against him that focuses on his air defenses and his command and control structures, and I think this time we need to really hit him where it hurts. We need to take out his oil and refinery facilities."

"General," started the president, "you know I can't do that. The environmentalists will go nuts . . . my own party will attack me."

"That may be, sir, but you ask those environmentalists what they think will cause more damage to this planet. A couple of thousand barrels of spilled oil or a nuclear deto-nation over Tel Aviv, or God forbid, Washington." Flood leaned forward, setting his large forearms on the table. "Sir, the only way he can afford to buy these weapons is through his oil revenues. We need to hit him in his wallet, and if you're worried about Turkey and Jordan we can throw a couple hundred million more dollars in aid their way after we're done."

The president looked to Kennedy for her opinion. "General Flood makes a very forceful case, and in princi-ple I agree with everything he's just said. Unfortunately, however, we have to take politics into consideration. Right now your administration hangs on to a razor-thin mandate. If you lose that mandate by alienating the base of your own party you could become ineffective both domestically and abroad."

Michael Haik eagerly jumped in. "I agree with Irene one hundred percent. As much as I'd like to, we can't go after his refineries. The outcry would be horrendous."

"So go ahead and bomb a hospital full of innocent people," replied the president in disgust, "but don't do anything to hurt Mother Earth. It's the stupidest damn thing I've ever heard."

"Sir, I'm not saying I agree with it," said Haik. "I'm just stating the political reality."

"Well it's a shitty reality, and one that I'm very tempted to try and change."

"Sir, if I may," interjected Kennedy. Looking to Colonel Gray she asked, "How difficult would it be for your men to bring one of the nukes back?"

"That depends how big it is."

"I'll have my people give you an accurate answer by this evening, but for the sake of our discussion, let's assume at the very least you could remove the part of the weapon that we're most interested in."

"You mean the warhead, of course."

"Essentially."

Gray thought about it for a moment. "If the weapon hasn't been assembled, my guess is one man could carry the warhead, but if it has been assembled . . . then things could get tricky. We'd have to spend time trying to dismantle the weapon to get at the warhead, and on a mission like this we'd prefer to get in, plant the charges and be out in a minute or less."

"I understand, but it's conceivable that you could pull it off?"

The army officer thought about it again and said, "Yes. I think we probably could."

Kennedy turned back to the president. "Sir, if we were able to get our hands on one of the weapons, I know our scientists could trace the plutonium back to the reactor where it was created. There is also a good chance we could trace most of the other parts back to their origination."

Haik saw an even better use for the captured weapon. "And we could hold one hell of a press conference. There would be nowhere for Saddam to run. We'd have caught him red-handed, and the U.N. would have no choice but to be outraged." Haik looked at General Flood with a grin. "You could bomb all the refineries you wanted as long as you had proof that you stopped Saddam from having an operational nuclear weapon." Haik looked back to the president. "There isn't a politician in this town who wouldn't be behind you, sir."

21

MILAN, THURSDAY EVENING

Outside the bar, Rapp and Donatella fell into stride, Rapp on the left, Donatella on the right. It was an old professional habit. Both could shoot, stab, or punch with either hand but Rapp favored his left and Donatella her right. They walked south on Via Brera. It was nearing eight o'clock in the evening. The streetlights were on. A quick thunderstorm had coated the ground with a film of water that gleamed beneath the numerous restaurant lights and passing cars. There were other people about, but not many. It looked as if the rain had sent almost everyone indoors.

It was obvious that Donatella had been shaken by his words in the bar. Rapp looked over his shoulder; her attitude and his natural instincts were telling him that all was not well. His pistol with the silencer attached was right where it should be in case he needed to get at it quickly. "If you're not going to tell me where we're going, then tell me who hired you."

Donatella's pace did not slow. The collar of her stylish black trench coat was turned up and her chin was set firmly in the downward position like a fullback about to steamroll a linebacker. "I don't think I can answer that question, either."

Rapp didn't like the answer. "You can't or you won't."

"What's the difference?"

"You know what the difference is," replied Rapp in an obviously irritated tone. "Do you know who hired you, or not?"

She laughed bitterly. "Oh, I know who hired me, but I don't know who hired him."

Rapp didn't say anything for a while and then asked, "Who gave you the target profile?"

She shook her head. "I can't answer that."

"Why? Is the person connected to Mossad?"

"Don't ask me any more questions for a while. I need to think."

Rapp could manage to maintain his silence for only a few steps. "Where are we going?"

"Back to your hotel. I want to meet your girlfriend."

Seeing no humor in the comment, he said, "That's not going to happen. I think you'd better get serious about this, Donny. This problem is not going to go away. This Cameron guy you killed had twenty years with the CIA. Some very important people want to know why he was meddling in an operation and who he was working for."

"I thought you were going to protect me."

"I can't protect you unless you tell me who hired you to make the hit."

"Then we have a problem, because I don't think I can tell you."

Rapp grabbed her by the arm and yanked her to a stop. "Donny, I'm not fucking around. Irene Kennedy knows you killed Cameron. She can prove you were in the country. She has you on surveillance video leaving Cameron's office at George Washington University and she knows of at least three other people who you've killed by shoving a pick in their ear. She is prepared to take this all the way to the top if need be. I'm over here as a personal courtesy to see if we can keep this thing as quiet as possible."

Donatella pulled her arm from Rapp's grip and started walking again. "Thanks for nothing. If you really want to do me a favor you can go back to Washington and tell Irene that I had nothing to do with this."

Rapp followed a step behind, his temper starting to boil over. "Donny, you'd better get real about this, and you'd better start showing some fucking gratitude. If it wasn't for me you'd have been snatched off the street and you'd be sitting in a dark basement with psychotropic drugs coursing through your veins and a black bag over your head."

Donatella turned around and stuck her finger in his face. "Don't threaten me."

Rapp slapped her hand out of the way, and leaned in close. "What in the fuck is wrong with you? You know the rules. You're a goddamn freelancer. You took a rush job and killed somebody who had been meddling in the business of the CIA, and now the CIA wants some answers."

"Well, they'll have to get them somewhere else, because I'm not talking." Donatella turned and walked across the Via Senato.

Rapp stood with his fists clenched at his side and watched her enter the big park known as the Giardini Pubblici. After a brief moment of indecision he followed. She was headed for her flat and away from the hotel. Rapp jogged across the street and yelled for Donatella to wait for him. She didn't, and kept going at full speed through the park with her head down. A short while later Rapp caught up to her and tried a different tack.

"Donny, I'm sorry I had to be the bearer of bad news, but I'm here to protect you. Whoever you're afraid of I can help."

She gave him a disbelieving sideways glance and kept walking.

"You don't believe me. You don't think I can protect you? Donny, give me the name of the person who got you into this and I swear I will make sure nothing happens to you."

"Just . . . don't talk for five minutes. That's all I'm asking for right now. Just don't say another word until we get to the other side of the park."

Rapp was about to hit her with another argument but held back. Donatella was a very headstrong woman. She would have to decide for herself that the best thing would be to tell him who had hired her. After taking a deep breath Rapp grabbed her hand and squeezed it. He did not envy the position she was in. Whoever had hired her had neglected to mention who was looking for Peter Cameron.

Holding hands, they continued across the park in silence. The whole time, Rapp tried to think of ways to get Donatella to give him the information he needed. When they finally reached the other side of the park, Rapp said, "Donny, I'll do whatever it takes to protect you. I can have you on an Agency plane bound for the U.S. by morning. I'll give you my personal guarantee that nothing will happen to you."

She took a second to glance at him, but kept walking. "I can protect myself just fine."

"I didn't say you couldn't, I'm just offering my assistance."

"If I were to take you up on that offer, I'd have to give all of this up. I love this city. I love Italy. I don't want to go hide in America."

Rapp thought about her predicament and decided to make a drastic offer. "Donny, you tell me who you're afraid of, and I'll pay them a little visit. One way or another, I'll make sure they're never in a position to do you any harm."

The thought of Mitch Rapp flying to Tel Aviv to threaten Ben Freidman made her laugh. If there was ever a man who would be so bold it would be Rapp.

"You think that's funny?"

"No, I don't think any of this is funny. What I do think, is that you need to slow down for a second. I'm not saying I won't give you what you need, I'm just saying I need a little time to figure out how to do it."

During the silent walk across the park Donatella had tried to figure out a way to give Rapp the info he needed without telling him that Ben Freidman was her handler. She felt an awesome sense of loyalty to Rapp, and if they were talking about anyone other than Ben Freidman, she'd tell him. But they weren't. They were talking about the director general of Mossad. If the CIA were to find out that the head of Mossad was arranging hits in their own backyard they would have an absolute conniption. No, she had to find another way to give Rapp what he wanted. She couldn't simply give them Ben's name. He had snatched her from the clutches of heroin addiction and imbued her with a sense of self worth that she would have never found on her own.

Donatella knew Mitch well enough to know that he wouldn't rest until he found out who had hired Cameron to kill him. Somehow she would have to convince Freidman to tell her who had taken the contract out on Cameron's life. It was the only way out. She would send Freidman an encrypted e-mail when she got back to her flat and with any luck she'd have an answer by morning.

Donatella was about to speak when Rapp squeezed her hand in three quick successions. Her eyes immediately began sweeping from left to right, looking for trouble. Mitch had seen something and the hand squeezing was their signal that someone was watching them. They were just around the corner from her flat. As Donatella searched for what Rapp had seen she was slightly irritated that she didn't notice it first.

This was the third time Rapp had noticed the car. The first time was near Donatella's office earlier in the day, the second was when they'd left the bar and then now. Rapp broke into casual conversation. If anyone was listening to them via a directional microphone he didn't want to tip them off. "Are you free for lunch tomorrow?"

"I think so."

"Should we meet at eleven-thirty?" Rapp gave her hand a quick squeeze.

"That sounds fine." Donatella's eyes searched the street. Twelve o'clock was straight ahead. Eleven-thirty would be a click to the left. She could barely make out the form of a man slumped behind the steering wheel. The man was parked in the perfect position to keep an eye on her street and the one they were now walking on.

"That photo shoot you were talking about earlier?"

"Yeah."

"I've run into that photographer three times this week."

"Really," said Donatella. Mitch had no idea who the photographer was, so she knew he was telling her this was the third time he'd seen the car.

They took a right onto Donatella's block. Rapp kissed her on the cheek and quietly whispered in her ear, "Are you carrying?"

Donatella smiled at him and said, "Always, darling. How about you?"

"Of course."

When they reached the stoop in front of Donatella's flat Rapp placed his hands on her shoulders and mouthed the words, *Who hired you?*

"I'll tell you tomorrow. I have to take care of something first."

"I'd rather know now."

"I'm sure you would," replied Donatella with a playful grin. "Maybe you could come upstairs and coax it out of me."

She placed her hands firmly on his hips and gave him a lustful smile that sent a jolt of electricity through his groin. Rapp was in the process of trying to ignore her flirtations and figure out who would be watching them when Donatella planted a passionate kiss on his lips. Rapp's first reaction was to push her away, but caution got the better of him, and he remembered they were being watched.

Donatella's tongue in his mouth brought back a wave of emotion. It was like a slide show of erotic memories flashing before his eyes in an instant, and then suddenly there was a larger than life image of Anna Rielly. The vision of his future wife had the correct effect and Rapp casually extricated his ex-lover's tongue from his mouth.

"Oh, I'm tempted to come up," Rapp said for the benefit of any listeners, "but I've got some things I need to take care of before work tomorrow." He gave a slight head jerk in the direction of the car they had discovered just moments ago.

"I understand. Maybe tomorrow night I can talk you into staying." Knowing she had a captive audience, she pulled Rapp close and playfully planted another passionate kiss on his lips. He went along with it for a moment, and then, when he began to push her away she bit down on his lip just hard enough to cause some pain.

Rapp didn't find it funny at all. He was too busy trying to figure out who was watching them. If they were watching him, if they were watching her, if it was a coincidence, if they'd been sent by the same person who hired Peter Cameron or if Kennedy had sent some people from the Rome station to keep an eye on him. If the last were the case, there would be hell to pay when Rapp got back to Washington. He didn't like people looking over his shoulder while he worked. In typical Rapp fashion he decided he would find out what was going on sooner rather than later. Opening his jacket he grabbed his mobile phone and showed it to Donatella. He mouthed the words, *I'll call you in ten seconds. Don't go into your apartment.*

This time it was Rapp who delivered the kiss. It was quick and his tongue stayed in his mouth. "I had a great time. Have a good night's sleep, and I'll call you in the morning." Rapp turned and walked back in the direction from which they had just come. He only glanced at the car to make sure it was still there. When he got to the corner he took a left and headed away from the car. Instantly he picked up the pace, and took out the small black earpiece for his mobile phone. When he reached the next block he turned right and crossed the street. As soon as he was out of sight of the man watching Donatella's flat he broke into a sprint. While running he dialed Donatella's mobile phone number and counted the rings. When Donatella finally answered he was almost to the end of the next block.

"Don't go into your apartment."

"Why?"

He could tell by her tone that she was intentionally baiting him. "Don't argue with me. Just let me check something out first." Rapp slowed down to make a hard right turn.

"I can take care of myself. Don't worry."

Rapp's breathing started getting heavier. "Just give me a minute."

"If anyone is dumb enough to be waiting for me in my apartment I feel sorry for them."

"Okay," Rapp crossed the next block. He was halfway there. Two more blocks and he would be behind the man sitting in the car. "I'll make a deal with you. You tell me who hired you, and then you can go into your apartment."

Donatella laughed at him. "You're in no position to be making deals."

Her flat was on the fourth floor. Rapp knew she rarely used the elevator and she surely wouldn't tonight. Not with the possibility that someone was waiting for her. "I'm almost there. Just give me half a minute."

"Too late. I'm at my door."

"Donny, tell me who hired you. Don't do this to me." The line went dead. "Shit." Rapp commanded his legs to go faster, but there was nothing more. His lungs burning, he rounded the next corner and threw away any pretense of finesse in what he was about to do.

CAPITOL HILL, THURSDAY MORNING

NORBERT STEVEKEN HAD decided to leave his car on the street near the Hart Senate Office Building rather than risk finding a new space over by the Rayburn House Office Building. The Senate offices were in three buildings on the north side of the Capitol and the House offices were in four buildings on the south side of the Capitol. As the cold November wind whipped at his tan trench coat he realized that what had looked to be a relatively short jaunt across the Capitol grounds was more like a half-mile trek.

By the time he reached the Rayburn Building his cheeks and ears were bright red. The former FBI special agent checked his weapon with the Capitol Hill police officer in the lobby and proceeded through the metal detector and up the stairs to Congressman Rudin's office.

Steveken was not looking forward to the meeting. If it were anyone other than Hank Clark he would have said no, but he couldn't do that to the senator. The man had done too much for him. If Steveken went through his client list, he'd bet almost two-thirds of it was a direct result of Clark.

Steveken told himself he could handle it. He'd keep the meeting short and then he'd get to work doing some research on Brown. The office door was open and Steveken stepped into the tiny waiting area. A plump woman with a massive gray bun of hair looked up over her spectacles and said, "Yes?"

Steveken smiled and said, "Hello."

The old battleax gave him the once-over and said, "May I help you?"

"I'm here to see the congressman."

"Do you have an appointment?"

"Nope." Steveken could see where this was going.

"The congressman doesn't take visitors without appointments." The woman looked back down at her work in hopes that the man before her would leave.

"I think he'll see me."

"Is that right," she said with an edge to her voice.

"Yes. We have a mutual friend who asked me to stop by and talk to the congressman."

"And who would that mutual friend be?" The tone was still there.

Steveken bent over and placed both hands on the desk. He'd seen enough career bureaucrats over the years to know how to handle this woman. "That's none of your business. Now I'm a very busy man. So why don't you get off your ass and go tell the congressman that Norbert Steveken is here to see him." He stayed bent over, his face hovering just a foot from the testy receptionist's.

The woman pushed her chair back and stood. In a huff, she walked around her desk, opened the door to Rudin's office and then slammed it behind her. With arms folded Steveken waited alone in the lobby. He listened to the muffled shouts coming from the office and looked around the reception area. The place was a dump compared to Senator Clark's office. Its décor, the level of cleanliness or lack thereof, spoke volumes about the chasm between the two men.

A moment later Congressman Rudin appeared from his office with the old battleax on his heels. Her face was still flushed with anger. Rudin grabbed his overcoat from a coat tree and shouted over his shoulder. "I'm going to be gone for a while."

"When will you be back?" she demanded.

"I don't know." Rudin looked at Steveken and with a jerk of his birdlike head, he signaled for his visitor to follow.

Steveken winked at the congressman's assistant and then followed her boss out the door. Out in the hallway he had to pick up the pace to catch up with the craggy old congressman.

"I don't want to talk in my office." Rudin whispered the words over his shoulder.

Like most law enforcement officers, active or retired, Steveken studied people. For better or worse he'd developed the habit of sizing them up in short order. Occasionally, though, he'd meet someone who really piqued his curiosity. As he and Rudin descended the stairs, he thought the congressman might be one of those people.

Steveken reclaimed his weapon from the Capitol Hill police and went outside to catch up. Rudin was already halfway up the block standing impatiently, gesturing for Steveken to hurry. Steveken started toward him and to his irritation, Rudin began to walk again. He quickened the pace and two blocks later he pulled up alongside the congressman from Connecticut. Steveken caught up and asked, "Where are we going?"

"Coffee. There's a little place up the street a ways." A half minute later Rudin said, "I don't like talking in my office."

"Yeah, you said that." Steveken had decided he was going to have to jerk Rudin's chain a bit.

"It's those bastards out at Langley. I don't trust them a bit."

Steveken couldn't believe what he was hearing. He knew the CIA was capable of doing some pretty bizarre stuff, but there was no way they were stupid enough to bug a congressman's office. Steveken looked over both shoulders. "It must really freak you out to talk like this out in the open."

Rudin looked around. "Why?"

"Directional microphones. They can pick up everything we say, even whispers."

Rudin mumbled a few things and then pointed ahead saying, "The coffee place is up here. Just past Second Street." They traveled the rest of the way in silence.

Rudin entered the shop first and approached the counter. A young white woman with dreadlocks and a pierced nose paid little attention to the congressman as he ordered an extra large cup of French Roast. In deference to his bladder Steveken ordered a small cup. Rudin's coffee arrived first. He grabbed his cup and went and sat at a table near the back. Steveken noted that he'd made no effort to pay for his coffee. Steveken gave the woman three dollars and told her to keep the change. He joined the congressman at the table and took off his trench coat.

He gave Rudin a chance to thank him and when he didn't, Steveken said, "You're welcome."

"Huh?"

"For the cup of coffee."

"Oh, yeah . . . thanks." Rudin clutched the tall cup with his bony hands and took a sip. "Hank says you're very good at what you do."

Steveken said nothing. He just stared at Rudin.

"We don't have much time," said the congressman. "Kennedy starts her confirmation hearing tomorrow."

"What is it that you're looking for?"

"Are you familiar with congressional oversight in terms of the intelligence community?"

"Somewhat."

"Well, Thomas Stansfield, thank God that bastard is finally dead, he didn't much believe in congressional oversight. He tried to keep us in the dark as much as possible, especially when it came to covert operations."

"And what does this have to do with Kennedy?"

"She's one and the same. She's the female version of Stansfield."

"I've heard she's pretty sharp." Steveken blew on his coffee.

"Oh God," grimaced Rudin. "Don't tell me you believe that."

"So what are you telling me? That she's stupid?"

"No, she's not stupid. She's far from stupid."

"So she's pretty sharp."

"I suppose, but that has nothing to do with this. The

bottom line is that the CIA needs to be reined in, and the best chance we have of doing it is right now. Before she becomes entrenched."

"What proof do you have that she's broken the law?"

Rudin looked like he was about to jump out of his own skin. "I don't have any, you idiot. That's why I'm talking to you. You're supposed to get me the proof."

One of the things Steveken liked most about working for himself was that he could be selective about who he took shit from. If a client was paying him a lot of money, he'd been known to let some stuff slide, but the smaller the fee the less crap he was willing to take. Rudin wasn't paying him a cent, and Steveken doubted the man would ever send a client his way. At least not any he'd want.

"How in the hell did you ever get elected?"

"What?" snarled Rudin, utterly confused by the question.

"You and Broom Hilda, your receptionist, you're two of the most socially retarded persons I've ever met."

"What?" Rudin couldn't believe his ears.

"I'm doing this as a favor to Senator Clark." Steveken pointed his thick index finger at Rudin. "You're not paying my tab. Hell, you won't even buy me a cup of coffee. I'm the one doing you a favor by meeting with you. You should be buying me the cup of coffee, not the other way around." Before Rudin could react Steveken changed gears. "But I'm not going to cry over a couple bucks, so let's get down to business. If you want me to help, you have to answer my questions. And while you're at it, it might be a good idea to avoid calling me an idiot." Steveken gave Rudin a patronizing smile and said, "So . . . tell me how you think Kennedy has broken the law."

22

The flat was very nice. It was tastefully decorated with the perfect mix of antiques and modern amenities. The walls were covered with original paintings by artists that Rosenthal did not know. Nor did he care to know. It was all irrelevant shit to him. He'd been sitting in the dark now for over two hours waiting for the woman to return, and he was growing impatient. Sunberg was positioned across the room from him on the living room couch. Yanta was out on the street in the rental car following the target.

The file Rosenthal had received from Freidman said nothing about a security system, but Rosenthal had learned the hard way that the files were rarely as up-to-date as they should be. So instead of picking the lock and running the risk of getting caught in the hallway, and possibly setting off an alarm, Rosenthal went in search of the caretaker's flat in the basement. He asked the seventy-six-year-old man if there were any available units in the building. The old man told him that there weren't any at present, but he expected one to open up after the first of the year.

Rosenthal told the caretaker that he was in town from Rome, and would be moving to Milan in February. He then pulled out a wad of money and said he was willing to put down a cash deposit today if the unit was acceptable. The caretaker leapt at the opportunity to rent the flat after one showing, and the two men ascended to the top floor of the building.

While they were upstairs poking around, Jordan Sunberg picked his way into the caretaker's flat and found the file on Donatella Rahn. Fortunately there was no security system, and even more fortunately there were three copies of the key to her flat. Sunberg checked the other hooks. Some of the flats had four copies and others had only two. There appeared to be no system, but just to make sure, Sunberg found a drawer filled with spare keys and grabbed one. He then took one of the keys to Donatella's apartment and replaced it with the one from the drawer. After checking to make sure he didn't disturb anything that might be noticed, he left the caretaker's flat and waited down the street for Rosenthal.

For his part, Rosenthal gave the old man the cash deposit and told him he would stop by the next morning to fill out the paperwork. He of course would not be returning, and he hoped if the police came around asking questions the old man would say nothing of his visit for fear of having to turn the cash over as evidence. Either way, he wasn't worried. Rosenthal and his team would be out of the country by midmorning, and he doubted any description given by the old caretaker would be detailed enough to give him real problems. In Rosenthal's opinion it was a gamble well worth taking.

Israel, because it was a country surrounded by enemies, had little compunction when it came to using assassination as a means to secure the foundling country's interests. During the country's brief existence they'd had some fantastic successes and some horrible failures. The successes were not always publicized. Rosenthal knew that better than anyone. Some of his best work had never been noticed by anyone other than the most senior Mossad officials. Rosenthal was determined to keep it that way.

He told himself to be patient, despite the fact that just minutes before Yanta had radioed that the target and her date had left the bar and were walking in their direction. Everything looked like it was going well and then Yanta lost them when they entered the park. He'd driven around to the other side and was waiting for them to emerge.

The blackout gave Rosenthal time to think through several contingencies. If she invited her date up for a drink, or by the looks of what he'd found in her nightstand, more than a drink, it would be the man's unlucky, not lucky night. Rosenthal had no compunction in killing an innocent bystander. There were those in his profession who would argue with him, but very few of them had shared his success. If she did not come home tonight, if this man lived nearby and they were walking to his place, he would have to consider hitting her on the street in the morning. There would be some increased risk in killing her in the open, but it wasn't that difficult. He'd done it before. Walk up behind her, move to pass her on the left side, place the silencer against her back and fire three times. Keep walking and never look back. The gun would be exposed for no more than two seconds. The impact of the bullets would knock the wind from her, she'd be incapable of screaming and her heart would stop beating before she hit the ground.

Rosenthal looked at his watch. Freidman had been very specific that this had to be taken care of quickly. He was tempted to leave the apartment and go find them. Take care of it right now and get out of the country. It was dark; there'd be few witnesses if any. It just might be worth it. As he was mulling it over, his earpiece crackled with the voice of Yanta.

"They've just come out of the park and are headed your way."

"Roger," whispered Rosenthal. "Can you get ahead of them and watch the street in front of the flat?"

"Yeah, but I'll have to lose sight of them for a block."

Rosenthal weighed the risk, and decided it was almost certain that they were headed back to her flat. "Go ahead and break contact. Get into a position where you can see them coming and watch the front of the flat."

"Roger, I'm on my way."

Rosenthal looked across the room at Sunberg and nodded. The two men stood and stretched. "Are you ready?"

"Yep," answered Sunberg.

Rosenthal had gone over the plan with him three times. It wasn't complicated. They were at opposite ends of the living room, their fire directed at diagonal angles where their target would enter the room. The lights were off, just as they'd found them. "Remember, wait for her to enter the room, and then we take her."

RAPP WAS RIGHT; Donatella avoided the elevator and took the stairs. And true to her profession, she never went anywhere without a weapon. Donatella chose her handguns like most women chose handbags, different ones for different occasions. Her pistol of choice was the Beretta 92F 9-mm, but fully loaded the weapon was too large and heavy to carry around in a purse. For everyday use she carried the Walther PPK with a silencer. The weapon was light, only 20 ounces, and short. Its one drawback was a lack of stopping power. It fired the small .22 caliber round, which wasn't going to knock anybody down with a body shot, but as long as you hit them in the head it didn't make any difference. And Donatella rarely missed what she was aiming for.

As she ascended the staircase she kept the pistol concealed in the folds of her coat. It was cocked and the safety was off. There was no need to check and see if a round was chambered, because she never carried a gun without a round in the chamber. She spoke to Rapp over her mobile phone as she went. At each landing she paused briefly to listen and check the next flight. She had a slight buzz from the two martinis, but the walk home in the crisp night air had helped to awaken her senses. That, and the man sitting in the car down on the street. Rapp didn't have to spell it out for her. Someone didn't like loose ends, and they were willing to keep killing until the trail went cold. There was one other option, and that was why she wasn't telling Rapp what he wanted to know. The U.S. was an ally, but that only went so far.

The CIA was not beyond lying to get what they wanted, and there could be no doubt that they'd love to find out who her controller was. The man sitting in the car could be someone sent to kill her, or he could just as likely be an employee of the CIA, either sent to kill her or scare her into telling Rapp who had hired her. Maybe that's why Rapp saw the man before she did. Because he knew the man was going to be there. Welcome to the paranoid world of spying.

By the time she reached the fourth floor she'd hung up on Rapp, and she'd made up her mind. If anyone was waiting for her in her flat they were fair game. She'd go in shooting. She stood silently in the shadows of the open stairwell for a few moments, patiently searching for a sign that someone was waiting for her. She put the cell phone away and for a second thought of taking her boots off so she could make it down the hall without noise. Then she realized if anyone was in her flat they would have already been alerted by the man on the street.

Donatella took off her coat and retrieved a knife and

her keys from her purse. She threw her coat over her shoulder and started down the hall. When she reached the door to her flat she stood off to one side and placed the key in the lock. She turned the key and pushed in the door. The four-panel door swung open by itself while she stayed in the hallway protected by the heavy door frame. With one eye peeking into the narrow foyer, she looked at the credenza on the right to see if anything had been disturbed. The three framed photos and the flower arrangement were as she'd left them.

She reached in and turned the light on and then before stepping into the narrow foyer, she peered through the crack where the door was connected to the frame to make sure no one was waiting behind it. It was clear. She entered her flat, the heels of her boots announcing very clearly that it was a woman. She paused for a moment and then reached out with a second key and locked the closet on her left. Clearing closets was a two person job, and even then it was a good way to get killed. She set the keys down on the credenza along with her purse, and then with a deep breath to steel herself, she walked toward her living room as casually as her nerves would allow.

Her pistol was up and level in her right hand, and the knife was in her left, reversed so the blade was hidden against her forearm. Even now just several feet from the end of the foyer she could see no more than half of the rectangular shaped room. All four corners were hidden from her sight. If she were waiting in someone's apartment she knew exactly where she'd be positioned. With her left hand she flipped the switch up and the ceiling light and two lamps in the room flickered to life.

Donatella paused briefly, listening for the sound of movement, her gun pointed where she thought her assassin might come from, but there was nothing. Pulling her coat from her shoulder, she swung it underhand and launched it into the room where it landed on the arm of the couch just to the left. Like a gymnast, Donatella followed the jacket into the room with a diving forward somersault. In midair she heard the telltale sound of a subsonic round leaving the end of a silencer. It had come from the direction she'd anticipated. In the split second it took for her to hit the ground she knew the assassin had missed. Donatella rolled forward between the couch and a chair and sprang to her knees. Her silenced Walther was up and rapidly moving toward the source of the shot.

Before she'd come to a stop she found her target and fired a single well aimed shot. The only thing she noticed about the man was his dark hair and his gun coming to bear on her. Up on one knee, Donatella spun to her right as her eye caught some motion, and moved her arm quickly to acquire a second target. Before she could get off a shot she felt the stinging impact of a bullet slamming into her right shoulder. The shot knocked her off-balance and she started to fall. In slow motion she watched her gun drop from her unresponsive fingers, and then she felt something slice through her hair.

23

Rapp rounded the last corner and instead of taking a hard right and coming up directly behind the car, he crossed over to the other side of the street. He was breathing hard from the sprint but ignored the pain. He was too close to getting the answer he desperately needed. Rapp saw the car up ahead on his right as he ran down the sidewalk in a slight crouch. His eyes scanned the parked cars and sidewalk for any signs of trouble. There was no turning back.

He was close now. He kept his eye on the car at the next corner and then slowed enough to cut in between two parked vehicles. He darted out into the street at the perfect place. He was in the car's blind spot, moving toward it quickly. Rapp drew his gun with his left hand and took aim. With ten feet to go he squeezed the trigger.

The bullet leaving the thick black silencer barely made a noise, and the safety glass window breaking on the driver's side wasn't much louder. At least from the exterior of the car, but from the inside it was considerably louder. The man sitting behind the wheel jerked spastically in reaction to the shattered glass. His arms flew up in a vain attempt to stop the thousands of broken pieces from hitting him.

Rapp was now at the window. It had taken less than a second for him to fire the shot and get to the door. The man's hands were up shielding his face, and the glass was still tumbling from his lap to the floor of the car. Rapp reached in with his right hand and grabbed the man's wrist. Rapp's pistol was still in his left hand and he reached in to smack the man with the butt end of the grip. He aimed for the man's temple. Just before the hard metal made contact the man yelled, and then his body went limp from the sharp blow.

Quickly, Rapp unlocked the door and opened it. He immediately removed the man's gun from his hip holster, and threw it into the backseat as he continued his search. While looking for a backup weapon it occurred to him that he'd almost missed something. He'd been breathing so hard, and the adrenaline was coursing through his veins so fast, that it didn't register what the man had yelled, and more importantly, what language he had yelled it in. The man had sworn in Hebrew.

ROSENTHAL'S PISTOL WAS trained on the woman. He slowly approached her from his corner of the room. She was on her butt, her body limp and leaning against the side of the chair. Her pistol was a good eight feet away sitting in the middle of the hardwood floor. Rosenthal was pretty sure she was dead. He'd hit her once in the shoulder and then in the head. He'd put one more in her just to make sure.

With his gun still aimed at her he called for his partner through clenched lips, "Jordan." There was no answer. "Jordan, can you hear me? Are you all right?"

Rosenthal tried to make sense of what had just happened. How had she known they were waiting for her? What had he done wrong? How would he explain to the colonel that he had lost Jordan Sunberg? Rosenthal was pondering these questions when out of nowhere came a loud noise over his earpiece and then the voice of David Yanta swearing in Hebrew. Rosenthal stopped dead in his tracks. Yanta was a professional, and knew that under no circumstances were they ever to speak in their native tongue while on a mission. For him to make such a mistake someone had to have surprised him. Rosenthal had lost one man and maybe two. He was jolted by the horrible sinking feeling of going from the hunter to the hunted in just seconds. With one hand on his lip mike and the other holding his gun he began to call in earnest for Yanta to check in.

DONATELLA HAD LANDED on her butt. She was leaning against the chair with one of her legs bent under her. Her shoulder hadn't begun to throb yet. It was too early for that, but she felt a stinging sensation on the back of her scalp. One of the shots must have grazed her. Her head was tilted down, her chin resting on her chest. She looked dead, or at the least, unconscious. She didn't dare move, not without her pistol. The man would have to come closer.

With her hair hanging down in front of her face she cracked her eyes ever so slightly. She looked for her Walther, but it was nowhere in sight. She heard the man's steps as he approached her. She'd have to act dead. Donatella tried to discern if there were any more of them. The man called out someone's name, but there was no response. That must have been the one she'd killed with the headshot.

Donatella took a quick inventory of her body. Her right arm was useless, but she still had both her legs and her left hand, which was thankfully still holding on to the knife. The man would not be able to see the weapon since she held the blade flat against her forearm.

The man took another step forward. "David, come in. Can you hear me?"

He was checking with his partner on the street. That was good; he was distracted. The shoes came another step closer and the man was standing right in front of her. Through her hair she could see the gun that was pointed at her head. Donatella knew what she had to do. She jerked her head away from the gun and brought her left hand up at the same time. The razor sharp blade sliced through the flesh and tendons of the man's wrist. The silenced gun thudded to the floor before a shot could be fired.

Donatella's next move was a vicious kick that just barely caught the man's groin, but nonetheless sent him retreating across the room. In that fleeting moment

Donatella abandoned the knife and lunged for the man's gun. The man realized his mistake and stopped his retreat. With his life in the balance, he stepped forward and dove for the gun. Donatella beat him to it by less than a second. She grabbed the gun with her left hand just as he landed on top of her. The force of him hitting her sent them skidding across the hardwood floor. It was her good arm against his good arm.

Donatella wrestled to get free and Rosenthal struggled to keep her down. She was on her back, and he was on top of her. He was stronger and had the leverage. The gun started to move closer to Donatella's head. Her brain sent signals to her wounded right arm to do something. With incredible effort it began to twitch. Donatella felt herself losing her grip on the pistol and she lashed out.

The man's head was just above her. She opened her mouth wide, lifted her head off the floor and bit down as hard as she could. After just a second she could taste the warm salty blood of the man's right ear dripping into her mouth. The man growled in pain, but did not release his grip. Donatella kept her jaw locked and started shaking her head violently. In her teeth she could feel the ear tearing away from the man's head. His groan turned into an all out scream, but his grip stayed firm.

The thought occurred to Donatella again that she was going to die, that this man was too tough for her. It was this feeling of absolute desperation that caused her right arm to move, and when it did it bumped into a familiar object. Donatella closed her eyes, as her fingertips searched the familiar shape. After what seemed like an eternity she had it in her hand. With agonizing pain she picked it up and released her bite on the man's ear.

His head snapped around, his ear barely still attached, flapping loosely down by his neck. He looked at her with

absolute rage in his eyes. Her sweaty left hand lost the battle over his gun and he twisted it from her grip. Any feeling of accomplishment or celebration that he might have
felt was short-lived. Donatella stuck her silenced Walther
.22 against the bloody spot where the man's ear should
have been and pulled the trigger. Rosenthal's head jerked
violently, his eyes opened wide with the horror of what
had just happened and then his whole body went limp.
Donatella did not have the strength to move. She just lay
there, covered by the body of the man she'd killed.

24

FOUR SEASONS HOTEL, MILAN,
THURSDAY EVENING

Anna felt a little off kilter. She'd woken on her own
at five past nine, a little surprised to find that
Mitch hadn't returned. Not overly alarmed, she
went into the bathroom and stepped into the shower.
Mitch had said he had some business to take care of, but
that he'd be back around eight to take her to dinner. Anna
stood in the marble shower and let the warm water bring
her back to life. She tried to figure out what time it was in
Washington, and if she'd just taken a long nap or had a
short night's sleep. She wasn't awake enough yet to figure
it out, so she gave up after a couple of weak attempts. She
was in Italy to enjoy life and hopefully to start a new one.
Time didn't matter for the next six days. She would sleep
when she wanted to sleep, she would eat when she
wanted to eat and she would have sex often.

By the time she got out of the shower she'd gone back on her first promise. She toweled herself off and squinted at the clock sitting on the nightstand in the other room. It was 9:20 and despite what she'd just told herself, time mattered. Her job was a series of deadlines, and they were deadlines you couldn't miss. When Tom Brokaw tossed it to you in the middle of the nightly news you were live in front of millions of people. Deadlines were there to be kept. It had been pounded into her psyche from day one of her first journalism course at the University of Michigan.

Professionally she was good at keeping deadlines, but personally she struggled. This was a source of great irritation between her and Mitch. For very real reasons, he was a worrier. He was rarely late, and when he was, he called. She was constantly late for everything but the news and it drove Mitch nuts. The talons of fear began clawing at her. She was getting a taste of what he felt. It would be one thing if Mitch was just another tourist, but he wasn't.

Standing in front of the mirror she began applying lotion to her skin. She worked her way from top to bottom, rubbing the lotion in more vigorously as she went. By the time she reached her feet she was mad. She was mad at Mitch for being late, and she was mad at herself for allowing herself to get upset. She kept telling herself to relax, but it didn't work. To help pass the time she got dressed. She had no idea where they were going to dinner so she put on a nice pair of dress pants, a white camisole and a sheer gray blouse. With that done the clock was quickly approaching 10:00.

With few other options she opened the mini bar and made herself a vodka tonic. Anna alternated between sitting and sipping her drink and walking out onto the balcony and sipping her drink. The Four Seasons had a beautiful courtyard. From the room's balcony she could look down at the people dining on the terrace of the hotel's restaurant. They sat under white umbrellas and dined by candlelight. A young couple, about her age, began dancing to the music of a string quartet. It was all very romantic and it depressed her. She went back inside and poured herself another drink, a stiff one.

She sat down in front of the TV and turned it on. She stared at the screen but it didn't really register. Her mind was off and running, trying to solve bigger problems, trying to decide if maybe she was making the wrong decision. Why would any woman want to live the rest of her life with so much stress?

The doubt sneaked up on her, and she began asking herself just what in the hell she was thinking when she'd allowed herself to fall in love with Mitch Rapp. There were a lot of obvious reasons. He was an incredibly gentle and sensitive man, especially considering what he did for a living. He was, without exaggeration, the sexiest man she'd ever known. His rugged good looks were backed up by a confidence and intellect that feared nothing. He was a lover like no one she had ever experienced. When they went to bed it felt as if their bodies were made to be with each other. And he had saved her life and countless others. She could place no value on that. He was a phenomenal person, but he had his faults, or more precisely, he had one major fault.

Rielly knew what it was like to grow up in a home where you worried if a loved one might not return after a day's work, or if the next knock on the door might be your father's best friend coming to tell the family that Dad had given his life in the line of duty. Rielly's father had just retired from the Chicago Police Department after thirty years. As a little girl she vividly remembered lying awake at night hearing sirens and worrying that Daddy

wouldn't come home, crying as she thought of never seeing him again. Her parents did their best to protect her
and her brothers from the fears, but they were unavoidable. Chicago was a big city and with it came some pretty
rough crime and with that came dead cops. They saw it
on TV, they saw it in the papers, and the nuns made them
pray for the deceased officers and their families at St.
Ann's, her Catholic grade school. It was not a nice part of
her childhood.

Anna loved her father dearly. He and her mother had
done a wonderful job raising her and her brothers. Two of
those brothers had followed in their father's footsteps and
were now patrolmen with the Chicago PD and the other
brother, the black sheep, was an attorney.

Anna had always told herself she'd never marry a cop.
Despite the fact that her mother and father had made it,
she'd seen enough of her father's friends to know the
stress from their jobs more often than not made marriage
a failed venture. And Mitch's job, if that's what she could
call it, was ten times worse. Cops were meant to keep the
peace and enforce the law. Occasionally they had to draw
their weapon, but rarely did they have to shoot someone.
If they did it was usually because someone was shooting at
them. During these dark moments of doubt, Anna was
forced to admit who Mitch Rapp really was. He was an
assassin. When he went to work he went with the intent
to kill. He didn't wait for anyone to shoot first, he went
with his gun cocked and drawn.

She looked up at the door and wished he would walk
through it right now before she went any further down
this path. She wished that he would hold her tight and tell
her that this last piece of business was taken care of. That
he was done with the killing and the field operations and
was ready to take a desk job at Langley. She held the

sweaty glass so tightly she thought it might break. Tilting her head back, she took a big gulp and finished her second drink. She got up to pour another, and as she walked toward the minibar, she prayed that Mitch wouldn't let her down. She didn't want any more nights of worrying, wondering if he was on his way to meet her or if he was already dead.

THE MAN MOANED and started to move. Rapp tore his headset off and threw it on the seat. Keeping the gun pressed against his head, Rapp took his free hand and undid the man's belt and pants. Then grabbing him by his jacket collar, he yanked him from the car and slammed him against the rear door of the sedan. He'd already checked his breast pocket for ID and had found nothing. Rapp took this as a sign that he wasn't a cop.

"Who do you work for?" asked Rapp in Italian. The man looked at him through dazed eyes and told Rapp to go fuck himself. Without hesitation Rapp brought his knee up and delivered a vicious blow to the man's groin. He tried to double over, but Rapp kept him pinned against the car.

Rapp repeated the question, and this time the guy spat in his face. Rapp brought his head back and snapped it forward. His brow landed on the bridge of the man's nose, instantly crushing it and sending a stream of blood running down the man's face.

Grabbing him by his jacket collar, Rapp swung the man around and yanked the back of the jacket down so his arms were pinned against his sides. He then pushed him forward and started marching him across the street toward Donatella's flat. The man moaned in pain and spit blood from his mouth. His unbuckled pants fell from his waist and he was forced to grab them.

"Keep walking." Rapp's pistol was stuck in the small of the man's back right on the spinal column. One wrong move and the guy would lose the use of his legs for the rest of his life. With his free hand, Rapp hit the send button on his mobile phone and listened through his earpiece as it began to ring.

After an eternity, a very out of breath Donatella answered. In a clipped voice, Rapp asked, "Is everything all right?"

"No." There was obvious pain in her voice.

"Hold tight. I'm on my way up. Can you buzz me through the door?"

"Yeah."

Rapp pushed the man in the back and drove him forward. "Move it." When they got to the door, Rapp told Donatella to buzz him in. The elevator was waiting for them, but Rapp ignored it. Shoving the man toward the stairs he said, "All right, numb-nuts, let's double-time it up these stairs. If you slow me down or try anything stupid you're dead." With that they started up the stairs, Rapp pushing the man every step of the way.

When they reached Donatella's apartment the door was cracked. Rapp pushed the man into the flat and closed and locked the door behind them. When he entered the living room he saw a body on the floor and Donatella sitting on the couch with blood on her face and neck.

"What in the hell happened?"

"There were two of them waiting for me. The one on the floor, and a second one over there behind the couch."

Rapp didn't bother asking if they were dead. "Are you hit?"

Donatella nodded.

"Where?"

"My shoulder."

Rapp could tell by her posture that the wound was more than a graze. His mind was scrambling to prioritize what had to be done. A gunshot wound was serious business. They would have to get a doctor, and not just any doctor. They'd need one on the payroll. One who wouldn't report it to the authorities. The first thing he had to do though, was secure the man he'd dragged up from the car. With one hand still on the guy's shirt collar, Rapp flipped his gun in the air and caught it by the barrel. He then swung it, smashing the grip into the back left side of the man's head. His knees went limp and Rapp lowered his unconscious body to the floor.

Stepping over him, Rapp knelt down in front of Donatella. "Are you hit anywhere else?" he asked incredulously as he looked at all the blood on her chin and neck.

"No. This is his." She jerked her head toward Rosenthal's body. "I bit his ear during the struggle."

Rapp started peeling back her jacket so he could get a look at the wound. Donatella winced in pain. Rapp asked, "Any idea who these goons belong to?"

"No."

After he'd eased the jacket off her shoulder, he found the bullet hole in her shirt and tore it open so he could inspect the wound. He quickly realized by the size of it that he was looking at an exit wound. His other hand slid around the back and felt for the entry wound. He found it with his forefinger and was pleased that there was very little blood coming from it. "What would you say if I told you I think they're Israelis?"

"I'd tell you you're crazy."

"Well, the one I dragged up here, when I jumped him . . . he swore in Hebrew. And then when I pulled him out of the car he spoke in Italian."

"What does that prove?"

"I don't know. Why don't you tell me?" While Donatella thought about it, Rapp continued to check her shoulder. He tried to calculate the trajectory of the bullet and announced, "It passed clean through, which of course is good, but I think it did some pretty bad damage."

"I'd say," muttered Donatella as another wave of pain washed over her.

"Where's your first-aid kit?"

"In my bedroom closet. Top shelf, right side."

Before leaving the room, Rapp yanked the cord off the nearest lamp and then tied the wrists of the man he'd knocked out. "I'll be right back."

Donatella watched Rapp go down the hall to her bedroom. When he was gone she whispered several swear words to herself and looked at the bodies on the floor. It *was* a big deal that Rapp had heard the man swear in Hebrew. Donatella didn't recognize any of them, but they were Mossad. They were personal recruits of Ben Freidman. She'd seen the type before. As Donatella linked things together, she saw that she was painted into a very tight corner. Her life in Italy was over, and for that fact, so probably too was her life. She needed a way out, and she didn't mean finding a way to spend the rest of her life on the lam. She'd seen others try it. Very few succeeded. They usually slipped up somewhere along the way or were forced to live such a shitty life that it wasn't worth it. No, she'd worked too hard for everything. She wasn't going to just throw it all away. She needed leverage. She needed a way to negate Ben Freidman's significant power. She thought of what Rapp had said earlier. That he could protect her. That he could take it all the way to the top. She wondered briefly how high all the way to the top was.

The man on the floor began stirring. Donatella wondered what information he would provide when Mitch went to work on him. At that moment she made a difficult decision. She would be the only one with the secrets, and if Rapp wanted them, he would have to come through on his promise. He would have to give her her life back.

The silenced Walther was still in her left hand. She heard Rapp coming back down the hall. Donatella raised the weapon, took aim and fired a single shot into the top of the man's head.

25

"What in the hell are you doing!" snarled Rapp as he stood in the hallway, staring at the smoke wafting from the end of Donatella's silenced pistol. His own gun was aimed at her head, and he was holding the first-aid kit in his other hand with some towels under his arm. "Put your gun down right now, Donatella!"

Acting as if his request was tiresome, she tossed her weapon to the floor and sank back into the couch. Rapp crossed over to her and kicked her weapon to the other side of the room. He set the first-aid kit and the towels on the coffee table, looked at the man with the fresh bullet hole in the top of his head, and then turned back to Donatella. "What in the fuck was that for?"

"We were going to have to kill him sooner or later." She looked away from Rapp and closed her eyes. "I didn't want you to have to do it."

"The hell you did."

"I did you a favor."

"My ass you did." Rapp pointed his pistol at the man whose hands he'd just tied. "You knew him, didn't you?"

With her eyes closed and a grimace on her face, she shook her head.

"Bullshit, Donny."

"Stop your stupid arguing and give me a shot of morphine." She reached out for the kit with her good hand. For this exact reason Donatella possessed a military first-aid kit, complete with battle dressings, sutures, clamps, surgical staples, penicillin, morphine and much more.

Rapp snatched the kit away from her and said, "I came all the way over here to help you, and you haven't given me shit. You'd better start giving me some answers."

"You didn't come over here to help me, you came over here to help yourself."

"Oh, is that right, you little ingrate? If I hadn't stepped in, the Agency would have grabbed you off the street and done God only knows what to you."

"For all I know, these guys were sent here by the Agency."

"Yeah, Donny, these guys were sent here by the Agency," Rapp said in a mocking tone. "That's why you executed this sap right here."

"I don't know them."

"Bullshit, Donny. I know you well enough to know you wouldn't have just executed this guy if you weren't afraid he'd have something to say."

"I don't know any of these guys." She grimaced as another wave of pain washed over her. "Give me some goddamn morphine."

"You might not know these guys personally, but you sure as hell know who sent them."

"Maybe."

"Maybe, my ass, Donny. I'm done fucking around. You're gonna tell me right now who hired you to kill Peter Cameron, or I'm walking out of this apartment and out of your life."

"I think you're walking out of my life whether I tell you or not."

"Fine." Rapp grabbed his mobile phone.

"Who are you calling?"

"The Agency. I'm done with you. I'll baby-sit you until they get some people over here to pick you up."

"Hey . . . hey . . . put the phone away for a second."

"Why? Give me a good reason."

"Because I need you. Because I saved your life once."

"Ain't that convenient. I've saved your life twice and tonight makes three. If you want to get the ledger out, I think it's you who owe me."

Donatella held her fist up against her forehead and closed her eyes as another wave of pain washed over her. "Just give me the kit, and I'll give myself the damn shot."

"Donny, what in the hell is wrong with you? I came here to help you. Why won't you trust me and tell me who hired you?"

"Give me the shot, and I'll tell you."

"Nope." Rapp shook his head.

"Fine." Donatella tried to get off the couch, but Rapp pushed her back down.

"Where do you think you're going?"

"Mitch, either give me a shot, or get the hell out of my way."

"No way, Donny. You can either tell me who hired you, or you can tell one of the Agency's doctors."

After letting out a moan, she said, "All right . . . fine. Give me the shot, and then I'll tell you."

Rapp looked at her, trying to discern her sincerity. "Do you know who hired you?"

"Yes, dammit! Now give me the damn shot!"

Rapp finally relented and set the kit down. He opened it and found an ampule of morphine. He took the small glass container and held it in front of Donatella's face. "This is your last chance. I'm going to give this to you and then you'd better tell me who hired you to kill Peter Cameron. If you don't, you're going to wish you would have." Rapp stabbed the ampule into her thigh and the painkiller was released into her bloodstream.

It didn't take long for Donatella to begin to relax. "Thank you."

"You're welcome." Rapp grabbed a pair of scissors from the kit and began cutting the sleeve from Donatella's bloodstained blouse. His biggest fear now was that she'd lose consciousness from the loss of blood. "Where do you want to start?"

"What do you mean?" Her eyes were getting glassy.

"Who hired you, Donny?"

"Oh . . . we're back to that again."

"Yep." Rapp grabbed one of the towels and started wiping the blood away. "Who hired you, Donny?"

"Oh . . . Mitch, I'm in a lot of trouble."

"I can help. I promise you I'll protect you." Rapp placed one of the towels on the couch. "Here . . . lie down." He gently lowered her onto the towel. He began cleaning the wound. "Whatever kind of trouble you're in, I promise I can help you get out of it." Rapp doused the wound with iodine. Thanks to the morphine, Donatella never felt the sting.

"You have to promise me, Mitchell. You have to promise me that no matter how bad this gets you'll stand by me."

Rapp tore open a packet of coagulant powder and sprinkled as much of it into the wound as possible. "Donny, do you trust me?" He looked into her beautiful brown eyes.

Donatella blinked. "Yes, but . . . I'm warning you . . . this is going to get very ugly."

Rapp shrugged and began packing gauze into the bullet hole. "It can't be any worse than some of the crap we've already been through."

"Oh, yes it can. You have to promise me that you won't leave my side until I'm safe. You have to take me to America."

After thinking about it Rapp said, "That shouldn't be a problem."

He finished packing the wound and applied a field dressing to the front of her shoulder. Gently, he rolled her onto her side and started cleaning the entry wound. "I'm waiting, Donny."

Donatella was tired. Too tired to continue the fight. She owed much to Ben Freidman, but if he'd sent these goons to kill her, she owed him no more. She had neither the strength nor the assets to fight him on her own, and any hope of going to him and proving her loyalty was childish. Ben Freidman was a ruthless man who would do anything to save his own ass.

Donatella sighed and said, "It was Ben Freidman."

Rapp let her roll onto her back. He had to see her face. "You mean to tell me Ben Freidman, the head of Mossad, ordered you to kill Peter Cameron?"

"Yes."

"Holy shit," muttered Rapp. He pushed Donatella back onto her side, and went back to work on the wound. He and Kennedy had ruled the Israelis out. As far as they could tell, there was no motive for them to try and kill

Rapp. They must have missed something. Those in the know around Washington knew that no group was better at penetrating U.S. intelligence assets than Israel. In many ways they were America's most ungrateful ally, but they almost always worked toward the same goal when it came to counterterrorism.

"Was Cameron an agent for Mossad?"

"I have no idea."

"Then why would Freidman want him dead?"

"I don't know. You'll have to ask the person who hired us."

"What do you mean, 'hired you?' You said Freidman ordered the hit."

"I'm freelance now, but Freidman still handles my contracts. He sets everything up, takes care of the money and keeps a third of it."

"Cheap bastard. So technically Mossad has nothing to do with this."

"No. We're completely separate."

"Donny, I don't think you're very separate when you were trained by them, used to work for them and Freidman is the current director general."

"Mitchell, I'm telling you Mossad had nothing to do with this. Someone approached Ben with a rush job, and they were willing to pay a lot of money to have Cameron taken care of quickly."

"How much?"

"Half a million."

Rapp stopped what he was doing momentarily. Half a million bucks was a lot of money for a contract on a former civil servant. "Did you get the money?"

"Yes."

Rapp placed a field dressing on her back and then gave her a shot of penicillin. "How do you feel?"

"Fine." She smiled crookedly. "I don't feel a thing."

After helping her sit up, Rapp asked, "Do you think you can walk?"

"At your service."

"All right. I'm going to get you a new shirt from your room, and then we need to get out of here." Rapp stood. "Do you still have a bag packed?"

"Of course. Bedroom closet, bottom right side."

"If you can think of anything else, now's the time. You might not be back here for a while." Rapp hurried into the bedroom and reappeared less than a minute later with a bag over his shoulder, and a blouse and black sweater in hand.

Donatella looked at the dead bodies on the floor. "What are we going to do about these guys?"

"I'll make a call and have it taken care of."

Rapp helped Donatella change into her new blouse and sweater and then helped her put on her coat. He threw some of the medical supplies into the bag and grabbed her pistol from the floor. After finding her purse, he put in a fresh magazine and gave her the gun. Rapp grabbed Donatella with one hand and threw the bag over his shoulder. They left the apartment, locked the door and took the elevator down to the first floor. As they went out into the cool night, Rapp scanned the street for danger. They headed toward the hotel and he briefly wondered how he would explain Donatella to Anna. He tried to tell himself that she'd understand, but something told him it was wishful thinking.

26

Donatella wasn't saying much. Rapp had her gripped firmly under her good arm. He would have liked it if they could have walked a little faster, but at least he didn't have to carry her. Rapp wasn't too sure how long she'd last. She'd lost a fair amount of blood. There was no way around the problem; that blood needed to be replaced. They could worry about the wound and possible infection later, but for now he needed to get her stabilized. Fortunately, the streets were not very crowded. If there were any more trouble out there he'd stand a good chance of seeing it coming.

The worry that more Mossad agents might be lurking in the shadows had kept him from using his phone. He had to keep one hand on Donatella and the other on his gun. Conversely though, he needed to alert Kennedy. He needed to tell her what he'd found out, and if there were more Mossad agents about there was a strong case to make that he should call Kennedy immediately and tell her what he'd discovered. If he and Donatella went down in a hail of bullets Kennedy would never discover the truth.

Rapp decided the risk was worth taking. At the next corner he stopped and leaned Donatella against a building. "Hold tight for a second."

He released the grip of his pistol and grabbed his earpiece and phone. In a perfect world he would have preferred a more secure form of communication, but his digital satellite phone would have to do. He'd been told the

phone was secure, but he knew better. There was very little the National Security Agency couldn't pick up if they
put their minds to it. What he had to say was for
Kennedy's ears only. Yes, the NSA was supposedly on his
team, but they had their own problems just like the CIA
had theirs, and unfortunately in this particular case Ben
Freidman had been very good at cultivating agents within
Washington's various intelligence agencies.

Security be damned, he had to make the call. He
would have to use innuendo and personal information to
communicate the message. Rapp punched in a special
number, one that he'd used very rarely over the last ten
years. As it rang, he grabbed Donatella by the arm and
they started walking again.

A man answered on the other end with a no-nonsense
tone. "State your business."

"This is an alpha priority call. I need to speak with the
DCI immediately."

"Are you on a secure line?"

"No."

"I have your number. Hang up and stay off the line."

Rapp pressed the end button on the phone and turned
to check the street behind him. Two men had appeared
out of nowhere and they were moving fast. Rapp
squeezed Donatella's arm and whispered, "Look sharp. We
might have company."

SITUATION ROOM, THURSDAY AFTERNOON

THE PRESIDENT LIKED Colonel Gray's plan, and he liked
it even more after Kennedy came up with the idea of
bringing back one of the nukes. It was not without great
risk, however. Launching cruise missiles was one thing.
Anybody with or without moral character, anybody with

or without some intestinal fortitude could give the order to send in the cruise missiles. It did not test a leader's skills one iota. Sending in the planes was the next level and involved some real risk on America's part. The last thing anybody wanted to see was an American airman on Iraqi TV. Putting troops on the ground, though, that was some serious business. Especially sending them into Baghdad.

The president eyed Colonel Gray. "Do you know where you'd land the helicopters?"

Gray produced a map and walked it down to the president. Standing over his left shoulder he said, "Right here, forty-eight miles southwest of Baghdad. We know this area is deserted."

"Why is it deserted?"

"See this building right here?" Gray stabbed his index finger at the photo.

"Yes."

"It used to be a chemical weapons factory. We bombed it, and now the area is under quarantine."

Hayes looked surprised and asked, "You're going to send your men into an area that's under quarantine?"

"We bombed it eight years ago, sir. We've sent people back into the area and had the soil and air tested. It's safe."

The president was tempted to ask when this was done, but instead accepted the colonel's answer. "Is there anything else in the area we need to worry about?"

"Just the main road between Al Musaiyih and Baghdad." Gray again pointed out the spot with his finger. "There's a secondary road right here, that leads to an abandoned chemical factory."

"So you'll use the area to unload the cars." The president studied the photograph. "What if you get there and it's occupied?"

244 / VINCE FLYNN

"Then we move onto our secondary landing area here." Gray pointed out the next spot.

"Sounds complicated, Colonel."

"This isn't the part that worries me, sir."

"What is?"

"Baghdad, sir. I don't have anybody who's ever set foot in the city. I'd like to find someone who knows their way around, someone who can get into the city before the op and check things out. Someone who can meet my team there and lead them to the target and back out of the city."

"Do you have anybody in mind?"

"I do, actually." Gray looked at Kennedy. "There's a certain individual who I've worked with from time to time who knows his way around this part of the world very well. We could really use his help."

The president looked at Kennedy. "Who is he talking about?"

"Iron Man."

"That might be a problem," replied the president.

"Why?" asked a disappointed Colonel Gray.

"Iron Man is in the process of, how should we say this," the president looked to Kennedy, who finished the sentence.

"He's retiring from the field."

Instead of showing disappointment, a sly grin spread across the Delta Force commander's face. "Guys like Iron Man don't retire. Give me five minutes with him, and he'll be begging me to go on this op."

The president folded his arms across his chest and said, "I hope you're right, Colonel."

As General Flood began to reiterate his position on the air strikes, Kennedy's digital phone beeped. She turned away from the group and answered the call. She listened for only a few seconds, ended the call and abruptly stood.

There was a secure phone in the Situation Room but she didn't want to talk in front of the others. "Excuse me, Mr. President, but there's something I have to take care of." The president consented with a curt nod and Kennedy quickly left the room in search of a secure phone with some privacy.

AT THE NEXT corner Rapp took a right turn and pushed Donatella into the first storefront he could find. He drew his weapon and waited for the two men to round the corner. Several seconds later they appeared but continued straight instead of turning. Rapp watched them cross the street and disappear. It was probably a false alarm.

The ringing of his phone caused him to jump slightly. He pressed the call button and said, "Hello."

"It's me. What's up?"

"We've got some big stuff happening. You know that hunch we had about my old friend?"

"Yes."

"We were right."

"Who was she working for?"

"Her old employer."

There was a pause before Kennedy replied. "Say that again."

"Do you remember who hired her originally?"

"Yes."

Rapp looked up and down the street. "They had some type of a freelance arrangement. He set up the contracts, and she did the work."

"Are we talking about my counterpart over there?"

Rapp could tell Kennedy was having a hard time believing this. "That's correct."

"Are you sure?"

"Yes, and there's more, but we need to talk in person."

Rapp looked at Donatella. Her eyes were closed, and she was leaning against the glass door. He was losing her. "I need a place cleaned up. Do you understand?"

"I think so."

"And I need a doc."

"For you." There was concern in Kennedy's voice.

"No, for someone else."

"Anna?" The concern grew.

"No, the other person we were talking about."

"How serious?"

"She'll be all right, but someone needs to look at her in the next hour or so."

"I can take care of that."

There was a moment of hesitation before Rapp spoke again. "I need to be brought in." He wasn't used to asking for help in this way.

"I can call the office over there and have it taken care of immediately."

"Be careful who you choose, and I don't want to be taken back to the office. Do you understand?"

"Yes." Rapp was telling her he didn't want to be taken to the embassy. "Where will you be?" she asked.

"Do you remember where I'm staying?"

"Yes."

"That's where I'll be."

"All right. And by the way, something has come up on this end. We need to get you back here immediately."

"That's probably for the best, but the travel arrangements need to be very private and I'll have company."

"I understand. I'll get to work on the other stuff first and call you back in fifteen minutes."

"All right." Rapp patted Donatella on the cheek to see if she'd open her eyes, and she did. He grabbed her under the arm again and they headed off for the hotel.

27

Rielly was at her wit's end. Her third vodka tonic had been consumed and she'd switched to water. She'd gone from concern to anger, back to concern and then back to anger. That's where she was now, her fertile imagination playing out all of the possibilities as to why Mitch was late. None of the scenarios were good. It was in this moment of despair that she made up her mind. She loved him too much to just walk away, but if she was going to marry him some changes would have to be made.

No longer did she think it was good idea for him to take the job in the CIA's Counterterrorism Center. He needed to sever all ties with that godforsaken place. If they were going to get married and have children he would have to take a normal job like normal people. Rielly made up her mind. She didn't like giving ultimatums, but she was going to. It was worth it. She couldn't live the rest of her life in fear that every time her husband was late something terrible had happened.

She was pulled from her moment of decisiveness by a sound at the door. She did not leap to her feet. She kept her cool, and calmed herself for the ensuing battle. When the door opened she stared in utter confusion at the sight of her boyfriend entering the room with an extremely attractive woman on his arm. She could tell from the look on Mitch's face that something was not right.

Rapp closed the door, turned the dead bolt and latched

the chain. He continued past Rielly and into the bed-room. "Anna, I need your help." He set Donatella on the bed and moved immediately to the French doors that looked down onto the inner courtyard. Rapp shut and locked the doors and drew the curtains. He turned to find Rielly standing in the doorway, arms folded, in her defiant pose.

Rapp moved back toward the bed saying, "Honey, I'm sorry I'm late, but something came up." He bent over Donatella and forced open her eyelids. Her pupils were dilated and her skin was getting clammy. In Italian he asked her how she felt. Donatella told him she was tired.

"What in the hell is going on, and who the hell is this?" From where Anna was standing it looked like Mitch had brought home an inebriated whore.

Before Rapp could answer Donatella blurted out, in English, a response to the second part of Rielly's question. "I am his lover."

"What?" snarled Anna.

Rapp grimaced and then began shaking his head as he went toward his girlfriend. "That's not what this is all about."

Anna seized on the fact that he didn't confirm or deny the woman's claim. "How well do you know this woman?"

He put his hands up in an effort to calm Anna. "Very well, but that's not what this is about."

" 'Very well,' " spat Rielly. "What in the hell does 'very well' mean?"

"We had," Donatella slurred her words, "wild and pas-sionate sex for many years."

Rapp cringed and waved his hands back and forth. "Don't listen to her."

Anna's skin was flushed with anger. She yelled, "Excuse me, but I was under the impression that you were going to take care of some business, and now you show up two hours late with this drunken tramp! I think you have some explaining to do!"

Rapp grabbed Anna by the shoulders. "Lower your voice."

She tried to break free from his grip, but couldn't. "Let go of me."

Rapp held her tight. "Anna, she isn't drunk. She's been shot. She's on morphine, and I think she's slipping into shock, so if it's okay with you I'd like to discuss this later." Rapp didn't wait for an answer. He released Anna and walked into the living room. He opened the mini bar and grabbed a bag of cookies and a bottle of water. He came back to the bed and propped Donatella up against the headboard. "Here." Rapp held the bottle of water to Donatella's lips. "I don't know how long it'll be until a doctor gets here." She drank half of the bottle and then Rapp handed her a cookie. When she was done with the cookie she drank the rest of the water. Rapp laid her down on the bed and shoved some pillows under her legs to get her feet elevated. He covered her with a blanket and checked her eyes again. Hovering above her face he whispered, "Everything is going to be fine. I want you to just lie here and rest. No more talking. Just rest."

Rapp turned around and found that Anna had again adopted her defiant pose. This time, however, there was a scowl on her face that told him he was in trouble. Rapp grabbed Anna by the arm and brought her into the living room. He closed the doors to the bedroom and said, "I know you're mad, but I can explain."

In an extra catty tone she said, "Please do."

"That woman and I used to work together. We were—"

Anna interrupted him. "Have you ever slept with her?"

Rapp looked her in the eye. The thought occurred to him that he should lie, but he knew it was wrong to keep a secret like this from her. "That's beside the point. It has nothing to do with this—"

"Answer the question." Anna took a step toward him and poked him in the chest. "Have you ever slept with her?"

"Yes, but it was—" Rapp was blinking in frustration, trying to figure out a way to make her understand.

She brought her hand up fast and slapped him across the face. "You bastard."

Rapp's demeanor changed instantly. He grabbed Rielly by the wrist and stuck his face within inches of hers. Very slowly, clearly and deliberately he said, "Don't ever hit me again! I don't hit you, you don't hit me!"

Rielly yanked her hand free. "Don't change the subject. We come to Italy to get engaged, and you take off on *some meeting.*" Rielly mocked him by making quotation marks with her fingers. "*To take care of some final business.* What was that final business? One more screw with your old girlfriend?"

Rapp closed his eyes. "It wasn't like that. We used to work with each other."

"And you used to screw."

"Yes, but that was before I met you."

"Yeah, right. I screw everyone *I* work with."

"Stop it."

"No. Do you actually expect me to believe this crap? You keep all of these secrets from me because you say it involves national security." Rielly was getting louder. "And then you go have a drink with this gal who you used to work with. Now I'm no spy, but I sure as hell wouldn't think that the fact that you and this girl used to fuck each other is a national secret." She folded her arms across her chest and looked at Rapp with hatred in her eyes.

"Anna, please don't do this. I love you. I have never cheated on you, and I will never cheat on you."

"Then why didn't you tell me about her?"

"She was before you. I don't ask you about any of your old boyfriends."

"Excuse me, but I don't fly to foreign countries to have secret meetings with my ex-boyfriends. I don't show up in our hotel room with one of my ex-boyfriends who just happens to have been shot!"

Rapp took a step back and tried to figure a way out of the mess. "Anna, my darling, you have to trust me on this. I did not cheat on you. I will never cheat on you. This was official business."

Rielly wasn't buying any of it. "What did you have to talk to her about?"

After hesitating Rapp said, "I can't talk about it."

"How did she get shot?"

"There were some men waiting for her in her apartment."

"Oh, so you went to her apartment. Did you have sex?"

"No."

"Oh, that's right, you couldn't because these men were waiting for her. But you would've, right?"

"No, I would not have," Rapp said patiently.

"Bullshit. Who were these men? Why were they waiting for her?"

"I can't talk about it, Anna."

"The hell you can't. I am so sick of your secrets. I am so sick of this double life. I'm so sick of worrying that you're going to get killed every time you walk out the door."

Rapp moved toward her. "I just have to see this last thing through," he moved to put his arms around her, "and then everything will be fine."

Rielly blocked him and stepped away. "No." She began shaking her head. "No, it'll never be over. I can't live like this." She moved toward the door, tears welling up in her eyes. "I can't do this."

Rapp held out his hand for her. "Anna, I love you. I promise I'll make everything right."

She stopped by the door and wiped some tears from her face. Turning, she faced Rapp and said, "I love you, too, but I know now I can't live this way." She grabbed her purse and her jacket. He moved toward her and she held up her hand. "Don't!" Rapp stopped. "I had my doubts before tonight. This . . . this mess only confirmed what I already feared. I can't be married to you." Rielly opened the door and without looking at Rapp she said, "Don't follow me. I think it's best if we don't see or talk to each other." With that she went into the hallway, and the door closed behind her.

Rapp stood in the middle of the room unable to move. He didn't know if he'd ever felt such pain. The woman he loved more than anyone in the world had just told him she would not marry him, that she did not want to talk to him or see him again. None of it made any sense. This was supposed to be one of the happiest times of his life and it had just turned into one of the worst. He couldn't just let it slip away like this. As Rapp started for the door, his phone rang. He stopped, thought about not answering and then decided he had to. It was Kennedy.

28

The last vestiges of daylight were slipping over the horizon, but the wind was still gusting. A small beagle darted off the path and scampered through the dry leaves that covered almost every inch of the park. The dog found a sapling with a yellow ribbon tied around it and lifted his leg. His owner puffed on a pipe and watched. It looked like they had the park to themselves. Jonathan Brown's outward appearance didn't show it, but he was nervous. So much so that he'd dug through the boxes in his basement and broken out his old pipe. He just hoped the boys from Langley's Office of Security hadn't decided that today was the day to follow him. Or even worse, the counterespionage people over at the FBI. They followed everybody from time to time, no matter how senior.

The beagle finished relieving himself and trotted back to the path. The owner and dog started winding their way through the park again. Brown had obsessed all day about the risks involved with the meeting. He wondered if it was a good idea to meet in a park so close to his home. That's where they'd busted the traitor Robert Hanssen, in a park right by his house. Brown couldn't remember exactly, but he thought he'd even been walking the family dog. He looked down at Sparky for a moment as if the pooch might be a bad omen. Brown shook his head and told himself he was being paranoid. Hanssen had been spying for the Russians. Brown wasn't spying for anyone. He was simply trying to do the right thing. He wouldn't be breaking any laws by meeting with this Steveken fellow. At least none that he knew of. The retired judge cringed at the use of such poor reasoning. It was one of the first things he'd learned in law school. Ignorance of the law is no excuse.

When accepting his job at the CIA, he'd had to sign a National Security nondisclosure document. The heinous contract was so long, and cast such a wide net, that Brown was sure the CIA would be able to find him in violation of something. Whether or not he could beat those charges was up for debate. With his reputation as a jurist, he would stand a good chance of being regarded as an honest man who was trying to right a wrong.

Work had been depressing and stressful of late. Kennedy was taking a position that had been promised to him. Brown knew that she and the other deputies had hidden things from him. They didn't trust a federal judge with no practical experience in the spy trade, and that was fine. He'd see how quickly they changed their tune when he became director. He would clean house, and bring in people who were loyal to him, people who would do things by the book. And then when the time was right he would move into Clark's administration for one of the top spots.

The wind died down for a second, and it was then that he noticed the footfalls of someone on the path behind him. Nervously, he looked over his shoulder and saw a man approaching. Sparky darted off the path again. Brown stopped and turned so he could get a good look at the man. There was a casual recognition in the eyes of the person as he approached, a slight nod as a precursor to a verbal greeting. Brown had no idea what this Steveken looked like. A horrific thought flashed across his mind. What if this was a trap? Brown's pulse quickened. Peter Cameron had just disappeared several weeks ago. Maybe it was Brown's turn. The deputy director watched as the man smiled at him and began to extract something from the pocket of his trench coat. Brown flinched and brought his hands up.

Steveken was not nervous about the meeting. He'd thought it through and came to the conclusion that he was doing nothing even remotely illegal. He was a former special agent for the FBI helping a U.S. congressman look into any illegalities that may or may not be occurring at the CIA.

As Steveken withdrew his right hand from his jacket he saw Brown flinch. He stopped several steps away and asked, "Judge Brown, how are you?"

Brown lowered his hands and said, "Ah . . . fine."

"I'm Norb Steveken."

Brown took his hand and said, "Hello."

"Someone who respects you very much gave me your name."

"Oh really," said Brown tentatively. "Who was that?"

Steveken shrugged off the question. "He doesn't want to get involved in any of this, but he said you're a man of great integrity and honor."

"You seem to have me at a bit of a disadvantage, Mr. Steveken. What is it you do for a living?"

"I run a security consulting business here in Washington. Before that I was with the FBI for eleven years."

"Oh," Brown announced with genuine trepidation.

"If you have a few minutes, I'd like to ask you some questions."

Brown didn't respond, he simply turned and started

down the path. Steveken fell in beside him. "Judge Brown, I'm going to be blunt with you. I followed some of your cases while you were on the bench. I know that you ran your courtroom by the book. You had a reputation for being very hard on the Bureau."

"Your former employer sometimes thinks they don't have to follow the rules like everyone else."

"You'll get no argument from me, Judge." After a few steps, Steveken asked, "What about your new employer, Judge? Do they like to play by the rules?"

"That's an interesting question." Brown watched Sparky dart off the path again. "Who asked you to come see me?"

Steveken didn't answer right away. He thought about ignoring the question but decided if Brown was going to trust him he'd have to take some gambles. "Congressman Rudin."

"Ah . . . Albert. He's no fan of my current employer."

"Would that be the federal government or the CIA?"

"No, he's a big believer in the federal government, it's the CIA he takes issue with."

"Congressman Rudin seems to think Dr. Kennedy is a bad choice to be the next director."

"Dr. Kennedy is a very competent person."

"So I've heard. Does she like to play by the rules, or does she like to bend them from time to time?"

Brown looked warily at the man Senator Clark had told him to expect. "What are you getting at, Mr. Steveken?"

"You were awfully hard on the FBI. I'm just wondering if you have a new set of standards or if you're using the same ones you had when you were on the bench?"

"Are you questioning my integrity, Mr. Steveken?"

"Not at all, your honor. I know the difficult position

you're in, but I'm here to tell you that it's only going to get worse. If Kennedy is confirmed next week, you're stuck."

"This is a dangerous game you're asking me to play."

"It doesn't have to be. The congressman doesn't want you to get dragged into this. In fact, he thinks you should be the one going through confirmation right now. Not Kennedy."

"That changes nothing. Let's just say hypothetically that I'd seen some things. If I went before the congressman's committee I'd never get another job in this town."

"The congressman knows that. He has no desire to ruin your reputation and turn you into a whistle blower. All he's looking for right now is enough information to slow down Kennedy's confirmation." Steveken stopped and grabbed Brown by the arm. "Something legitimate that he can take to the press. Something from an unnamed source at Langley."

"He wants to slow down Kennedy's confirmation or derail it?"

Steveken grinned. "I'm sure he'd prefer to derail it. I've already told you, he'd rather see you at the helm."

Brown started walking again. "I'll need some time to think about this."

"I'm sorry, Judge, but we don't have a lot of time. The Senate Intelligence Committee is scheduled to vote on Monday afternoon."

Brown stopped abruptly and extended his hand. "It was very interesting meeting you, Mr. Steveken." Brown pumped his hand twice and then leaned in close. He whispered, "Come back tomorrow evening, and we'll talk some more." With that, Brown released Steveken's hand and walked away. In the darkness of the coming night a smile creased his lips. The real world of plotting and trading secrets was far more exhilarating than he'd ever imagined.

THE UNITED STATES Air Force executive jet was on approach for landing. It had left the U.S. Air Force Base in Aviano, Italy, just prior to sunup. There were only two passengers on board, one was sleeping, and the other had been and wished he still was. He'd slept for the first part of the flight, but despite badly needing more, he could not attain the elusive state of rest. His mind simply would not allow it. There was too much to think about.

Mitch Rapp stared out the window at the dark countryside beneath. Porch lights, streetlights and headlights dotted the predawn rural Maryland countryside. He had to admit that the power of the United States was, at times, awesome. Five minutes after Anna had stormed out of their hotel room, a van was waiting for Donatella and him by the side door. There was no time to go after Anna, no time to write a note, no time to try and reason with her. He had to get Donatella out of Italy fast.

Waiting for them outside the hotel was a man who introduced himself only as Chuck. The Agency had sent him. Twenty minutes after leaving the hotel, Rapp and Chuck were carrying Donatella through the back door of a clinic on the outskirts of Milan. They were met by a doctor who was on the CIA's payroll. The elderly man recleaned, packed and dressed Donatella's wound. He typed her blood and replaced two liters through an IV. He gave her more antibiotics and another shot of morphine for the pain. After just two hours at the clinic, the doctor gave Rapp an extra liter of blood plasma to bring with him and specific directions on how to monitor her blood pressure. He told Rapp that her wound was not life threatening and that as long as she continued taking her antibiotics and didn't exert herself for the next four or five days, she'd be fine.

They left the clinic shortly before one in the morning and began their journey across the northern part of Italy, passing through Verona and Venice and then heading north toward Udine. Donatella slept during the entire three-hour drive. Rapp could not afford to. He'd never met this Chuck fellow before, and he wasn't about to trust his life with a complete stranger. When they reached the base they were waved through security and escorted to the waiting plane. Within minutes they were airborne and headed for America, no customs, no police, no video cameras.

Rapp had virtually passed out after takeoff. He and Donatella were alone in the spacious cabin portion of the plane. The flight crew had been told not to disturb their two passengers. A little over four hours into the flight, Rapp had woken up suddenly. He was agitated and disturbed. He'd been having a nightmare. Anna was in his dream. She was in his house with another man. Someone he'd never seen before. They were happy, laughing, holding hands and kissing. Rapp was outside looking in. Anna noticed him in the window and shook her head at him as if to say, *You had your chance and you blew it.* It hurt. He loved her dearly, but the way she'd handled things back at the hotel had given him pause.

Staring out the small window of the plane he was rocked by a barrage of emotions over the entire disaster. He was mad at Donatella and her crazy Italian passion. She didn't need to tell Anna that they'd been lovers. It was hardly the time for the confession. Rapp would like to have thought that it was the morphine talking, but he knew Donatella well enough to know that she was more than capable of such verbal confrontations when she was sober. He could be mad at her for her lack of tact and timing, but that was it. In light of the information he'd been given by her, he had to let the other stuff go, and besides, she'd been very loyal over the years.

As the landing gear locked into the down position, Rapp realized that part of him resented Anna for not understanding the severity of the situation. Hell, she didn't even wait around to let him explain. People had died, Donatella had been shot, and he had just been given a piece of information that would impact the national security of the United States in ways he could only begin to imagine. The news that the head of Mossad was involved in the assassination of a former CIA employee was very serious. A lot of questions needed to be answered. Was Peter Cameron a spy for Mossad, a double agent? Was Ben Freidman acting on his own when he'd ordered the hit, or was he taking orders from someone else? One thing was for certain; things would get worse before they got better. Rapp had gone to Italy to get an answer. All he wanted was a name from Donatella, and he had been foolish enough to think that one name would end it.

Instead, he found himself embroiled in what could become an international crisis. It was clear that Donatella needed to be protected, and she had to tell her story to Kennedy. He'd had no choice other than to get her out of Italy and back to the U.S. as quickly as possible. It was obvious by what had happened at her apartment that Freidman wanted her dead, and Rapp knew that he would not stop until he got what he wanted.

This was the way the last ten-plus hours had gone. He'd bounced back and forth between the crisis with

Freidman and his disintegrating relationship with Anna. His past was pulling him in one direction and his future was vanishing over the next ridge.

As far as Rielly was concerned he saw little hope. He could not tell her what was going on. He couldn't even get into the details of his past with Donatella. Yes, they had been lovers, but that was over. He did not care who Rielly had slept with before they met. He trusted her, and it hurt that it wasn't mutual. It hurt that she didn't understand the complexities of his life. He wasn't walking away from an accounting job after a decade. In his line of work you didn't just simply hand in your two week notice and spend your remaining days hanging out in the break room and taking long lunches. In his world there were no coffee breaks, no long lunches, hell, he didn't even have a desk to clean out. It was a dirty, thankless profession and Rapp knew it sounded trite, but somebody sure as hell had to do it. He was trying his best to get out, and it was all for the sake of his future with Anna.

He was angry at her for not appreciating his sacrifices. He'd killed for his country, he'd bled for his country and they hit one little bump in the road and she was gone. He'd even killed for her once, but he wasn't about to hold that over her head. He would never stoop so low. She either loved him, or she didn't. And right now it looked like she didn't. Rapp didn't know a lot about love, but he knew a lot about commitment and loyalty, and in his mind one of the worst things you could do is run away from your partner. People who really love each other stay and work it out. They don't run. Not Rielly, though, she didn't even give him the chance to explain.

He kept telling himself to withhold judgment on Rielly until he had some time to calm down, but he couldn't help it. The more he thought about her storming out of their hotel room the more it angered him. He had to ask himself if that was the type of woman he wanted to be married to and it scared him that he didn't know the answer. He loved her so much it hurt. It pained him that they were so close to having their life together and then, wham, their whole dream was derailed by one bizarre night in Milan.

Rapp was not good at grays. He liked black and white. Gray made for indecision, and indecision in his line of work was what got you killed. The plane was now floating just above the runway. He was almost home on American soil. The wheels gently touched down and Rapp decided on a plan of action. Rielly would have to wait. He wanted out, but he couldn't just abandon Kennedy. She was his friend, and unlike Rielly, he wasn't about to abandon her. He had to see this other business through, and then he would go to Rielly and explain everything. If she truly loved him, she would accept his apology and give one of her own. If she didn't, no matter how painful that proposition seemed, it was for the better. He would have to move on with his life.

29

ANDREWS AIR FORCE BASE,
FRIDAY MORNING

Irene Kennedy checked her watch. She stood at the door of a large gray metal airplane hangar. Her armor-plated limousine was parked outside about forty feet away. Her security detail was relaxing, leaning against the black gas-guzzler. She sipped hot black coffee from a large travel mug and looked out across the tarmac. The sun wasn't up yet, and despite winter's approach it was surprisingly warm and humid. The air was stagnant with pockets of low lying fog hugging the tree line at the end of the runway. Andrews Air Force Base was a busy place, but not where Kennedy was situated. The hangar that the CIA leased from the air force was on a remote part of the base.

There was a 7:00 A.M. meeting at the Pentagon, and Kennedy needed some one-on-one time to prepare Rapp before the Special Forces guys got their hands on him. Not only did they need to discuss the Iraqi matter, she also wanted more information on Donatella and Ben Freidman. Rapp had given her very few details. She thought that he might fill her in once the plane was over the Atlantic, but she'd been wrong. Whatever else Rapp had to say about her counterpart in Israel, he would not trust to even the Air Force's secure communications equipment, and she didn't blame him. Information of this nature not only needed to be kept from the prying ears of foreigners but also from certain groups in America. When Kennedy had tried to press for details, Rapp had only one word for her: Pollard. The innuendo was clear. Jonathan Pollard was an American caught spying for Israel in the eighties. Pollard's treason had compromised every communiqué sent and received by the U.S. Navy for almost a decade. Israel was masterful at recruiting agents in the U.S. and Kennedy firmly believed there were more Jonathan Pollards out there.

It was human nature to think that only other people had problems. Many parents were slow to believe that their little darling could be causing trouble in school. Other people's children did that. The intelligence community worked the same way. When the navy was caught with a spy in their midst, the air force, the army, the CIA, the FBI, and everybody else pretty much shook their heads and said, "they blew it." Well, Kennedy was a realist. Everybody spied and that pretty much meant everybody was spied on. She remembered the dark days at Langley when Aldrich Ames had been caught by the FBI. Morale was not good during that period, but Kennedy always hearkened to something her boss had said. Thomas Stansfield had been the deputy director of operations at the time. His job, as it had been for over fifty years, was to recruit spies in foreign countries. During the Ames fiasco he had told a conference room full of whining CIA executives that it was the cost of doing business. You can't go into a boxing ring and expect to never get hit, and you can't be in the spying business without getting spied on.

Stansfield had been a big man. He knew how to stay above the petty everyday dealings of Washington. He used to say that ninety-nine percent of the talk in Washington was utterly worthless. To him the key was to take nothing personally and remember the old axiom: whatever goes around comes around. Well, he couldn't have been more prophetic when it came to the Ames case. It was no secret that the FBI and the CIA did not always get along. During the fifties, sixties, seventies and eighties the battles were legendary, and the Ames case only deepened the divide. The FBI adopted a very overt smugness toward the CIA. With Ames, the FBI gloated over how talented they were and how inept the CIA was. Stansfield had said to Kennedy and his other people, "Don't worry, the FBI has a few Aldrich Ameses of their own, they just haven't caught them yet."

Stansfield had been right, and almost seven years after

the Ames case the CIA returned the favor to the FBI when an agent in Moscow told his CIA controller about an FBI special agent named Robert Hanssen. It was the FBI's turn to suffer the humiliation of a traitor in their midst.

All of this was a reminder to her to be cautious. Kennedy took a sip of coffee, and appreciated Rapp's paranoia. They had to communicate via long distances. There was no way around it. They were, after all, in the information exchange business. They just had to be careful who they exchanged the info with. Rapp had made the right call in waiting to tell her in person. Ben Freidman had eyes and ears all over Washington, and she was certain he had a few in Langley, too.

The previous night's sleep had been restless. Kennedy hadn't mentioned the Freidman business to anyone, not even the president. She needed to get a better handle on things before she did that. First, she would have to put her most trusted people on analyzing the damage Peter Cameron may have caused as a double agent for Israel. The group would have to ascertain if there were any others at Langley who could be linked to Cameron. After that the job would become interesting. Kennedy had already begun to form a plan that would give Ben Freidman a taste of his own medicine. The true test of spying was not to simply expose someone. There was another option, one that required real talent.

Kennedy heard the car first and then looked to her left. The white van was rolling down the tarmac toward the Agency's hangar. She had been expecting it. As the vehicle neared she pointed inside the hangar and watched as the nondescript vehicle rolled past her. The van contained three individuals whom she knew Rapp would approve of. They were former Navy SEALs. The leader of the group was Scott Coleman, a former commander of SEAL Team 6. He'd brought with him two of his most trusted operators, Kevin Hackett and Dan Stroble. Rapp had worked with them before. If the president and the Special Forces guys got their way, Rapp would be leaving the country very quickly, and that meant somebody was going to have to baby-sit Donatella. It had to be somebody who Rapp trusted implicitly, and that meant the guys from the CIA's Office of Security were out of the question.

Coleman approached Kennedy and extended his hand. In his late thirties he was still lean, and even a casual observer would notice that he was someone not to be messed with. The former naval officer had a very interesting past. He had killed both abroad and at home, and not all of it was sanctioned by the U.S. government.

Kennedy took his hand. "Thanks for coming on such short notice."

Coleman looked at her with his blue eyes. "No offense, Irene, but you don't look so good. Have you had any sleep lately?"

"Not enough I'm afraid, but I'll make it."

"So what's this all about?"

"Mitch is bringing someone back from Italy."

"Who?"

"The woman who killed Peter Cameron."

Coleman looked at her with genuine surprise. He'd been with Rapp when they'd discovered Cameron's body in his George Washington University office. "Woman?"

"Yes."

"Is she coming back of her own free will, or is he dragging her back?"

Kennedy didn't answer immediately. At some point she had to decide how much she would reveal to Coleman.

She trusted him, but the events of the last several weeks had reinforced the need to know axiom of spying. Theirs was a world where the less that was said, usually the better. In response to Coleman's question she replied, "Yes, she is. Other events that have occurred have driven her into our arms."

"What's that supposed to mean?"

"I don't want to get into it just yet. When they get here we'll know more."

THE PLANE PROCEEDED to the Agency's hangar where the large doors were closed and the engines cut. Kennedy had directed that her own detail stay outside. She didn't want anyone getting a glimpse of Donatella. She wanted no record that the woman was in the United States. Donatella was a very valuable card, and Kennedy knew she would be most effective if no one knew she had her.

The door to the plane opened and Rapp stuck his head out. He waved to Kennedy and Coleman and then he went back in. A few moments later he appeared with a pale and weak-looking Donatella and helped her down the steps. Donatella was wearing a white sling over her bad shoulder.

Coleman whispered to Kennedy, "It looks like she didn't come of her own free will."

Rapp walked across the smooth cement floor. He looked all around the hangar, checking the exits and looking to see who was there. He was in operation mode. Nothing would get past his heightened senses.

He stopped a few feet short of Kennedy and Coleman and said, "This is Donny."

"How is her wound?" asked Kennedy.

"Pretty good, so far, but we should have it checked again."

"I'll make the arrangements," pronounced Kennedy.

Gesturing to his boss, Rapp turned to Donatella and said, "This is Irene Kennedy."

Without lifting her eyes Donatella said in a raspy voice, "I know."

"And this is Scott."

Donatella lifted her eyes for only a second, but said nothing.

"It's really nice to meet you, too," replied Coleman.

Rapp smiled. "Donny is usually a wonderful person, but the last day's been a little rough."

"I called on Scott and the boys to protect Donatella until we figure out what to do. In the meantime you and I have some business to attend to."

Donatella became animated and spoke to Rapp in Italian. "I am not leaving your side."

"That's not possible." Rapp put his hand on her good shoulder and held her hand. "I've trusted Scott with my own life. He and his people are good."

"But *he* has people inside the Agency." She was clearly referring to Freidman.

"Scott and his people don't work for the Agency."

Kennedy did not like not knowing what they were saying. "Translate, please."

Rapp told her of Donatella's concerns. Kennedy almost winced when he told her that Donatella had said, *he has people inside the Agency.* She remained cool and said, "I assumed that he did, and that is why my own security people are outside right now. I've called on Scott because he is someone I trust, and more important, he is someone who Mitch trusts."

Rapp could tell that Donatella was still not enthralled with the idea. "Donny, you have to trust me. In order to help you I have to do some things. I have to meet with some people and you can't be seen. We need to keep you under wraps until the time is right."

Reluctantly she relented, and they walked over to the van. Coleman introduced Donatella to his two men who said only hello. When they had her buckled in, Rapp asked for a moment alone with her and the others walked away.

Rapp brushed a curly black lock of hair from her face. "Donny, don't do anything stupid." She scowled at him. "I'm serious," he said. "These guys can protect you. They're good."

Looking out the window she sized them up. "Military."

"Yep. Retired Navy SEALs."

She sized them up again.

"I know what you're thinking and I want you to get it out of your head right now. They are my friends. Don't even think about running. If you kill them I will kill you." Donatella would not look him in the eye, so Rapp grabbed her chin and made her look at him. "I'm serious. I want you to give me your word that you won't kill any of them. Give me your word that you won't try to run. I can help if you trust me." Rapp looked into her tired eyes. "Do you trust me?"

She did not answer right away, but when she did it was sincere. "Yes, I do."

"Good. Now promise me that you won't hurt any of them."

"I promise." Donatella was looking down.

"Look me in the eye and mean it."

"I promise."

"Good." Rapp retrieved Donatella's silenced pistol from his jacket and handed it to her. "You gave me your word."

"And I meant it." She wasn't able to pull the slide back so she asked, "Is it chambered?"

"Of course."

She looked at the weapon and said, "Thank you."

"No problem. I know you'd do the same."

"I would, you know," she said a little defensively.

Rapp touched her cheek. "I know, and don't be sad, Donny. I'm going to get you your life back." Rapp kissed her on the forehead. "I'll be checking in with you later. Be nice to Scott and the boys."

Rapp got out of the van and went over to the group. "I need to tell you guys a few things about Donny. First of all, she's armed and second of all she's really good."

None of the former SEALs spoke, but Kennedy did. "I don't think that's such a good idea."

"I'm sure you don't, but I do. If I were in her shoes, I'd want to be able to protect myself. And besides, if something goes down, believe me, you want a gun in her hand."

"I don't like it," replied Kennedy firmly.

"Well, you're going to have to live with it, because I don't think we're going to get it back from her." Rapp and Kennedy were very close. Sometimes, like this, when Rapp spoke to her like they were siblings Kennedy thought they'd gotten a little too close. She'd learned over the years to not take it personally, though. Mitch was a one-man show, and when things got tense the traits that had helped him to survive in the field for all these years came to the forefront. He showed little patience, he was controlling and any pretense of civility or respect for a superior was thrown out the window.

Rapp shook Coleman's hand and said, "Thanks for helping out. Be really careful with her, Scott. She's frightened right now and you know what frightened animals do."

Coleman nodded. "Do I need to worry about her taking off?"

After thinking about it, Rapp said, "No. As long as she feels safe, she'll stay put."

"We'll have to make sure she stays safe, then."

"Where are you taking her?"

"Eastern shore of the bay. Irene has all the info."

It was just like the old SEAL to pick a spot on the Chesapeake. Rapp held up his phone. "You've got the number for this, right?"

"Yep."

"All right, call me if you need anything."

"Don't worry, Mitch. I won't let anything happen to her."

Rapp slapped Coleman on the arm and said, "I know you won't."

He walked with Kennedy and Rapp over to the small door and punched the green button that opened the large hangar doors. He went in and got into the van and Kennedy and Rapp walked outside and got into the limousine. Alone in the backseat of the limo Rapp blurted out the question that had been eating away at him. "How is she doing?"

"She's fine. She stayed at the Four Seasons last night."

Before leaving Italy, Rapp had asked Kennedy to have someone keep an eye on Anna. "What did she do today?"

"She left the hotel and went to the Duomo." Kennedy turned to the side so she could better observe Rapp. "My person tells me she's been very emotional. He's seen her crying on three separate occasions."

Rapp dropped his head into his hands. He did not like to hear that she was in pain, but at least she still cared enough to cry.

"Do you want to tell me about it?"

He shook his head slowly.

"I think you might have to."

272 / VINCE FLYNN

"Why?"

"I need to know what she knows."

"Irene, Anna isn't going to say anything."

"I disagree, but my real concern is what Ben Freidman will do when he discovers his men have gone missing."

Rapp thought of the three dead bodies in Donatella's apartment. "Did you get that taken care of?"

"I've been told it's no longer a problem." Kennedy studied Rapp for a moment and said, "I'd feel better if Anna was back here in the States."

Rapp thought he would too, but was reluctant to put any pressure on her. She had said some very hurtful things, and although they were spoken in the heat of the moment, they all had a ring of truth to them. In a solemn voice he said, "I can't ask her to come back."

"Why?"

"I don't want to get into it."

"Is there anything I need to know?"

Rapp shook his head.

"What happened between you and Anna?"

"I don't want to talk about it."

Kennedy was reluctant to say what was on her mind, but felt she couldn't let it go. "What were you thinking when you decided to bring her along?"

That I wanted to ask her to marry me. That I wanted to get out of this shitty thankless job before it sucked all normalcy from me. I was thinking all of that and much more, thought Rapp. He couldn't say it to Kennedy, though. He was too proud. It was time to be tough. Anna had let her true feelings be known. He had been a fool to think that she would marry him. Beautiful, smart Anna Rielly. There were guys all over America who would jump at the chance to marry her, guys with normal jobs, good jobs, guys that could offer stability. Guys who would be willing to move to New York when and if the time came. He'd been a fool for even dreaming of marrying her. An utter idiot for thinking that he could have what other people had. Love had clouded his otherwise good judgment, and Rapp had ignored one simple fact. He was a killer, and killers didn't marry women like Anna Rielly.

Embarrassed that his personal life had interfered with his professional life, Rapp was determined to put an end to this line of discussion and get down to business. "I don't want to talk about Anna."

"Well, I would like to know—"

Rapp cut her off. "I said I'm not going to talk about it, Irene. I made some bad decisions. It's over. Let's move on."

Rapp's words gave Kennedy great concern. "When you say it's over, you don't mean it's over between you and Anna?"

"That's exactly what I mean."

Rapp replied with an intensity that told Kennedy it would be unwise to probe further. It was clear that more had happened in Milan than she knew. Kennedy decided that if Rapp wouldn't call Rielly, she would. With Ben Freidman in his current state of mind she didn't think it was wise to simply let Anna roam about Italy. She would make arrangements to bring Anna home and then she would talk to her.

30

General Flood's office was located in the E Ring of the Pentagon on the second floor. He'd arrived at work well before sunup. He didn't usually come in so early, but the Iraqi problem was weighing heavily on his mind. The president had made it very clear that he wanted to keep a tight lid on the recent developments with Iraq. If Saddam got even the slightest whiff that they were on to him the nukes would be moved, and their chances of ever finding them would vanish. This presented one hell of a problem for General Flood and his people. How do you prepare to wage war without telling your own people? In this regard Saddam had done the U.S. military a great service. He had provided them with the best peacetime live-fire training ground the U.S. had ever seen.

Since the end of the Gulf War the U.S. military's Central Command had kept a very active presence in the region. Most notably they enforced the northern and southern "no fly zones." On a lesser note, the army and Marine Corps regularly conducted exercises in the deserts of Kuwait and Saudi Arabia.

On the clandestine front, the air force and navy conducted almost nonstop photographic and electronic aerial surveillance of Saddam's kingdom. In addition to the military intelligence that was gathered, the National Security Agency and the National Reconnaissance Office probed deep into the heart of Iraq with their billion-dollar satellites orbiting the earth. The Middle Eastern dictatorship had become enemy number one of the U.S., and with such distinction came great attention.

Back on the ground a full-time contingent of Delta Force commandos and Green Berets had been added to the region. They trained regularly with the Special Air Service, Britain's elite commando unit. The American and British commando units had made a habit of ignoring the Iraqi border and running operations that penetrated hundreds of miles into the Iraqi desert. They did not seek out Iraqi troops, but they had been known to engage them from time to time and the battles were very lopsided.

It was all part of a coordinated strategy, to keep the U.S. troops sharp and the enemy wary. The men manning the Iraqi air defenses were loath to turn on their targeting radar for fear that a patrolling U.S. fighter might slam a missile down their throats. The unlucky Iraqis charged with operating in the deserts of southern Iraq and the mountains of northern Iraq had heard one too many stories about their comrades going out on patrol and never returning. The few survivors who did make it back told stories of being ambushed in the middle of the night by men they never saw or heard. Morale in the Iraqi military wasn't good.

But for General Flood it was the opposite. His men were well trained, well equipped and ready to go. The Iraqi theater was one massive ongoing drill. The wealth of information that was collected was constantly fed to air force, navy, Marine Corps and army experts who continually updated their target assessments. The result was that an effective and concise battle plan was never more than twelve hours away.

In essence, Flood did not need to let a half million

American troops in on the secret. All he needed to do was tell the Joint Chiefs that the president wanted options. That Saddam had once again pissed off President Hayes. None of this was unusual. Since the Gulf War a single year hadn't passed without some type of military action being leveled against Baghdad's Bad Man. Flood could tell the Central Command that he wanted them to put together a comprehensive bombing plan, and he would have a preliminary report on his desk within the hour. The whole force would be ready to strike in a day or less. General Flood wielded a mighty stick.

It was no small comfort to him that his front line troops were ready to commence such a large operation on such short notice. It gave him the peace of mind to tackle a far more complicated problem, the problem of trying to steal three nuclear weapons out from under Saddam's nose.

His intercom buzzed and one of his four administrative assistants announced that his visitors had arrived. Flood said to show them in. He stood and as he buttoned his green jacket, he looked down at the shelf of brightly colored ribbons on his barrel chest. He remembered in detail how each one had been obtained. Many of them were B.S. Given to him for things that he thought had little to do with soldiering, but there were a few that he was very proud of.

A strange thought occurred to the general. *How many ribbons and medals would Mitch Rapp have been awarded if he'd been in the army instead of the CIA?* Flood had seen some great soldiers in action over the years, and there was no doubt in his mind that Mitch Rapp was one of them. Maybe the best. Flood desperately wanted to believe in Rapp's abilities. He'd told no one of his dreams lately, but they horrified the old soldier. He had been visited in his sleep by the specter of nuclear battle. On a nightly basis he found himself looking out over a charred battlefield. The golden soft sand of the desert was burnt and black. The bodies of his soldiers were strewn about, thousands of them, charred from the heat wave of a nuclear detonation.

General Flood had never met Saddam face-to-face. He'd never even talked to the man, but he'd studied him and felt he knew him well. Or at least he knew his type. The pages of history books were sprinkled with megalo-maniacs just like him. It seemed that every century could count a half dozen as their own.

Flood was willing to risk his entire career to make sure Saddam never got the chance to use those weapons. This would be the biggest gamble he'd ever taken. Sending a dozen Delta Force commandos into the heart of Baghdad, during the middle of an air strike, to steal three nuclear warheads was pushing the odds a bit. If the mission failed the critics would stone him from the bleachers and then they would go after the president. At a bare minimum he wanted Rapp leading the way. The man with the Midas touch. He had a way of succeeding where others failed.

Irene Kennedy entered the room first. Her small stature was perfect for her profession. She was not the first person noticed in a crowd. Mitch Rapp, on the other hand, was a different matter. In his black leather jacket and two-day-old beard, he stood out like a sore thumb. Fortunately, General Flood's staff practiced discretion with his visitors, especially when they arrived before 7:00 A.M. and were in the company of the director designate of the CIA.

Flood met them midway across his large office. "Good morning, Irene."

"Good morning, General."

Flood reached out for Rapp's hand. "Thanks for coming in to see me, Mitch."

"Not a problem, sir." Rapp liked Flood, so he lied. There were other things that he would rather be attending to, but he would hear the man out.

"Please, sit." Flood motioned to an arrangement of two couches and several chairs on his right. There was a small table in the middle. On top was a basket of muffins, a coffeepot, sugar and cream and several cups, as well as side plates. "I figured you'd be hungry, Mitch. Help yourself to whatever you want." Flood leaned forward and poured a cup of coffee. "Irene?"

"Please." Kennedy took the cup, but passed on the muffins. "Thank you."

Rapp poured himself a cup and took a muffin. "Irene tells me you have a little bit of a problem."

"I'd say so. How many times have you been in Baghdad?"

"Before the war I spent a lot of time there, but since the war I've only been back three times."

The general looked at Kennedy. "How much does he know?"

"Unfortunately, I didn't have time to brief him. We had some other things that we needed to discuss."

Flood didn't bother to ask what, but he was a little surprised that they could have something else cooking that would take priority over his current problem. "Mitch, you're about to become part of a very select group. The Joint Chiefs don't even know what I'm about to tell you. The president has asked us to keep an extremely tight lid on this."

"Understood."

"A week ago one of our allies came to us with some pretty damning intelligence that Saddam is about to go operative with three nuclear weapons." Flood stopped so Rapp would have a chance to absorb the seriousness of the problem. To his surprise Rapp smiled.

"I knew it."

"Knew what?" asked Flood. "Don't tell me you already knew."

"No. I just knew sooner or later it would come to this. That's why I disagreed when we stopped back in 1991. We should have gone all the way to Baghdad and ousted the nut bag."

"You don't need to tell me. I was over there with my Rangers preparing a nighttime assault on several bridges when the truce was announced. We could have been in Baghdad in two days, but the man who previously occupied this office, in his infinite wisdom, convinced President Bush to stop. Thanks to him I am now confronted with a much bigger problem than the invasion and occupation of Kuwait."

"How much time do we have?" asked Rapp.

Flood looked to Kennedy. She turned to Rapp and said, "This information was provided by the Israelis. We have a little more than a week to take the bombs out, or they will do it themselves."

In light of his recent trip to Italy, Israel was not at the top of his favorite country list. Rapp was tempted to say, *let them,* but kept his mouth shut. When he and Kennedy were alone he would probe deeper in regard to the veracity of the intelligence provided by Israel. "I assume we know where the bombs are?"

"Yes." Flood got up and went over to his desk. He came back with a file containing aerial photographs of the target. "We don't have anybody on the inside, but we've been told they are located here." Flood pointed to a building circled in red. "That's the Al Hussein Hospital."

Kennedy added, "About a year ago they built a hardened bunker under the hospital."

Rapp looked up. "Saddam figured we'd never find it, and if we did, we wouldn't have the balls to bomb it."

"Exactly," Kennedy answered.

"Do you know where the hospital is?" Flood asked.

"Yeah." Rapp threw the photos on the table. "I've been in the area before." Not one to beat around the bush, Rapp added, "So, where do I fit in?"

Flood sat back down and let out a sigh. "We've already put a plan in front of the president to take out the bunker with some new bombs that are designed to penetrate command and control structures."

Rapp didn't like the idea of dropping a bunch of bombs on a hospital. He liked the people of Iraq. They were caught between an inhumane dictator and a superpower that was hell-bent on destroying them. "What are the odds for success?"

"Good. My fly-boys tell me they can virtually guarantee the destruction of the facility."

"Then why am I here?" Rapp knew at least part of the answer, but he wanted to hear it from Flood. He'd done this type of stuff before. Sneak into a country, sit on a rooftop and paint the target with a laser designator. The fly-boys weren't quite as good as they liked to advertise. When they really needed to hit something, they usually put someone on the ground first.

"Several reasons, actually. First of all, your old friend Colonel Gray asked for you. Apparently he thinks you're pretty good at your job." Flood grinned. "And as soon as the president heard your name mentioned, he insisted that you be involved."

"In what capacity?"

"Bombing the target has some drawbacks."

"Like killing a bunch of innocent civilians?"

"Mitch, we didn't put those nukes under that hospital."

"I know we didn't. I'm just pointing out the shitty reality of the situation."

"As always I appreciate your frankness, and I agree with you. So do a lot of others, and that's one of the reasons we're working on a second plan."

Rapp raised an eyebrow. "And would that involve Colonel Gray?"

"Yes, it would. The colonel has come up with a bold but ingenious plan." Flood went on to explain the use of the white cars to ferry the Delta team into Baghdad under the cover and mass confusion of an all-out aerial bombardment. He also told Rapp that the president hoped one of the bombs could be brought back as proof that Saddam was working on acquiring the ultimate weapon of mass destruction. Flood ended by saying, "This plan is quite a bit riskier than simply bombing the facility, but it offers two distinct advantages."

"We don't have to kill a bunch of innocent noncombatants."

"Exactly, and we also make sure that the bombs are taken out. We could bomb the facility and still never really know if all three weapons were in the structure at the time."

Rapp leaned back, thinking about the plan, trying to calculate the odds of success, the areas where it was weak. There was no doubt that Colonel Gray had come up with one hell of a plan. After a lengthy period of silence, Rapp looked at Kennedy and said, "So, one more time, where do I come in?"

31

She'd returned to the hotel after midnight, relieved to find that Mitch and the bitch from hell were gone. Rielly was in no mood for confrontation. The feeling of relief was short lived, however. It lasted as long as it took to take one lap through the suite. Mitch's bag was gone, and there was no note. No letter saying he was sorry. No letter saying he blew it and that he loved her dearly, that he would do whatever it took to make it up to her.

Rielly had collapsed on the bed in a huff of tears. She couldn't understand what had happened. How two people with so much attraction and genuine love for each other could part so quickly. The tears turned to anger, as she placed all the blame squarely on Rapp's shoulders. She did blame herself for one thing, however. Allowing herself to fall in love with a man who would just walk out on her was the dumbest thing she'd ever done.

Rielly was well aware of the fact that she'd told him to get out of her life, but if he truly loved her, he would have ignored her request and proved his love. He hadn't, though. He'd left with the little Italian slut, and he hadn't even bothered to leave a note. A simple sorry would have gone a long way.

When Rielly awoke the next morning she was still in her clothes from the night before. A hangover gnawed at her, the result of the three vodka tonics and the three glasses of wine she'd downed at a bar after she'd stormed out of the hotel. Her eyes were puffy from all the crying and in general she felt like shit, both emotionally and physically. Before entering the shower the thought occurred to her to go home, to just pack up and get the hell out of Italy.

By the time she got out of the shower she was resolved to stay. She would not simply run home. None of this was her fault. She had six days of vacation left and she was going to enjoy it. Rielly dressed with a determination to make the best of the trip. To enjoy her day in Milan and then head south for warmer weather and a few days in the sun.

The day had turned out to be a real roller coaster of emotions. There were tears and determination, longing and anger, second-guessing and righteous indignation. Anna Rielly was, in short, miserable. She'd explored the Duomo, the magnificent cathedral of Milan that had taken over 400 years to complete. The awe-inspiring beauty of the church could move even the most emotionally stable person. In Rielly's fragile condition the tears flowed frequently, and she found herself asking God why. Why had he allowed her to fall in love with Mitch Rapp? Of all the men in the world, why him?

God didn't answer her question. After spending the entire morning at the Duomo she moved on to shopping. That helped for a while, but all too frequently she found herself looking at clothes and wondering if Mitch would like them. All in all the day had proved one thing to her. That she loved Mitch Rapp more than she had ever realized.

Her last act of bravado was to go out for dinner. Anna Rielly was nothing if not stubborn, and she'd be damned if she was going to sit in her room and pout. The concierge at the hotel got her a reservation at Leo, a nice restaurant within walking distance of the hotel. The place was known for great fresh fish and an unpretentious atmosphere. Rielly dressed conservatively for the evening. She didn't want to sit in her room and hide, but she had no desire to attract the attention of any male company.

Upon arriving at the restaurant she was seated at a table for two by the front window. She ordered a glass of Foradori Pinot Noir and began perusing the menu. She was there for all of five minutes when a man approached her table. He asked Rielly if he could join her, and she politely declined. For dinner she ordered penne with prawns and grilled razor clams and a second glass of wine. It was delicious. Midway through her meal a second man approached her table and sat. He was dressed nicely in a dark suit and tie. He looked to be around fifty. Rielly was immediately irritated, and was about to tell him to get lost when something unusual happened.

"Good evening, Ms. Rielly. I apologize for intruding like this, but a mutual acquaintance asked me to give you a message."

Anna's heart leapt. "Mitch?"

"No." The man casually looked around the restaurant. "Dr. Kennedy." Extending his hand he said, "My name is Tino Nanne. I work at the consulate here in Milan."

"The U.S. consulate."

"That's correct."

Rielly lowered her voice. "Is everything all right with Mitch?"

"I wouldn't know, Ms. Rielly. I've only been told to give you a message."

Eagerly, Anna asked, "And what is that?"

"Dr. Kennedy thinks you should return to the U.S."

Anna was instantly taken aback. "What do you mean?"

"I know next to nothing. I've simply been told to give you a message. Dr. Kennedy, for reasons unknown to me, thinks you should return to the U.S. immediately."

"You work for the CIA?"

The man winced at the acronym and looked around. "I work for the State Department, and please be careful about what you say."

Rielly, always the reporter, was used to asking what she wanted whenever she wanted. "I think you know more than you're telling me."

"I know a lot of things, young lady." The man stood. "But as far as you are concerned, and why you're supposed to return to the States, I know nothing." He reached inside the breast pocket of his suit coat and grabbed a business card. "If you need anything, call me." He placed the card on the table and left the restaurant.

TEL AVIV, FRIDAY EVENING

BEN FREIDMAN WAS busy pecking away at his computer. The younger people at Mossad called it surfing the Web; he called it doing research. Freidman did not look natural in front of a keyboard. His bald head, broad shoulders and thick forearms were more suited for heavy labor. His stubby index fingers pounded away at the keys. It was slow going but it worked. A cigarette dangled from his lips, a curved hunk of gray ash ready to break free at any second. At the last second Freidman snatched the cigarette from his mouth and deposited the spent vice in an ashtray. He grabbed his small four-ounce coffee cup in his meaty hands and gulped down the remaining few ounces of thick black coffee.

"Adriana!" He yelled his assistant's name without taking his eyes off the screen. "More coffee, please." Freidman

was worried. It had been a full day since the hit was to
have taken place. Rosenthal was to have e-mailed him the
results of the operation, and as of yet there was nothing.
He was now checking the online version of Milan's newspaper, looking for what would undoubtedly be a big
story. So far he'd come up with nothing.

It was possible that Rosenthal had killed her and dis-
posed of her body without anyone knowing. That was
what Freidman had asked him to do. Maybe Rosenthal
had run into a few problems and it was taking longer to
get out of Italy and back to Israel. Anything was still possible, but with each passing hour of silence, the chances
that things had gone according to plan diminished. At this
stage Freidman had no choice but to try to stay calm,
despite the fact that his gut told him Donatella had not
gone down without a fight.

He'd trained her. He should have known better. It was
the damn money Senator Clark waved in his face. He
should have firmly told him not to worry. That he knew
Donatella, and she would keep her mouth shut. Freidman
had to be honest with himself, though. It was more than
just the money. Donatella was a bit of a loose cannon and
sooner or later, he figured he'd have to deal with her. She
knew too many of his secrets, and with her temper there
was no telling when she would explode and take him
down with her.

No, Freidman decided. It hadn't been a mistake to go
after her. It had been a mistake to not send more people.
Freidman needed to start working on a cover story.
Rosenthal couldn't go missing for too many more days
without some people starting to ask where he was. Why
had he sent Rosenthal to Italy? That would be the first
hurdle to overcome. He felt confident that he could come
up with a pretty good lie to handle that problem, but if

Donatella was still alive, and she started making waves, he could be in big trouble. Freidman grabbed his phone and punched in an extension.

A moment later a woman answered and he said, "I need you in my office right now." He hung up and wondered how much he'd have to tell this one. Not much, he decided. She could go to Milan and start digging around. Hopefully, Rosenthal would contact him and report that the mission was a success, before she even got there. Freidman knew the chances of that happening were between slim and none.

32

CAPITOL HILL, FRIDAY AFTERNOON

The motorcade of two government sedans and a limousine pulled up to the loading dock of the Hart Senate Office Building. Normally they would have used the front of the building, but today it was swarming with media. Dr. Irene Kennedy emerged from the limo. Her detail quickly escorted her into the building and brought her to the second floor. One of the staffers from the Senate Intelligence Committee was waiting for them. The man showed Kennedy into one of the private witness rooms at the rear of room 216 and then left her alone. Her detail also stayed outside. Kennedy wanted a few minutes of solitude before the confirmation circus started.

She used the room's private bathroom to wash her hands and check her makeup. She'd applied an unusually heavy amount today knowing that she'd be on TV. She touched up her lips a bit and put some more powder on her nose and forehead. Looking into the mirror she told herself, *No matter what happens stay calm, and don't be afraid to say, I don't know.*

Kennedy left the bathroom and took a seat at the small conference table. She knew all of the men on the committee. She'd sat in front of them countless times before and answered their questions. The only thing that was different about today was the media. Kennedy had just gotten settled in when there was a knock on the door.

Senator Clark entered with a warm grin on his face. "Irene, how are you?" Clark closed the door.

Kennedy stood. "Just fine, Mr. Chairman."

"Irene, how many times do I have to tell you, it's Hank when we're alone like this." He placed a hand on her shoulder. "I could never get your boss, God rest his soul, to call me by my first name, but he was twenty years my senior so I cut him a little slack." Clark winked at Kennedy. "You don't have that excuse, so from now on it's Hank when we're alone. All right?"

Kennedy nodded. "All right, Hank."

"Good. Now, are you nervous at all? Is there anything I can get you before we go out there?"

"No, I'm fine, thank you."

Clark looked down at the diminutive Kennedy and felt a pang of sorrow for her. He really did like her. It was too bad that she was going to have to go through this. "I don't expect things to get rough. Most of the men out there like you, and with the president and myself backing you, the votes are already there. You might get a few tough questions from Schuman, but don't sweat it. That's just him grandstanding in front of the cameras."

"I know. I've seen him do it plenty of times."

"I'll do my best to keep him in line along with any others who might get a little unruly, but ultimately it's up to you to handle them."

"I know. I've done this before, Hank."

"But you've never done it in front of all these cameras and reporters." There was no smile on his face. "Be very careful what you say in front of this crowd. One slipup and they'll pile on."

Kennedy showed no fear. "I know."

"Well, you're the only show this afternoon, so when you're ready, we'll go." Clark pointed toward the door with his thumb.

"I'm ready."

Clark gave her another warm smile and then wrapped his arms around her for a hug. "Good luck out there." He released her and said, "Let's go make history."

Kennedy followed him out of the room. The hallway was crowded with people. Every single one of them stopped talking when Clark and Kennedy appeared. The senator towered above everyone, even the men from Kennedy's security detail. He continued through another door and Kennedy followed him out onto the side of the dais located at the front of the hearing room. Clark gestured for Kennedy to head out to the witness table and he continued up to take his place at the center of the long U-shaped bench with the other senators.

The gallery was filled with reporters and TV crews. Today was an historic moment. The first woman ever nominated to run the CIA was about to begin her confirmation hearing. The hearing was not scheduled to be aired live by any of the networks or major cable outlets other than C-SPAN, but every network was there to get a clip for what would be the lead story on the nightly news.

As Kennedy approached the witness table she was

nearly blinded by camera flashes. She'd left an entire entourage back at Langley. The people from legal and public relations had wanted to sit at the table with her, or at the very least in the first row. They wanted to be there to help manage a situation in case one arose. Kennedy had declined all requests. It was a point of pride that she go through this alone. No photo ops of men whispering in her ear, as if she couldn't answer a question on her own. Kennedy had looked forward to this day for a long time. She wasn't always sure it would happen, but that didn't stop her from dreaming. As the political climate changed in Washington over the last two decades she began to realize that within her lifetime it was likely that a woman would head the CIA. It was inevitable. The old boy network that had run the Agency during its first fifty years wouldn't like it one bit. Kennedy's potential to men like Allen Dulles and William Casey would have been to get them a cup of coffee and maybe type a few letters. They were different men from a different generation.

Kennedy looked up at the senators seated in their high back leather chairs. They were her judges. Sixteen men in total, not a single woman among the group and all but one of them a millionaire. This didn't bother Kennedy in the least. She was in good standing with almost all of them, and the few that she didn't know well, were not the type to cause problems. One or two of them might try to grandstand, but she could handle them. For the most part they respected her, and she respected them. None of it was personal. That's what she kept telling herself. This was the business of government.

The photographers sitting on the floor between the witness table and the dais continued snapping photos. As Senator Clark looked down from on high, Kennedy returned his smile and nodded that she was ready. It was comforting to have an ally chairing the committee. For some unknown reason, at that exact moment she felt a nagging fear creep up on her. She was finally here, literally days away from taking over as the director the most powerful espionage agency in the world, and she couldn't shake the feeling that something was going to trip her up. She had two very serious issues to deal with right now, and she certainly couldn't let the committee know about either of them. They would know soon enough about the problem with Iraq, but the president had been adamant that everyone act as if it were business as usual. There would be no request for a delay in the hearings so she could deal with these monstrous problems. She would have to sit here for the remainder of the day and answer an unending stream of questions, the vast majority of them mundane or self-serving.

Senator Clark gaveled the room to order and greeted Kennedy by lowering his mouth to the microphone. After taking care of a few housekeeping matters he asked the relatively young director designate to rise, raise her hand and repeat after him. Kennedy did so, and as she raised her right hand, the flashes once again erupted. These were seasoned photographers, and Kennedy knew why they wanted that shot. They needed it in case she was ever caught lying. If that happened they needed the photo to run under the headline, *CIA Director Lied to Congress.* Kennedy recited the pledge and told herself to be very careful. There were so many lies, so many places where she could be tripped up.

WOLF TRAP PARK, VIRGINIA,
FRIDAY EVENING

STEVEKEN WAS FREEZING his ass off. If he'd been thinking, he would have worn his long underwear; but he hadn't been, of course. It was the first really cold night of the sea-son and he'd been caught off guard. Without gloves he kept his hands shoved into the pockets of his trench coat. At least he'd zipped the winter liner into the jacket the day before. The temperature was already down into the thirties and was supposed to get below freezing. It was really dark out, much darker than the night before. Steveken had been at the park for almost thirty minutes, not so patiently waiting for the judge to arrive. Since his meeting with Brown the night before, he'd done some digging, and it wasn't into Irene Kennedy's career. It was into the judge's.

Some of his old friends at the Bureau were more than willing to talk. Not wanting to lie, Steveken told his contacts that Brown was being considered for a job and the prospective employer wanted a simple background check done. A picture formed pretty early in his calls, and it wasn't far from what he remembered hearing about Brown. He was not well liked by the FBI. He was considered a very liberal judge who'd been known to throw entire cases out on minor technicalities. Steveken had even been turned on to one former federal prosecutor who said Judge Brown was the most self-righteous and pontificating judge he'd ever tried a case in front of. There hadn't been a lot of positive things said about the man, but Steveken had to admit his sample was biased with people from law enforcement, the exact type of people you would expect to hate a liberal judge. There was one person though, of the nine people he'd talked to, who had surprised him—a retired judge who had worked with Brown on the court of appeals, a judge who had a reputation for being every bit the liberal. The man had told Steveken that Brown would sell his soul to advance his career.

Steveken had yet to decide what to do with that information. If Senator Clark asked he would probably give it to him, but he doubted he would pass it on to Rudin. The congressman from Connecticut was one of the least likable people he'd ever met.

Conversely, he'd watched a little bit of Kennedy's testimony on C-SPAN and he'd been impressed. She seemed very likable, and had handled herself well. It was also obvious that no one had tested her. Steveken figured that was due to Senator Clark keeping everyone in line. He'd given his word to the president, and there would be no wild accusations thrown at Kennedy without some proof to back them up.

Steveken wasn't quite sure what to make of the things Rudin had told him about Stansfield and Kennedy. The crass old man didn't have a shred of proof, but at the same time, Steveken fully believed the CIA was capable of every single accusation that Rudin had leveled. The truth was the CIA had to deal with a lot of shitty people. The types of people, who under normal circumstances you'd never even consider entering into a partnership with. But the problem was, the CIA wasn't asked to deal with normal situations. They were asked to associate with drug dealers, arms dealers, dictators, despots, terrorists and thugs, just to name a few. And when you do business with people like that you're going to get your hands dirty sometimes.

Thanks to Rudin's irritating personality, Steveken found himself in the awkward position of feeling empathy for Kennedy and the CIA. Part of him hoped Brown wouldn't show up tonight. Part of him hoped that he'd be able to meet the old prick for lunch, tell him he came up empty, and then stick him with the tab. Steveken laughed to himself in the cold darkness as he imagined the sour look on Rudin's face.

Something caught Steveken's eye. He looked off into the distance and saw a red orb glow bright and then disappear. A moment later it was back, like a firefly picking its way through the darkness. It kept getting closer. Steveken heard the tapping of a dog's feet on the asphalt right about the time he smelled tobacco. It was a pipe, he realized. Brown had been smoking a pipe the night before.

Brown stopped several feet away, and in the glow of his pipe, Steveken thought he noticed a hint of smugness on the man's face. "Good evening, Judge."

"How are you tonight, Mr. Steveken?"

"Cold. You're running late tonight."

"I had to gather some things for you."

Steveken resisted the urge to put his hand out. "So what do you have?"

Brown hesitated for a moment and then said, "Let me give you some advice." He reached into his jacket and extracted a large manila envelope. "Don't open this. Just hand it to Congressman Rudin, and tell him you have no idea what's in it." Brown gave the envelope to Steveken and added with emphasis, "Under no circumstances are you to tell him where you got this." Brown looked him hard in the eye. "The man who gave me this information just up and disappeared two weeks ago. I'm assuming he's dead."

Brown didn't give Steveken a chance to reply. He started back down the path and said, "Do yourself a favor and get rid of that package as quickly as possible. Congressman Rudin will know what to do with it."

With his mouth slightly agape, the normally talkative Steveken found himself at a loss for words. He just stood there with the envelope in hand watching as Brown disappeared into the darkness. When the judge was too far away to hear, Steveken mumbled, "Thanks for nothing." He had the distinct feeling that he was being played, but he owed Clark too much to do anything about it.

33

THE WHITE HOUSE, FRIDAY EVENING

As night fell on Washington the limousine approached the White House. Rapp didn't like coming here, too many cameras, too many reporters, and too many people who liked to talk. Besides, in his present state he looked like someone who would like to assault the president, not meet with him. He hadn't accepted the mission yet, but he knew which way he was leaning. It would be a quick insertion, and because of that he couldn't shave, at least not until he knew what his cover would be. If he had to go in across the desert and play the role of a nomad, he would need a scruffy beard to pull it off. After missing several days with the razor it was already thick. He was wearing his black leather jacket, and in an attempt to fit in a bit he was wearing a blue U.S. Secret Service baseball hat.

As the limousine pulled up to the southwest gate of the White House Kennedy leaned over to Rapp and said, "Have you ever noticed the president paces when he's upset?"

Rapp had to think about it for a second. He seemed to remember that the president was prone to standing in meetings, but not the pacing part. "I've noticed he stands a lot."

"He stands because his back bothers him," she said in her clinical tone. "That doesn't mean he's mad. When he starts pacing, that means he's mad."

Kennedy was a frequent visitor to the White House, and the limo was allowed through the heavy gate without inspecting the passengers. Before the vehicle came to a stop Rapp asked, "So, do you think he's going to do some pacing?"

After rolling her eyes, Kennedy said, "I think this is going to infuriate him like nothing I've ever seen." The limo stopped in front of the awning on West Executive Drive. "It's a good thing we're meeting in the Situation Room. That way he can scream his head off, and no one will hear a word of it."

Rapp let Kennedy get out first and he followed close behind, keeping the brim of his hat tilted down. When they went through the door Jack Warch, the special agent in charge of the president's Secret Service detail, was waiting for them with his hand extended palm up. Rapp took his weapon from his shoulder holster, checked to make sure the red dot was covered and then handed the gun over to Warch. Warch thanked him and the three of them started down the hallway.

"Nice hat," Warch said with a grin.

"I earned it," Rapp backhanded the Secret Service agent in the stomach, "by bailing your ass out."

Warch laughed. "No arguments here."

"Hey," said Rapp. "When are you going to trust me to carry in this place?"

"It's procedure, Mitch. You know that."

"Yeah, but come on. I've fired more rounds in this place than your entire detail."

Warch was quiet for a moment as he thought about the hostage standoff that had taken place not so long ago.

Rapp had bailed everyone out, that was for certain. "Let me talk to the president about it. We'll see if he'll make an exception."

They turned into the area of offices known as the Situation Room and stopped at a heavy reinforced door with a camera mounted above it. Warch punched his code into the cipher lock and opened the door. Immediately on the left was the soundproof conference room. "He's in there waiting for you."

Kennedy and Rapp found the president alone, sitting at the head of the table with his back to the door. The president stood immediately and grabbed Rapp's hand. "Mitch, thank you for coming. I really appreciate it. Irene tells me you've been doing some traveling."

"Yeah," Rapp had no desire to get into the subject of Italy, at least not the personal aspect of his trip. He sat one spot farther away from the president and Kennedy took the seat between them. President Hayes asked if either of them would like anything to drink. They both declined.

Hayes plopped himself down in his leather chair. The man looked tired. There were dark circles under his eyes and his hair was slightly mussed. The white sleeves of his dress shirt were rolled up and his top button was undone. It looked like the crisis was getting to him.

Hayes picked up his reading glasses and twirled them around. "Irene, I heard you did a nice job on the Hill this afternoon."

"It seemed to go smoothly."

"Good." Turning his attention to Rapp the president said, "General Flood tells me he talked with you this morning."

"That's right."

"So what do you think?"

"I think we have one hell of a problem."

"We sure do," replied the president, "and that's why I want you involved." The commander in chief of the world's sole superpower stared unflinchingly at one of his best offensive weapons.

Rapp already knew his answer. His day had been filled with a repeating chain of thoughts: Anna, Donatella, and Baghdad. It had gone like that over and over. As soon as he stopped thinking about one it was on to the next. He didn't know it, but he'd already started to build walls around the Anna issue. His feelings were hurt, and his defense mechanisms had kicked in. His undying love had been damaged. He'd begun to question Anna's loyalty and sense of commitment. Maybe she wasn't the one for him. Not if she wouldn't give him the common courtesy of allowing him to explain himself. The more Rapp thought about her storming out in Milan, the more distance it put between them. If she couldn't understand the importance of what he did, he was better off without her.

That, at least, was the flimsy conclusion he'd come to the last time he'd thought of her. It had been several hours earlier. He'd gone to his home on the bay to get some things, and he was instantly awash in memories of Anna. Everywhere he turned there were reminders of her. They were too painful to deal with, so he pushed them from his mind. He hurriedly gathered his things and left. He refused to admit the truth to himself. That he would give or do almost anything to get her back. Rapp was too busy putting up walls. Sealing off that part of his life so he could deal with more urgent problems.

"We really need your help on this one, Mitch," the president pleaded.

For the most part, Rapp had already made up his mind. For a lot of good reasons he didn't want the hospital bombed by the air force. The Iraqi patients and the medical staff inside should be spared if at all possible, and on an almost equal footing was the fallout from the bombing. Every terrorist group in the Middle East would receive an influx of cash and recruits as a result of the military action. The evil United States of America would be blamed for everything. No one would dare question Saddam's despicable act of placing the facility under a hospital. The anger would be directed toward America. Leveling the hospital would create more problems down the road. He'd seen it before.

These were the reasons he would give to the president and Kennedy, but there was a third. It was one that he would never speak of. It was one that only a warrior would understand. Colonel Gray knew it without question. The challenge, the thrill of such a mission was something that very few would ever experience. This operation was the sort that could shape history. It would be written about years from now as either one of the greatest Special Forces successes of all time or one of the most spectacular blunders. It would be looked at as the Mount Everest of covert operations. For Rapp to walk away from such a crusade was unthinkable.

He looked at President Hayes and said, "Sir, you can count on me."

President Hayes let out a sigh of relief. "You'll never know how comforting it is for me to have you involved."

"I'll do my best."

"I'm sure you will. Any ideas yet, on how you're going to get in?"

"I've got a couple, but I want to run them by Colonel Gray first."

"Understandable."

"Sir," interjected Kennedy. "There's something else we need to discuss with you."

Hayes could tell by the tone of her voice that it was serious. He leaned back in his chair and formed a steeple with his hands. "Let's hear it."

"We know who killed Peter Cameron."

The president bounced forward immediately. "Who?"

"Her name is Donatella Rahn. She used to work for Mossad, and now she's what we refer to as an independent contractor."

The president cocked his head to the side. "You said she used to work for Mossad."

"That's correct, sir."

"What in the hell is she doing killing former employees of the CIA and American citizens?"

Rapp spoke up. "She didn't know who he was, sir. She was simply hired, wired a sum of money and given the basic information on her target. Nowhere in the information did it say that Cameron used to work for the CIA."

"Who hired her to kill Cameron?"

Rapp didn't feel it was his place to answer the question so he turned to his boss. Kennedy scratched the tip of her nose with the back of her hand and said, "We don't know who took the contract out on Cameron, sir, but we know who Donatella's handler is." Kennedy looked down briefly, taking a moment to steel herself against the ensuing explosion.

"Who?"

"Donatella's handler is Ben Freidman."

"What?" the question spat from the president's mouth as if it had a bad taste to it.

"Somebody, we do not know who, contacted Ben Freidman and took out a hit on Peter Cameron. It was a rush job and it paid well. Freidman in turn gave the job to Donatella."

"And she succeeded!" The president stood and started pacing. "How in the hell did we get this information?"

"Mitch has worked with Donatella before."

The president stopped and spun around. Looking at Rapp he said, "You've worked with this woman. What in the hell is that supposed to mean?"

"When she was with Mossad, sir, we conducted several operations against Hezbollah." Rapp was not the type to be unnerved by a little emotion, even if it came from the president. "I have a lot of trust and respect for her, sir."

Rapp's words caused the president to back off a bit. Turning to Kennedy he asked, "What in the hell is Ben Freidman doing involved in something like this?"

"I'm not sure, sir."

Before she finished her answer Hayes had resumed his pacing. "Why is it that I get this horrible feeling that Israel has been meddling in the affairs of this country?"

"I'm not so sure, sir." Kennedy spoke carefully. "We have debriefed Donatella and she claims—"

"What do you mean, debriefed? We have her?"

"Yes. She's here in the U.S. Mitch brought her back from Italy. That's where she lives."

"What?" The president was beet red with anger.

Rapp thought it was time to weigh in. "Sir, we had a suspicion that Donatella may have been involved in Cameron's death, so I went to Italy to talk to her. While I was visiting her there was an attempt on her life. It would appear that she had outgrown her usefulness to Colonel Freidman."

Hayes stopped pacing and stabbed his index fingers onto the surface of the table. "Irene, does the attempt on Mitch's life in Germany and the assassination of Peter Cameron have anything to do with this crap going on in Baghdad?"

After hesitating, Kennedy replied, "I don't think so, sir, but I'm looking into it."

Now Hayes's face was really red. "Well, what do you say I pick up the phone and call Prime Minister Goldberg?"

Kennedy shook her head. "I don't think that's a good idea, sir."

"Well, I do," snapped Hayes. "I don't like it when our allies are involved in the assassination of Americans." Hayes pointed and added, "Especially when it happens less than a mile from the White House."

Kennedy decided it was time to be more forceful. "Sir, you'll get no disagreement from me. Ben Freidman is going to have to answer some very tough questions, but as of right now I don't think the problem in Baghdad has anything to do with this. Our satellite images tell us that something unusual was built under that hospital. Most likely some type of a hardened bunker. Also, the information on the North Koreans checks out, and we know Saddam has been working toward this goal for some time. As far as the other issue is concerned, Donatella tells us Freidman set this deal up with her when she left Mossad. Freidman takes a third of the contract and everything is run through him. Donatella says the fee on Cameron was a half a million dollars. She claims Israel would never pay that kind of money."

"Then who in the hell did?"

"I don't know, sir."

Hayes threw up his arms in frustration. "Great. Do you have any ideas on how to find out?"

"Yes, I do. When the time is right we're going to ask Ben Freidman."

"And you expect him to give us a straight answer?"

"Yes, I do, sir. And I expect quite a bit more from him as well."

Hayes eyed her for a second. What she had just said

reminded him of Thomas Stansfield. "Would you like to let me in on your plan?"

"No." Kennedy shook her head. "You have enough to worry about with the situation in Baghdad. When the time is right you're going to play a very active roll in getting the truth from Ben Freidman. Trust me."

34

FORT BRAGG, NORTH CAROLINA,
SATURDAY MORNING

Early the next morning Rapp boarded a CIA Learjet for the relatively short hop from D.C. down to Fayetteville, North Carolina. In his possession were two large duffels and a garment bag. The duffels contained various weapons and ammunition that he might need for the mission, plus a few necessities. He did not plan on returning to D.C. until the mission was over. In the garment bag was a surprise. It involved something he'd been perfecting for years.

As the plane took off, Rapp looked out the small window and allowed himself to think of Anna one last time. He told himself this really would be it. He would need absolute focus and clarity in everything he did until the nukes were taken out. It was painful to think of her. He wondered where she was. If she was on her way back to America or sitting in the sun on the terrace of the breathtaking villa he'd rented on the Amalfi Coast. He imagined lying beside her, his arm under her head, his hand on her naked hip, their legs intertwined, her gorgeous green eyes staring dreamily at him, her perfect lips turned up in a blissful smile. She looked so happy in his dreams, the way he'd seen her on so many occasions before. Why couldn't it have stayed that way?

His hopes, his dreams for a normal life were in tatters. He'd been a fool for ever thinking he could have that life. He was a killer. Men like him didn't marry someone like Anna. They were oceans apart. She was worried about who he'd slept with before they met, and he was trying to find out who had hired Peter Cameron to kill him. It was almost comical when you took a step back. When he looked at it this way it caused him to think Anna was selfish or at least self-absorbed. She couldn't understand the commitment and sacrifices he'd made, and if she couldn't do that, they had serious problems. Sure, she'd been appreciative that he'd saved her from being raped and probably killed. His secret life with the CIA was fine, just so long as it involved saving her, but in any other light it was horrible and intolerable. And to end it all over something so sophomoric as jealousy was pathetic. Maybe she wasn't the woman for him.

That's how Rapp came to grips with his dashed dreams. Anna had always told him it was fate that he'd intervened that horrible night in the White House. Well, maybe it was fate, and maybe it was fate that things had fallen apart in Milan before he'd asked her to marry him. To a certain degree he really believed in fate, or at least that things happened in life for a reason. If they were truly meant to be together she would be there when he got back.

COLONEL GRAY WAS waiting for Rapp when the plane landed at Pope Air Force Base, which was adjacent to Fort Bragg. He was in his green camouflage fatigues, a beret and black jump boots that were polished to perfection. Despite the late autumn chill he had his sleeves rolled up to the middle of his muscular and tanned forearms. Unlike most of his men Gray kept his hair short, since he didn't go into the field anymore. Delta Force operators were given a special dispensation by the Army on hair regulations. The intent was to allow them to blend in with the general population when they were deployed.

Gray, in his mid-forties, was still in peak physical condition. He jogged five miles five days a week and still managed to keep up with the new recruits on the obstacle course. To keep his skills sharp he fired over two hundred rounds a day on Delta's various ranges. Gray believed in leading by example. The man did not have a pretentious bone in his body.

As Rapp stepped from the plane Gray rushed forward to help him with his bags. They stowed Rapp's luggage in the back of the colonel's Humvee and jumped in.

"Thanks for coming down, Mitch. I really appreciate it. I got a little worried the other day when I heard you were looking at retiring."

Rapp shrugged off the question and not wanting to get into the details of his disastrous love life, he simply said, "I'm getting old, Colonel."

"The hell you are. You're old when you get to be my age. You're still a young pup."

Rapp figured Gray was in his mid forties, still relatively young by any normal standards, but by Special Force's standards he was ancient. "Where are we off to this morning?"

Gray wrestled with the steering wheel on the Humvee like he was a city bus driver. He turned it around a corner and hit the gas. "I want to show you something before I bring you over for the briefing."

A minute later they pulled inside a massive airplane hangar where an equally massive C-141 Starlifter was being loaded with equipment. The colonel shut off the Humvee, and he and Rapp jumped out. Near the rear of the plane were three vehicles sitting under gray tarps. Gray approached the last one and pulled the tarp off. Underneath was a white Mercedes-Benz E-Class sedan.

"What do you think?"

Rapp was smiling. "No offense, Colonel, but the army isn't exactly known for throwing money around. How did you get your hands on these?"

Gray opened the driver's door. "We do the DEA a lot of favors. We help train their SWAT guys and in general help them with tactical training."

"And?"

"I told them if they ever come across any Mercedes sedans to let me know. We got them cheap."

"Drug seizures?"

"Yep. And that's only half of it. They're armor-plated. Some crazy Colombian drug dealer down in Miami owned them. A white one, a black one and silver one. We painted them all white." Gray gestured to the other side of the car. "Get in. I want to show you a few things."

Rapp got into the front passenger seat, and looked at the dash. Colonel Gray was pointing to a computer screen beneath the radio on the dashboard. "The car comes standard with a GPS map system. We brought in some techno-weenies from the National Reconnaissance Office and had them program the system for every street in Baghdad and all the main and secondary roads leading in and out of the city."

Rapp nodded. "You have them in all three cars?"

"Yep."

"That's huge. No more Mogadishus." Rapp was

referring to an operation in Somalia back in 1993 when things went horribly wrong for a task force of U.S. Special Forces. After grabbing several top lieutenants of a war lord, the ground element of the force came under fire and got lost in the maze of streets that crisscrossed the Third World hellhole. Even with a command helicopter circling high above the city giving the ground element directions on how to avoid roadblocks and get out of the war lord's stronghold, the convoy continued to take wrong turns. Taking heavy fire the group was pinned down for the night. By the time the operation was over eighteen soldiers were dead and dozens more critically injured. Despite killing over 400 Somalis the operation was looked on as a disaster back in Washington.

"The windows are all bulletproof, the tires are self-sealing and we added sunroofs to the backseat so the men can fire the heavy equipment while moving."

Rapp looked around the vehicle admiringly. He thought he knew the answer but he asked anyway. "Why didn't you go with limos?"

"We thought about it, and even fooled around with the idea a bit, but it really complicated the mission profile. If we used the limos we would either have to drive them in across the border, which presented some problems that we wanted to avoid, or we would have to load them on C-130's and either drop them by pallet and parachute, or land the planes in Iraq and offload them, which for obvious reasons we didn't like. One of my men who'd been pouring over reconnaissance photographs noticed that not all of these caravans are limousines. Some of them use sedans. Several in particular use these Mercedes E-Class sedans."

"Those are the ones used by his son Uday," added Rapp.

"The sadistic little bastard?"

"Yep."

"Where'd you get that info?"

Rapp grinned. "I have my sources."

"I'm sure you do." Gray studied Rapp for a moment with his shrewd eyes, wondering how far he should push. "Does the fact that Uday uses these cars hurt or help?"

"Oh," said Rapp, "I think it helps."

"What do you know that I don't?"

"I'll tell you later, when you give me the briefing. For now I'd like to hear the rest of what you were saying."

"Going to the sedans simplified things greatly for us. They fit into the Chinooks that we use for deep penetration operations. Using the Chinooks we can fly in under radar and land exactly where we want."

"Perfect. I'm impressed, Colonel."

"Well, let's hope you still are when you've heard the briefing."

HIDDEN AMONG THE tall pine trees of North Carolina is a military compound known as the SOT. It stands for Special Operations Training Facility. The eight-mile perimeter of the compound is surrounded by a double fence topped with razor wire. The no-man's-land between the two fences is loaded with microwave sensors and cameras. Inside the fence line, tall earth berms conceal the movement of the people who train at the hundred million-dollar facility. The men who occupy the area are referred to as operators. The SOT is home to Delta Force, the U.S. Army's ultrasecret counterterrorism Special Forces unit.

The SOT itself sits within Fort Bragg, the massive military reservation that is home to the John F. Kennedy Special Warfare Center and the Special Forces Command;

the home of the Green Berets. It is from the Green Berets that Delta Force gets its operators, the best of the best. Security around the facility is very tight. Rarely is a civilian allowed entrance, but in the case of Mitch Rapp, Colonel Gray, the commanding officer of Delta Force, was more than willing to make an exception.

The guards at the gate allowed Colonel Gray through with a salute. They didn't bother checking the credentials of the other man in the front seat of the Humvee. Half a mile later the vehicle braked to a quick stop in front of Delta's headquarters building. Rapp grabbed his garment bag and on the way in Gray confided in him saying, "I envy you young guys. This is going to be the op to end all ops."

Rapp smiled back but didn't say anything. He didn't need to. Gray was right. Instead he asked, "What's on the schedule?"

"I have my team assembled. I want to give you a full briefing, have you poke a few holes in the plan, and then try and figure out the best way to coordinate our activities. We're due to ship out at fourteen hundred, so we don't have much time."

Rapp followed him down the hall to a conference room. He draped the garment bag over a chair and took a seat next to Gray at the head of the table. Gray took a moment to introduce Rapp to the team's commanding officer. "Mitch, this is Major Berg."

Rapp stuck out his hand. "Nice to meet you, Major." The man looked to be in his mid thirties. Old enough to have served in the Gulf.

"Same here. The colonel speaks very highly of you."

Rapp accepted the compliment with a nod and sat back to listen to the colonel.

"This is Mr. Kruse," bellowed the colonel to the other

twelve men sitting around the table. They all knew Kruse was not his real name and none of them would bother asking what it was. Gray continued. "He's spent a lot of time in the Middle East. Probably more than all of us combined." The colonel made eye contact with each of the twelve men. "I've worked with him personally before and can attest to his skills as an operator. I went all the way to the top to request that he help us with this."

The men were impressed. It wasn't often that their CO handed out such compliments. Rapp eyed the twelve men at the table. It was obvious what they'd been trained for. There wasn't a pair of blue eyes to be found. Not even hazel. All of the men had brown eyes, jet-black hair and thick black mustaches. A few of them also had beards. They were all dark-skinned, and as was the case with Rapp, after applying a healthy dose of deep brown self-tanning lotion, they would pass for Arabs.

Rapp didn't have to ask about language skills. He doubted any of them spoke Arabic as well as he did, but they would all be fluent. Many of them would also speak Farsi and Kurdish. These men were trained specifically to operate in the Middle East. Rapp knew the breakdown of the unit. Twelve men: one commanding officer, who was Major Berg, a warrant officer and the rest sergeants. They were what was known in the Special Forces business as Operational Detachment Alphas. Delta Force referred to them as simply "Teams." Each individual had been in the army for at least ten years. There were two weapons specialists capable of stripping, cleaning and firing almost every gun and rifle known to man, two engineers who specialized in explosives, two medics who could work at any emergency room in the country, two communications specialists whose equipment would allow the group to talk to their command via secure satellite uplink from anywhere in the world, an intelligence specialist and an operations specialist who was in charge of keeping everyone supplied and in line. The last man was the senior sergeant of the group.

They were all the best at what they did, but that wasn't enough for Delta Force. Every man in the unit was trained almost to the level of their counterparts to do every single job in the unit. If someone went down on an operation, someone else needed to be able to step into their shoes and finish the job. What was often lost in the jumble of acronyms and sterile military references was the fact that these men, in addition to their highly technical skills, were lethal killing machines. The medics weren't just medics. Both of them were sniper qualified, as were the weapons sergeants and the communications sergeants. First and foremost these men were trained to shoot. Each man on the team, including their commander, fired over 2,000 rounds a week, week in and week out, fifty-two weeks a year. Their skills were kept honed for just this reason—that on a moment's notice they would be sent into action.

Colonel Gray introduced each team member, and then asked Rapp, "I know General Flood gave you a brief overview of the mission. Do you have any questions before I get into the details?"

"I assume the team will be wearing SRG uniforms?" SRG stood for Special Republican Guard. This was the elite unit within the Republican Guard that was in charge of protecting Saddam, his family and his palaces. The unit was made up of men entirely from the towns of Tikrit, Baiji and al-Sharqat, all towns with clans that had proved their undying loyalty to Saddam over the years.

"Yes. They'll be in SRG uniforms with U.S. Army uniforms underneath, in case they're caught."

"Good. General Flood told me a little bit about what you had in mind for me." Rapp paused while he thought about his own plan. "With the time constraints we're up against, I think it would be difficult to get me into the country without running the risk of setting off some alarms. I have no safe house to operate from, and the few contacts that we do have in Baghdad, I wouldn't be comfortable using. Not for this sensitive of an operation." Rapp grimaced. "This would be just the type of thing an agent would flip for. The person would be Saddam's new best friend. And if that happened, you guys could plan on a nice welcoming party when you landed."

Gray had been under the impression that Rapp thought he could help. Slightly irritated, he asked, "So you don't think you could scout out the target?"

"Oh, I think I could. I also think there's a chance I'd get caught, which would then compromise the entire operation. At any rate I don't think it's worth the risk. I think your men are better off driving into Baghdad like they own the place."

"But we don't even know what the door to this facility looks like," protested one of the engineers.

"I can't get you that kind of info. If it's concealed like we think it is, there'll be a normal entrance from the alley and the real door will be down a flight or two. There's no way I could go to Baghdad and get all that information for you, without someone getting suspicious."

"Then if you don't mind me asking," started the colonel, "why in the hell did you fly all the way down here?"

"Because I have something else to offer," Rapp replied confidently. He looked evenly at each man and then asked, "Who is the most feared man in all of Iraq?"

Gray thought about it for a second. "Saddam, of course."

"Who is the second most feared man?" asked Rapp.

The colonel shared a look with his men. No one spoke for a long while. Finally one of the sergeants said, "Saddam's son Uday."

"Correct." Rapp pointed at the sergeant. "Some would argue that he is the most feared man in Iraq. He's always been a bit of a sadist, but in 1996 there was an attempt on his life. He was shot ten times and survived. Since then he's become a real bastard. No one is safe from him. His own friends have been tortured by his hand. Teeth pulled out, fingers cut off, eyes gouged out, servants hobbled . . . he even killed his own brothers-in-law."

"Saddam Kamel and Hussein Kamel," said the sergeant.

"That's right. Uday is feared by *everyone,* including his own family."

"So how does he fit into this?" asked Gray.

"Like you, Colonel, I've done some experimenting in my spare time. Your plan, by the way, to use the white cars to transport the team, is pure genius."

"Thank you, but I can't take credit for it. It was Sergeant Abdo." Gray pointed to the man who had been answering Rapp's questions.

Rapp looked at the man approvingly. "Nice work, Sergeant."

"Thank you." Abdo placed his forearms on the table and asked Rapp, "Where are you going with this Uday thing?"

"Saddam is not the only person who travels around Iraq in white cars. His sons Uday and Qusai also travel in similar fashion. Uday, in fact, has a fleet of white Mercedes sedans. He has a real penchant for wanting to appear hip, and he sees the sedans as a way to separate himself from the older limousine-riding members of the family. At any rate, just pulling up to the side door of the hospital in white cars does not guarantee that they'll let you into the facility."

"But if we have Uday Saddam Hussein with us," interrupted Sergeant Abdo, "they will open the door without question."

"Exactly," smiled Rapp. He was beginning to like this Sergeant Abdo. "Uday has become a bit of an obsession of mine. I've studied videotapes of his rare public appearances; satellite intercepts of his phone conversations, virtually everything that we have on him. I know the way he walks, with a pronounced limp in his right leg. I know the way he speaks, I know his gestures, and I know where each of his scars are located. I know how to imitate him to perfection."

35

ARLINGTON, VIRGINIA,
SATURDAY MORNING

Steveken hadn't slept too well. It was the package. After his meeting with Brown he'd returned to his town house. He didn't call Rudin right away. He set the letter-size manila envelope on his coffee table and twisted the top off a cold bottle of Anchor Steam. No TV, no music, just him and the package of secrets. If Brown hadn't dished out his unsolicited advice, there was a good chance Steveken would have just passed the package along and left it at that. But the arrogant man had to dole out his wisdom. If he wasn't so full of himself, he might have realized that such a warning might only serve to entice him into looking inside the package.

It was during his third bottle of Anchor Steam that Steveken came full circle with his logic and pondered the possibility that Brown was using reverse psychology on him. After all, who in their right mind tells a former special agent not to look at something? It's in a fed's very fiber to want to find things out, to crack the unsolved case. By the time the eleven o'clock news came on, Steveken had pretty much decided that whatever was in the package wasn't worth knowing. This was the type of stuff that you could get subpoenaed over. And getting subpoenaed wasn't good for future business. There was also the chance that things could get really ugly. It was not outrageous to assume someone would be willing to kill to keep the information in the package from becoming public knowledge, and if he didn't know what was in the package, there was no reason for anyone to want to kill him.

For a brief moment he had thought of looking into the envelope and then transferring the material to a new envelope, but decided against it. There was also the option of discarding the package into the nearest Dumpster and telling Rudin he'd come up empty. As far as Brown and Rudin were concerned, he was impressed with neither. A sense of professionalism, however, and his gratitude to Clark, made him decide not to dump the package. Finally, at 11:30 he called Congressman Rudin and told him he'd come up with something. Rudin wanted him to come over to his row house on Capitol Hill immediately. Steveken told him he'd meet him at 7:00 A.M. at the Silver Diner on Wilson Boulevard in Arlington. As he predicted, Rudin wanted to meet someplace closer to his house. Steveken, emboldened by the three beers and a growing dislike of Rudin, repeated the name of the establishment and the time and then hung up.

He arrived the next morning at 6:30 A.M. with a copy of the *Post* and the package. As was fitting for the meeting, he picked a corner booth and sat facing the door. Steveken was in jeans, a blue ski jacket and a Penn baseball cap. He was one of only eight customers in the place and the youngest by a good twenty years. When the waitress showed up he ordered a pot of coffee, a large glass of orange juice, a side of hash browns, a side of links and a tall stack of blueberry pancakes.

Steveken drank his orange juice and scanned the paper. Below the fold on the front page was a headline that read *Historical Confirmation Hearing Begins.* Under it was a picture of Dr. Kennedy with her right hand raised. The article was pretty standard background-type stuff. It said Kennedy joined the CIA after her parents were killed in the U.S. embassy bombing in Beirut back in 1983. It encapsulated her career with the Agency, and talked about her successes since becoming the director of the Counterterrorism Center. It mentioned that she had overwhelming support on the Hill with the noted exception of Congressman Albert Rudin of Connecticut, the chairman of the House Intelligence Committee. Fortunately for Kennedy, the article pointed out that Rudin had no say over whether or not she would be confirmed.

His pancakes and sides arrived and he went to work on the food. He intended to be done by the time Rudin arrived. Steveken came to the conclusion that Kennedy was probably a pretty decent person. Losing your parents to some crazed car bomber would be no fun at all. He found himself looking at the package and again wondering what was inside. His thoughts were interrupted by the obnoxious sound of someone loudly clearing his throat.

Steveken looked up and saw Rudin standing in front of

the hostess stand, with a white handkerchief. He placed it over his large nose and began to blow. Every patron in the place turned to see who was making so much noise. Steveken shook his head and shoved another stack of syrup drenched pancakes into his mouth. He made no effort to alert Rudin to his presence. The man was ten minutes early, and Steveken hadn't finished his meal yet.

With only eight people in the place, Rudin eventually found him. He sat down in the booth and unzipped his puffy down jacket. Not bothering to say good morning, he asked, "So, what do you have for me?"

Steveken ignored his request and asked, "Why do you hate Irene Kennedy so much?"

Rudin looked shocked. "What are you talking about?"

"Kennedy . . . Dr. Irene Kennedy." He held up the paper and showed Rudin the photograph. "Why do you hate her so much?"

Rudin glared at the young man and said, "You told me last night you had something for me. Now hand it over. I'm a very busy man."

The waitress was headed their way so Steveken flagged her down. He pointed to Rudin. "What do you want?"

"Nothing, I'm fine."

"Nonsense." Looking up at the waitress, he said, "Bring him the same thing you gave me."

"But I'm not—"

Steveken held out his hand and silenced the congressman. He repeated the order and shooed the waitress away. With an arched brow he looked at Rudin and said, "You don't do this much, do you?"

"Do what?" he snapped.

"Clandestine meetings. You come in the door and start honking your nose so everybody in the whole joint turns around to see who's making the racket. You sit down and

tell the waitress you don't want anything. Well, if you
don't want anything then why in the hell are you here?"
Steveken waited half a second to see if Rudin had anything stupid to say and then added, "This is classified
information." He held up the package and saw Rudin's
eyes get as big as a pervert's in a strip joint. "Pull your
head out of your ass, and get with the program." On the
outside, Steveken looked very serious, but inside he was
laughing.

Rudin had seen the treasure and couldn't take his eyes
off it. He mumbled, "Sorry," and stuck his hand out for
the envelope.

Steveken set it back down on the booth seat and said,
"Under the table dummy. People are looking."

"Oh." Rudin put his hand under the table.

"Not yet," said Steveken. "We have to go over a couple
things first."

"Like what?"

Steveken stabbed his fork into a sausage link and
shoved half of it into his mouth. He washed it down with
some coffee and asked, "Why do you hate Kennedy so
much?"

It was obvious that Rudin didn't want to answer the
question, but it was also obvious that he needed to play
along until he got what he wanted. "She's a liar, and I
don't like public servants lying before congressional committees. It's very bad for a democracy."

"You mean a republic."

"What?"

"Never mind." Steveken wolfed down his last two
bites of pancakes and wiped his mouth. At he looked at
Rudin he made a final decision concerning how he
would handle things. "I want to be very clear about this.
I don't know what's in this package. I haven't looked

because I don't want to get involved." He flashed Rudin the inside of his jacket and said, "I'm taping this meeting as proof. Whatever you have up your sleeve, I don't want to be involved in it. I got this from Jonathan Brown. You have any questions, you go to him." Steveken slid the package under the table and Rudin eagerly snatched it. Sitting back, he watched the congressman tear open the top and sneak a peek at the contents. He wasn't actually taping anything, but that wasn't important. Rudin would believe the threat. He'd given Brown up out of a sense of fair play. If he wanted to destroy Kennedy he should have to show his face.

The waitress dropped off Rudin's orange juice and coffee. "Your food'll be up in a minute."

When the waitress left, Steveken got up and grabbed his paper. Rudin looked at him and asked, "Where are you going?"

"I'm a busy man, Albert," he pointed at his own eyes and then at Rudin, "but I'm going to have my eye on you." He started to walk away.

Rudin called after him, "Hey, you forgot to leave some money."

Steveken smiled and said to himself, "No, I didn't."

36

Tel Aviv, Saturday Afternoon

Surly was probably the best word to describe Ben Freidman's mood. He'd just left his wife and was on his way into the office. He'd sent a katsa to Milan to look into the disappearance of Rosenthal and his people, and that trusted agent was back. Unfortunately, it sounded like she had little to report. As the armor-plated Mercedes raced through the suburb of Ramat Aviv, Freidman looked out the window at the ocean and wondered how in God's name three highly trained agents just disappear. The problem, Freidman knew, was that they didn't just disappear. There was only one logical explanation after this long: Donatella had killed them. This presented a challenging problem for the head of Mossad. Three kidons can only go missing for so long, and then people start asking questions.

The Mercedes turned away from the ocean and rocketed up a steep hill toward a bland six-story concrete building with antennae bristling from the roof. The driver had radioed ahead and the popup barrier at the gate was down. The car raced through the entrance leaving the Uzi-toting security personnel in a cloud of dust.

When Freidman reached his office he found the katsa that he'd sent to Milan waiting in his outer office by herself. Freidman rushed past her like a tank racing toward the front lines. Without a word, he waved for her to follow. When she entered his inner sanctum he closed the door and sat behind his desk. The katsa did not sit. She stood practically at attention in front of his desk. Freidman yanked open his top drawer and retrieved a pack of cigarettes and a lighter.

He puffed on the cigarette and offered the pack up to the woman. She declined with a shake of her head. "So, tell me, Tanya. What did you discover for me?"

The woman's posture and demeanor spoke of military training. She was small with dark features and wore no makeup. "I found some things at the safe flat, but other than that, there was no sign of them."

"And the woman I told you to check on?" Freidman ran one of his meaty hands along the top of his bald head.

"I called her office and they said she was out, so I took the opportunity to stop by in person. I pretended that we were old friends and that I was just passing through Milan for the day. I put on a big show about how disappointed I was and asked if I could leave a note. While I was leaving the note I asked where she was off to this time. They told me they didn't know. She called in abruptly on Friday to say she needed to take some personal time."

Freidman puffed on his cigarette and tried to piece things together. Friday would have been the day after Rosenthal was supposed to have hit her. She was on the run and Rosenthal, Yanta and Sunberg were all dead. Damn, she was good. Freidman chided himself for not sending more people, or better yet, doing it himself. Donatella would have trusted him. He could have got her to let her guard down and then taken her. The problem was he had rushed into it and now the mess was compounded.

"Did you check her flat?"

"Yeah. It was spotless. Nothing unusual or out of the ordinary."

Freidman thought for a while longer and finally said, "All right. Thank you for looking into this for me."

"No problem, sir. Am I excused?"

"Yes, but I want you to keep quiet about this entire matter."

"Yes, sir." The woman turned and left the office.

Freidman spun his chair around and looked out at the blue water of the Mediterranean. There would be an official investigation, one way or another, and it would look much better if he were the one to launch it. He would have to make Donatella out to be a psychotic who had betrayed Israel by freelancing. He could even go the CIA and apologize for Donatella killing Peter Cameron. He could say that she had broken away and was doing freelance work. *Yes,* he told himself, *that was the path to take.* Always mix fact with fiction for the most believable story.

CONGRESSIONAL COUNTRY CLUB, D.C.,
SATURDAY MORNING

IF HE WAS in town, and it was Saturday, he was doing one of two things: either playing golf or getting a massage. Since the temperature was still below freezing he had opted for the massage. When he pulled up the long drive of the club in his Jaguar XK8 coupe shortly after nine, he spotted three brave souls standing on the first tee. Huddled in stocking caps, they were a testament to golf's addictive nature.

Hank Clark had two overriding principles or philosophies in life. The first was to never allow any single thing or person to control him, and the second was to succeed at any cost. He could have adopted a puritan lifestyle and banned all vices from his life, but that would have been too easy. Clark had seen alcohol destroy his mother. He knew what it could do to a person, to a family, but instead of running from it, he was determined to conquer it. Clark's competitive nature could not stand boredom, and it detested simplicity and complacency. Life was to be lived, not wasted cowering in a corner avoiding every vice as if it might jump up and drag you down into hell.

Clark took things on, but always in a well thought out way. He'd been an all-conference pitcher for the ASU Sun Devils. That was when he learned to control his emotions and outthink an opponent. Where a football player is taught to get pumped up and attack the ball carrier, Clark learned to think clearly, get his competitor to expect one thing and then deliver something else. He was a master at blindsiding people without them ever knowing he had a hand in their demise.

As he lay facedown on the massage table, he was trying to figure out how to take these last few steps. He was so close, but this was where it would get tricky. The important thing to keep in mind was to let things happen. Not to force anything. The wheels were set in motion, the game was rigged and the odds were in his favor. All he needed was for Albert Rudin to make one last-ditch effort to derail the Kennedy nomination, and based on the conversation he'd had with Deputy Director Brown he could expect to hear from Rudin shortly. The package had been delivered last night and Clark knew that Steveken wouldn't disappoint him. By now Rudin had his grubby little hands on the info and he was probably close to having a coronary. With that satisfying thought Clark began to doze off. The waterfall music played softly in the background and Lou the masseur was kneading away at his legs. Life was good.

THE DOOR FLEW open, thudded against the wall, and bounced back. Albert Rudin stood silhouetted in the light of the men's locker room staring into the relative darkness of massage room number two. "Hank! Are you in there?"

Clark, startled by the interruption, pulled from a deep sleep in the wink of a second, bolted up onto his elbows and growled, "What the fuck!"

"Hank, I need to talk to you immediately!" He stepped into the room.

Through unfocused, sleepy eyes Clark said, "Albert, what in the hell are you doing?"

"I need to talk to you alone! I have something very important to show you."

"I'm in the middle of a massage," snarled Clark, still not quite awake.

"I don't care." Rudin stepped forward, thrusting the manila envelope in front of his face.

"Albert, whatever you have can wait until I have some clothes on. Now get the hell out of here!"

Rudin had never heard Clark so upset. Reluctantly, he retreated from the room and closed the door. He looked down at the envelope in his hand. He desperately wanted to show the contents to someone, and Hank Clark was the obvious choice. He'd been looking for him for the past two hours. He'd called his house, his office and his cell phone. No one at the house answered, no one at the office knew where he was, and he didn't answer his cell phone. The club was a lucky guess. Rudin saw the senator's gleaming Jaguar in the parking lot and practically ran into the building. The locker room manager told him Clark was getting a massage. Without putting any further thought into it, Rudin had raced off through the maze of lockers like a rat in search of a piece of cheese.

Standing alone in the bright lights of the locker room Rudin now saw the error of his ways. He checked his watch. It was 9:55. Clark wouldn't be that much longer. Rudin began walking. He'd waited this long to destroy Irene Kennedy, he could wait a few more minutes.

THERE WAS A small lounge in the men's locker room; two couches, several chairs, a television and two phones. This was where Rudin had decided to wait. It was a good thirty minutes before Clark showed. His salt and pepper hair was slicked back and he was wearing a pair of dress corduroy pants, a button-down shirt and a cashmere sweater. Rudin popped out of his chair looking slightly low-rent in his wrinkled khakis, faded flannel shirt and overstuffed down coat.

Clark had decided to act as if the intrusion into his hypnotic massage had not happened. There was no sense in revisiting the issue. After all these years Rudin wasn't about to change. Clark did not greet the congressman. He simply said, "Let's grab a cup of coffee."

Rudin shook his head emphatically. "Let's talk outside. In your car." He looked around the small lounge like the walls had ears.

Clark understood Rudin's paranoia. He was the one who had encouraged it. "All right."

They left the club and went to the parking lot without speaking. Rudin took every step like he was on point during a patrol behind enemy lines. Clark played along and kept his mouth shut. He'd anticipated Rudin's behavior. From thirty feet away, he pressed the button on his keyless remote. The headlights flashed once. Clark climbed in behind the wheel and Rudin got in on the passenger side.

From the folds of his down coat Rudin extracted the envelope and said, "You're not going to believe what is in here." He offered the envelope to Clark.

Clark didn't take it. He instead asked, "What's in it?"

"The information I've been looking for," replied Rudin with glee.

Impassively, Clark nodded for him to elaborate.

"Have you ever heard of an organization called the Orion Team?"

Clark just shook his head no.

"It's a secret organization that was started by that bastard Thomas Stansfield, and headed by Irene Kennedy." Rudin spoke their names with great hatred. "They've been running covert ops in the Middle East for over a decade, and they haven't said shit to us." Rudin stabbed his finger into his own chest. "They've fucking lied to us, Hank, and I have proof. Right here! Look!" Rudin pulled some papers from the envelope. "I have a list of people they've killed. There's account numbers where legitimate money has been diverted to fund these operations. There's even mention of Special Forces units being used to support these *fucking* antics."

"This is absolutely shocking."

"I told you she was no good. Just like her old boss Stansfield."

"I can't believe it," said Clark. "Where did you get this?"

"From your guy," said Rudin defensively. "That Steveken fellow."

"And where did he get it?"

"That's the best part," said Rudin excitedly. "He got it from Jonathan Brown . . . Judge Fucking Brown. Can you believe it?"

That was not the answer Clark was expecting. "Have you talked to anybody else about this?"

"No! You're the first person."

"Well, do yourself and Brown a favor and don't mention his name to anyone." Clark was trying to figure out how in the hell Rudin had got Brown's name.

"Why?"

"Because the second you mention his name they'll destroy his reputation." Clark was thinking quickly, trying to come up with a logical reason. "Think of his name as your ace in the hole. The longer you wait to show it, the more valuable it'll be."

"Or the longer you wait to play it." Rudin tried to pass the envelope to Clark.

"No. I believe you. When you get a chance make copies for me and send me the whole thing." Clark wasn't about to put his fingerprints on classified documents.

Rudin was a little disappointed, but pleased to hear that Clark trusted him enough to take his word. "So what are you going to do on Monday?"

The senator placed a hand on his chin and looked out the front windshield. Quietly, he said, "I'm not sure."

Rudin was sure. It's all he'd been thinking about for the past three hours. Kennedy's confirmation hearing was going to turn into an inquisition. "Hank, what do you mean you're not sure? You're going to get her under oath, and you're going to nail her ass to the wall!"

"Oh, don't worry, if this information is as damaging as you say, that'll happen," he said reassuringly. "I'm just trying to make sure we have all of our bases covered first." Clark looked at Rudin and asked, "Are you still scheduled to appear on *Meet the Press* tomorrow?"

"Yeah."

Clark paused briefly and said, "All right, here's what we're going to do."

37

MARYLAND, SATURDAY EVENING

A steady drizzle fell from the night's black sky, and the cab's headlights cut a perfect but limited swath through the darkness. In the backseat Anna Rielly sat feeling her determination wilt away. She wasn't sure what she wanted to happen, but she knew she had to meet him face-to-face. She couldn't run. She loved him too much; she'd poured too much of her heart into the relationship. There were too many things that needed to be said. And besides, as a matter of practicality she had to get her car.

The trip back from Milan had been a long one. Thankfully, the American Airlines ticket agent had been kind enough to honor Rielly's first-class ticket without charging her for changing the return date. It probably helped that she recognized Rielly as the NBC White House correspondent. What made the flight so miserable was that she was seated next to a forty-some-year-old man from Baltimore who spent the majority of the flight trying to put the moves on her. She heard his life story at least once, and several chapters that he deemed extra important were repeated. The experience did nothing for her resolve. Like most people with any sense, she didn't like dating. If this was what life held for her, maybe she was better off spending a few fitful nights waiting for Mitch to come home. She knew that wasn't true, but in the midst of the excruciating flight the thought occurred more than once.

With a few days to cool off, Anna had settled in on her main problem with Mitch. How well did she really know him? The question of course could be asked, how much did one really know anybody, but she didn't buy into that esoteric philosophy. She knew her family and her friends very well, and she thought she knew Mitch well, but she would have never thought him capable of doing what he did in Milan.

Rielly knew why they went to Italy. They went there to get engaged. Mitch had a little business to take care of first, and then they were off to start the rest of their lives together. The big problem was, his business involved meeting with an ex-lover. She tried to put the shoe on the other foot. What would Mitch have done if she'd gone off to meet secretly with an ex while they were on vacation together? It didn't take Rielly long to come up with an answer. He'd blow his top.

Then why should she be so understanding? She kept coming back to the same question and the same answer. Mitch lived a different life. Secrets were part of his existence, and what made this worse was that Anna was a reporter. She had an overwhelming need to find things out, to dig, to uncover the hidden, the forgotten, and the neglected. She wanted to know things, while Mitch was content with just being there. One of his favorite lines was that talking is overrated. She'd asked him about his previous lovers one night, and he had steadfastly avoided the discussion. She had finally said, "Don't you want to know about the men I've dated?" and Rapp had claimed that he didn't. This only served to arouse her curiosity more. There was no past with the man. It was an aspect of Mitch that drew her in and drove her nuts. He only wanted to talk about the present, and the future.

As the cab neared his house, the house that just a few days earlier she'd thought of as theirs, she felt butterflies in her stomach that rivaled the ones she'd had on her first live remote. Out of nervousness she hoped he wasn't home, and out of hope she wished he were. The coward in her wanted to grab her stuff and leave. Not give him the satisfaction of showing that she cared enough to talk about it. She could sneak in, grab her stuff and avoid any confrontation whatsoever. There was another voice from within, though not quite as strong as the first, that was telling her she had overreacted. Telling her that she could trust Mitch, and that whatever had happened in Milan could be explained.

When the cab pulled into the driveway, Rielly spotted her car parked next to the garage and noticed that the front light was on as well as one upstairs. She paid the cabbie and stood in the rain as he got her bag from the trunk. After a moment of indecision she wheeled her bag over to her car and hefted it into the trunk. Then standing under the narrow eave in front of the garage she peered through the small square window. Mitch's car wasn't there. Her heart fell and after a moment of melancholy thoughts she decided to go inside and see if there was a note.

Anna unlocked the front door and punched in the code for the alarm. The first thing she saw was Mitch's large Travel Pro black-wheeled suitcase. The same one he'd taken to Milan. It was on the floor and open. He was home, or at least he'd been home. She closed the front door and went into the kitchen. The breakfast bar was bare and again she felt her heart shrink a little. This was the spot where he would have left a note. There was none. Next she checked the answering machine. All she got for her trouble was a red zero telling her she'd again come up empty. She felt a brief sense of panic.

Snatching the handset from the cradle she called her apartment and checked her messages. The first one was from the phone company, asking her if she'd like to take advantage of a new long-distance calling plan. That was it. With a lump in her throat she called her work number and quickly skipped through five messages, none of which were from Mitch. She slammed the handset down and started for the stairs. The first tear trickled down her cheek as she reached the bedroom, their bedroom.

The bed was unmade. She tried to remember if it was that way when they'd left for Italy. It wasn't. She clearly remembered it had been made. In frustration she grabbed one of the pillows and threw it against the wall. Not even a note. It was bad enough that he didn't leave her one in their hotel room, but this was inexcusable. She'd misjudged him. With salty tears streaming down her face she went into the bathroom to gather her things. If he could be this cold and impersonal after all they'd been through, then so could she.

WASHINGTON, D.C., SUNDAY MORNING

SENATOR CLARK WAS in the kitchen of his mansion on Foxhall Road in the Wesley Heights neighborhood of Washington. The large château style home was the senator's castle. The front of the house was covered with ivy that looked like it had been there for a century or more and the double front door looked big enough to drive a small car through. Four stone chimneys jutted above the hipped slate roof, two at each end. The 9,000-square-foot home sat on three perfectly landscaped acres, and was surrounded by an eight foot, black wrought iron fence.

On Sundays the help was off so he was on his own for breakfast. After popping an English muffin into the toaster he poured himself a tall glass of fresh squeezed orange juice and took several gulps before heading out to get the papers. In slippers and a silk robe he dared the November morning chill and walked the almost 200 feet from his front door to the large black wrought iron gate that kept unwanted visitors out. Caesar and Brutus, the senator's golden retrievers, joined him on the walk.

It promised to be a good morning. His two regular Sunday papers, the *New York Times* and the *Washington Post,* were waiting for him in plastic bags. Clark returned to the house in time to hear the bell on the toaster announce that his muffin was done. He dropped the papers on the table and grabbed the muffin. He put raspberry jam on one half and peanut butter on the other. It was the same thing every Sunday, orange juice and a muffin first and then coffee with the paper. Rituals were a good thing.

Wife number three was never involved in this little ritual because she never got out of bed before ten on Sundays. And he doubted that he'd see her before noon today. She didn't just have one too many glasses of wine last night; she'd had one too many bottles. He was going to have to talk to her about laying off the booze. The campaign for the presidency would be in full swing about a year from now, and it wouldn't do to have her stumbling around making an ass out of herself. As he took a bite of the peanut butter-covered muffin, he asked himself what he was thinking when he married her. Unfortunately he knew the answer. She was very attractive, and in politics it never hurt to have a good-looking lady on your arm. If the boozing didn't get better, though, he'd have to figure something out. Again he contemplated the idea of her having a little accident. It might drum up the sympathy vote. No, Clark decided, as tempting as it was they always blamed the husband when there was foul play.

He finished his breakfast and headed into his study with his coffee and two newspapers. The study was located in the southern wing of the house and was decorated in the style of his home state. It was filled with expensive Western art and antiques. Balanced on two pegs above the fireplace mantel was an 1886 Winchester .45–70 lever action rifle. Every time Clark looked at the weapon he was reminded of Peter Cameron, the man he had hired to kill Mitch Rapp. Whenever Cameron had visited the study he had drooled over the unique weapon. It had been presented to President Grover Cleveland as a wedding present, and was the first of a limited number produced. The historical significance of the piece and the perfect condition it was in made it very valuable. On top of the mantel were two Frederic Remington sculptures, *The Bronco Buster* on one side and *The Buffalo* on the other. And above it all was one of Albert Bierstadt's breathtaking originals depicting a group of Indians on horseback riding across the plain. Across the room in a glass bookcase was a complete set of signed first editions by Ernest Hemingway.

Clark was unusually excited this morning and it wasn't because the Redskins were playing the Cowboys. It was because Albert Rudin was appearing live on *Meet the Press*. Clark checked to make sure a fresh tape was in the VCR, and then sat down in his worn leather chair. He turned on the TV and placed the thick copy of the *Times* on the footstool. There were five more minutes before show time so he scanned the famously liberal editorial page, for a few laughs.

When the music for the show came on Clark put the paper down and hit the record button. He sat and grinned as Tim Russert's voice announced the topics to be covered on the hour-long show. First up were Chairman Rudin of the House Permanent Select Committee on Intelligence and Congressman Zebarth, the committee's ranking minority. Both men were in their sixties and had spent thirty-plus years each in Washington as representatives.

Russert started the segment by introducing his guests and saying, "Congressmen, this is truly a historical week in Washington. For the first time in its fifty-plus-year history a woman has been nominated to head the Central Intelligence Agency. What are your thoughts?"

Congressman Zebarth jumped on the question first. "Dr. Kennedy is more than up to the job. She's been very effective as the director of the Counterterrorism Center, and she knows her way around Langley. I think the president has made a great choice, and I look forward to working with Dr. Kennedy in the years to come."

Russert turned to address Rudin. His eyes were open wide, he had a bit of a grin on his face, and his head was cocked slightly to one side. He knew practically every politician's politics, and hence, nine times out of ten he knew the answer before he asked the question. "That's one heck of an endorsement coming from a Republican." Russert knew his guest detested the president's nomination.

Rudin's face looked as if he'd just bitten into a bad piece of fruit. "I have no problem with a woman running the CIA, in fact I think it's about time we give one a shot. God knows the men we've had running the place haven't given us much for the trillions of dollars we've pumped into it."

"So, you don't agree with the president's nomination," suggested Russert with a faint smile.

"No, I don't. I've been warning the White House for months that Kennedy is not the type of person we Democrats want to be associated with." Rudin spoke with conviction.

The gossip was all over town that the president had taken Rudin to the woodshed about the Kennedy nomination. Russert was a little surprised that the congressman from Connecticut would so publicly disagree with Hayes after what he'd heard. "And why do you think Dr. Kennedy is such a poor choice as the next director of Central Intelligence? You seem to be the only person on the Hill who disagrees with her nomination."

"The only one who publicly disagrees," Rudin was quick to add. "For reasons I can't figure out, this president and his administration have forced this nominee down our throats without doing their research."

In a strange twist of politics Russert looked to Zebarth, the Republican, to defend a Democratic president. "Congressman Zebarth?"

"As I've already said, I think Dr. Kennedy is more than qualified for the job, and to be honest with you, Tim, I'm getting a little tired of my friend's innuendos and implications. Just once I'd like to see him back up his charges with some real evidence, or leave Dr. Kennedy alone. The woman has worked hard for this country, and she deserves a little gratitude." This sounded so reasonable that it made Rudin look like a bully.

Hank Clark was on the edge of his seat. Zebarth had just lobbed a big fat hanging curve ball. Clark clapped his hands together and said, "Come on, Albert. If there's ever a time to hit one out of the park, it's now."

Rudin reached under the table and produced a file. With a grim look on his face he shook his head and said, "I feel a little bit like Winston Churchill today, Tim."

Clark frowned at his TV and said, "Don't get carried away here, Albert."

"I've been warning my colleagues for years about what was going on at the CIA. I've been harping that we need more oversight. I've been complaining that we weren't getting the truth from Director Stansfield when he testified before my committee, and the same goes for Dr. Kennedy. No one has listened to me; even my own party has shunned me. Well, I'm here today to say that thanks to my vigilance we are about to avoid a huge mistake."

"What are you saying, Congressman Rudin?"

"I have here in this file," Rudin waved it in the air for emphasis, "proof that Dr. Kennedy has lied before my committee. I have proof that she has launched covert operations without notifying Congress or seeking our approval. I have proof that she has committed perjury before Congress and that she has obstructed justice."

Over the years Congressman Zebarth had heard an unending litany of baseless accusations from his colleague. To his ears, Rudin's diatribe sounded like a last ditch effort from a desperate man. "Albert, I've heard you say this many times before, and frankly I think it is despicable that you continue to assassinate the character of this fine woman."

"I'll tell you what's despicable," Rudin fired back. "A Congress that refuses to do the work the American people sent them to Washington to do. A Congress and a White House," he added with emphasis, "that refuse to make even the slightest effort to protect the Constitution."

Zebarth, an old-school Virginian and a throwback to the days when the rules of debate truly ruled the day, was genuinely insulted by Rudin's blanket accusations. "Albert, if you have any proof of wrongdoing by Dr. Kennedy, I suggest that you produce it right here and now. Otherwise, attempt to have some dignity and cease these unending character assassinations."

"I find your use of the word assassination rather amusing," snarled Rudin.

At home, in the solitude of his study, Clark realized how poorly Rudin came off on TV. It would make the senator look all the more stately when he began asking Kennedy about the accusations in front of a huge national audience tomorrow.

"Tell me, Congressman Zebarth, have you ever heard of an organization called the Orion Team?"

Zebarth balked at the question and refused to answer.

"It is a clandestine organization that was founded by

Thomas Stansfield and run by none other than Dr. Irene Kennedy. An organization that for the last ten years has waged a secret war in the Middle East without a single member of Congress being notified."

Sounding disinterested so as not to give Rudin's words any weight, Zebarth asked, "And how did you discover this secret organization?" Beneath his calm exterior Zebarth was ablaze. He knew of the Orion Team. He was one of a select group of congressmen and senators who had told Thomas Stansfield to take the battle to the terrorists.

"Since my own committee has refused to allow me to investigate the CIA, and President Hayes has also tried to silence me at every turn, I had to proceed on my own. Through my own diligence, and at great personal sacrifice, I found a very senior person at the Central Intelligence Agency who was willing to talk to me. Someone who is as disturbed as I am over the abuses that were committed by Thomas Stansfield and continue to be perpetuated by Irene Kennedy."

A name meant nothing by itself. If that was all Rudin had, it wasn't enough. Glancing down at the file on the table, Zebarth felt the urge to call his colleague's bluff. "If you have proof, I'd like to see it." He pointed at the file.

Rudin was more than willing to oblige. He whipped open the file saying, "I have the names and dates of people that this organization assassinated. I have proof that U.S. Special Forces personnel were involved in some of these operations, and I have this." Rudin produced a black-and-white photograph. "His name is Mitch Rapp. He is an American citizen who was trained by the CIA and has been the Orion Team's top operative for almost a decade. He has killed over *twenty* private citizens in various countries around the Middle East. He is an assassin, he is a criminal and he should be prosecuted, as should Irene Kennedy and every single person who has anything to do with this abomination." Rudin paused just long enough to retrieve something else from the file. "I have bank records that show how money was diverted out of congressionally funded programs and into this organization known as the Orion Team." Rudin pointed an accusatory finger at Zebarth and said, "There are too many politicians in this town who haven't been doing their job," he turned his hard stare on Russert, "and I'm here to tell you that that is going to end!"

Russert was so shell-shocked all he could manage to say was, "These are very serious accusations, Congressman Rudin."

"Yes, they are."

"Are you going to hold hearings into the matter or will you hand it over to the Justice Department?"

Rudin glanced sideways at Zebarth briefly and then back to the moderator. "Since my own committee has been unwilling to look into the matter, and since Irene Kennedy is set to testify before the Senate Intelligence Committee tomorrow, I'm going to turn this evidence over to Senator Clark and see if, *for once,* someone can get some straight answers from her."

In his study, Clark had risen to his feet in pure elation. Albert Rudin had just given him everything he'd been working for. At 1:00 P.M. tomorrow, Clark would gavel in one of the most dramatic and anticipated confirmation hearings America had ever seen. Clark had been in on the decision to found the Orion Team, but as part of that arrangement Thomas Stansfield had agreed to fall on the sword if anything should go wrong. Kennedy would do the same. Clark would stay above the fray and look statesman-like when his colleagues went after Kennedy tomorrow.

The television audience would be huge and that was just the start. The story would be on the cover of every magazine and the front page of every newspaper. His face and name would be burned into the minds of practically every single voter in the country. This is what would launch him on his presidential bid.

38

SAUDI ARABIA, SUNDAY EVENING

Rapp stood on the edge of a natural rock escarpment staring out at the wrinkled rolling terrain, toward Baghdad. He was dressed in tan desert fatigues. This place was called Oasis One by the Pentagon. Very few people knew it existed. It was located directly on top of the Saudi-Iraqi border, a mere two hundred miles from Baghdad. The rock formation that made up the natural perimeter of the forward base jutted from the red sea of sand like a volcanic island in the middle of an expansive ocean. Rapp was the only civilian who'd ever been to the base. The military personnel who occupied the rock island didn't even refer to it as a base. The men in black berets called it a forward staging area, or raiding area. This was Special Forces country, and true to their colorful personalities, they did not refer to the base by its official and top-secret name: Oasis One. The snake eaters called it the Snake Pit. There was even a hand-painted sign hanging over one of the caves that said, Welcome to the Snake Pit. Drinking is Encouraged.

Special Forces types were different. They actually

seemed normal to Rapp, but in relation to the rest of the military they were a breed apart. They prided themselves on making their own rules, and when they'd arrived at the old marauders' outpost they made it a point to set up a bar. All U.S. military personnel in Saudi Arabia were strictly forbidden from consuming alcohol. This did not deter the Green Berets, Delta Force Commandos, Navy SEALs and helicopter pilots who occupied the outpost.

They had arrived at the Prince Sultan Air Base the previous evening after traveling nonstop from North Carolina with several in-flight refuelings. Three huge military cargo C-141 Starlifters had made the trip. In addition to the team that was tasked to go into Baghdad, Colonel Gray had brought along an additional 100 Delta Force Commandos. Part of that force would be assigned the vital role of backup in case the primary team got bogged down and needed to be pulled out, and for the remainder of the force, Colonel Gray had something special planned.

Due to the secrecy surrounding the mission they flew in under the cover of darkness and landed at the eighty-square-mile Prince Sultan Air Base, located sixty miles south of Riyadh. The American portion of the base sits inside the Saudi Air Base and is a highly secure facility, in great part due to the tragic 1996 bombing in Dhahran, which killed 19 U.S. servicemen. Special Forces personnel are constantly coming and going from the base, but rarely does such a large force arrive unless an exercise is scheduled. For this reason the force left the base within hours of arriving. It was still dark when the helicopter pilots of the army's 160th Special Operations Aviation Regiment and the air force's 1st Special Operations Wing began ferrying the commandos off the Prince Sultan Air Base and up to the northern frontier. The bulk of the force was delivered to Oasis One and other units were distributed along the frontier at predetermined locations that U.S. Green Berets had already prepped.

The U.S. military had learned many lessons during the Gulf War, chief among them, that it was vital to have equipment positioned before a conflict starts. This was a lesson they had also learned painfully during both World War I and World War II, when German Wolf Packs sent millions of tons of vital equipment to the bottom of the North Atlantic. After World War II the military minds of the day got it right and a large portion of U.S. armor and artillery stayed in Europe.

When Saddam Hussein invaded Kuwait in late July of 1990, the U.S. was completely caught off guard and had to move fast for fear that Saddam might seize the moment and take Saudi Arabia. Initially, the only thing President Bush could do was send elements of the 82nd Airborne Division. Several thousand lightly armed men against 150,000 of Saddam's Republican Guard. The brass at the Pentagon knew that the elite troops of the 82nd Airborne Division would hold out against Saddam's large force of heavy armor for a day or two at best.

Logistically, the problem for the U.S. was not moving troops to the battlefield. Wide body airplanes such as 747's and C-141's could ferry ten thousand–plus troops a day into the region. The problem lay in transporting the U.S. Army's armor divisions and their supreme M1A1 Abrams main battle tank. Each of these behemoths weighs 54 tons and cannot be flown to their theater of operation; they must be shipped by vessel, and then transported by train or flatbed truck to the front. And the Abrams is only a small but crucial part of an armor division's equipment. Armored personnel carriers, tracked reconnaissance vehicles, towed artillery, tracked artillery, rocket launchers, self-propelled antiaircraft guns, combat engineering vehicles, and spare parts and ordnance for every vehicle meant having to move millions of tons of equipment and supplies halfway around the world. This takes months and makes for many sleepless nights while planners wait to build a force strong enough to resist attack.

After the Gulf War the U.S. military did the smart thing, and with the approval of several Arab Gulf States they created depots for their heavy equipment and left it in the theater. The Special Forces took this basic idea and carried it a step further. Not only did they keep equipment such as helicopters and desert fast attack vehicles in the region, they used it as a live-fire training ground for their operators. Unknown to the public and most of the military was the fact that since the end of the Gulf War, U.S. Special Forces personnel had continued to operate in southern and western Iraq. They had created a series of outposts along the northern frontier between Saudi Arabia and Iraq that allowed them to operate without interference from their host country. Saudi Arabia knew something was up, but chose to turn a blind eye. Saddam, too proud to admit that a handful of American soldiers were harassing his supposed elite troops, didn't dare say anything to an international community that had little sympathy.

The bases were originally established as quick response combat search-and-rescue outposts, or CSAR, as they were referred to in military jargon. The farther to the north these bases were located the quicker the CSAR crews could get to a downed air crew. During the Gulf War many of these operations were conducted from the small airport at Ar Ar, forty miles from the border. General Campbell, the commander of the Joint Special Operations Command, pushed to have these bases moved farther to the north. In the case of Oasis One, they were literally on the border.

In recent years the Iraqis had begun firing more frequently on coalition flights that were enforcing the southern no-fly zone. Unlike his predecessor, General Flood believed in the capabilities of Special Forces. The previous chairman of the Joint Chiefs was loath to use the highly trained warriors. Fortunately, Flood thought it made as much sense as owning a Corvette and never taking it out of the garage. As Iraq became increasingly aggressive against coalition flights, General Flood took the leash off the Special Force's units arrayed across the northern frontier. They began launching raids across the border, harassing Iraqi army units, ambushing them and then disappearing into the desert. Green Beret, Delta Force and Navy SEAL snipers began eliminating Iraqi officers at distances approaching a mile. This harassing of the enemy had greatly affected the morale of the Iraqi units and a lessening of their desire to patrol so close to the border. The end result was some much appreciated breathing room for the Special Forces units arrayed across the northern frontier.

Rapp peered out from his perch. Long shadows fell from the escarpment as the sun prepared to slip over the western horizon. He could feel the heat escaping from the arid desert. The temperature would drop thirty degrees in the next two hours. Rapp looked at the patches of darkness below, stretching out to the east toward Baghdad and possible death. There was no fear, just anticipation and maybe a few regrets. He wished things had worked out between him and Anna, but they hadn't. They never would. They were from two different worlds, neither willing to give theirs up completely, and for that they would always be apart. The conviction was back. The fight in Milan had at least given him that. He had made a difference, and was about to make a huge difference. There were hundreds of innocent people sitting in the Al Hussein Hospital who were depending on him. They would never know him, they would never even know he had saved their lives, but he had to try.

A light breeze twisted the sand at the bottom of the escarpment into a funnel and carried it away. Rapp wondered if somewhere in his past there wasn't a relative who had come from this part of the world. Maybe it was just the similarities between the ocean and the desert. They were both awesome in power, they held a subtle, expansive beauty that could trick the human eye into seeing things that were not there, and they could be incredibly inhospitable if you didn't pay attention. The footfall from behind pulled him from his trance, and he turned to see Colonel Gray approaching through the narrow crevice.

"Beautiful up here, isn't it?" asked the wiry leader of Delta Force.

"Very."

"A perfect natural fort." Gray placed a hand on the rock and looked down the hundred-foot sheer drop to the desert floor.

"What did you have to give the Bedouins to get it from them?"

"Nothing. They used to launch raids from this place across the border into Iraq. They'd steal anything they could get their hands on. Saddam got fed up and in eighty-nine he cleared the rats' nest out and poisoned the well. The Bedouins left and have never come back."

Rapp nodded. Water dictated all travel in the desert. "Have you put any more thought into tonight?"

"Yeah. I think you're right. The men have the infiltration and extraction down. No sense running another exercise and risking an accident. We'll give everybody a chance to get some rest and save up for tomorrow night."

"You've talked to Washington." Rapp kept his eyes on the desert.

"Yep."

"And it's on?"

Gray cocked his head and grinned, "You know how they like to change their minds. For now it's on."

"Good. We can't afford to have this compromised. The longer we wait around the better chance there is that someone will talk."

"Not my men," said a defensive Gray.

"It's not your men I'm worried about. It's the blowhards back in D.C." Rapp added quietly, "We need complete surprise to pull this off. I told the president your men could handle it. Another day or week of training will only give us a marginal benefit, but if the word leaks out somehow, we're fucked." Rapp looked off into the distance toward Baghdad. "If they know we're coming, no amount of training is going to save us."

39

SOUTH LAWN, THE WHITE HOUSE,
SUNDAY AFTERNOON

The day was still as Marine One descended ominously from the gray sky. The wheels landed perfectly on the three disks that had been put down to keep the heavy helicopter from sinking into the lush grass. The fire engine was in place just in case something went wrong and the Secret Service was out in full force to dissuade anyone from trying anything stupid. The meet-and-greet at the rope line had been canceled. When the president left and returned to the White House on Marine One, his staff often arranged for friends, family, and donors, of course, to watch. Depending on how busy the president was he would sometimes stop and shake hands. The meet-and-greet had been scheduled for 7:00 P.M. Due to a certain congressman's interview on *Meet the Press,* the president was returning early from Camp David, and he was in no mood to shake anyone's hand.

The hatch opened and President Hayes appeared almost immediately. He was wearing a pair of olive dress slacks, a white button-down and a blue blazer. He saluted the marine standing at the foot of the helicopter and wasted no time heading for his office. As he motored quickly across the South Lawn, his staff tried frantically to keep up. Several of them attempted to talk to him, but he wasn't having any of it. He had one thing on his mind right now, and he wasn't going to talk about it outside.

When he reached the Oval Office he slammed the door closed and glared at his chief of staff, Valerie Jones. "Where the hell is everybody?"

"Dr. Kennedy is downstairs in the Situation Room. The others should be here any minute."

The president looked as if his head was about to pop off. "Have you seen what he has?"

She shook her head. "But I've heard it's pretty serious stuff."

The president knew it was. He'd authorized some of it. "Valerie," he spoke through gritted teeth. "I want to be very clear about this. I want Albert Rudin destroyed. By tomorrow morning I want him working out of a broom closet on the fifth floor of the Capitol. I want to call in every political favor we're owed, and I want Rudin to feel like he's a leper."

Jones placed her hands in front of her as she were about to pray and then separated them and made a cautioning motion. "I don't think——"

"I don't want to hear excuses," snapped the president. "I just warned him. Remember?"

Jones nodded. She knew the president needed to vent and being the chief of staff meant that she was the chief ventee. "Yes, I remember."

"Well, the little prick went out, and despite my warnings, he continued to try and meddle in the affairs of the Executive Branch."

"He is the chairman of the House Intelligence Committee, sir."

"And he's a damn Democrat," yelled Hayes. "He's supposed to be on our side. I'm not supposed to have to worry about congressmen from my own party attacking me!"

"Sir, I know you're upset, but I need to caution you."

The president held up a hand like he was a traffic cop. "And I know you're my chief of staff, and you're trying to prevent me from doing anything stupid, but this time around, Valerie, there is no turning back. Albert Rudin has committed the cardinal sin of politics. He's stabbed his own president in the back. Everybody is watching now and only one of us is going to survive this."

Jones blinked several times and finally nodded. She would have to try again later when he had calmed down a bit. "What do you want me to do?"

"I want the damn party leadership over here." The president pointed at the ground and started for the door. "I'm going downstairs. When they get here let me know."

Jones started walking with him. "Do you want me to

come with you?" She was a little afraid of what the president might say without her in the room.

"No!" Hayes said with zero room for negotiation. He left the Oval Office and went down one floor to the secure Situation Room. When he entered the conference room he was a little surprised that in addition to Kennedy, General Flood, General Campbell and a half dozen of their staff members were also in the room. All three of them were leaning over the table looking at a series of maps. Upon seeing the president they stopped what they were doing and stood up.

"Gentlemen, I didn't know you were here. If you'll excuse us for a moment, I need to speak with Dr. Kennedy alone."

The military men were all aware of what had happened on *Meet the Press*. Especially the part where Rudin had mentioned the use of Special Forces personnel. They knew before the week was out they'd likely be summoned to the Hill to answer some very pointed questions. The timing couldn't be worse.

As the military men filed out of the room, the president gestured for Kennedy to sit. She did so and Hayes remained standing. He placed his hands on the table and with genuine sorrow, looked at Kennedy and said, "Irene, I'm sorry. I'm sorry you've been dragged into this."

Kennedy smiled and said, "Mr. President, I'm sorry I've dragged *you* into this. Albert Rudin hated me long before you became president."

"No, I don't mean that. I'm talking about what we asked you to do back in eighty-eight. The formation of the Orion Team." He shook his head. "We never thought that one of our own would blow the cover."

"Sir, I was aware of the risks when I took the job. If it were offered to me again, I wouldn't hesitate for a second."

Hayes's bowed his head. "I know you wouldn't," he said softly. "That's all the more reason you don't deserve this."

Kennedy had expected some of this. It was politics, and it was never rougher than during a confirmation fight. She'd spent much of the day analyzing her future, and it didn't look so good. Especially in regard to becoming the first female director of the CIA. The pressure on President Hayes to pull her nomination would be immense. Kennedy wouldn't make him do it. She would withdraw her name from consideration before it came to that, but she didn't think it would. She guessed from the president's beaten posture that he thought it was over. He didn't know what she did, though. She'd lived most of the last fifteen years thinking ahead of the pack, and so had Thomas Stansfield. The deceased former director had anticipated that a day might come where the Orion Team's cover would be blown. The original senators and congressmen who had asked him to take the war to the terrorists had demanded that Stansfield act as a firewall. If word ever got out that the CIA was assassinating people in the Middle East, the agreement was that Stansfield would take full blame and make no mention of the senators' and congressmens' involvement. This had been the initial agreement.

Without telling the senators and congressmen, Stansfield had decided to amend that agreement over the years. He had created a series of dummy files that he kept in the safe in the director's office. The files contained letters of notification to the House and Senate leadership, all of them dated within twenty-four hours of the start of covert operations run by the Orion Team. This was what was required by law and ultimately what Congressman Rudin was so irate about. In addition to the dummy files, Stansfield had passed along a wealth of information about a number of influential lawmakers on the Hill—the type of information they would like kept secret. Kennedy saw a chance in what, just hours earlier, had looked like a hopeless situation.

Hayes brought his gaze up and asked, "How in God's name are you going to testify tomorrow?"

"I'm not sure I'm going to, sir."

There was a brief pause while the president wondered if she would withdraw her name. "I wish there was a way we could fight this, Irene."

"Oh, there is," Kennedy replied with an understated confidence.

"How?"

"It's going to involve some risks, sir, but I think it will work."

The president studied her, wondering how she could possibly get out from under Rudin's sights. "I'm listening."

"Whatever Congressman Rudin has in that file that he was waving around today, it is classified material."

"And?"

"It is classified material that he received from an employee of the CIA. Someone, sir, has committed a crime by passing along that information."

"How?"

"If they are an employee of the CIA they have signed a national security nondisclosure document, sir."

The president looked skeptical. "It's bigger than all that, Irene. The press is involved."

"Please hear me out, sir. Much of what the Orion Team did, originally, was handled outside the CIA. Over the last year, Director Stansfield went to great lengths to legitimize the actions of the team. Giving Mitch a legitimate personnel file was just part of what he was up to. He created a real paper trail of classified documents documenting what the team has done. He has a list of senators and congressmen who were informed every time the team was sent into action."

The president was frowning. "How legitimate is this?"

"It's not a question of legitimacy, sir."

"Sure it is. What if they deny ever signing such a document?"

"They won't," Kennedy said with a steady voice.

Hayes took the hint. The rumors about Stansfield keeping files on people were true. "You mean they might be afraid of what would come out if they didn't go along?"

"Maybe." Kennedy stayed evasive, but got her point across.

The president seemed ill at ease with this course of action.

"Sir, all of this is legitimate enough for you to ask FBI Director Roach to seize that file and any copies that Rudin has made."

Wincing, the president asked, "You are asking me to have the FBI bust into the home of a U.S. congressman?"

"Yes, I am."

"You can't be serious. The press will—"

"Sir," interrupted Kennedy. "Rudin didn't exactly play fair with you on this one. He, or someone close to him, has broken the law. Normally, we would gladly turn a blind eye to it, but he has forced our hand by purging top secret information on national TV."

The president stubbornly crossed his arms. "Where is this whole thing going to take us, Irene?"

"If I go up to the Hill tomorrow and answer questions, I'll be crucified. If I withdraw my name from the process, Rudin will hold hearings within a week, and I'll be cruci-

fied. Either way it's going to happen, and under both scenarios, sir, your presidency will be guilty by association."

"We're screwed." Hayes stood tall as if he needed a full
breath of air. He placed his hands on his hips and continued, "And of all the times for it to happen, it has to come
along right now when this whole Iraqi thing is about to
heat up."

"There is a third way, sir," she suggested.

"I'm all ears."

Kennedy began carefully laying out her plan. They
would need the FBI to raid Rudin's home and office. The
uproar from the other politicians and the press would be
unavoidable, but predictable and ultimately short-lived,
for Kennedy had something very bold planned for Albert
Rudin, something that would in all likelihood end his
career.

40

OVAL OFFICE, SUNDAY EVENING

Clark put on a suit for the meeting. It was in his
plan to call the president and talk to him about
the news created by Rudin. If he was going to
keep the president in the dark about his involvement, it
was best to act sympathetic and see if there was anything
he could do to help. There wasn't, of course. He had the
president and the Democrats boxed in. Kennedy was
going to become the lightning rod for one of the most
sensational hearings ever launched.

The president had surprised him slightly by calling him

first. He asked Clark to come over to the White House. Hayes made it known it was extremely important that they talk tonight. Clark worried briefly that his name might have somehow been dragged into the mess. If that was the case he could handle it, but it would, of course, be much better if the president never knew of his involvement.

The president's chief of staff escorted the senior senator from Arizona into the Oval Office and left. The president closed the classified documents he was looking at and set his reading glasses on his desk. Hayes had also put on a suit. He rose to greet the man whom he thought was his ally.

"Hank, thanks for coming in." He stuck out his hand.

"No, problem, Bob." The two men had served in the Senate together, and Hayes preferred to be called by his first name when no one else was around.

"Let's take a seat over here." Hayes gestured to the couches by the fireplace. "Can I get you anything to drink?"

"No, I'm fine, thank you." Clark unbuttoned his suit coat and sat.

The president took the opposite couch and said, "Well, your old buddy Al Rudin has created one hell of a mess for us."

Clark was very conscious of the president's tone. He worried briefly that he might know more than he was showing. Clark let out a sigh and said, "Tomorrow is going to be a circus."

"There's no doubt about that." The president leaned back and draped his right arm over the back of the couch. "How are you going to handle it?"

"That's a good question. As you might imagine my phone hasn't stopped ringing since this morning. Every reporter in town wants to know what's going to happen tomorrow. Practically every member of my committee has called; most of them are furious. They all pretty much feel the same way. If there is any truth to what Albert said on TV this morning, Dr. Kennedy is toast."

This was no great revelation to the president. His chief of staff had already talked to several of the Democratic senators on the committee and they were already trying to distance themselves from the president and his nominee. The president used the moment of frankness to ask a question that he normally would not. With a sly grin he asked, "And just what is your party leadership saying?"

Clark stared unwaveringly at the president. "They want your balls, and they want me to serve them up on a silver platter."

Hayes stared back. "Are you going to?"

Clark blinked and looked away. "You know I don't like this crap, Bob."

"You didn't answer my question."

Clark kept up his act of looking torn. "I'm not going to call your capabilities into question."

"But someone else on your committee will." The president moved his head in an effort to get Clark to look him in the eye. "Senator Jetland perhaps?"

"Bob, this is beyond us. I have a tremendous amount of respect for you, but you know how this works. There's blood in the water, and the sharks are circling."

"I'm sure they are." There was a trace of amusement in his voice. Hayes was silent for a while and then said, "Hank, you've been a good colleague over the years, so I'm going to give you a warning. Do yourself a favor and delay the hearings for a day or two."

"There's no way I can do that." Clark shook his head vigorously.

The president wondered how far he should go and

after brief reflection decided that he didn't have to go far. The battle lines had been drawn. It was Republican against Democrat with Albert Rudin in the middle, a very dangerous place to be in Washington. "From one friend to another, Dr. Kennedy is going to be very tight-lipped tomorrow. Do yourself a favor and go easy on her."

"How tight-lipped?"

"Invoking the national security nondisclosure document that she signed when she went to work for the CIA, she is going to refuse to answer any questions in an open hearing."

"I have a lot of respect for Dr. Kennedy, but this is beyond that. If she cops that kind of an attitude, she's going to give me no other choice but to go after her."

"Don't," warned the president.

Clark frowned. "You remember the deal. If the Orion Team was ever found out, Stansfield and she were to fall on their swords." He paused to let the weight of his words sink in. "She needs to do the right thing and come before my committee and admit fault. I'll do everything I can to protect her."

"Well, she's not going to do it tomorrow, so be smart and go easy on her." The president stood. "As one friend to another, Hank, I'm giving you fair warning. Take the high road tomorrow."

Clark looked up at the president and wondered what he could possibly have up his sleeve. The man was clearly checkmated, and he had the gall to bring him into the Oval Office and think that he could intimidate him. Inwardly, Clark wanted to laugh in his face, but outwardly, he acted as if he was carefully considering the president's words. Clark stood and said, "I'll take your warning under advisement."

SITUATION ROOM, SUNDAY EVENING

THE PRESIDENT LEFT his meeting with Clark and went back downstairs where the secretary of defense, the national security advisor, Irene Kennedy and the Joint Chiefs awaited him. The secretary of defense Rick Culbertson had returned from Colombia just that morning and was briefed personally by the president on the situation in Iraq. Security was so tight around the ultimate target that the president had made the decision to keep the inner circle very small. The only member of the Joint Chiefs who knew was General Flood. To the individual heads of each branch, there was to be no mention of the Al Hussein Hospital and what lay beneath it.

The president entered the room and before anybody could stand he said, "Stay seated, please." Hayes took his chair at the head of the table and looked to General Flood at the opposite end. He nodded once.

The chairman of the Joint Chiefs proceeded to distribute a briefing to each person at the table. "Gentlemen," Flood was speaking mainly to the Joint Chiefs, "you will be happy to know that in light of the recent aggressive behavior of the Iraqi air defenses the president has given the green light to go in and clear them out. If you'll open your briefings you will see a target list." Target lists for the Iraqi theater were updated on a daily basis as aerial, satellite and human intelligence was fed into the system. The military men at the table hadn't seen a list this comprehensive since the war. Eyes bulged and murmurs could be heard as the warriors flipped through over a dozen pages of targets. Each target was given a designation, a description, a GPS number identifying the exact location and the type of ordnance and delivery vehicle that would be used against it.

General Flood continued. "At twenty-one hundred tomorrow evening, Saudi time, we will commence operations against Iraq. The attack will proceed as follows. The first wave will consist of A-10's, Apache attack helicopters, F-117 stealth fighters and cruise missiles." Flood did not need to go into detail. Each officer had seen the plan outlined a thousand times. The first wave goes in undetected and takes out the air defenses, and then the second wave, consisting of bombers and attack fighters, goes in to take out the hard targets. The men sat stoically and listened to Flood. None of them asked a single question or added a thought. It was all predetermined. The men and women stationed in and around the Gulf trained for this 365 days a year. The military machine was in place. All that needed to be done was to flip the switch.

Flood finished his thumbnail sketch of the plan and said, "I apologize for not giving you more warning, but there are some other circumstances that figure into this. It goes without saying that we don't want to tip our hand on this so let's be real careful. Are there any questions?"

The admiral and three generals shook their heads. "Good," Flood said, "I'll let you men get back to your commands and put things in motion." As the men got up to leave Flood added, "I should be back in my office within the hour, if you need to speak to me."

When they were gone, the president held up his briefing book and said, "General, I don't see the safe corridor blocked out. How are we going to keep our Delta boys from getting bombed?"

"When the aviators go in for their final briefing they will be handed one of these." Flood held up a map of Baghdad with a portion of it blocked out in red. "Nowhere on their target lists will there be a site within this red zone. They will be given specific instructions before takeoff that they are not to drop bombs within this area."

"Won't they get a little suspicious?"

"Since the Chinese embassy incident they're used to being told to stay away from certain areas, but this cordon that we have marked off here," Flood pointed to several roads going in and out of the city, "this is pretty unusual."

"So they might wonder?" asked the president.

"Yes, sir, some of them will, but you have to remember they're going to have a lot on their minds."

"Sir," interjected Kennedy. "The hospital is in the Al Mansur district of Baghdad. It's very upscale and is home to several embassies, most notably the Russian embassy, the Jordanian embassy and the Pakistani embassy. It also happens to be where the Iraqi Intelligence Service and the Republican Guard are headquartered. It is not unusual for us to stay away from this area when we conduct strikes."

The president seemed satisfied with Kennedy's explanation of the red zone in the middle of Baghdad, but he still thought the corridor snaking out of the city to the south and west looked a bit unusual. "General, if one of these fly-boys saw a caravan of white cars screaming down the road in the middle of the air raid, what do you think their reaction would be?"

"They would radio the nearest AWACS and report the cars." The AWACS was the Air Force's Airborne Warning and Control System, used to coordinate attacks and vector fighter aircraft to intercept hostile targets.

"You don't think they might take the initiative and strafe the cars?" he suggested.

The general thought about that and then said, "They might."

"That's not going to work," announced the president.

"No, it isn't," agreed Flood as he tried to come up with a solution. After a moment of deliberation he looked at the president and said, "Sir, I think we're going to have to let our people know that we will have troops on the ground."

The president winced at the idea. "Right now?"

"No, we can wait until the last possible moment, and at no point do we have to mention a thing about the nukes."

This sounded better to the president. "What about the white cars?" He looked to Kennedy for an opinion.

She kept her face expressionless while she thought about it. "I think we have to tell the pilots about the cars. They simply offer too much of a temptation. I respect their training, and I respect the command and control that the military has in place, but the bottom line is, these fighter jocks are cowboys. They're taught to push the envelope and take risks. Those white cars represent the same thing to our pilots that they represent to the Iraqi people. They are Saddam or at least the possibility of Saddam." She paused to give the president a chance to absorb what she'd said. "I know if I were one of those of those guys, and I thought I had a chance to take out Saddam, there's a good chance I wouldn't wait around for some AWACS controller to give me the green light."

The president leaned back in his chair and stubbornly folded his arms across his chest. Kennedy could see that he was struggling with the idea of letting too many people in on the secret. History was replete with stories of advantages that had been lost because someone had talked. Having worked in the CIA for more than fifteen years, she was acutely aware of the importance of guarding knowledge. Conversely, though, history also had many examples of knowledge that was too protected. The

CIA's own James Angleton had practically incapacitated the entire Agency with his paranoia. Thousands of U.S. sailors and airmen died at Pearl Harbor because the powers that be in Washington were too afraid to disseminate intercepted Japanese messages that made their intentions very clear. At some point you had to let go and trust your people.

"Sir, if we alert the aviators and AWACS controllers an hour prior to the start of the bombing, I'm confident we won't compromise the mission. Even if, and it's a big if, Iraqi intelligence can intercept and decipher our communications, they can't move that fast. An intercepted message like this has to get kicked up the chain of command, and right about the time it would get to anybody who may or may not do something about it . . . the bombs will start falling."

The president finally relented. "All right. We tell the troops one hour before the bombing starts, but that's it. No earlier."

41

CAPITOL HILL, MONDAY AFTERNOON

The nation's capital was in a state of frenzy that could only be brought about by scandal. And this wasn't just any scandal; this one involved the CIA, lying to Congress, diverted funds and the assassination of foreigners. Normally this would be more than enough to cause a media storm, but an early morning development had upgraded the story to a full-blown hurricane. At the crack of dawn, with search warrants in hand, special agents from the FBI had raided the home and office of Congressman Rudin.

The congressman had spent the entire morning ranting and raving in front of every camera and microphone he could find. Like all seasoned politicians he stayed on message, and his message was, "Constitutional Crisis." On the *Today* show, Rudin had complained bitterly that the executive branch was trying to bully the legislative branch with jackboot tactics that were reminiscent of 1930's Germany. He protested to anyone who would listen that the bedrock of the Constitution was being cracked asunder, that the separation of powers was being trampled on, and that the congressman from Connecticut wasn't alone.

In the new age of twenty-four-hour cable news, scandal ruled the day. There wasn't time to check facts or sources; there was barely time to think. Though there were a few wise politicians who stayed on the sidelines waiting to see what was what, by and large this was a group with a very healthy set of egos. It was almost impossible for them to turn down an opportunity to be seen and heard, so with 100 senators and 435 congressmen, the media had no shortage of opinions, almost all of them in the defense of Congressman Rudin. The thought of federal agents seizing files from their offices and homes was enough to rally most of his colleagues soundly behind the legislative branch. Despite his obnoxious personality Rudin was winning. Pundits and politicians alike agreed that President Hayes had miscalculated. Whatever he'd hoped to accomplish by raiding the congressman's home and office had backfired. Public sentiment was firmly in Rudin's corner.

This was the mood Kennedy faced as her motorcade approached the Hart Senate Office Building shortly before 1:00 P.M. Her security detail was planning on bringing their charge around the back of the building and through the loading dock, but Kennedy had shot down the idea. Despite their vehement protests she informed them that they would be dropping her off in front of the building, where no less than ten news trucks with large satellite dishes were parked, and several hundred protestors were loudly exercising their First Amendment rights.

Kennedy understood media manipulation as well as anyone in Washington, and she was not going to be seen slinking into the back of the Senate building between two Dumpsters, surrounded by a cordon of stocky armed men. She would walk right through the mass of screaming protestors and pushy cameramen, and she would look like she had nothing to hide.

There was too much going on, when the three cars pulled around the corner, for the protestors and media types to notice. The caravan came to a quick stop and the car doors flew open. Kennedy was on the curb surrounded by four of her bodyguards before the mob knew she was there. The Capitol Hill police had been kind enough to keep the walkway and entrance clear. They were halfway to the door before anyone noticed, and inside the building before the screaming started. They were waved through the security checkpoint and metal detectors and picked up an additional escort of four Capitol Hill police officers for the trip up to the committee room.

Set up in the broad hallway outside room 216 were correspondents from every network plus the cable news shows. One correspondent who worked for one of the more sensational cable news shows announced that Dr. Kennedy's cortege had arrived. The not so subtle implication was that she was on the way to her own funeral.

They continued up the sloped ramp and into the hearing room. At the door Kennedy shed the wall of muscle and steel and continued down the center aisle by herself. All of the senators were already seated and looking down at her from on high, atop a U-shaped bench draped in front with crimson bunting. Kennedy's small witness table was covered with a simple green tablecloth, and her chair was blue molded plastic with metal legs. It was the same style that the members of the gallery were sitting in.

The wall of marble behind the senators looked like a Rorschach test gone bad. Kennedy took a moment to study the seal mounted in the middle of the marble monstrosity. She had an overwhelming sense of calm as the flashes erupted around her. Her strength came from knowledge. One of the tenets of the intelligence business was to deceive your enemy, to get them thinking one thing, while you're planning something else. That's what this was about. It was her last gambit.

The upper galleries were bristling with black camera lenses and microphones. The room was packed, and the entire event was being carried live on national television. The senators on the dais with their phalanx of staffers behind them were peering down at her as if she were a mass murderer. Today Kennedy was the wounded animal. The vultures were circling and the hyenas were closing in and they all had their eyes on the diminutive Irene Kennedy. With a national TV audience, the stakes were high. Political careers would be made today, and for them to do that they would have to destroy the career of a public servant who, for fifteen years, had worked tirelessly for the cause against terrorism.

Senator Clark smacked the wooden block with his gavel. He looked tan and handsome in his dark wool suit and deep claret colored tie. The room ignored him, so he tried again with much greater force and better results. The talking trickled to a drip, and then there was silence. Clark looked down at Kennedy and was briefly reminded of his meeting with the president the night before. The odds were the president was bluffing, but there was a chance he might not be. Clark told himself to move cautiously. Like a king in a game of chess, he decided to let others move out into the field of battle before him.

"Dr. Kennedy," Clark started in a deep somber tone, "I'd like to remind you that you are still under oath."

"I'm aware of that, Mr. Chairman." Kennedy made Clark look like a giant, sitting at the table all by herself.

"A lot has happened since we spoke on Friday." Clark glanced down at a piece of paper before him. It was a pre-determined gesture that he thought would look good on TV. "I was wondering if before we resumed with our questions, you would care to respond to the accusations that were made against you yesterday by Congressman Rudin?"

Kennedy opened her mouth, but she never got the words out. Despite outnumbering her significantly, the other senators on the dais were not about to let Kennedy go on the offensive and set the agenda. Five of them instantly began vying for Clark's attention.

"Excuse me, Mr. Chairman!" bellowed Senator Jetland. He repeated himself four more times until he'd drowned out the others. Having silenced his colleagues, he didn't bother to wait for the chair to recognize him. "I think our purposes would be better served today if we were allowed to ask the nominee some very pointed questions." The senator from New Mexico gave Kennedy a sidelong glance and continued saying, "Now, we were supposed to start at ten this morning but things were pushed back to one, and it's now," Jetland glanced at his watch, "ten minutes past. I would suggest that if Dr. Kennedy has a statement, it can either be entered into the record, or if there's enough time left over at the end of the day, she can read it then."

Despite the lust for blood, several of the senators wanted to hear what Kennedy had to say. They recognized what Jetland was up to and did not want to look like bullies. They began to intervene on Kennedy's behalf, but were interrupted.

The surprise came from the witness table. "If that's what Senator Jetland would prefer that's fine with me." Kennedy was calling him out. Jetland was a showboat who'd been an undependable ally of the CIA for some time. He also served on the judiciary committee, to which he devoted the bulk of his time. The only time he got involved in Intelligence issues was when it meant that he might get some headlines. He also happened to be one of President Hayes's harshest critics.

Again, not waiting to be recognized by the chair, Senator Jetland grabbed the pedestal of his microphone and said, "That is very kind of you, Dr. Kennedy. I would like to start out by asking you what was the extent of your involvement in the raids that were conducted at the office and home of Congressman Rudin this morning?"

"Could you be a little more specific, please?"

A faint smile spread across Jetland's face and he asked, "Did you advise the president or Director Roach of the FBI, or anyone at the FBI for that matter, that they should launch this raid against Congressman Rudin?"

All eyes turned to Kennedy. She leaned forward and said, "Yes, I did."

Shocked whispers rustled through the gallery. Senator Clark banged the gavel twice before the room fell silent. Kennedy added, "I advised both the president and

Director Roach that they should serve Congressman Rudin with a search warrant."

Senator Jetland placed both elbows on the table and said, "I find it very disturbing that you would launch a vendetta against a member of the House of Representatives after he went public with certain allegations that might be damaging to your career." He glared at Kennedy.

Unfazed, Kennedy sat silent for a moment and then asked, "Is that a question or a statement, Senator Jetland?"

Jetland was not amused. "You can treat it as either. Just please respond to it in a *truthful* manner."

"The only thing I'd like to respond to is your choice of the word vendetta." Kennedy spoke in her trademark clinical fashion. Her tone was even and respectful. "I have no vendetta against Congressman Rudin. I think the record would show that it is the congressman who has a vendetta against the CIA."

"So that excuses you ordering the president to have Congressman Rudin treated like a criminal?"

"Senator, one does not order the president to do anything. Especially not this president. President Hayes is—"

Jetland cut her off. "Have any federal agents broken down your door lately, to rifle through your personal effects?"

"I wasn't aware that they broke down the congressman's door." Kennedy knew they hadn't, and wasn't about to let Jetland get away with the implication.

"You didn't answer my question, Dr. Kennedy. Let me rephrase it. Have any federal agents seized your files at the behest of Congressman Rudin?"

"No they haven't, sir."

Jetland treated this admission as a victory and took the chance to look around the bench at his colleagues. "I find it to be just a bit of a coincidence that after Congressman Rudin goes on TV and accuses you of some very serious violations, you in turn advise the president, and the director of the FBI, that they should conduct a raid on the congressman."

Kennedy looked up with her doelike eyes and said, "It is my job to advise the president."

"Thank you, Dr. Kennedy," said Jetland in a patronizing tone. "I appreciate the remedial civics lesson. Now let's get to the heart of the matter. What was your reason for advising President Hayes to treat Congressman Rudin like he was a criminal?"

Kennedy took quite a long time to answer the question. So long that it was obvious that she did not want to. Finally, she said, "I'm sorry but I can't answer your question, Senator Jetland."

Jetland's brows furrowed for the cameras, and he scowled at Kennedy's defiance. "You can't or you won't?"

"I won't." Kennedy held her ground.

"Are you claiming executive privilege, Dr. Kennedy?"

"No, I'm not, Senator. For reasons involving national security I cannot and will not answer your question."

Kennedy's reply tripped the senator up a bit and it took him a moment to form his next question. Recovering loudly, Jetland asked, "Congressman Rudin appeared on *Meet the Press* yesterday, and he leveled some pretty serious accusations at you. Would you care to comment on those accusations?"

"No."

"And why not?"

"For reasons involving national security."

"How convenient," sniped the senator.

Kennedy calmly replied, "I don't think there is anything convenient about national security."

"Yes," bellowed the senator from New Mexico, "I'm sure you're willing to go to great lengths to protect what you consider to be this nation's national security. Even break a few laws along the way, perhaps?"

In her no-nonsense manner Kennedy asked, "Again, is that a statement or a question, Senator?"

"I have a question for you," spat the senator. "Do you think this committee will confirm your nomination if you refuse to answer our questions?"

"No." Kennedy shook her head.

"Am I to assume then, that you no longer want the job as director of the Central Intelligence Agency?"

"No, you would be wrong to assume that."

"Then you still want the job?"

"Yes."

Jetland threw up his arms in a theatrical gesture of frustration. "Well, Dr. Kennedy, I hate to be the one to tell you this, but you can't have it both ways. If you want to be the next director of the CIA you'll have to answer some pretty tough questions, so let's get back to the task at hand." Jetland flipped open a file and said, "Congressman Rudin claims to have information that was provided by one of your co-workers. I know Congressman Rudin, and have no reason to doubt the authenticity of his information, so for now I'm going to believe him." Jetland repositioned his chair and settled in. "I find that when we get into these types of discussions it's easy to get lost or confused, so I'm going to make this real simple and clear for everyone." Jetland held up a photograph and showed it to Kennedy. "Here's a face. It's always nice to put a face on a problem. This particular problem has a name and it's Mitch Rapp. Now according to Congressman Rudin and his source, this man has worked for the CIA for the last ten years, and he's no clerk," the senator added with an arched brow. "He's allegedly responsible for the deaths of over twenty people. Twenty people!" Jetland paused to give everyone a chance to think of the bodies. "Could you confirm or deny for us whether or not this man is, or has ever been, employed by the CIA?"

Kennedy looked at the photograph, and thought it was very fortunate that Mitch was far away from a TV in the middle of a desert right now. With great concern on her face she replied, "Senator, for reasons of national security I cannot answer your question."

Jetland shook his head in frustration. "That is entirely unacceptable!"

Kennedy nodded as if to say she understood. After glancing at her watch she shocked the entire room by standing. She looked up at Senator Clark and said, "Mr. Chairman, I have something I must attend to. I apologize that I couldn't respond to the committee's questions today, but there are some extenuating circumstances at play. My reluctance in no way should be seen as an affront to the committee or the Senate. The president will contact you within the next day in regard to my status as a nominee. Thank you for your time and consideration." With that Kennedy turned and left the room to wide eyes and a chorus of whispers.

42

Oasis One was a flurry of anxious activity as helicopters were prepped and equipment was checked. The briefings were all completed and the team was ready to go. Rapp emerged from the command trailer wearing his Special Republican Guard uniform and took in the scene before him. The air was stifling inside from all the cigarette smoke. Colonel Gray and his staff were listening intently to the status reports from the mission's advance element. An MH-53J Pave Low helicopter from the air force's 20th Special Operation Squadron was already across the border and on its way to Scorpion I. The big helicopter was carrying a twelve member air force STS team made up of combat controllers and pararescue personnel. The team specialized in securing landing sites and evacuating wounded and downed aviators. They were a crucial part of the mission, especially if things went wrong. To bolster their effectiveness, Colonel Gray had sent along four of his best Delta snipers.

The desert sky was bright with stars. Rapp looked up in search of the moon only to find a sliver of white. For his part of the mission he would have preferred cloud cover, but he knew the fly-boys dropping their paveway guided bombs from above 10,000 feet would appreciate the clear skies. Rapp scratched the thick stubble on his face. He'd trimmed it up along the neckline and cheeks, just like Uday Hussein did. The red and gold epaulets on his green uniform bore the rank of general. Rapp found it comical that Uday, who was only thirty-seven, had already reached such a high rank. Welcome to the crazy world of dictators. He had a black leather belt strapped to his waist with two holsters. Uday fashioned himself a bit of a cowboy and was known to carry two Colt .45 caliber nickel-plated pistols. To complete the outfit he was wearing a black beret with the insignia of the SRG on the front and a bright red cravat that conveniently concealed his throat mike. For two reasons Rapp had opted not to wear an American uniform under the Iraqi one. The first was that Rapp was a good twenty pounds heavier than Uday, and putting an extra layer of clothes on under the SRG uniform would have only made the disparity more obvious. The second reason was more fatalistic. If they were caught, they would be tortured and killed no matter what uniform they were wearing. He was also wearing a Kevlar vest and an encrypted radio with a throat mike and an earpiece. Each member of the team was wearing the same radio. This would allow them to stay in communication throughout the operation.

Rapp looked out at the scene before him. Oasis One was a comforting site. It showed a lot of initiative by the military, something they weren't always known for. The rock formation rose out of the desert floor approximately 100 feet and was bowl shaped, with a slight opening at the southwestern end. The bowl was over 500 feet across at its center. The interior of the bowl was covered by desert camouflage netting. More than 100 yards of it was stretched tightly from one side to the other. Underneath the netting sat four highly advanced MH-47E Chinook helicopters with ground crews climbing over the airframes checking every inch of the complicated birds to make sure they were in perfect condition. The twin rotor behemoth was the new workhorse for the army's 160th SOAR.

The 160th SOAR, based out of Fort Campbell, Kentucky, is widely regarded as home to the best helicopter pilots in the world. The only other aviators who can give them a run for their money are the men from the air force's 1st Special Operations Wing, and they too would be involved in tonight's operation. Both units owed their current peak performance to a tragedy that had occurred more than twenty years earlier. On April 24, 1980, the United States Special Forces community suffered their greatest defeat in an operation code-named Eagle Claw.

Eagle Claw would painfully reveal the inadequacies and shortcomings created by decades of interservice rivalries and a general reluctance on the part of military leaders to properly fund the Special Forces. The mission on that fateful night was to rescue the fifty-three hostages held at the American embassy in Teheran. The Ayatollah Khomeini and his Revolutionary Guard had seized the embassy and its personnel some six months earlier. Time had run out on President Carter, and if he wanted to spend four more years at 1600 Pennsylvania Avenue, the hostages had to be brought home.

The operation would be the first time the army's supersecret Delta counterterrorism force would see action. On that cold April evening, five C-130 transport and refueling planes were to rendezvous with eight RH-53D Sea Stallion helicopters at a sight known as Desert I. The Sea Stallions were then to refuel and take on the Delta operators for the trip to a site in the mountains outside Teheran. Unfortunately, the mission was scrubbed after two of the eight Sea Stallions got lost en route to Desert I, and a third suffered mechanical difficulties. There were not enough helicopters left to get the job done, so the plug was pulled. That was when a bad situation got worse, drastically worse.

As one of the Sea Stallions maneuvered into position for refueling, its main rotor hit an EC-130E, and both the helicopter and plane burst into flames. With fire shooting into the night sky, the team had to make an emergency departure leaving behind all the helicopters and the burning plane.

In the wake of the disaster the military formed a review group that was aimed at pacifying critics in the media and on the Hill. Admiral James Holloway chaired the group, and fortunately for the Special Forces, the admiral didn't pull any punches. The group produced a document that eventually became known as the Holloway Report. It laid bare the inadequacies of operation Eagle Claw. At the top of the list was the subject of helicopters. The report stated that if future covert missions were to stand a chance, the military had to greatly improve its helicopter operations.

The result was the formation of a covert aviation unit named Task Force 160. Forty highly qualified candidates were selected to make up the task force. Of those original forty pilots more than a half dozen perished in training accidents as they pushed their flying machines to the limit in the worst of weather conditions. It was during this time that they became known as the "Night Stalkers." By the early nineties the force had grown to approximately 400 aviators. This was also when they took on their official name, the 160th Special Operations Aviation Regiment, or SOAR. The aviators and airmen of SOAR train constantly, in the worst of conditions, and do so while hugging the earth at speeds of over 120 mph. This is why they are the best helicopter pilots in the world.

Rapp had put his life in their hands on many occasions, and although they'd brought him to the brink of vomiting on at least three occasions, there was no other group of aviators he trusted more. He watched the flight crews work on their helicopters under red filter lights. The scene before him looked like something out of a futuristic sci-fi movie. He could see the pilots sitting in the cockpits of the big MH-47E Chinooks. They too were working under the faint glow of red filter lights. Because they would be flying with night vision they could not expose their expert eyes to bright light for at least an hour prior to takeoff. There would be no Desert I disasters with these guys.

Rapp knew they were going through their extensive preflight checklist. The advanced Chinooks came at a price tag of $35 million apiece. Each bird was capable of carrying thirty troops or a variety of other payloads. They were equipped with the Enhanced Navigation Systems, or ENS. Using twenty separate systems such as Doppler navigation, automatic direction finders, attitude director indicators, GPS, and a bevy of compasses and gyroscopes, the ENS tells the pilots exactly where they are at all times. They were also equipped with highly advanced terrain-following/terrain-avoidance radar and forward-looking infrared imagers or FLIR. This integrated system allowed the aviators to fly deep penetration missions while skimming the surface, in the worst of weather conditions, and land exactly on a target within seconds of their stated extraction or infiltration time.

Three of the four Chinooks were loaded with the white Mercedes sedans. The team would split up and ride with their vehicles—four Delta operators in each chopper plus Rapp in the middle helicopter. The fourth Chinook was there as a backup in case something went wrong with any of the others.

His detached solitude was broken by the door to the command trailer opening and Colonel Gray's gruff voice loudly barking out orders. A second later Major Berg, the commander of the assault team, appeared at Rapp's side.

In Arabic the major asked, "Are you ready, Uday Hussein?"

Rapp grinned. Looking at the choppers he replied in Arabic, "Yep. Let's go win one for the Gipper, rah rah, sis-boomba."

Major Berg smiled, showing a bright set of white teeth accented by a thick black mustache. "The advance team is halfway there. No problems so far."

"I suppose it's time to saddle up?"

"Yep. Dust off in five minutes." Berg stood silent for a moment and then added, "Last chance to back out."

"You couldn't pay me enough to miss this one."

The door to the command trailer flew open and Colonel Gray appeared in the doorway. "Major Berg, get your men and load 'em up!" The colonel approached Rapp and stuck out his hand. "Good luck, Mitch. I wish I was going with you."

Rapp knew he meant it. He took Gray's hand, and over the roar of the big Chinooks engines coming to life, he thought about giving the colonel a message for Anna in case something went wrong. After a moment of hesitation he decided against it. He thanked the colonel and then headed off to grab the rest of his equipment.

SITUATION ROOM, MONDAY AFTERNOON

KENNEDY WENT STRAIGHT from Capitol Hill to the White House. Her testimony had ended so abruptly that it had caught the media off guard. They'd settled in for the afternoon expecting hours of cantankerous questions and evasive testimony. When she'd left the Hart Senate Office Building just thirty minutes after she'd arrived, the majority of the cameras out in front of the building were unmanned. There were still a number of photographers who tried to hold her up as she left the building, jumping in front of her bodyguards as they escorted her to the director's limousine. The beefy security detail pushed the photographers aside like blockers on a kick return. Kennedy was safely tucked away in her limo twenty seconds after walking out on the committee.

When she arrived at the White House her blockers stayed outside with the vehicles, which was unfortunate because, between the entrance on West Executive Avenue and the Situation Room, she was practically tackled by Michelle Bernard, the president's press secretary.

"Irene, would you mind telling me what in the hell that was all about?" Bernard had one of the most stressful jobs in Washington.

Kennedy sidestepped her and motioned for Bernard to follow. Kennedy liked her, and didn't envy the position she was in. "What has the president told you?"

"Nothing," she half snapped. "That's the problem." Bernard looked over both shoulders to make sure no one from the press was within earshot. "The jackals are all over me, and I look like an idiot. I can't confirm or deny a thing. I look like I'm completely out of the loop."

"That's not such a bad spot to be in, Michelle."

Bernard ignored the advice and asked, "How bad is it?"

As they rounded the corner, Kennedy waited for two White House staffers to pass and then said, "Get ready for a long night."

"It's that bad?"

"I didn't say that, I just said it's going to be a long night."

Bernard gave her a wary glance, and then asked, "How the hell can you be so calm? I mean for Christ's sake, Irene, they're getting ready to burn you at the stake."

Stopping at the outer door to the Situation Room, Kennedy punched her code into the cipher lock and said, "Don't worry, no one's going to be burned at the stake." Kennedy pulled open the heavy door and said, "I promise I'll be able to tell you something by tonight. And trust me, until then it's better that you don't know what's going on." Kennedy let the door close behind her and opened the first door on her left.

The secure conference room was packed. General Flood was there with four of his aides, Secretary of Defense Culbertson was present, Casey Byrne, the deputy secretary of state, was there as well as Michael Haik, the NSA. The president was at the head of the table in his usual spot. He looked over his shoulder to see who had entered the room. When he saw it was Kennedy he immediately stood.

"Irene, great job. You handled Jetland like a pro."

"Thank you, sir. We've bought ourselves a little time, but I'm afraid not much. What's the status on the operation?"

"Take a seat here." The president grabbed a chair and wheeled it over to the corner of the table. They both sat. Kennedy was seated between General Flood and the president. Flood had a phone in each hand, one to his left ear and the other poised to be held against his right.

The president pointed to one of three large screens on the wall. "That's a live image from an AWACS patrolling over northern Saudi Arabia." The screen showed most of Iraq, Kuwait, the northern part of the Persian Gulf and the northern and eastern part of Saudi Arabia. The image was being fed via satellite from an E-3 Sentry Airborne

Warning and Control System. These were the air force's big Boeing 707's with the large rotodomes mounted above the fuselage. "The advance element is on the ground." Hayes pointed at the screen. "See the blue triangle just south of Baghdad?"

Kennedy squinted to make sense of the jumble of electronic markings on the screen. After a moment she located the site just west of the Tigris River. "Yes."

"They arrived less than five minutes ago. They've secured the area, and we've given the green light for the assault team to go in."

"That's the assault team there?" Kennedy pointed to four blue triangles closely grouped about halfway between Baghdad and the Saudi border.

"Correct."

"Have any of our allies called to ask what's going on?"

"I just got off the phone with the British PM. I called him. I didn't tell him about the nukes, but I said something serious was up. I'm going to call King Fahd just before it starts, as well as the Russian president, then after that it's a long list."

"So no leaks so far?"

"No." The president rapped his knuckles on the table twice.

The secrecy involving the operation had been amazing, thanks to two factors. The first was the short time period between receiving the information and launching the operation. The entire thing had been put together in just six days' time, a true testament to the readiness of the military. The second factor was entirely unintended. Thanks to Congressman Rudin's appearance on *Meet the Press,* Washington and much of the world was focused on the scandal. The president had cleared his schedule and spent the entire day in the Situation Room, an action that would normally set off warning bells in capitals all over the world. But today the foreign intelligence officers who normally paid attention to such things assumed President Hayes had dropped everything to try to salvage the Kennedy nomination.

Kennedy's eyes drifted beyond the airspace around Baghdad and noticed the massive air armada that was forming up over northern Saudi Arabia and the Persian Gulf. She knew the battle plan by heart. They'd gone over it from top to bottom this morning. The blue triangles that were massing on the Iraqi borders were U.S. jets that were suckling up to big KC-135 tankers and topping off their tanks. Closer to the border were formations of AH-64 Apache attack helicopters that would be led into battle by air force MH-53J Pave Lows. Air force JSTAR ground surveillance radar planes had given them pinpoint locations of surface-to-air missile sites that the Iraqis had hidden throughout the desolate terrain south and west of Baghdad.

In the northern Persian Gulf the Independence Battle Group was on station twenty-five miles off the Kuwaiti coast. The carrier's planes were in the air and were bolstered by two squadrons of Marine Corps F/A-18 Hornets flying out of Kuwait. In the opening salvo of the operation the battle group's surface ships would launch more than 100 cruise missiles. In addition, a flight of B-52's out of Diego Garcia in the Indian Ocean were forty minutes away from being in position to launch a payload of eighty-four cruise missiles.

With so many planes in the air questions were bound to be asked, so in an effort to keep a lid on things, earlier in the day, U.S. military attachés in embassies around the Persian Gulf informed their host countries that the U.S. would be holding a surprise readiness exercise commencing at 1900 local time. The Pentagon ran readiness exercises like this several times a year to keep the troops sharp and to keep Saddam guessing.

General Flood hung up both phones and said, "Mr. President, the flight of F-111's are airborne, refueled, and can be over the target twenty minutes after you give the word."

The military planners had decided that eight F-111's would create enough redundancy to ensure the destruction of the target. They were confident that they could achieve total destruction with just two planes and were hoping to use the remaining six to visit some other targets that they had carefully chosen. The eight F-111's were all carrying a single Deep Throat, GBU-28/B superpenetrator bomb. If Rapp and the Delta Team failed, the hospital would be leveled.

The president didn't want to think of that option right now. "What's the status on the ground team?"

"Everything looks good so far. They're proceeding without incident, and the advance element has reported the area secure."

The president looked over at the center screen for a moment. "Give me the time frame again."

"They should touch down in," Flood looked at the screen, "approximately seven minutes. It takes them a minute or two to unload the cars, and then it's almost a mile to the main gate of the facility. From there it's three miles to reach Route 144, the main road between Karbala and Baghdad. After that it's a straight shot, thirty-two and a half miles to the hospital. If they don't run into any trouble, it's supposed to take them twenty-six minutes to get to the hospital from the time they reach Route 144."

"They should be at the hospital in about forty minutes," Kennedy offered.

"And they want the bombs to start falling just after they get to the hospital?" asked a skeptical president.

"Yes. That's Mitch's idea."

"Why?"

"I don't know, but he said he can handle it either way, he'd just prefer if the bombs started falling about a minute after they've arrived."

The president was having difficulty understanding the reasoning behind Rapp's rationale. The entire thing was looking more and more complicated to him. He was sticking his neck out further than he'd ever intended. If Rapp and the Delta team failed, he was done. The combination of the Kennedy scandal and dead American troops would be his death knell.

Sensing his apprehension, Kennedy grabbed his arm and said with sincere confidence, "Don't worry, sir. Mitch will not fail."

Slowly the president nodded. "I hope you're right."

43

IRAQ, MONDAY NIGHT

The four helicopters knifed their way through the cooling desert air like a snake slithering across the sand. They were not flying a straight route to Scorpion I, the designation for the abandoned chemical weapons factory outside of Baghdad. Instead, a predetermined course had been plugged into the Chinooks' advanced navigation systems, allowing them to avoid all villages, major roads and Iraqi radar sites. Cruising at just

100 feet off the desert floor, with only three hundred feet between each chopper, and flying at speeds of over 120 mph, there was almost no room for error.

In the cargo area of the second Chinook Rapp tried to think of none of this. When they were in the air it was all out of his control. From his seat he looked up at the two door gunners. They mere both manning 7.62-mm mini-guns capable of cutting a vehicle in half. When fired at night, the guns looked like they were spewing fire. Air rushed through the open hatches and down the fuselage creating a roar that battled the loud engines and thumping rotors. The Mercedes sedan was blocking his view of a third gunner at the rear ramp, but Rapp knew he was there wearing a safety harness and holding a sling mounted M60 machine gun to further bolster the heli-copter's firepower. The car was secured to the floor of the chopper with four high-test tie-downs. One of the Delta operators was sitting behind the wheel ready to back it out as soon as they hit the ground. The three gunners were all wearing flight helmets, with night vision goggles and comlinks so they could tell the pilots and navigator what they saw. The gunners literally flew with their heads outside the airframe.

The big helicopter bucked, banked and dove its way through the air. There was nothing smooth and steady about the ride. Most people could handle it for a few minutes, like a ride at an amusement park, but to suffer through it for an hour or more could be incapacitating, throwing one's senses into such a jumble that the slightest touch or movement brought on nausea and vomiting. Rapp was used to it, as were the Delta operators.

One of the door gunners suddenly left his post and went to each man, grabbing their shoulder and holding up five fingers. They were almost there, and when they hit the ground, Rapp's chief responsibility would be to stay out of the way and let the Delta boys do their thing. Rapp went down his mental checklist one more time. He visualized how everything would go once they got to the hospital. He knew exactly what to do to get the team in, and it had nothing to do with firepower.

A few minutes later Rapp felt the helicopter begin to slow. They were close. Suddenly, the big bird banked hard to port and flared out, dropping its ass end toward the ground. The harsh maneuver didn't worry Rapp. He couldn't see out the window, but he knew what was going on. It had all been covered in the briefing. The air force STS team had prepped the landing strip in the parking lot of the abandoned factory and set up four equally spaced infrared strobe lights that could not be seen by the naked eye, but through night vision goggles they were as bright as a lighthouse's beacon. All four of the behemoths would touch down within seconds of each other directly on top of their strobes.

They hit with a thud and the Delta boys were instantly on their feet. The engine on the Mercedes purred to life, and the straps were snapped free. Less than five seconds after hitting the ground the car was backed down the ramp and clear of the helicopter. Rapp exited the chopper on the heels of the Delta boys and jumped into the front passenger seat.

The three cars sped away instantly into the pitch black night. Rapp didn't hesitate to put on his seat belt. The car's automatic headlights had been disabled and wouldn't be turned on until they reached the main road. Rapp could barely make out the car in front of them. Fortunately, the sergeant driving the vehicle was wearing night vision goggles.

The cars sped down the drive and forty-five seconds

later they reached the main gate. As they motored through, Rapp glimpsed a man holding the gate open. He would be one of the air force guys sent to cut the lock and secure the perimeter. About a quarter mile down the road Major Berg's voice came over their secure radios.

"On my mark, turn on your headlights. Three . . . two . . . one . . . mark."

All three drivers snatched their night vision goggles from their faces and turned on their headlights. It was crucial that they do this at the same time. If done while wearing the goggles it would cause temporary blindness. With the road now illuminated the team relaxed just a notch. Major Berg's voice came over the team's secure radios again and said, "Nice work, guys. Twenty minutes to Baghdad and then the real fun starts."

CAPITOL HILL, MONDAY AFTERNOON

HANK CLARK HAD his white shirtsleeves rolled up. His elbows were placed on his desk and his fingers kneaded his temples. He wished he were in his hide at the Capitol, but he would have never made it over there without being accosted by the media. As it was, his outer office was a complete zoo. There were at least three reporters with TV crews in tow demanding to speak to him, and there were another five or so print reporters just waiting for the chance to shove their damned Dictaphones in his face.

He should have been happy with the way things had gone, but something was bothering him. Clark couldn't figure out what he was missing, but he had the feeling that something was afoot. Kennedy's testimony, or lack thereof, had been a surprise, but nowhere as big a surprise as the FBI raiding Rudin's office and house. Clark hoped Steveken had the sense to make himself scarce. Rudin would not cooperate with the FBI, he hated them too much, but if the charges were real Rudin might give Steveken and Brown up to save his own skin. And then there was the president telling him that for his own good he should go easy on Kennedy. Then Kennedy shows up today and starts talking about national security. Something was going on, but he couldn't figure out what.

There was a sudden loud ruckus in the outer office. Clark was about to get up to investigate, when his door flew open and Rudin barged in. The bone-thin congressman slammed the door closed and stormed across the room gesturing wildly with his hands. "I knew you wouldn't answer your damn phone, so I came over here. What in the hell happened?"

Clark took a deep breath and stifled the urge to tell Rudin to shut up. "What did you want me to do, Albert?"

"I wanted you to tear her head off."

"I don't think that would have played too well on TV."

Rudin stopped in front of Clark's desk. "I don't care how it would have played, Hank. The damn bitch admitted that she advised the president to raid my house. My fucking house!"

"I thought Jetland did just fine."

"Have you lost your mind? He came off looking like a pompous overbearing ass."

Clark was tempted to ask Rudin if he'd watched any tapes of himself lately, but instead said, "And that's exactly what I would have looked like if I'd gone after her."

Rudin's disagreement was apparent on his twisted face. "You should have never let her walk out like that. I don't get it." He threw his arms up in the air. "I did my part yesterday, and you just sat there."

"Easy, Albert." Clark pointed to a chair and said, "Take a seat. You're way too worked up. Kennedy's done." The senator wasn't so sure, but he recognized the need to say something to mollify Rudin.

"Oh, there's no question about that. The president better start looking for a new nominee." Rudin sat. "You know, before all this started I would have been satisfied to just end her career, but not now." The bags of loose skin under his jaw jiggled as he shook his head. "I want her in jail."

"I don't blame you," Clark lied. "If she'd advised the president to raid my house and office I'd be furious."

"Does that mean you're going to let me hold hearings?"

Clark smiled slyly. "I think there'll be more than enough for both our committees to handle."

The two men took a moment to gloat over the destruction of Kennedy. It was cut short by the voice of Clark's personal secretary emanating from the phone.

"Senator, President Hayes is holding on line one."

Clark's eyes opened wide in an exaggerated show of surprise. "Thank you, Debbie. I'll grab it in a second." Looking at Rudin he asked, "What do you think this is about?"

Rudin clapped his hands together and gleefully announced, "He's calling to withdraw her nomination. What else?"

Clark thought he was right. With Kennedy out of the way he could breathe a sigh of relief and help select Brown as the next nominee. Beyond that, he would still be able to hold hearings. He could explain to the president that it was needed to balance out what would undoubtedly be a rabid persecution of Kennedy by Rudin and the House Intelligence Committee.

Finally he reached out and grabbed the handset. "Mr. President."

"Hank, I don't have much time so I'm going to make this real quick. In about ten minutes we're going to start bombing Iraq. I've already informed the leaders of both houses. I've also signed a Presidential Finding authorizing lethal force for U.S. Special Forces personnel who are in the area. I can't get into any specifics right now, but we're trying to put together a briefing for later tonight. Please do me a favor and keep this under your hat until the story breaks."

"Absolutely, Mr. President."

"Thanks, Hank. I'll be in touch."

The line went dead and Clark slowly hung up the phone.

Rudin was still gloating. "What did he say? Did he pull her nomination?"

It took Clark a moment to answer. "No. He called to inform me that we're ten minutes away from bombing Baghdad."

"What?" screamed Rudin. He jumped out of his chair. "There's no way. He can't . . . I can't believe he's—"

"He can and he is," said Clark firmly as his mind raced to figure out what was going on.

"It's *Wag the Dog*. It's all a diversion to get the media to ignore Kennedy."

The congressman's words gave Clark pause. He thought about it for a moment as Rudin paced back and forth in front of his desk spewing obscenities. Clark knew Robert Hayes pretty well, and he didn't take him for the type to put soldiers and airmen into harm's way just to divert attention from a political crisis, but the presidency did funny things to people's morals. Looking at the red-faced Rudin, Clark decided to bait him a bit. "Do you really think he'd do that?"

"You're damn right he would! He'd sell my fucking

party down the river to save his own ass!" Rudin stopped and jabbed his thumb into his chest. "And I'll be damned if I'm going to let him do it. I'm going to go tell every reporter who'll listen that this is a farce!"

"You do what you need to do, Albert, but you're going to wait until the bombs start falling before you say a word."

44

BAGHDAD, MONDAY NIGHT

Rapp had given the members of the Delta team one piece of serious advice. They were true professionals, men who did not take well to outsiders telling them what to do, so he was careful how he said it, but he was firm. He told them, "Be bold, be arrogant, and if anybody gets in the way, threaten to kill them." This was the way of Uday Hussein. He had learned it from his father, and young Uday had bested him. Saddam had no heart, but it seemed at least that there was some logic to his use of force. It was used to rule, to keep his subjects cowering. If the people cowered they couldn't look up long enough to strike back. Uday, on the other hand, seemed to take perverse pleasure in maiming and killing innocent people in the most random of ways.

Saddam tolerated Uday's brutal behavior for three reasons. The first was that Saddam himself was no saint, the second was that Uday was his son, and the third was that Uday's sadistic behavior served a purpose. It helped to spread fear among even Saddam's most senior people. The message was clear, don't screw up or you'll end up as Uday's evening entertainment.

The stories were well-known throughout Iraq and in the western intelligence agencies. In 1995 Saddam's two sons-in-law, Hussein Kamel and Saddam Kamel, defected to Jordan with Saddam's daughters. After a short period Saddam convinced them to come back to Baghdad. He promised them that he had forgiven them, and that the important thing was that they were family. Upon their return to Baghdad, Uday convinced his father that they needed to make an example of them. Saddam was swayed by his son. Uday then proceeded to torture them for hours on end, kill them, and then as a final message to all the people of Iraq, he burned their houses to the ground. He did it all in front of his sisters, who were allowed to live.

Then there was the story of a friend who had dared to criticize the son of Saddam. Uday had a string tied around the man's penis and then forced three bottles of gin down his throat. The man died an excruciating death. Just a year earlier his father had sent one of his top advisors to talk to Uday about certain affairs of state. Uday felt the man was too condescending, so he had his testicles cut off and fed to his dogs. The man was allowed to live as a reminder to all that Uday was to be treated with absolute respect. Rapp had told all these stories and more to the Delta boys so they could understand the real fear that Uday Hussein strikes into the hearts of all Iraqis. It was this fear that they were depending on to get them into the facility.

The cars had proceeded without difficulty up Route 144. The six-lane highway was very modern and relatively quiet as the clock approached 11:00 P.M. The few cars and trucks that they encountered moved quickly out of the way as the caravan of three white Mercedes sedans rolled past at 75 mph. When they reached the city limits they turned onto the Abu Ghurayb Expressway, another six lane thoroughfare that would carry them into the heart of Baghdad and right through the very teeth of the enemy. On the left was the sprawling Abu Ghurayb munitions factory and on the right was the main barracks for the Republican Guard, over ten thousand shock troops ready to put down any revolt launched against Saddam.

Suddenly Rapp noticed the lead car begin to slow a bit. Looking ahead he saw a police cruiser in the middle lane. He spoke decisively over the team's comnet. "Don't slow down. There isn't a cop in this country who'd pull over one of these caravans. Speed right past him."

The Mercedes all had deeply tinted windows so it was impossible to see in. As they passed the police cruiser Rapp looked over at the officer. Just as he thought, the man didn't dare to even glance at the speeding luxury sedans.

The computer mapping in the car was very nice. The system was uplinked to the Global Positioning System and showed them their exact location on a map of the city. Their course to the hospital was also clearly marked in green. As an extra precaution each member had also memorized the location of the hospital and the streets leading to and from it.

The lead car hit its right turn signal and began to move over. Their exit for the hospital was coming up. As they reached the top of the ramp, and prepared to turn onto Shari' Arba'at, Rapp saw a flash off in the distance. For a split second he thought it was lightning, but it was quickly followed by three more. The strikes were not coming from the sky, they were erupting from the ground. Suddenly fiery streaks appeared in the night sky, and Rapp realized they were cruise missiles. It was an amazing sight, like a low-level meteor storm. Bright flashes began popping to the south of them, each one moving closer until they could hear the explosions. The drivers kept moving toward the hospital. When they reached Shari' Al Mansur they took a left and sped down the road. Several blocks later they passed the Russian embassy and had to race around cars that were stopped in the middle of the road.

At that exact moment, a block in front of them, a blur of fire-breathing cruise missiles screamed overhead less than a hundred feet off the ground. The cars shook from the noise, but continued on even faster. The hospital was only blocks away. Over the comnet Rapp said, "Major, did you see the crowd gathering in front of the Russian embassy?"

"Affirmative."

"The locals know it's safe to go there during an air raid. The street might be blocked by the time we get out of here."

"Roger, we'll go with the secondary route. Did everybody get that? On the way out we're switching to the secondary route."

The drivers all confirmed that they'd received the order and the group pressed on. The explosions started occurring closer by the second and Rapp briefly wondered if they'd all lost their minds to volunteer for this operation. He'd specifically asked that the bombing start minutes after they'd arrived at the hospital, not before. His greatest fear was that the underground facility would go through a standard lockdown procedure when the bombing started.

They made one last turn, all three vehicles skidding around the corner. The side entrance to the hospital was up ahead on the left and the street was empty. Rapp didn't know if this was a good sign or a bad one. The cars skidded to a halt and twelve doors instantly flew open. Each man had a job. In the backseat of the first and third vehicles Delta operators popped up through the sunroofs and set up their Heckler & Koch 7.62-mm machine guns on tripods. The heavy weapons would eviscerate anything short of an armored personnel carrier, and if one of those or, God forbid, a tank showed up, they had three LAW 80 antitank guided missiles. The three drivers stood next to their vehicles, leaving the engines running. Each carried an M4A1 carbine with an advanced combat optical gun sight, and an M203 40-mm grenade launcher affixed under the barrel grip. The driver from the middle car would cover the door after the entry team went in.

The remaining seven Delta operators and Rapp moved quickly toward the door. Each man with the exception of Rapp carried a Heckler & Koch MP10 suppressed submachine gun. The weapons were silent 9-mm close-quarter killing machines. They were the best weapon available for the job, and if not for Rapp, they would have been left behind. The original plan had been to use AK-74's and AKSU's, the standard weapons of the Special Republican Guard, but Rapp had intervened, explaining that Uday was a gun nut and the men on his personal detail carried the best weapons money could buy.

The Delta operators and Rapp moved toward the nondescript metal door en masse. None of them knew what to expect on the other side. The lead man shoved open the door just as an earthshaking explosion occurred from a bomb strike nearby.

The Iraqi soldier standing in the small room had a wall phone to his ear and a machine gun slung over his shoulder. His eyes were wide open with fear from either the explosion or the sudden arrival of the Special Republican Guard unit.

Whichever the case, Rapp did not wait around to find out. Remembering his words to the Delta operators, Rapp pushed his way through the men, limping like Uday Hussein would, and in Arabic yelled, "Hang up the phone!"

The man mumbled something quickly into the phone and nervously placed it in its cradle. Snapping to attention, he saluted Rapp and said, "General Hussein, we are under attack by the Americans. We must get you down to the shelter."

"I know we are under attack, you idiot! That is why I'm here. Take me to the bombs."

Without hesitation the guard turned and inserted a key into a riveted steel door. He yanked it open and gestured for the man he thought to be Uday Hussein to enter. Rapp did so and stepped into a slightly larger room. The guard nervously inserted another key into a box on the wall. Two heavy doors slid back to reveal a large freight elevator. Everyone piled in and the guard pressed one of two buttons.

Rapp asked, "Is Dr. Lee here?"

The guard would not look Rapp in the eyes. "I'm sorry, General Hussein?"

"The Korean," he yelled.

"Yes, I think so," the man answered nervously.

"Who were you on the phone with when I arrived?"

"Headquarters, General."

"Why?"

"They are sending more men over just in case."

The Delta operators on the street could not hear what the Iraqi soldier was saying, so Rapp said, "Headquarters is sending men! Those idiots! All they'll do is attract attention to this place."

The elevator stopped and the doors opened. Two

guards were waiting for them. Both were at attention with their rifles at port, standing one on each side of a huge blast door. The guard who had ridden down with them asked, "I can call headquarters, General, and tell them not to send the men."

"Yes, do that!" Rapp yelled. He continued forward, marching with his fake limp through the blast door into a cavernous room, at least 100 feet by 300 feet, with twenty-foot ceilings.

Major Berg appeared at Rapp's side and in Arabic whispered, "Cameras."

Rapp looked up and in one sweep found four of them. He pulled the major close and said, "Deploy your men. Leave two of them here to take care of the guards." Rapp heard a loud humming noise and turned to see the large blast door moving.

"Stop!" screamed Rapp. "I gave no order to close that door!"

The guard at the wall smacked a red button with the palm of his hand and snapped to attention. Rapp barked at him, "Call headquarters and tell them I'm going to cut the balls off of the idiot who decided to draw attention to this place!"

The guard ran for the nearest phone and snatched the handset from its cradle. Rapp looked the length of the chamber and spotted a clean room against the far wall. Inside the glass-walled, environmentally controlled room he could see several people in white lab coats and hairnets. Rapp set out for the room with Major Berg and four of the operators. Rapp burst into the room and looked at the five Korean men covered from head to toe in surgical garb. "Dr. Lee!"

One of the men came toward them waving his arms. Rapp assumed it was Dr. Lee. In heavily accented English he said, "No . . . no . . . you can't come in here dressed like that."

Rapp drew one of the nickel-plated .45's, cocked the hammer, pointed it at the doctor's head and screamed, "No one tells me what to do!"

The scientist stopped in his tracks and lowered his head. "I'm sorry."

"Where are the weapons?" he yelled. Rapp had no idea if Dr. Lee had ever met Uday, but the disguise appeared to be working so far.

"The weapons?" asked the Korean.

"The bombs, you idiot! The Americans know about them. An air attack is under way and one of our spies tells us they are preparing to drop one of their special bombs on this place."

"But they aren't ready."

"I don't care if they aren't ready!" Rapp pointed to a cart on the other side of the room. "Put the crucial parts on that cart immediately! We have to get out of here fast!"

Dr. Lee turned and started giving orders to his people in Korean. Rapp glanced over his shoulder and looked at the two Delta operators who specialized in explosives and had been briefed on what to look for. With a head jerk from Rapp the two men set out to keep an eye on the scientists. Rapp grabbed Major Berg by the arm and walked back out into the large chamber. "Have your men leave one of the charges in that clean room." Each member of the assault team was wearing a satchel around their waist that contained enough C4 plastic explosives to level a house.

The major nodded. "Good enough. I'm going to put another satchel over by those canisters of liquid nitrogen."

"Make sure you save one for the elevator."

The guard who Rapp had told to call headquarters approached nervously. "General Hussein." The man stopped just out of Rapp's reach. "I'm sorry, but head-quarters reports that your brother Qusai has given the order to secure the facility with his troops. They want me to shut the blast doors."

This was big trouble. Qusai was Uday's older brother and their father's successor. "You incompetent fool!" Rapp lunged forward and slapped the man across the face. The guard dropped to his knees in a sign of submission. Rapp looked to Berg and mouthed the words, *Hurry up.* Addressing the cowering guard Rapp yelled, "Get up! You are coming with me."

Rapp marched the man back across the room and into the waiting elevator. They rode it back upstairs in silence. When the doors opened Rapp took one of his pistols and pointed it at the man's head. "Go back down there and help my men, and don't even think about closing those blast doors. If you do I will have your eyeballs cut out!"

Rapp left the elevator and went back out onto the street. As he emerged from the building two hulking armored personnel carriers came around the corner. The first thing Rapp heard was one of the Delta operators say. "Shit, we've got two Russian BTR-80's. Get the LAWs ready."

Rapp limped off in the direction of the steel monsters. Over the group's comlink he said, "Hold tight for a second, guys. Let me see what I can do." He stopped the vehicles halfway down the block by sticking out his hand and holding his ground. The vehicles stopped and one of the doors opened. An Iraqi colonel appeared wearing an SRG uniform. Rapp instantly knew he was in trouble. There was a good chance this officer had dealt with Uday on a more intimate level.

Rapp kept up the façade. "Colonel, get your men out of here immediately. My father has sent me on a special mission. If he finds out you were here he will have your head."

The officer stopped eight feet from Rapp and looked at him strangely. With a frown on his face he asked, "Uday?"

Rapp could tell by the look on the man's face that he had pushed his luck far enough. With lightning speed he drew his gun and fired a shot straight into the center of the colonel's forehead. The heavy .45-caliber round knocked the man from his feet and sent him to the street. Rapp stepped forward, screaming at the top of his lungs, "How dare you talk about my father that way!" He squeezed off three more rounds into the already dead body and spat on it. Then, looking up at the armored personnel carrier he waved his gun in the air and yelled, "Get out of here right now, or my father will have your heads!"

Quickly Rapp turned and limped back toward the cars. Over the team's comnet he said, "I sure hope you guys have got those rockets ready."

"Roger that," someone said.

"Then use them right now, before they have a chance to call in what I just did." Rapp watched as one of the Delta operators reached into the car and pulled out a LAW 80 rocket. He expertly extended it into firing position, stepped clear of the car and yelled, "Get down!"

Rapp dove for the pavement and before he hit the ground he heard the loud swooshing noise of the 94-mm rocket leaving the tube. A split second later there was an incredible explosion and the armored personnel carrier burst into flames. With debris still falling Rapp saw one of the other Delta operators run to the other side of the street with a second LAW in his hand. The man dropped to his knee in a doorway, acquired the second armored personnel carrier in his sights and fired.

Rapp covered his ears, the explosion lifting his body

off the ground an inch. After a moment he scrambled to his feet. As machine-gun fire erupted he raced for the building and yelled, "Major Berg, our cover's been blown, get up here ASAP!"

Rapp ran into the building and made it to the elevator. "Give me an update, Major."

"We've got the bombs, or at least the parts that matter most."

"Wax the guards and get up here," said Rapp with urgency.

"What about the scientists?"

"Fuck!" He'd forgot about them. He looked around for a moment and said, "Bring 'em all up, and do it fast."

"Roger."

Rapp went back to the street. The shooting, at least for now, had stopped. Nervously, he looked at his watch and swore under his breath, wishing the rest of the team was already up here. The Delta operators had fanned out a bit and were scanning in every direction, ready to shoot anything that moved. Rapp headed back to the elevator and paced back and forth until the door opened. When it did, two Delta operators raced past him with the cart. Next, Dr. Lee stepped off, loudly protesting in English that the components were too fragile to be moved like this.

Rapp delivered a well placed left hook to the scientist's jaw and grabbed him as he began to crumple. Tossing Lee over his shoulder, Rapp motioned for the other scientists to get off the elevator. They stood cowering in the corner as one of Major Berg's men threw his satchel charge into the elevator and pressed the button to send it back down. The doors closed and the whine of the elevator could be heard as the cable unwound. Rapp backed out of the room and yelled at the other scientists, "Do not leave this room or you will be shot!"

With that he closed the door, went through the small room and out onto the street. Rapp dumped Lee's body into the trunk of the last car and put a pair of flex cuffs on his wrists.

Berg appeared at his side. "What in the hell are you doing?"

"Dr. Lee is going to spend the next several years of his life telling us everything he knows about Saddam's nuclear weapons program."

Berg grinned. "Good idea. Now can we get the hell out of here?"

"Yep. Have one of your men close that door over there and set one more satchel charge with a thirty-second delay."

Berg barked the orders in Arabic, and his men went to work. One by one they retreated to the vehicles and loaded up. The gunners standing in the sunroofs covered the withdrawal until the last man was in. Each car did a head count and Berg gave the order to move out.

The cars sped away from the burning vehicles to the sound of air raid sirens and antiaircraft guns, punctuated by the heavy explosions of bombs. The night sky was ablaze with tracer fire and the streets were empty. The bombing had driven people for cover. Moments later they turned onto Shari' Al Urdun, another major thoroughfare, and punched it. Less than a mile later the road turned into Route 10, an empty six- lane highway. As Major Berg radioed Colonel Gray their status, the cars flew down the road at 110 mph toward the waiting choppers, safety, and success.

45

Colonel Gray had informed General Flood via secure satellite uplink that the team had achieved their primary goal without any casualties and was en route to Scorpion I for extraction. The room erupted in a premature show of excitement that was quickly doused when the president reminded everyone that they weren't out of the woods yet.

Hayes felt as if something was trying to eat its way out of his stomach. He was so tense he'd taken to pacing back and forth along one side of the conference table. While this may have helped the commander in chief relax a bit, it did little to comfort the others in the room. In the midst of the battle the president felt the walls closing in. This was, bar none, the boldest, most difficult decision of his political life. He knew without the slightest doubt that he'd made the right choice, but that didn't mean he had to like it. Somewhere in the back of his mind he knew that Israel had played him. They had sent Ben Freidman to Washington knowing full well that America wouldn't ignore the information. If Israel were to take matters into their own hands and bomb Iraq it would shatter the Arab coalition that was organized against Saddam. Israel knew Hayes would have to act.

This somehow tainted everything he'd done during the last week. Robert Hayes was a proud man, and he wanted to do the right thing for the right reasons. He didn't enjoy being played. He didn't enjoy being caught up in other people's schemes. In the midst of his pacing he came to a decision. Some things were going to change as soon as the mission was over. If it failed he was done. And not just kind of done, *really* done. The only way he was going to be able to put out the fire started by Congressman Rudin was with complete victory. Anything short of that and his enemies would ravage him. Hayes had no false illusions about the future. If Rapp and the Delta team failed to get out of Iraq with the nukes, he would be crucified.

As Hayes continued pacing he glanced over at the big board and stared at the five blue triangles west of Baghdad. If only they would start moving. The president's eyes shifted to one of the other TVs which was showing CNN. His eyes squinted in genuine hatred at the man on the screen. Congressman Albert Rudin was on the screen ranting and raving about the bombing. Hayes had already caught his act on MSNBC twenty minutes earlier. He was sure that before the night was over Rudin would make his *Wag the Dog* innuendo on every network and cable outlet in America. The irritating ass was already asking for hearings into the bombings.

It was at that precise moment that President Hayes decided he was going to destroy Albert Rudin. It was the first and only time he'd ever been moved to such thoughts in his twenty-five-plus years of politics. But now he savored the thought of the absolute and utter destruction of Rudin's political career. Rudin had been warned, not just by Hayes, but by the leaders of the party to back off and keep his mouth shut. He'd been admonished severely, yet he still continued. He would pay for his irritating insolence and stubborn self-righteousness. If Rapp and the Delta team could pull it off they would give Hayes the sword he needed to do the job, and if they failed, they'd be giving the sword to Rudin. Either way, only one of them would survive.

As Hayes turned to do another circuit behind the table, a sheaf of papers was shoved under his nose by his chief of staff, Valerie Jones. "Give this the once-over."

The president took the four sheets of paper without comment and began reading them. He was relieved to have something to take his mind off the mission. Midway down the first page he stopped, and holding the sheets against the wall, he crossed out a word and inserted a different one. He was reading a statement written by Jones and White House Press Secretary Michelle Bernard. The press room upstairs was packed to the gills with reporters and photographers who were waiting for Bernard to fill them in on what was going on. Hayes quickly finished reading the pages and made just a few changes.

He handed them back to Jones and said, "It looks good. Add one more thing at the end, though." Before Hayes could continue General Flood's baritone voice filled the room.

"Mr. President, the extraction has been completed and the team is en route to Saudi Arabia."

Hayes looked at Flood and then the big screen. The five blue triangles that he'd been so concerned about were finally moving. With a smile on his face he looked back to the general and asked, "Every single person has been accounted for?"

Flood smiled back. "Every single person."

Hayes felt like screaming for joy, but kept his composure. The extraction was the easy part. Surface-to-air missile batteries in the western Iraqi desert had just been pounded mercilessly for the last hour by planes and special forces personnel. The AWACS had reported that the missile threat to the planes had ceased. If there were any SAM sights left they'd be too afraid to draw any attention to themselves.

Turning to Jones and Bernard the president said, "Get upstairs and give the briefing, and when you're done tell them I'll address the nation tonight at nine o'clock."

Jones stood first and said, "Slow down for a second. We need to discuss this."

All the president could do was smile at his always cautious chief of staff. "It's all right, Valerie. I know what I'm doing."

"But, sir, you don't even have a speech prepared."

The president kept smiling as he ushered his two advisors toward the door. "Don't worry. I know what I'm going to say."

When he returned to the conference table General Flood motioned for the president to sit next to Kennedy. He leaned over and said, "Mr. President, we still have the flight of F-111's holding. What would you like to do?"

Hayes glanced over at the board for a second. He knew the secondary targets well. They'd selected four command and control bunkers and four of Saddam's expansive presidential palaces. The folks over at the National Reconnaissance Office had chosen the palaces from a list of over twenty. They'd done so after studying thousands of photos. The four that they picked were the ones deemed most likely to be hiding production facilities for weapons of mass destruction. The president knew the time would never be better to strike. He had to balance the potential loss of civilian life against the possibility of delivering a crippling blow to Saddam. The superpenetrator bombs would decimate their targets. After a brief moment of consideration the president looked at Flood and said, "You have my authorization."

Relieved by the president's decision, Flood brought the phone to his mouth and said, "It's a go."

Kennedy placed a hand on the president's arm. "Sir, we need to make some calls."

Hayes sighed. The list was long, and he had a lot of explaining to do. Kennedy suggested that they should call Prime Minister Goldberg first and the president agreed. A moment later the two men were talking via a secure satellite uplink.

"Prime Minister Goldberg," started the president.

"I've been waiting for your call, Mr. President," answered a slightly irritated Israeli leader.

"I'm sorry I didn't let you know about the operation in advance, but for obvious reasons security has been very tight."

Goldberg, in his typical short manner, chose not to acknowledge the president's reason and instead asked, "Do you have any news to report?"

"I do," replied Hayes. "Approximately an hour ago U.S. Special Forces personnel stormed the Al Hussein Hospital in Baghdad and achieved their primary objective. The weapons we were after are in our possession, and the facility has been destroyed without any damage to the hospital."

There was an incredibly long period of silence on the line before a heartfelt Goldberg replied, "Mr. President, the country of Israel is forever indebted to you."

The president smiled at Kennedy, who was listening on an extension. "That is very kind of you to say. I'm sorry I can't talk long, but I'm looking forward to our visit next week." The Israeli prime minister was due in town shortly for scheduled peace talks with the Palestinians.

"Are you sure my Arab neighbor will show up after what has happened tonight?"

"Oh, I'm sure Yasser will be here. I'm not going to sit on our little secret. I'm going to let all the world know what Saddam was up to."

There was apprehension in Goldberg's voice when he spoke. "I hope that my country's role in this will not be mentioned."

"I appreciate your concern, David, but that goes without saying."

"You are a great ally to the Israeli people, Mr. President."

"And Israel has been a great ally to the U.S." Hayes said this with considerably less conviction than Goldberg had. The president looked at Kennedy who mouthed a name to him. Hayes nodded and spoke into the phone. "David, would you do me a favor and pass along my gratitude and apology to Colonel Freidman."

"I would be happy to, but whatever in the world would you need to apologize for?"

"I gave him a bit of a chilly reception when he was in D.C. last week."

"Oh, don't worry about that," laughed Goldberg. "I don't think he expected you to be happy with the news he delivered."

"Well, that doesn't change the fact that I was less than hospitable. It was wrong to treat him the way I did and I would like to apologize. In fact, I think you should bring him along next week. America owes him a debt of gratitude, and I would like to thank him personally."

"In light of the efforts you've made, Mr. President, I think Colonel Freidman would be honored by such a request."

"Good then . . . tell the colonel that I look forward to thanking him in person next week. I have to run now,

David." The president listened to Goldberg thank him one more time and then he hung up the phone.

In an extremely rare show of emotion Irene Kennedy smiled and nodded her head in a show of satisfaction. "That was perfect, sir."

46

THE WHITE HOUSE, MONDAY EVENING

The president had spent much of the last four hours trying to reassure his chief of staff that he was making the right decision to address the nation from the White House press room. Jones wanted him behind his desk in the Oval Office in a controlled environment. She wanted him reading a carefully scripted speech from a TelePrompTer so there was no room for error. No surprises from an overzealous reporter who might be looking to make a name for her or himself. No slipups by the commander in chief on an important issue. The situation was already delicate enough, and there was little room for error.

President Hayes strongly disagreed with his chief of staff. He knew that the truly great speeches, the ones that won people over, were given off the cuff, from the heart. Not when reading from some TelePrompTer. Sure, the historians with all of their diplomas would fawn over the great written speeches, but not the people, not the populace. They wanted you to act like a fellow citizen, not a robot. That's what he would do tonight. He was at his best when he just stood up and let it fly.

The president was alone in the Oval Office, taking a moment to organize his thoughts before he went out in front of the cameras. On a legal pad he scratched out his major themes. Like a loosely scripted play he outlined the first, second and final act. It helped immensely that victory was complete. Rapp and the Delta team were safely back in Saudi Arabia with the nukes, and every air crew and special forces soldier was accounted for. His critics both domestically and internationally were still spouting off, taking him to task for the bombing. Either through innuendo or direct attack they were all saying the same thing; that he'd bombed Saddam for political cover. In a few minutes they would all look very petty.

A knock on the door interrupted the conclusion he was working on and then he remembered that he needed to speak to someone before the briefing started. "Come in." The president stood and walked around his desk.

Kennedy entered the room with a very nervous looking Anna Rielly. The president met them halfway and directed them toward the couches by the fireplace. Hayes imagined that NBC was wondering why the president had asked for a private meeting with their White House correspondent just minutes prior to addressing the nation.

"Ladies, please sit." Hayes sat on one couch and Kennedy and Rielly the other. "Anna, Irene tells me you've had a very difficult week."

Rielly, not wanting to talk about her personal life with the president, gave him a curt nod. The truth was it had been hell. If the entire matter in Milan hadn't been bad enough, she'd had to deal with the deluge of phone calls from family, friends and co-workers after Congressman Rudin had showed Mitch's photograph on national TV. The whole world now thought of him as an assassin.

"Well," continued the president, "after all you've been

through, I thought you deserved to know a few things before I go out there and address your colleagues." The president paused briefly and then began explaining the events of the last week to a shocked Rielly.

THE WHITE HOUSE PRESS ROOM, MONDAY EVENING

PRESIDENT HAYES BOUNDED onto the platform at the front of the room like the young man he once was. Irene Kennedy, General Flood, Secretary of Defense Culbertson and National Security Advisor Haik stood behind him against the blue curtain backdrop. His chief of staff and press secretary stood just off to the side by the door. Hayes looked supremely confident.

The president gripped the podium with both hands and took a moment to look over the gallery of reporters jammed into the small room. "This afternoon I gave the order for our forces in the Persian Gulf to attack Iraq. I did not inform our allies prior to commencing military operations, and I informed only a few members of my Cabinet and only a handful of senators and congressmen. This was intentional on my part, and if you'll bear with me for a moment I'll explain why I went to such great lengths to keep this attack a secret."

The president paused to sip from a glass of water sitting under the podium. He wanted the tension to build. "It should come as no surprise to any of us that Saddam Hussein has been on a quest to develop and obtain weapons of mass destruction for some time. Well, last week I was confronted with a horrifying reality. I was informed that Saddam was less than a month away from having three fully operational nuclear weapons." The president stopped and looked out across the hushed room. "It seems that for the past several years he has been developing these nuclear weapons with the help of Park Chow Lee, a North Korean nuclear physicist."

The president turned and nodded to Kennedy, who approached an easel and flipped over a piece of foam board, on which a photograph of the scientist was printed.

"Dr. Lee was on loan from the North Korean government," continued the president, "along with another half dozen scientists. In return for providing Saddam with these experts, the North Korean government was given some forty million dollars in crude oil. Dr. Kennedy will provide you with documentation to prove this when I'm done." Looking to Kennedy the president said, "Next photo please."

Kennedy moved the photo of Lee out of the way and replaced it with an aerial shot of a city. One building in the middle was circled in red. "Saddam went to great lengths to hide what he was up to. So much so that he placed the production facility for these weapons under the Al Hussein Hospital in Baghdad." The president paused again. "I don't need to explain to you his motives for doing this. Let's just say they were less than noble. None of this should shock any of us." The president shook his head with sad conviction. "Confronted with this untenable situation I was left with no other alternative than to take these weapons out. A man like Saddam Hussein, a man who has used poison gas on his own people, must never be allowed to obtain the destructive power of a nuclear bomb. At nine o'clock this evening, Baghdad time, we commenced offensive operations to take these weapons out and destroy the facility. U.S. Special Forces personnel conducted a daring raid on the facility at exactly the same time as an air raid started. I am pleased to announce that the operations were a complete success. The facility was destroyed and there were no civilian casualties. I repeat, no civilian casualties. In addition, the special forces team that conducted the raid was able to take the three nuclear devices with them when they were extracted. Those weapons are safely out of Iraq, and we are in the process of arranging an inspection by a U.N. team and any U.S. senator and congressman who is still in doubt as to the integrity of their president." The comment was a well aimed shot, but the president wasn't done. He wasn't even close.

"I am also pleased to announce that all U.S. personnel who were involved in tonight's operations have returned safely to their bases and ships. I apologize to our allies and our leaders on the Hill for not letting you in on this operation earlier, but I couldn't risk it for fear that the weapons would be moved. National security was paramount during every phase of this operation, and that brings me to the second reason for addressing you tonight.

"Just yesterday this entire operation was put in jeopardy by Congressman Albert Rudin when he went on TV and divulged classified top-secret information." The president shook his head in disgust. "Congressman Rudin, blinded by his irrational hatred of the CIA, and his zeal to destroy Dr. Kennedy, decided to give all the world the name and photograph of one of this country's top counterterrorism operatives. Many of you in the press have spent the last day trying to find out who this man is. Well, for reasons of national security, I can't tell you much about him, but I will tell you that he is the man who led the raid into Baghdad tonight. Without his bravery and selfless attitude this mission would not have been a success. His name is Mitch Rapp, and he has just completed his last mission, thanks to Congressman Rudin and his inability to put the national security of this country before his own petty vendettas.

"Many of you were shocked by the raids that occurred at the congressman's home and office this morning. Let me explain how they came about. Dr. Kennedy and I sat down with FBI Director Roach last night and showed him the classified files of Mr. Rapp's career with the CIA. I can assure all of you that the law was upheld by both myself and my predecessor. The file contains presidential findings authorizing the use of lethal force. In each and every case the leadership of both the House and the Senate were notified under the laws of Congressional Notification. *Technically* speaking, Congressman Rudin, as chairman of the House Intelligence Committee, is to be notified in a timely fashion of any covert action. Myself and my predecessor argued successfully to the leadership on the Hill, both Democrats and Republicans alike, that Congressman Rudin could not be trusted with such information. They agreed, and he was kept out of the loop. This was a difficult situation. We had to balance the needs of Congressional Notification and national security. We felt, and so did the House and Senate leadership, that we were fulfilling our obligation on both counts.

"With the high stakes of this current operation hanging in the balance we proved to Director Roach and a federal judge that laws had been broken. We moved quickly to have those files seized so the operation would not be further compromised by Congressman Rudin's brash and reckless behavior."

The president stopped and looked as if even he couldn't believe Rudin's stupidity. "I am sorry to say that Mr. Rapp's career in the field of counterterrorism has been damaged beyond repair, and as a consequence so has the national security of our country. The FBI will be investigating Congressman Rudin to find out just how much damage he's done, and they will explore filing criminal charges."

The president glanced over his shoulder and then said, "This was also why Dr. Kennedy was unwilling to answer questions on the Hill today. The operation in Iraq was already under way, and she did not want to lie to the committee nor did she want to say anything that might compromise the mission.

"Now before turning this over to Dr. Kennedy and General Flood I would like to thank our allies for their understanding, patience and loyalty, and I'd like to thank our soldiers, sailors, airmen and marines for their bravery and professionalism. And to Mitch Rapp, for once again putting his life on the line. The world is a safer place tonight because of all of you." With a sincere smile the president ended by saying, "Good night and God bless all of you." Without pause, President Hayes turned and left the room.

47

U.S. CAPITOL, MONDAY EVENING

A promising day had turned out to be a complete disaster. Hank Clark sat in the dark in his hide on the fourth floor of the Capitol. He had a large snifter of cognac in one hand and a cigar in the other. His chair was turned toward the open window with his feet up on the sill. Cold air rushed in from the outside to battle with the century-old radiator. It was just another example of government inefficiency. Smoking was officially forbidden in any federal workplace, but the people who wrote the laws sometimes chose to ignore them. Clark took a big puff from his Diamond Crown Figurado cigar and blew it out into the cold night air.

The combination of nicotine and high octane cognac had him buzzing. His mind was nearing that place where he desperately wanted to be, the place where booze actually elicits clarity of thought. It was difficult to both achieve and maintain, and very easy to overshoot and get lost in the sluggish orbit of drunken stupidity.

The senator's grand plans were in tatters, and he was trying to figure out how he'd been so badly outflanked. He was in full retreat, scrambling to salvage enough to fight another day. The president's move had been brilliant. His poll numbers would be near eighty percent by Friday and Mitch Rapp wasn't a national hero yet, but by the time the press got finished with him, he would be. Kennedy's stock had risen, too. She was seen as a cool professional in the midst of a crisis. The type of person we needed running the CIA. No one on the Hill was going to risk their career trying to take either of them down at this point.

Albert Rudin was all the example they needed. If ever a politician was finished it was Rudin. The president had just jumped from the bully pulpit and squashed him like a bug. The man was radioactive. By tomorrow morning he wouldn't be able to get a table at Burger King. He wouldn't have a single ally left in Washington.

Unfortunately, Clark knew Rudin well enough to know that the stubborn old bastard would not simply slink back to Connecticut and retire quietly. Washington was his lair, and the Democratic Party was his life. He would be a desperate man, and desperate men rarely think wisely. Rudin was now a major liability.

Clark took another sip of cognac and tried to assess the damage that the cantankerous congressman might cause him. It didn't look good. Clark could try to take the high road and dismiss Rudin's ranting and raving as those of a bitter beaten man, but the president would still wonder. And then there was the issue of Steveken and Brown. If the president was serious about the FBI pursuing a criminal investigation, they were in trouble, and that meant he was in trouble. Rudin had to be convinced to keep his mouth shut, or Clark would be up the ol' shit crick without a paddle. Money was the most likely way to solve things. He would approach Rudin on principle, and if that didn't work he'd have to pay him off.

Clark looked out the open window down the National Mall and puffed on his cigar. He tried to calculate his odds for success. Rudin was a cheap bastard. The money just might work.

Suddenly, someone began banging loudly on the office door. Sitting alone in the darkness Clark was so startled that he leapt to his feet. He placed a hand over his racing heart and tried to calm himself.

"Open this damn door, Hank! I know you're in there!"

It was Rudin. Clark wasn't so sure he wanted to talk to him yet. He stood in front of the open window afraid to move.

"I can smell your damn cigar smoke! Open this door right now!" Rudin screamed. "The FBI wants to talk to me tomorrow and they've advised me to bring a lawyer, Hank! I need to talk to you right now."

With great reluctance Clark set his drink down and turned on a desk lamp. He went to the door, unlocked and opened it. Rudin shouldered his way past Clark muttering obscenities as he went. Clark closed the door and turned to address the congressman. "Albert, I feel horrible about what happened tonight. I can understand the president's frustration, but I think he's crossed the line a bit."

"Understand his frustration," Rudin snapped with spit flying from his mouth. "He just fucked me over in front of the entire country, hell, the entire world, and all you can say is you understand his *frustration!* What about my frustration?" Rudin barked.

Clark made a calming motion with his hands. "I'm here to help you, Albert. Your screaming will accomplish nothing."

"Here to help me," he bellowed. "You're up here hiding. Fucking help me, my ass."

The senator sighed and told himself to stay calm. "You're right, Albert. I'm sorry."

"Well, sorry ain't gonna cut it. You're gonna make things right."

"Albert, I want to help you, but before I do that you have to admit to some blame here."

"Blame!" he screeched with an angry face. "The only blame I'm going to take is for listening to you. You were the one who sent that oddball Steveken to see me. You were the one who told me to go on *Meet the Press* and tell the world about Mitch Rapp. If I hadn't listened to you, I wouldn't be in any of this."

Clark's calm demeanor began to unravel. "Oh, Albert, I think you can take more than a little bit of the blame for the position you're in."

"Bullshit. I'm right and you know it."

"Everything the president said tonight was true. Especially the part about you having a vendetta."

"Fuck you, Hank." Rudin furthered his point by raising his middle finger.

Clark leaned in. "You'd better watch it, Albert. I'm probably the only friend you have left in this town."

The senator's size managed to intimidate Rudin enough to force him back a step. In defense he said, "I'm desperate! I'm a desperate man. You have to help me!"

Clark remembered his own earlier thought. *Desperate men do desperate things.* It was as if he'd been given a sign. The fog had cleared. Clark saw a way out of the entire mess. He placed a hand on Rudin's bony shoulder and said, "Come here. I want to show you something that I think will help."

Rudin hesitated at first, but Clark nudged him with his large hand. The two men walked over to the open window, and Clark pointed off in the distance toward the Washington Monument. It was bathed in a bright light on all four sides, shooting up out of the middle of the Mall as if it were a rocket ready for flight.

Clark gazed out window and said, "You fought the good fight, Albert. Just like Washington did, only you didn't have history on your side."

Rudin shook his head angrily and said, "History fucked me."

"Well, I'm going to make things right. You and I are going to go see the president in the morning, and I'm going to get him to call off the FBI." Clark patted Rudin on the back and said, "Don't worry, I'll take care of it."

Rudin's shoulders sank in relief. "Oh, thank you, Hank. Thank you . . . thank you . . . thank you."

"Don't worry about it." Clark patted him on the back again and said, "That's what friends are for." And with Rudin finally relaxed, Clark took a half step back and placed both hands in the middle of the wiry congressman's back. With one good push the senator sent Rudin toppling out the open window. There was a brief blood-curdling scream and then an instant later a dull thud. Clark stuck his head out the window and looked down some eighty feet to the stone terrace below. There lay Albert Rudin's lifeless body.

Clark went to his desk and grabbed his snifter, where he downed the remainder of the liqueur in one gulp. Next he grabbed his mobile phone from his suit coat and dialed a number. When a woman answered on the other end he said, "This is Senator Clark. I need to speak to the president immediately. Something terrible has happened."

48

MARYLAND, WEDNESDAY EVENING

Rapp arrived stateside with a genuine mix of emotions. He was still riding high from the operation and doubted that the pride he felt over the mission's success would ever wane. He had more than likely reached the apex of his career, and he could think of no better way to exit. Whether he liked it or not, Congressman Rudin had blown his cover. He was done operating in the field. Fortunately for the congressman, he'd taken the cowardly way out and jumped. As a result, it was much easier for Rapp to deal with the problem. There was no sense in hurting a dead man.

When his plane landed at Andrews a group of geeks from the CIA and the Pentagon were waiting to debrief him. Rapp told them it would have to wait, but they continued to press the point, so he told them to go to hell. Before leaving he spent a few minutes alone with Kennedy. She tried to bring up Anna, but he would have none of it. He had already made the mistake of combining his professional life with his personal life, and he would never do it again. She filled him in on what had happened since the president's address on Monday night. Virtually every magazine, newspaper and TV show had called the CIA's office of public affairs and asked for an interview with America's new hero.

"And what did you tell them?" asked Rapp.

"That there wasn't a snowball's chance in hell that you would do an interview."

"Exactly. You know me well."

"Too well."

She tried to bring up Anna again, but he cut her off. He was going to crawl into a hole for a few days, and when he was ready to come out, he'd call. Kennedy stood alone with a worried expression on her face and watched him drive away. She could tell that beneath Mitch's tough exterior he was hurting. She knew him better than he knew himself and Kennedy could see he was ready to crumble.

Rapp flew down the rural country roads of Maryland with a mixture of apprehension and excitement coursing through his veins. Before leaving Saudi Arabia, he'd called her apartment and left a message. "I'll be home Wednesday night. I miss you very much. It would mean a lot if you were at the house when I got there." He figured this was safe. He met her halfway, and now it was up to her.

As he returned to America the cruel irony of the situation began to set in. He'd been searching for that normal life, a wife, a family, true love, and now after all these years he was finally in a position to give it his all. Anna was that woman. Despite what had happened in Milan, he knew with all his heart that he wanted to spend the rest of his life with her, but he also knew he couldn't force it. Anna was a bit of a contrarian. She did not like being badgered.

She needed to come to certain conclusions of her own free will.

Rapp was not well versed in the affairs of the heart, and he was entirely unaccustomed to failure. He was someone who was supremely confident in his ability to handle any situation, but on this cool November evening there were cracks in his armor. An unfamiliar feeling was percolating just beneath the surface. It was the foreign emotion of vulnerability. He tried not to get his hopes too high, but he couldn't help it. He desperately wanted Anna to be at the house.

Turning onto his road he could no longer contain his excitement. He'd come too far, given too much, to be deprived of happiness. He knew with absolute conviction that Anna loved him. There were two sides to every story, and now, having had some time to think about Milan, he could see why she was so upset. He was bringing a lot of baggage to the relationship, and not your everyday type of baggage. Deep down inside he knew they were meant to be together. It was fate.

As he turned into the driveway and the headlights from his car swung around across the long front yard, they hit the house and then the garage. His heart sank in disappointment, and he stopped the car. It was eleven minutes past eight, and she wasn't here. Slowly he released the brake and rolled down the driveway. He stopped the car in front of the garage and got out. Not wanting to deal with his bags, he went straight for the front door.

Rapp unlocked the door and punched in the security code. He headed for the kitchen to check the answering machine. It was full. He swore to himself, and like an addict searching for a fix, began plowing through them one at a time, skipping over each new message as soon as

he heard it was someone other than Anna. With each passing message he sank further into despair until finally the
last one had been heard. He exhaled deeply as if part of
his soul had just left his body.

Turning, he went to the fridge and grabbed a beer. His
nerves were dead. He grabbed a jacket and went outside
onto the deck. For some reason he needed to see the
water. As he looked out across the dark bay he tried to
find an excuse for her. Why she wasn't there, why she
hadn't called and left a message. He felt pathetic, for not
facing the truth, for grasping at empty hopes. Needing to
do something, anything, to take his mind off the pain he
felt, he set off to get a few logs and start a fire.

Five minutes later he seemed to have found a brief
moment of relief. The flames licked upward into the chilly
night air and the bark on the birch logs popped and
crackled. The wind blew in off the bay and carried the
smoke with it. He took a sip of beer and looking into the
flames, he remembered that Anna had given him the fire
kettle for his birthday. He suddenly felt awash in a barren
sea of loneliness. He'd spent years hiding his inner
thoughts. Emotions were a luxury he could ill afford.
Anna had changed all that. She'd gently peeled away the
tough exterior to expose an array of feelings that he'd
never known. Now those feelings had turned against him,
and the pain was excruciating.

As he stared into the fire tears began to fill his eyes. He
leaned back in the Adirondack chair and wondered what
life would be like without her. The smell of her hair, the
touch of her skin, her enchanting green eyes, her smile,
her laugh, it was all gone and somehow he felt cheated.
His sacrifices had been great and this had been all he'd
asked for in return. A little happiness. A companion to
spend the rest of his life with.

Through the tears his analytical mind raced ahead in an attempt to see his future. He would survive, he knew that. Strip away everything else and he was the consummate survivor. The pain of this loss would diminish but not entirely heal. There would be no other women, at least not for a long time, and when and if he ever found one, she would never measure up to Anna. She was his one true love, and he had lost her. With tears streaming down his tired face he began to wonder if any of it was worth his sadness.

Rielly stood in the shadows near the side of the house and watched. She smelled the smoke when she got out of her car and came around the side of the house. She did not want to be there when he got home. She wanted to make a point. She wanted him to feel what she had felt. Now standing in the shadows, seeing the pain he was in, she couldn't take it anymore.

She stepped from the shadows and approached him. He stared up at her the way a child looks when they first awake from a long sleep. Gazing down at his tear-filled eyes, all she wanted to do was make his pain go away.

Reaching out, she cupped his face in her hands and said, "Darling, I'm sorry." He did not speak. He grabbed her, pulled her down onto his lap, buried his face in her chest and wrapped his arms around her. Rielly kissed the top of his head and ran her fingers through his short hair. "How did you feel when you got home and I wasn't here?"

"Like shit."

She gazed at him seriously. "I wanted you to know what it feels like to wait for me, to wonder if I'm going to come through the door, if you'll ever see me again. That's what I went through in Milan."

His head stayed buried in her chest. "It's no fun."

"No, it isn't." She grabbed his strong chin and lifted it toward her. "Now that you know how painful it is to be confronted with losing me, promise me that'll you'll never make me go through it again."

Without hesitation Rapp said, "I promise." They embraced in a long kiss and held each other as if they'd been apart for months.

After several minutes they stood and Rapp asked her to wait outside for a minute. He ran into the house and raced upstairs. A moment later he came back downstairs and out onto the deck. He grabbed Rielly by the shoulders and had her sit in the Adirondack chair. Kneeling in front of her he kissed her on the lips and asked, "Do you remember when we met?"

Rielly looked at him as if he were asking a trick question. It would be impossible for her to forget when they'd met. He'd saved her life. "Of course I remember."

"Do you remember what you said to me when the hostage standoff was over? That it was fate?"

Rielly smiled. "Yes."

"Do you still believe that?" he asked sincerely.

"Yes," she said softly.

"So do I." He cupped her face in his hands. "I think I was sent there to save you, so that later you could save me."

Still smiling, she tilted her head and asked, "How?"

"By spending the rest of your life with me." He reached into his pocket and pulled out a beautiful diamond ring. Grabbing her hand he gazed into her eyes and asked, "Anna, will you please marry me?"

Her eyes filled with tears of joy, and her bottom lip began to quiver as he slid the ring onto her finger. Not able to speak, she slowly nodded her head and bent forward to kiss him on the lips.

49

The president stood in front of the fireplace in the Oval Office. The cameras snapped away and flashes filled the room. On his left was Yasser Arafat, and on his right Prime Minister Goldberg of Israel. It had been a great week for Hayes. His poll numbers were through the roof. He had a mandate to get things done both in Washington and on the international stage. Even the press was fawning over him. There wasn't a country in the Middle East, including Iran, that wasn't relieved that Hayes had pulled the teeth from Saddam's arsenal. Saddam was screaming bloody murder over the raid, but no one was listening. Hayes had carried the day.

The president's chief of staff stepped in front of the press pool and said, "Okay, that's it for now. Thank you." Jones ushered them toward the door gesturing with her arms like she was moving livestock into a corral.

When the press was gone the president turned to his guests and said, "Something has come up that I need to attend to. It shouldn't take long. My chief of staff will take you into the Roosevelt Room and get things started."

Hayes smiled at both men and left the Oval Office. As soon as he reached the hallway, the smile vanished. He traveled by himself down to the basement. When he reached the Situation Room he entered and closed the door behind him. Irene Kennedy was sitting on one side of the table and her Israeli counterpart was sitting across the table.

Ben Freidman stood immediately and said, "Mr. President, thank you for your invitation to come to the White House."

Hayes stood behind his leather chair, his hands resting on the back. This was Kennedy's plan, and he was more than willing to play his part. "You'll excuse me if I got you to travel all this way on a less than honest pretense, but I don't think you would have made the trip if I'd told you the real reason I wanted to talk to you."

The smile melted from Freidman's face as warning flags went up.

"Sit." Hayes pointed toward the Israeli's chair. Reluctantly the intelligence chief sat. "Is there anything you'd like to get off your chest?" asked Hayes.

Freidman scrambled to come up with the source of the president's ire. He'd just spent the entire morning with Kennedy and it had been very pleasant. No sign whatsoever that something was wrong. He looked across the table for her assistance and all he got was an inquiring glance. He turned to the president and said, "I'm sorry, sir, but I'm not quite sure I understand."

"Oh, I think you do." Hayes was ready to burst. He knew what Freid-man's eventual excuse would be and he already didn't buy it. It was high time they started acting like true allies. "Does the name Peter Cameron ring a bell?"

Freidman was a professional liar by trade. He shook his head, and with absolute conviction said, "I don't think so."

The president scoffed at his answer. "How about Donatella Rahn?"

Freidman had been wondering where she'd gone and now he knew the answer. "Yes, I do, Mr. President. Unfortunately."

"Oh, why is that?" Hayes asked with feigned concern.

"I recruited her personally, to work for Mossad. She was very good in her day, but several years ago we lost control of her."

"Lost control of her?" asked Hayes.

"It happens from time to time in our line of work, sir." Freidman glanced at Kennedy. "We don't have the best retirement plan and there are people who are willing to pay a lot of money for someone with Donatella's skills."

Hayes glanced at his watch and then at Kennedy. "I don't have time for this B.S."

"Are you trying to tell us, Ben, that Donatella has not worked for you for two years?"

"That's exactly what I'm trying to tell you."

"You're a liar, and not a very good one." The president picked up the phone behind him and pushed a button. "Send them in." He placed the phone back and watched Freidman squirm.

A moment later the door opened. Donatella Rahn and Mitch Rapp entered the room. Donatella went around the table and sat next to Kennedy. Rapp stood next to the president and glared at Freidman.

The president asked, "Would you like to amend your story now?"

"I don't know what this woman has told you, but she cannot be trusted." Freidman's forehead was beginning to glisten with sweat.

The president laughed. "Somehow I think it is you who can't be trusted, Mr. Freidman."

"Mr. President, I beg you. You cannot listen to this woman. She has stabbed my country in the back. We have been hunting her for almost a year."

"For the sake of making some progress, I'm going to at least for now ignore your comment about Ms. Rahn stabbing you in the back. I would like instead to focus on something else. Explain to me why you've been paying Ms. Rahn large amounts of money and hunting her at the same time."

Freidman tried to act confused by the whole thing. "I have no idea what you're talking about."

"Irene." The president looked to Kennedy.

Kennedy produced a file, opened it and slid it across the table. They were the Swiss bank accounts that Freidman used to hide money from his own government. With Donatella's help, Marcus Dumond, the CIA's top hacker, had obtained this information and much more. The president asked, "Do you recognize these bank accounts?"

Freidman lied. "No."

"Good, then you won't mind that they were closed this morning and the money was transferred to us."

Despite trying to keep his cool, Freidman was showing signs of unraveling. He chose not to respond to the president.

The president looked to Rapp and nodded. Then he held his hand out and said, "Ms. Rahn, it's time for us to leave."

Rapp drew his Beretta from his shoulder holster and methodically twisted a thick black silencer onto the end of it. Donatella got up from her chair and took the president's hand. In response to the recent development Freidman let out a laugh that sounded a little more nervous than he would have liked.

"Mr. President, how naive do you think I am? You can't intimidate me like this." Freidman shook his head disbelievingly at Hayes. "You could never get away with killing me. Especially not here in the White House."

"Oh, Mr. Freidman, I think you underestimate my dislike for you, and I think you overestimate your importance to your government. All I have to do is show Prime Minister Goldberg what you've been up to and by the time I'm done, he'll be thanking me for killing you." Hayes opened the door and ushered Donatella out.

"Wait," said a nervous Freidman.

The president motioned for Donatella to go on without him and he closed the door. "Don't waste my time, Mr. Freidman."

"What do you want to know?"

Rapp asked the question. "Who hired you to kill Peter Cameron?"

Freidman squirmed. "That's a complicated question."

Rapp raised his gun and pointed it at Freidman's knee cap. "No it isn't."

He looked at the gun and then at the man holding it. There was absolutely no doubt in Freidman's mind that Rapp would pull the trigger. In the blink of an eye he made up his mind and said, "It was Hank Clark."

"What?" asked a shocked president.

"Hank Clark." Freidman looked at Kennedy and said, "Give me my money back, and I'll tell you everything I know."

Rapp turned to the president and said, "I'd like you to leave now."

Hayes, still reeling over the name he'd just heard, said, "But—"

Rapp grabbed the president by his shoulder and said, "Leave."

Hayes looked to Kennedy for guidance. She nodded and looked at the door. After a moment of hesitation he reluctantly left the room. When he was gone Freidman breathed a sigh of relief and said to Kennedy, "Good. Now we can deal."

"Wrong!" bellowed Rapp. He pointed his gun at

Freidman's leg and pulled the trigger. A bullet spat from the end of the silencer and grazed the Israeli's meaty inner thigh. Freidman lurched back in his chair and grabbed his leg in a mix of shock and pain.

Rapp moved the weapon back to Freidman's knee and through clenched teeth said, "I'm looking for a reason to kill you, so there ain't gonna be any negotiating. If you want to walk out of here alive, you're gonna tell us everything you know."

Clutching his leg in pain, Freidman nodded his head and began to talk.

EPILOGUE

The Cosmos Club was Senator Clark's kind of place, especially around Christmas. The mansion at 2121 Massachusetts Avenue was a bastion of wealth, class, intellectual discussion, fine food, cigars and liquor. It was the type of place that would have never allowed Congressman Albert Rudin through its doors. The century-old club had rules, and chief among them was a sense of decorum. Differing opinions were encouraged, but loud divisive arguing was not.

The senator's limousine was cued up on Mass Avenue with the other social elites of Washington. He was fifth in line with at least as many limos and cars behind him. Sally Bradley's annual Christmas party at the Cosmos Club was an event not to be missed. That was, unless you were wife number three. She'd gone home to Phoenix. Washington's cold gray December skies depressed her too much.

Clark was more than a little surprised at the lack of remorse and guilt he felt over killing Rudin. He found it very satisfying that he was the only person who knew the truth. Just three weeks after the death the case was ruled a suicide and closed. The police had been very easy to handle. Clark laid it all out for the detectives. Rudin had been depressed for some time, especially since a meeting he'd had with his party's leadership and the president several weeks earlier. They'd threatened to strip him of his chairmanship and do everything in their power to make sure he didn't get reelected. Rudin had been devastated. Blinded by his convictions, he tried to find a way to torpedo Kennedy's nomination. Clark warned him against it, but Rudin said he'd discovered something that would ruin Kennedy. That was when he went on *Meet the Press* with his accusations. The next night his world fell apart around him when the president gave his speech to the nation. Clark told how a panicked Rudin came to him and begged him to talk to the president. He'd pleaded with Clark to intercede and get the president to call off the FBI's investigation.

Solemnly, Clark told the investigators that he'd refused Rudin's plea. How he'd told Rudin that he had nobody to blame but himself for the mess he was in. "I didn't think he'd jump. The thought never occurred to me. Now I realize I failed him in his hour of need." Clark seemed genuinely remorseful and the police believed him. Much of his story was backed up by the president himself and even Rudin's wife had said he'd been in a dark funk for several weeks. Clark was never once treated as a suspect, and after a short investigation it was ruled that Rudin had committed suicide.

The feeling of having avoided near disaster was intoxicating. Knowing that he had fooled them all gave him a sense of omnipotence. His plans to run for the White House, however, were on hold. Ellis and his West Coast financiers were very upset that Kennedy had been confirmed as director, but there was nothing he could do about that. At least not for now. In the meantime he told Ellis that he would begin trying to find another mole at the CIA. Amazingly, neither Steveken nor Brown's name had been dragged into the spotlight. After Rudin's death the FBI just dropped everything.

President Hayes was untouchable at present. His numbers were so high, someone would have to be a complete fool to run against him. But that was now. Who knew what the political climate would be like in a year? Clark would hang around biding his time. He'd lived to fight another day, and his dream of someday occupying the Oval Office was still alive.

Clark's limousine finally pulled into the small drive and a doorman, resplendent in topcoat and top hat, opened the door. The senator got out of the car in his double-breasted tuxedo and entered the club. He looked tanned and rested from another weekend retreat in the Bahamas and was in the mood to have some fun. He proceeded to the magnificent Warne Lounge where a band was playing and most of the partygoers had gathered. Too many in fact. Upon seeing that they were five deep at the bar, the senator reversed his course and headed off for the Cherrywood Bar. A few folks tried to stop him on the way but Clark politely informed them of his predicament and told them he would be back. Fortunately, there were only a few wise souls bellied up to the curved granite bar.

He ordered a glass of Merlot and settled in. He'd finish this one and order another before he went back to join the revelry. He was about to begin making small talk with the bartender when an absolutely stunning blond in an ivory, beaded dress sauntered into the room. She cozied up to the bar one chair over from Clark and ordered a glass of Chardonnay.

When she looked in his direction Clark said, "How are you doing this evening?"

"Just fine, thank you." She turned her attention back to the bartender.

The woman had just a touch of an accent, but Clark couldn't place it. She was absolutely gorgeous, high cheekbones, full lips and a curvaceous figure with a tiny waist. Clark was already wondering what she looked like with her clothes off when he asked, "Are you enjoying the party?"

"Yes." She studied Clark for a second and said, "You look familiar. Have we met before?"

He smiled and took a big sip of wine. "Most certainly not. I'd remember that." Standing, he extended his hand. "I'm Senator Hank Clark."

"Oh, that's right." She took his hand. "I've seen you on TV." With a flirtatious smile she added, "You're much better-looking in person."

"Why thank you, and so are you."

The woman laughed and patted Clark's hand.

"And what is your name?"

"I'm Mary Johnson."

"You must not live in Washington, Mary, or I'm sure we would have crossed paths."

"You are correct, Senator. I'm from Richmond."

"So how'd you get mixed up with this crowd?"

The glass of Chardonnay arrived. "I was a sorority sister of Sally's daughter in college."

"Oh, great. Here, take a seat." Clark offered the stool next to him.

"Thank you." She sat and crossed her legs, the long slit in her dress revealing a healthy portion of her toned thigh.

Clark noticed the exposed flesh immediately and reached for his wine. He took a large gulp and smiled. "I love your dress. It's beautiful." He looked at the wedding ring on her finger, and then back down at her leg. "So where's your husband?"

She hesitated for a second and then replied, "He's down in Richmond. He doesn't like coming to these things. In fact, all he pretty much likes to do is work."

Clark moved a little closer and in a quieter voice said, "If I was married to you, I'd only have one thing on my mind."

"And what's that, Senator?"

"You." Clark polished off his glass of wine and ordered another.

The woman blushed at the compliment and reached into her handbag to retrieve a compact. She opened it and checked her makeup, applying some more powder to her nose. "So tell me, Senator, where is Mrs. Clark tonight?"

"She is, fortunately, back in Arizona for the evening."

The second glass of Merlot appeared and the bartender scurried off to help another customer. The woman pulled some lipstick out of her handbag and asked Clark, "Is that you in that photo over there?" She pointed over Clark's shoulder at a collection of black-and-white photographs on the wall of the bar. When Clark turned to look, she casually moved her lipstick over the senator's glass of wine and pressed a small button on the side. Several drops of a clear odorless liquid fell into the glass. The woman placed the lipstick back in her handbag and took a sip of her own wine.

When Clark turned back around he said, "Yes, I think that is me and some of my colleagues from the Hill." He lifted his glass of wine and took a sip.

The woman nodded and then stuck her hand out. "Well, Senator Clark, I feel like dancing. What do you say?"

"I'd love to." Clark took another sip and stood. He offered his hand to the woman and decided tonight was going to be a good night indeed. As he stared down at her full breasts peeking over the top of her tight dress, he once again tried to imagine what Mary Johnson would look like naked.

RAPP STOOD ALONE in his tuxedo near the bar in the ballroom. His black hair had been dyed mostly gray, and he sported a salt and pepper goatee. He adjusted the horn-rimmed glasses he was wearing and looked out over the crowd in search of Donatella. He'd sent her to follow Clark, and was waiting for her to return.

For the most part, Rapp had kept Kennedy out of the loop over the last three weeks. She knew what he was up to but didn't want any details. The president, he assumed, had conveniently decided not to get involved. Freidman had given them a good start on what Clark had been up to. For his help, Kennedy and the president would stay silent about what the head of Mossad had done. Freidman's money, though, would stay out of his reach for a while longer. Kennedy wanted it for leverage on some other things.

With Freidman's information they began looking into Clark's life. Rapp had done most of the surveillance and digging with the help of Donatella and a few other well trusted specialists. He'd been inside all three of Clark's homes and examined his financial and medical records in detail. He'd also taken the opportunity to insert certain things here and there to help explain the senator's upcoming death.

Just killing Clark wasn't going to work. It would have been easy, but doing it so closely on the heels of Rudin's apparent suicide would have raised too many questions. This was why Rapp had picked tonight. The more witnesses the better.

Through the festive sea of holiday revelers Rapp spied a blond-haired Donatella working her way toward him with Clark in tow. Several people tried to stop the senator, but he was too focused on the bombshell in front of him to slow down.

Donatella approached Rapp and whispered, "It's taken care of." Then turning back to Clark she said, "I'd like you to meet a friend of mine." Donatella stepped out of the way and left the two men facing each other.

Rapp looked at Clark's face for signs that the drug was

working its way through his bloodstream. A layer of sweat was forming on his lip and his eyes appeared to be agitated.

Clark stuck out his hand and said, "Senator Hank Clark. Nice to meet you." At that moment he seemed to lose his balance for a second.

Rapp grabbed his hand firmly. "My name is Mitch Kruse, Senator. I've been looking forward to meeting you for some time."

"What did you say your name was?"

"Mitch Kruse."

Over the loud music of the band Clark said, "I've heard that name somewhere before."

Rapp shrugged. "Tell me, Senator, did Congressman Rudin jump, or was he pushed out your window?" Rapp was still holding on to Clark's hand and wasn't about to let go.

Clark tried to pull away, but Rapp was too strong. "I don't find your attempt at humor very entertaining."

"There's nothing humorous about it, Senator. I think you killed him."

Clark tried to pull away again and swayed a bit. "I have no idea what you're talking about."

Rapp noticed a heaviness in the senator's speech. "Senator, you don't look so good." Still holding Clark's hand, Rapp stepped to the side revealing an armchair he'd been saving. "Here. Sit." Rapp guided him into the chair and took his glass of wine. He handed it to Donatella who wiped it with a napkin and set it on the bar.

Clark clawed at his bow tie. "Something isn't right. I'm having a hard time breathing." The words barely made it out.

"You're having a heart attack, Senator. Just try and stay calm, it'll all be over in a minute."

436 / VINCE FLYNN

There was horror on Clark's face. He tried to speak, but nothing came out.

Rapp leaned in real close and said, "By the way, Senator, my name isn't Mitch Kruse, it's Mitch Rapp."

There was a flutter of recognition in Clark's eyes, but he was too far gone to react.

"I just wanted to meet you face-to-face before you died." Rapp stepped away so he could see the look of absolute horror on Clark's face fade to a death stare.

With Clark sitting wide-eyed, Rapp turned and extended his arm for Donatella. She grabbed it and they walked across the dance floor to the sounds of music, conversation and laughter.

Turn the page to read an exclusive extract from
Vince Flynn's next gripping Mitch Rapp
adventure . . .

EXECUTIVE POWER

Coming soon,
from Simon & Schuster/Pocket Books

PRELUDE

The sleek gray craft sliced through the warm water and humid night air of the Philippine Sea at twenty-five knots, its twin engines rumbling toward its destination with a guttural moan. The boat was in violation of international law and at least one treaty, but the men on board didn't care. Technicalities, legalities and diplomacy were for other people to sort out, people who sat in comfortable leather chairs with Ivy league degrees mounted and framed on their office walls. The men standing on the deck of the Mark V special operations craft were here to get a job done, and in their minds, it was a job that should have been taken care of months ago.

The low profile Mark V special operations craft was designed to sneak in under radar. It had been designed especially for the United States Navy SEALs and it was their choice of platform when running maritime insertions. It was eighty-two feet in length but the boat only drafted five feet when it was fully loaded and dead in the water. Instead of the standard screw it was propelled by two waterjets. All of this allowed the boat to maneuver very close to the beach with great precision.

Five men wearing black flight helmets and night vision goggles manned four .50 caliber machine guns and a 40mm grenade launcher. Eight other men dressed in jungle BDUs and floppy hats sat on the gunwales of the rubber combat raiding craft they would soon launch off the Mark V, and went over their equipment for at least the tenth time. Their faces were smeared with warlike green and black camouflage paint, but their expressions were calm.

Lieutenant Jim Devolis looked down at his SEAL squad and watched them go through their last check. He'd observed them doing it countless times before and for some reason it always reminded him of baboons picking bugs from each other at the zoo. They meticulously examined their H harnesses to make sure every snap was secure and all grenades taped. The communications gear was checked and rechecked. Fresh batteries had been placed in everyone's night vision goggles and along with backup batteries the expensive optical devices were stowed in waterproof pouches attached to their H harnesses. Weapons were sand-proofed with condoms secured over the muzzles and a bead of silicone sealant around the magazines and bolt covers. The only person wearing a rucksack tonight would be the squad's medical corpsman, and Devolis sincerely hoped they wouldn't be needing his expertise. The group was traveling light tonight. No MRE's, only a couple of Power Bars for each man. The plan was to be in and out before the sun came up. Just the way the SEALs liked it.

The tension grew as they neared the demarcation point. Devolis was glad to see that the jaw jacking had subsided. It was time to get serious. Turning his head to the right and down, his lips found the tube for his neoprene camel water pack and he sucked in a mouthful of fresh water. The men had been drinking all the water they could hold for two days. Hydration before an op in this part of the world was crucial. Even at night the temperature was still in the mid eighties and the humidity wasn't far behind. The only thing that was keeping them from sweating through their BDUs was the breeze created by the boat as it cruised at twenty-plus knots. Once they hit the beach, though, that would change. They had a two mile hike ahead of them through the thick tropical jungle. Even with all the water they'd drank in the last two days each man on the team would probably lose five to ten pounds just hiking in and out.

A firm hand fell on Devolis's shoulder. He turned to look at the captain of the boat.

"Two minutes out, Jim. Get your boys loaded up."

Devolis nodded once and blinked, his white eyes glowing bright against the dark camouflage paint spread across his face. "Thanks, Pat." The two men had practiced this drill hundreds of times back in Coronado, California at the headquarters for Naval Special Warfare Group One.

"Don't go wandering off on me now," Devolis said with a white grin.

The captain smiled in the manner of someone who's confident in his professional ability. "If you call, I'll be there gun's *a' blazin*."

"That's what I like to hear." Devolis nodded and then turned to his men. With his forefinger pointed straight up he made a circular motion and the SEALs instantly got to their feet. A moment later the boat slowed to just under five knots.

The Mark V, in addition to being extremely fast, also came with a slanted aft deck which allowed it to launch and receive small craft without stopping. Without a word the men grabbed the sides of their black CRRC with the forty horsepower outboard leading, and walked down the aft ramp. The men stopped at the end of the ramp just shy of the Mark V's frothy white wake and set the rubber boat on the nonskid deck, the lower unit of the outboard hanging in the water. A crew member from the Mark V held onto the rubber boat's bow line and looked for each man to give him a thumbs up. All eight men were low in the boat clutching their hand holds. One by one they returned the sign.

The call came over the headset that the launch was a go and the crewman tossed the bow line into the boat. A second crewman joined the first and together they shoved the black rubber boat down the ramp and into the relatively warm water. The small rubber boat slowed instantly, the SEALs hanging as far to the aft as possible to prevent the bow from submarining. The boat rocked gently in the wake of the Mark V and no one moved a muscle. The men lay perfectly still, listening to the ominous moan of the Mark V as it sped away. Not one of them had any desire for the boat to return until they needed it. They looked forward eagerly to carrying out their mission. Unfortunately, they were all unaware that thousands of miles away they'd already been fatally compromised by someone from their own country.

1

Anna Reilly drifted in and out of sleep, the warm sun enveloping her in a lazy hazy dream. Her bronzed skin glistened with a mixture of sweat and sunscreen. A slight afternoon breeze floated in off the ocean. It had been the perfect week. Nothing but food, sun, sex and sleep. The ideal honeymoon. A small resort on a remote Caribbean island with their own secluded cabana, gravity pool and beach. Total privacy, no TV, no phones, no papers, just the two of them.

She opened her eyes a touch and looked down at her wedding ring. She couldn't help but smile. She was like a little school girl again. It was a perfect diamond set in an elegant platinum Tiffany setting. Not too big, not too small, just right. Most importantly, though, it was from the right man. The man of her dreams.

She was now officially Mrs. Anna Rapp. He had been a little surprised that she'd taken his name without so much as a word of debate. She was a feminist, after all, with definite liberal leanings, but she could also be an old fashioned romantic. She could think of no other man she respected more. It was an honor to share his name and she wanted the world to know that they were now a family. In addition, she could also be very pragmatic. She had no desire to see one day her grandchildren running around with four last names. Professionally though, she would keep her maiden name. As the White House correspondent for *NBC* she already had name recognition and a solid career. It was a good compromise and Mitch didn't object.

Amazingly, the entire wedding had gone off without a hitch. Reilly couldn't think of a friend who didn't have at least one big blowout with her fiancé, or mother, or mother in law while planning her wedding. For her part, Anna had always clung to the romantic notion that one day she'd fall in love and have a big wedding back at St. Ann's in Chicago. It was where her parents had been married, where she'd been baptized and confirmed, and where she and her brothers had gone to grade school. But in the months after they got engaged she could see that this was an idea Mitch was less than enthusiastic about. It wasn't that he was unco-operative. He told her that if she wanted a big wedding back in Chicago, that is what they'd do, but she could feel his apprehension. He didn't have to state it. Mitch Rapp did not like being the center of attention. He was a man who was used to working behind the scenes. The strange truth was that her husband had been a covert operative for the CIA since the age of twenty-two. And the harsh reality was that in some circles he was known as an assassin.

In the month's before their wedding, during the confirmation hearing for Mitch's boss at the CIA, a member of the House Intelligence Committee had leaked Mitch's story to the press in an attempt to derail Irene Kennedy's nomination as the next director of the Central Intelligence Agency. The president had come to both Rapp and Kennedy's defense and a version of the truth was released to the media. The president told the story of how Rapp had led a team of commandos deep into Iraq to prevent Saddam Hussein from joining the nuclear club. The president called Rapp the single most important person in America's fight against terrorism and overnight the politicians lined up to shake his hand.

Rapp had been thrust into the spotlight, and he didn't do well. Having survived for years because of his ability to move from city to city, and country to country, without being noticed, he was now recognized virtually everywhere he went. There were photographers and reporters who hounded him. Rapp tried to reason with them at first. A few listened, but most didn't. Not one to let a problem fester, Rapp arranged to have a few noses smashed. The others took the hint and backed off.

There was something else, though, that worried Rapp a great deal. He was now a marked man. Virtually every terrorist from Jakarta to London knew who he was. Bounties had been placed on his head and Fatwas, Islamic religious findings, had been thrown down by dozens of fanatical Muslim clerics across Arabia, Asia and the Pacific Rim. Thousands if not millions of crazed Islamic zealots would gladly give their lives to take him down.

Rapp worried incessantly about Anna's safety and had even asked her if she was sure she still wanted to spend the rest of her life looking over her shoulder. Without hesitation she had said yes and told him not to insult her by bringing it up again. He had stoically honored her request, but it didn't stop his worrying. He'd also taken some serious precautions, having ordered her a customized BMW with bullet proof glass, Kevalar lined body, and shred proof tires. They were also in the process of building a new house on twenty acres outside D.C. in rural Virginia. Anna had asked more than once where the money came from to pay for all this, but Rapp had always deflected her questions with a joke or change of subject. She knew he was a man of many means, and in the end she reasoned that there were some things she was better off not knowing.

When they sat down to plan the wedding Rapp brought up a laundry list of security concerns that would have to be addressed. As the weeks passed Anna began to realize that he simply would not be able to enjoy the day if they held such a large wedding. She made the decision then to have instead a small private ceremony with their families and a few close friends. The news had been received well by Mitch.

The event was held where they'd met. At the White House. Anna's entire family, her mom and dad, brothers and sisters in law and seven nieces and nephews were there. Mitch's only surviving relative, his brother Steven, was best man while Anna's long time friend Liz O'Rourke was the matron of honor. Dr. Irene Kennedy and a few of Rapp's friends from the CIA were present as well as a select group of Anna's media friends. Father Malone from St. Ann's was flown in to officiate and the president and the first lady were the perfect hosts. President Hayes also used his significant clout to make sure there wasn't a mention of the wedding in any of the papers or on TV. It was agreed by all that it would be wise to keep the identity of Mrs. Mitch Rapp off the front pages.

The guests all stayed at the Hay Adams Hotel, just a short walk across Lafayette Park from the White House. They celebrated well into the night and then the bride and groom were taken by the Secret Service to Regan National Airport where they caught a private jet to their island. Courtesy of the CIA they were traveling under the assumed identities of Troy and Betsy Harris.

Anna sat up and looked over the edge of the patio down at the beach. Her husband was coming out of the water after a swim. Naturally dark skinned to begin with, after a week in the sun he looked like he'd gone native. The man was a prime physical specimen, and she wasn't just thinking that because she was married to him. In his twenties he'd been a world class triathlete who competed in events around the world. He'd won the famous Iron Man competition in Hawaii twice. Now he was in his mid-thirties but not much had slipped.

Rapp sported some other physical features that had taken Reilly a little getting used to. He had three visible bullet scars: one on his leg and two more on his stomach. There was a fourth that was covered up by a thick scar on his shoulder where the doctors had torn him open to get at the bullet and reconstruct his shoulder socket. There was an elongated knife scar on his right side, and one last scar that he was particularly proud of. It was a constant reminder of the man he had sworn he would kill when he started on his crazy journey into the world of counter-terrorism. It ran along the left side of his face, from his ear down to his jaw line. The plastic surgeons had minimized the scar to a thin line, but more importantly to Rapp, the man who had marked him was now dead.

Rapp stepped onto the patio, water dripping from his shorts, and smiled at his bride. "How ya' doin' honey?"

"Fine." She reached out her hand for him. "I was just dozing off a bit."

Rapp bent down and kissed her and then without saying another word he jumped into the small pool. He came up and rested his arms and chin on the edge. "Are you ready to go back tomorrow?"

She shook her head and pouted prettily for him.

Rapp smiled. She really made him happy. She was smart, funny and drop dead gorgeous. She could be a bit of a ball buster at times, but he supposed any woman who was going to put up with him had to be able to assert herself or it'd be only a matter of years before he screwed everything up.

"Well, we'll just have to stay a little longer then," he said.

She shook her head again and put the pouty lips back on.

Reaching across the patio for the bucket of iced Red Stripe, he laughed to himself. He'd called her bluff. She needed to get back to work or the network would have a complete shit fit. If Rapp had it his way she'd quit. The exposure was an ever increasing risk to her safety. But Anna had to come to that conclusion all on her own. He didn't want to wake up ten years from now and have her go nuts on him for making her throw her career away. His only consolation was that her current assignment at the White House meant close proximity to more than a dozen well armed and supremely trained Secret Service agents and officers.

"Would you like a beer, honey?"

"Sure."

Rapp opened one, handed the ice cold bottle to Anna and then opened one for himself. Reaching out with his bottle he waited for his wife to do the same. The two bottles clinked together and Rapp said, "To us."

"To us," she replied with a blissful smile.

They both took a drink and Rapp added, "And lots of cute healthy babies."

Anna laughed and held up two fingers.

Rapp shook his head. "At least five."

She laughed even louder. "You're nuts."

"I never said I wasn't."

They sat there basking in the sun, talking about their future for the better part of an hour, teasing each other playfully about how many kids they were going to have, how they were going to be raised, what names they liked and what they would do if one of the kids was as stubborn as either of them. Rapp refrained from sharing his opinion as she talked about what she would do with her job after they had a baby. It was one of those new things he'd learned about relationships. He understood that she was talking it out, and not looking for him to throw in his own two cents.

For her part, Anna kept her promise that she would steer clear of digging for details on the goings on at Langley. Rapp knew that if they were going to survive in the long run he would have to share certain aspects of his job with her, regardless of what Agency policy dictated. Anna was too curious to spend the rest of their lives never discussing what he spent the majority of the week doing. The general subjects of terrorism and national security were fair game, but anything involving specific intelligence or covert policy was off the table. Having been silent for so many years Rapp actually found it satisfying to be able to share his opinions with someone who had a decent grasp of the issues.

They opened two more beers and Anna joined him in the water. They clung to the edge of the gravity pool and looked out at the ocean, their elbows and chins resting on the edge, their legs gently floating behind them. They laughed about the wedding and their week of seclusion and avoided mentioning that it was about to end. Rapp could tell that Anna was getting tipsy. She weighed only 115 pounds and the combination of beer, warm sun and a lazy breeze meant a siesta was on the cards.

After a little while she kissed him on the lips and swam to the other end of the small pool. Climbing out, she stopped on the top step and pulled her hair into a loose ponytail. As she twisted it with both hands the water cascaded down her smooth back and over her tiny white bikini bottom. With a flirtatious glance over her shoulder she began to unhook her top. "I'm going to go take a nap. Would you like to join me?" Keeping her back to him, she slipped off her bikini top and draped it over the hammock hook to her right.

Needing no further encouragement, Rapp set his beer down and hoisted himself over the edge. He followed his wife into the bedroom, losing his swim trunks along the way. His eyes never left her body, and for a brief moment he found himself wishing they could stay on this tiny island forever.

When they got back to Washington it wouldn't be like this. There would be fires to be put out and plans to be put into action. He watched Anna slip out of her bikini bottom, and the problems awaiting him in Washington vanished. They could wait, at least for another day. Right now he had more important things on his mind.

POCKET
BOOKS

Protect and Defend
Vince Flynn

With Iran on the brink of developing a nuclear weapon, Israel is
forced to react. But by destroying Iran's main nuclear facility,
Israel has triggered an international crisis. An outraged United
Nations condemns the attacks, while Iran swears vengeance
against Israel and her chief backer: the USA.

Enter Lebanese master terrorist Imad Mugniyah, who's spent
the past decade picking his targets and preparing his cells for
this exact moment. All he needs is approval from Iran's
Supreme Council, and he will strike at America's soft
underbelly and make her bleed like never before.

With the US on high alert, the President calls on the one
man ruthless enough to counter the fanatical terrorist. Meeting
violence with violence, CIA operative Mitch Rapp tracks his
mark across Europe to America, where they are pitted against
each other in a hunt only one of them can survive.

ISBN 978-1-84739-080-6
PRICE £6.99

POCKET
BOOKS

Act of Treason
Vince Flynn

There are two weeks to go to the US presidential election when
the hot favourite, Josh Alexander, is ambushed by a terrorist
bomb. He narrowly escapes, but members of his entourage are
not so lucky. Alexander is carried to victory by a sympathy vote.

On the surface it appears to be the work of al-Qaeda. But
the CIA director Irene Kennedy is presented with classified
information so toxic she has no option but to call on Mitch Rapp,
America's top counterterrorism operative: the one man reckless
enough to follow the evidence to its explosive conclusion.

ISBN 978-1-4165-0269-2
PRICE £6.99

POCKET
BOOKS

The Third Option
Vince Flynn

Mitch Rapp, the CIA's top counterterrorism operative,
is sent on his final mission, to eliminate a European
industrialist who has been selling sensitive equipment to
one of terrorism's most notorious sponsors. But he doesn't
know that the ultimate target of this mission is himself.

Set up by forces within the US who do not want the next
Director-elect of the CIA to take over, and therefore need a
disaster for the present regime, Mitch refuses to die . . . the
conspirators have made an awful miscalculation. They have
enraged one of the most lethal and efficient killers the
CIA has ever produced. Now they will pay.

ISBN 978-0-7434-6823-7
PRICE £6.99

**POCKET
BOOKS**

This book and other **Vince Flynn** titles are available from
your bookshop or can be ordered direct
from the publisher.

Please send cheque or postal order for the value
of the book – **free postage and packaging within the UK**
to SIMON & SCHUSTER CASH SALES
PO Box 29, Douglas Isle of Man, IM99 1BQ
Tel: 01624 677237, Fax: 01624 670923
E-mail: bookshop@enterprise.net
www.bookpost.co.uk

Please allow 14 days for delivery. Prices and availability
subject to change without notice.